Selkie

BY BRANDI KENNEDY

Text copyright ©2013
Brandi Kennedy
All Rights Reserved

A LETTER FROM THE AUTHOR

The first part of this book, "To Love A Selkie," was initially published as a stand-alone novel in December 2012, but the tragic ending was extremely difficult for readers to take, and so when Annie and Malik returned to my thoughts in the early days of 2013, I didn't ignore them. When the idea for a "sequel" came to me, I didn't ignore that either.

Now, the "sequel" has been written -- but in that writing, it seemed Annie and Malik still weren't finished with their story. The continuation of Annie and Malik began as a combination of "they-weren't-done" and "popular demand," and now, Selkie is the first book in my upcoming Selkie Trilogy! There is a war coming in the Selkie world, and Annie and Malik are caught up in the eye of the storm. Get ready, the battle is coming.

I hope you like the much-demanded extension of the story, and I hope that you'll be as excited as I am to see what happens next as the trilogy unfolds. Don't forget, if you like it, review it!

DEDICATION

*All my life, I have carried a dream in my heart.
And I am so incredibly thankful to those who have helped me to bring my dream to life.*

To my children, Josephine and Eden Lily, who spent so much time not minding when I told them I needed time to write ...

To their dad, who is my partner and my tech, who helped me figure out the computer when I wanted to break it, and who made so much of this possible by being supportive ...

To my sweet puppy, Chance, who spent so many days patiently waiting at my feet for me to finish "working" ...

To my friends who read for me, helped with plot issues, character issues, and storyline issues ...

To the one from the who believed in me when I couldn't believe in myself, who saw something strong in me for so long that I started to see it too ...

To my favorite cousin, Dana Fetters, my ever so awesome editor, who lent her time and helped me clean up the garbage in my work ...

To Lauren Bearzatto, who loved Annie and Malik right from the beginning and helped to see them get where they are now ...

And to the fans who demanded more of the story ...

*Thank*You*

PART ONE: TO LOVE A SELKIE

Driving along in the dark, Annie struggled to keep her emotions in check. It had been a long and weary two hundred and sixty four mile drive from Boston, with only the sounds of her aged and cranky car engine for company. That and the brutal inner voice that refused to give her aching heart even a moment's rest. A tear slipped down her cheek, and she wished again for a working radio. Music had always been soothing to her, like a free medicine that she could carry everywhere. But with a dead phone battery and a dead car radio, she'd been cut off from her favorite form of therapy, the music that she loved. Lately she'd been thinking a new car was in order.

"First things first," she whispered to herself. "First things first." It had become her motto over the past several months, a little mantra that she held onto, tucked away in her heart for the desperate moments when life on her own would rise up suddenly to suffocate her in fear. It helped her remember that she needed a plan, and it helped her remember to follow it.

So far, the plan was simple. The plan was to run away, to lick her wounds, to heal and repair herself without the pitying, patronizing looks she kept catching on the faces of her friends. They all meant well but Annie felt misunderstood, as if even women who had been through what she was now suffering couldn't possibly understand her pain. Annie needed to be alone, she needed quiet time to process, she needed new scenery, new inspiration. She needed to find who she was, now that she was no longer defined emotionally as "wife."

Even now, months later, whenever she closed her eyes she was accosted with the same image; she felt she would never escape the vision of her husband on the dining room table with Teresa, the neighbor's wife. They had been friends, Annie and Chase had often had dinner with Teresa and her husband Mark. They'd gone to movies together, to parties, amusement parks. Annie and Teresa had shared so much over the years, but never had she expected to find herself sharing her husband. Never had she expected her husband to betray her in that way, to throw away all that they had shared together, and still she could not stop punishing herself internally for all the things she felt she'd done wrong in her marriage.

Shaking her head, Annie sighed and banished her negative thoughts. She banished her sadness for what seemed like the millionth time. She checked her GPS and then took the recommended left turn, pulling into the driveway of the beach house she had rented on an indefinite lease. As a popular author of over twenty suspense novels, with a contract to write several more, she was free to travel and could write from wherever she chose to exist. For now, Annie was on hiatus. She hadn't worked since the divorce, and the only character she needed to develop these days was her own.

Annie shifted the car into park, cut the lights and killed the engine. She gathered her purse, the takeout bag from the fast food joint she'd visited, and her overnight bag. These were the only things essential for just now, and with a passing glance at the other things in the car, Annie shook her head. Her luggage could be carried in later. Passing the shoulder strap of her overnight bag over her head, she found the key to the house and hit the lock button on her car fob.

Swiping away another detested tear, Annie headed up the driveway to the house, taking in the manicured lawn and the hydrangea bushes surrounding the perimeter of the house. Bordering the hydrangeas, flowers and other greenery filled a narrow but beautiful bed Annie couldn't wait to get her hands dirty in.

A light upturning of her lips at the sight of the house reminded Annie that she was alive, that she was talented and beautiful, either as a wife or as a successful single woman. Most emphatically of all, she reminded herself that she was worthy in her own right, completely apart from the cruel words her once loving husband had thrown her way in the divorce. Chase may have been a liar and he may have been a cheater, but she refused to give him the power to break her God-given spirit. She had run to Maine because she needed privacy, but she fully intended to heal and move on, to remember who she'd been as a younger woman, and to revive herself now as a still young woman of thirty-two.

Shuffling her bags into one hand, she deftly slipped the key into the door and smoothly turned the lock. A quick twist of the doorknob and she was in; beginning a new life in a new town, rebuilding her broken heart into something strong again.

***

It had been a hard night. Annie had spent an emotional evening in the silence of the roomy house though she had come in determined to be strong, and to pretend that even though she was alone, she wasn't hurting. She had been so determined to pretend, even to herself, that Chase didn't matter. She had come in the door, turned and locked it behind her, and headed to the table there in the kitchen. She'd placed her things on the table, silently because there was no one to talk to, and then she'd taken her meager dinner to one of the sturdy chairs and settled in to eat.

She hadn't eaten, though, not for a while. Sitting there in that strong solid chair, Annie had been overwhelmed by the expanse of the table. It was a family table with six chairs, perfect for a happy loving bunch to sit together, enjoying a cheerful Sunday breakfast. But there she was, a lonesome divorcee with no handsome and loving husband to sit across from her, no sweet and perfect children to smile down upon.

"Well, it's just too big for one person, that's all," she'd muttered to herself, brushing away the ever-present tear. "But it'll be perfect for dinner parties, I guess, if I ever get around to having any."

Leaving the crumpled paper bag on the lonely table to keep the extra napkins and ketchup packets, Annie scooped up her overnight bag, her sandwich and the perfectly salted yet slightly cooled fries, and headed to the master bathroom. She'd finished her meal while she unpacked the overnight bag she always used for travel; a fry here and a bite there as she opened her makeup bag and set out her deodorant, her toothbrush and toothpaste, her minty floss and her makeup removal cloths.

She scooped a quick handful of water from the tap, slurping it from her palm to wash down her dinner. Moving on, she folded down the edges of her makeup bag, rounding them until the bag had become a sweet little countertop basket to house her modest makeup collection. Annie had never been a habitual makeup wearer, but had been addicted to mascara and lip gloss since the fifth grade. She also possessed a few natural shades of eye shadow and a blush so close to her skin tone that it was nearly invisible. There was a foundation stick she rarely used, an eyeliner pencil she'd never been able to apply correctly, and a small set of makeup brushes that she used by guesswork because she had no clue which brush was for which purpose.

Finally, Annie looked up to inspect her face, removing traces of makeup with one of the soft makeup removal cloths. She loved her clear green eyes; they were wide set and always wide open, accented by thin lines in the outer corners. She could remember her mother surveying her own blue eyes in the mirror so many years ago, muttering to herself about "crow's feet." She remembered, too, her father's cheerful answer. It was always the same.

"Darling," Annie's father would call out, "You can't help them! Those are laugh lines because I'm hilarious!" Right on cue, Annie's mother would smile. She would laugh a little to herself, and forget for a while that her face no longer bore the perfect smooth skin of her youth. Now, Annie's eyes looked much the same as her mother's had, little lines branching out away from the outer corners of the slanted green eyes that she had inherited from her father. Missing them all over again, Annie finished cleaning the rest of her face, wishing her parents had still been alive to turn to after the divorce. She'd often thought that that was the worst part of the whole situation; not only had she lost her husband and her best friend in one fell swoop, but to top it off, she'd had no family to turn to.

"Ah, well," she muttered into the silence, moving on to her hair. It was as thick and rich as melted chocolate, dozens of shades of red and brown in constant chaos over her head. Letting down her ponytail, she watched in the mirror as her hair fell into its usual cloud around her face. It was not straight enough to be truly straight, and not curly enough to even be wavy. She'd always been proud of her hair; thick and slick and healthy, her hair had always had beautiful color and texture all on its own, requiring very little of her attention each day. Manicured fingers guided a brush through her shoulder length tresses, and quickly worked the mass into a habitual braid for the night.

Brushing her teeth, Annie left the bathroom to double check the locks on the doors, then returned to spit a mound of white toothpaste foam down the drain of the sink. She stuck her tongue out at her reflection and smirked as a new thought struck her. Feeling for once free instead of abandoned, Annie reached back, pulled the tie from her braid and ran her fingers through her hair to free it. She kicked her sandals off, slid her jeans and panties all in one down her slender hips, and left them pooled on the bathroom tile. Throwing her t-shirt and bra on the pile, she headed for bed, loving how good it felt for once to just leave something for later. Chase had been a do-it-now sort of person, and he'd despised any untidiness within their household or lifestyle. He had also said it was impossible for him to sleep if she lay beside him unclothed, so the cool air of the house caressing her skin as she made her way into the bedroom was also entirely new.

A burst of rebellion had her skipping the silky nightgown in her bag; instead, she slid naked beneath the blankets, her hair an untidy spill on the pillows. Sleep came easily as it always had, but she woke often, cursing the hands that still unconsciously reached for a husband that was no longer hers.

A good night's sleep still didn't make anything better, and the morning was equally difficult for Annie. She woke alone, curled into herself in the middle of the big soft bed. She was tangled in the covers, one smooth naked leg bared and chilled in the morning air.

Rising from the bed, she smiled in the silence as no one berated her for the haphazard bundle of clothes on the bathroom floor, and for the moment, she decided to leave them lying. A shower brought her to her senses though, and when she was wrapped in a soft fluffy towel, she moved the dirty clothes into the neat little basket under the sink. She added mascara to the thick lashes of her eyes, smoothed gloss over her lips and slipped it into her pocket to be kept handy during the day.

Annie headed back to the bedroom, roughing her hair with the edges of the towel to dry it. She made the bed in the nude, then rifled through her bag and retrieved the panties she'd packed, scarlet with a soft lace trim, and a bra that matched. These had been a recent purchase, as Chase had always said that wives had "no business dressing in hooker panties." Slipping them on, Annie felt sexy even though she soon covered the scanty underwear with basic black slacks and a ruby red sleeveless top.

She'd discovered that what she wore underneath her clothes had just as much effect on her confidence as what she wore on the outside, and that discovery had her slowly amassing quite a collection of sweet but sexy underthings. After a little more searching, a white gold and garnet tennis bracelet twinkled on her right wrist, and simple matching garnet studs sparkled in her ears. She'd received the jewels as a birthday gift from her parents the year before they had died in a car accident, and she wore them often. Simple red strap sandals completed the outfit, and Annie left the bedroom to begin her first day in Maine.

Walking through the house, Annie headed for the kitchen, thinking hungrily of breakfast. The silence of the empty house ravaged her appetite though. Remembering that she hadn't yet been to a grocery store dropped her mood a little closer to the pit she'd been struggling to pull herself out of for months. She sometimes forgot to even eat, in an emotional struggle to avoid the loneliness of a solitary meal. Annie wasn't the kind of woman to stay desperate for company, but food was nearly always a social affair for her. For Annie, food was more than just sustenance; it represented togetherness and companionship.

For the last six years of her life, every morning had begun with lazy lovemaking with Chase, and Annie cooking breakfast while he showered. They would eat together, sitting close at the bar in their kitchen, and she'd send him off to work with kisses before heading into her office to write. Lunch was often with Teresa or some other friend, and dinners had usually been with Chase in some out of the way diner he'd found or heard about at work. Since the divorce, food had become a lonely affair.

Annie checked her purse and pulled out the book she'd been reading; since the divorce, she was never without one. Reading was how she coped with the loneliness of eating by herself; she had learned to eat simply and silently with one hand, while with the other, she turned the pages of whatever she was currently reading. She loved the ability to disappear into a world someone else had created and put on paper for her to become lost in. Checking her place marked in the pages of the book, Annie added the local bookstore to her shopping plan for the day. There was enough of the book left to get her through breakfast, but she was going to need something new to read by lunch.

***

The first stop of the day was a local coffee shop, not too big and not too busy. The service was personal, which was just the way she liked her coffee shops to be. Annie bought a giant muffin loaded with bits of nuts and berries, then ordered an iced coffee that could only be described as a most sinful dessert. Sweet, rich and creamy, the drink was cold and delightfully thick, drowning in the flavors of chocolate and caramel. It was a delicious breakfast, though as Annie peeked around at the other patrons of the intimate little shop, she could only imagine Chase's face, one perfect dark eyebrow raised in silent disapproval.

Defiantly, Annie took her time and enjoyed every last morsel of the sweet, fruit-filled muffin, smiling to herself as she tucked her book back into her purse. She'd finished the book just as she'd expected to, and she carried the remains of her coffee with her into the parking lot. Next to the coffee shop was a used bookstore, just the place to find a new bit of treasure to read over lunch. Annie loved all bookstores, but for her, used bookstores were like digging for buried gold, a mix of spectacularly fresh new books and well-loved, old worn ones. She also loved the idea of trading in the books she'd finished for different ones, as she rarely read anything more than once.

Walking in, Annie immediately fell in love with the atmosphere of the little bookstore. Behind one counter stood a slender and surprisingly petite girl who looked young enough to still be in high school. She wore simple black framed glasses, which perfectly accentuated the shape of her face and the sparkling blue of her eyes. Her smile was shy but eagerly inviting as she welcomed Annie into the store.

"Welcome to Well Worn Pages, have you been here before?" she asked, her easy smile causing Annie to smile in return.

"I hadn't before just now, but I think I'm already hooked. It just reeks of books and paper and ink in here; it's delicious. Do I need a card or something in order to trade?"

"Nope, nothing needed to trade but a finished book or three and a desire for something different to read. What you'll do is leave whatever you'd like to trade in one of our baskets with me, and I'll stamp your basket with a number. You'll have a matching stamp to hold onto until your number is called, then you come back to me. I'll let you know what your trade credit is, and after that, you're welcome to spend that credit the same as cash on anything in the store. And," the girl added with a wink, "you're welcome to use regular cash too. Any purchases go by that cashier over there." She pointed casually to a short, bored looking blonde behind another counter, near the exit door.

"Thanks," Annie said. "I actually do have something with me that I can trade; otherwise, anything I buy won't fit in my purse. I just finished it over at the coffee shop, actually. So I just leave it with you?"

"You sure do." The girl wore a name tag; her name was Stephanie. Reaching under the counter, she pulled out a miniature laundry basket with a label that bore the words 'Well Worn' on the side. She placed it on the counter, waiting while Annie pulled her book out of her purse. Dropping the book into the basket, she watched the girl print two identical stickers; she placed the first on the edge of the basket and the other on a laminated index card. Number seventeen. Annie thanked Stephanie for the card, memorized the number and turned away to browse while she waited. The loudspeaker boomed out that number nine was ready at the drop off counter, and Annie checked her number again, mentally calculating how many people were ahead of her in the system.

It took some time for Annie to find her way around the entire store. There were lots of books, beautiful blank notebooks and journals, audio books, CD's, and vinyl records; they even had video games, movies and old comic books. The more she walked, though, the more amused she was. It seemed she'd caught the eyes of a young man and his friend down one of the book aisles.

They were both young; she guessed they were maybe in their early twenties, and she'd first noticed them in a section that stocked used college textbooks. One was dark and the other rather fair in color; she'd whispered a quiet "excuse me" as she'd wandered past them on her way to the fiction section. She'd overheard an exchange between them as she left the aisle and turned the corner to wander up the next aisle. A short, interrupted whistle had caught her attention, a grunt and a gasp followed by a low, quiet chuckle and a whispered conversation. Walking up the next aisle over, she could still hear them clearly.

"So go for it," one boy was whispering. "I bet she has more experience in her pinky than that snob Sarah has in her entire body. Just go ask her, real women like that. And she looks like a tourist or something. I've never seen her before." The boy was getting slowly louder the more he talked. "Tell her you noticed her and want to offer to show her around the --"

The voice broke off with a thud and another gasp, a furious whisper. "Shut up! Women that hot don't even look at guys like us! Shut up before she hears you! But wow! That red shirt, though? Damn, she looked good, didn't she?" The first boy was still laughing when Annie quickly turned the next corner and stopped to catch her breath. Looking around, she found herself alone, so she took the time to check herself out in the reflection of the window. Sure, she looked nice enough, but she doubted she looked good enough to catch the young eyes of the boys in the next aisle.

She finally got lost in the fiction section, both flattered and flustered to have been the object of conversation, and still quite surprised to have been thought of as "hot." Being the abandoned wife and having her husband cheat on her had left her feeling decidedly unattractive, decidedly un-sexy, and most definitely not "hot."

Throughout her walk in the bookstore, Annie repeatedly reminded herself that each woman was attractive to a different type of man, just as each woman was attracted to a different type of man. Stifling her own sexuality all these years had certainly not been helpful in her effort to hold onto her own sense of self-esteem, but Annie had loved Chase with all her heart. Simple things that kept him happy like always being clothed and wearing simple cotton panties hadn't seemed such an important sacrifice at the time. It hadn't been until after the divorce that Annie had realized how low she felt about herself, how rarely she really felt sexy or attractive, though Chase had often told her that she was both, sexy and attractive.

Still, she had to admit that spending all that time feeling rather plain on the outside had really left her feeling quite plain on the inside as well, and that was just something she couldn't live with. On a whim, she left the fiction she loved so deeply, and headed for the self-help aisle.

Twenty minutes and twenty-four dollars later, Annie was in possession of enough material to keep her reading for the next month. She'd only gotten ninety-five cents in credit for the paperback she'd traded in, but she'd found several others that she'd been meaning to read, not to mention the small stack of self-help titles she'd been drawn to. The extra dollar she'd spent on a Well Worn Pages tote bag was looking pretty well spent too, as the little bag was the perfect size for all of the books she'd bought. Back in her car, Annie tucked the tote bag behind her seat, narrowly remembering to place one of the books in her purse for later.

"Okay," she muttered to herself in the quiet morning air. "Next stop, groceries." Adjusting the rearview mirror so that she could see her face, she checked her hair to be sure it was behaving, checked and reapplied her lip gloss, and then turned the mirror back to where she needed it for driving. She scooted low in her seat as the two boys came out of the store and breathed a sigh of relief when they elbowed each other to a Jeep on the other side of the parking area.

"Stop being an idiot," she said into the quiet as she fastened her seat belt. "They are only boys, and it isn't like you're looking for anyone. Jeez, they probably were just screwing around, it's not like you're a super model. Stop being narcissistic and get moving." Checking her mirrors one last time, Annie started the car.

Thankfully, the grocery store was much simpler than the bookstore. Annie loved food, and so she loved grocery shopping. A head of cabbage, some ground beef, olive oil, soy sauce, rice vinegar and a few seasonings made up her recipe for dinner, with leftovers to eat lunch and probably dinner the next day. A head of iceberg lettuce, a package of cherry tomatoes, a couple of cucumbers, some cheese and a bottle of dressing ensured that she had an easy go-to salad meal at any time. Greek yogurt, berries and granola were all she needed for simple breakfasts, and with that she had a great start at stocking her fridge. Hauling all of her groceries to the car, Annie headed home to eat a quick salad and make a list of anything else she might need for the house.

As hard as it was to be alone, Annie knew she was going to have to buckle down and get used to it. A woman simply couldn't shop all the time; there just wasn't sense in it. There was only so much hiking one person could do, and she knew that eventually she'd have to start staying home more to write again. This, of course, meant she'd have to be there, wherever she landed, alone in a home of her own, a place that had no connection to Chase or their life together. She'd have to conquer the sense of loneliness; she'd have to learn to live in the quiet.

Or maybe she'd just go out and buy a louder radio later. Besides, if she was going to take up the owner's option to buy the place, she needed to adjust to being there.

***

Annie had been reading one of her new books and it had her emotions in a complete tailspin. Sitting at the table with a plate of leftovers for breakfast, she'd been so engrossed in her reading that she had actually had to reheat her meal twice. Finally, she just scraped the leftover cabbage dish into the garbage and took her book with her out the back door.

There was a soft breeze and as Annie settled into one of the patio chairs, she brushed an errant strand of dark hair back, tucking it behind her ear. She crossed her ankles on the edge of the table in front of her and settled back into the pillows to re-read and soak in what she'd just learned.

It was a book about how sexy self-confidence was, about self-esteem being the most valuable trait that a woman could possess. The problem, Annie realized, was that she honestly hadn't known that she didn't already have that kind of confidence. She had always thought herself to be a confident and independent woman, one who could stand alone and who lived her own way, a woman who was always true to herself. Now, though, she could see parts of her life that had not been as she had believed them to be, and she was determined to do something about it. Annie had decided that she needed to figure out who she really was, and how to become more authentically herself. She held within her heart the hope that someday, she would meet a new man; that someday she would stumble upon a man who believed her to be as wonderful and beautiful as she herself was trying to believe that she was.

In the pages of the book, Annie had discovered several ways that she'd allowed her marriage to limit her, and that the entire situation was partially her own fault. The way she had allowed herself to stagnate in an effort to always be what Chase had once wanted, had probably been part of what had driven him to an affair in the first place. She only wished he hadn't taken up with the vivacious and fiery neighbor woman that Annie had so admired. It might have been nice to still have her best friend to talk to about her husband's betrayal, but since Chase had chosen Annie's best friend, she felt as if she'd lost them both. Still she could understand his choice in that too, if she was honest with herself.

Somewhere along the line, she had stopped being "Annie," and eventually she had drowned in being "Chase's Wife." In so many ways, she had allowed herself to belong to him, to behave as a possession and not as a partner; she'd stopped being her own woman. She wore what he approved of, not because he made her do it, but because she wanted his approval. She did and said and behaved as he wished, not because he said so or because he exerted his will over her, but because she wanted him to always choose her.

In the end, it had backfired. She had resented him for the things she had or hadn't done, telling herself that her dissatisfaction was his fault, and that all her perceived sacrifices had been for his sake. He had felt her silent anger and had returned it with his own; he'd filled himself up with his disappointment in her lack of growth as the years wore on, seeing her as being more and more stagnant as a woman while he grew beyond her as a man.

It had been hard to realize and admit those things; it had been harder still to admit that she had to release some of the anger she held toward her ex-husband. Annie couldn't honestly fault him for wanting more than an obedient servant. He'd wanted a partner, someone to match with, to spar with, to fight with, and to feel passionate emotion with.

He'd wanted someone who would be her own authentic self, who would never belong to anyone else. She didn't deny the fact that he had his own faults in their marriage, but she'd never before been willing to sit down and look at herself so honestly.

Still, she fought daily with the pain that he'd chosen to betray her with a beloved friend. More than that, the ache of her best friend's betrayal was like an apple stuck in her throat, one she couldn't seem to stop choking on.

"Argh! Enough of this," Annie suddenly said out loud, slamming the book shut. "I've had just enough of this for now. It's time to shut it down, let it sink in and go do something else." Still, as Annie carried the book inside and placed it on the kitchen table, she couldn't help taking another look at the back cover, and the short little quote listed there among so many others that had reached out to her right from the first moment.

"Happiness is not a goal," she read aloud to herself, trying to memorize the quote. "It is a by-product." She smiled, muttering, "Eleanor Roosevelt, what I wouldn't give to take you to lunch."

Annie left the book resting on the table and headed across the kitchen to the pantry, where she pulled out a small tote bag she liked to use as a lunch bag when she went hiking or to the beach. The bag was small enough to be light and easy to carry; it was large enough to carry everything she might want to take with her, and it had enough divided pockets to keep things separated neatly. The bag already held her favorite camera, a zipper pouch full of new batteries, and an extra lip gloss in case the tube of gloss she always carried in her pocket ran out or got lost. Into one pocket of her bag, she stuffed two bottles of water; another pocket lay empty, waiting to be filled with basic peanut butter sandwiches for lunch.

***

Parking in a slot on West Street, Annie slipped the straps of her tote bag over her shoulder and took the now familiar walk down Bridge Street to the sandbar. She'd made it with perfect timing; the tide was going out. It was already very low and the sandbar was well exposed. Stopping for just a moment, Annie removed her camera from her tote bag, checked the batteries and headed for the tide pools.

At low tide, the water inching further and further out to sea revealed little pools of magnificent life. Filled with tiny moving creatures, the shining pools of water were like miniature oceans, shallow enough to see and photograph, but still able to sustain, for a short time, the life that was always under the ocean. As a woman who had never learned to swim, Annie was both fearful and fascinated with the idea of all that hid inside the depths of the sea.

The gravel of the sandbar crunched underfoot as Annie surveyed the area. It was a perfect day and there was not much of a crowd, which meant Annie was free to photograph wherever and however she wanted. Creeping slowly over to a shallow pool, Annie perched on a rock and checked the settings of her camera. Looking out to sea, she started with easily beautiful photographs, shots of the water as the tide slipped away in a rhythm that had been the same since the dawn of man. She took photos as fluffy clouds passed over the sun and caused the rays of the sun to appear like a golden glowing halo around the border of the clouds.

Far out to sea, Annie watched boats cruise along the horizon; fishing boats and sail boats, tour boats and ferries. The ocean is a busy place along almost any coast; people floating here and there in various vessels, hunting food, fun or solitude. Out on the rocks, seals basked in the sun. Occasionally, one would roll off into the water with a splash, the furry grey body disappearing and then appearing again, water coursing down the fat creature as it bobbed in the water. The seals were too far away for good pictures with the camera that Annie had with her, but she planned to bring a better lens with her next time.

Annie sat watching until the tide had gone as low as it was likely to go, and then she turned her camera to the tide pools. Under the water, there was a flurry of motion; sea weeds twitched in the water, sea anemone writhed in the invisible current. Shrimp and snails moved under the water along with crabs and other small creatures she wasn't familiar with. There were several starfish there, bright and colorful among the tide pool, seemingly motionless.

Annie sat for what felt like hours, watching the tide pools and taking pictures of the things that lived beneath the ever-changing surface of the water. She sat in silence, occasionally moving from one pool to another and gradually working her way along the sandbar, stopping once to eat her lunch among the rocks.

Watching the rhythm of the waves, Annie was struck frequently by the feeling of sadness in the greatness of the sea. She put it off the first time, thinking her melancholy to be simply a by-product of her divorce; again and again the waves of loneliness crashed around her, though the sea remained mostly smooth and peaceful. The slow-motion world of the tide pools, the silence of the unusually quiet sandbar, and the general absence of the tourists all combined to produce within her heart an ache that seemed to swell with the now rising tide of the ocean.

The effect of this melancholy silence made Annie glad that she was alone in the moment, alone to process without fear of drawing notice from others. She spent time sitting and just looking out to sea, taking pictures occasionally in an attempt to capture the seals still frolicking in the distance. She was just enjoying being still, simply allowing her loneliness and feelings of sadness to wash over her. It was cleansing, to sink into herself and to allow herself to simply feel, without hiding from herself as she had been now for so long.

It had been several months since the divorce, and Annie had spent those months moving through life on auto pilot. During the divorce, Annie had been so thankful for the prenuptial contract she and Chase had agreed on before their marriage; it had meant that she kept her own money and everything else that she'd brought into the marriage. It meant that he got to keep his house though, and Annie had left everything that wouldn't fit in her car. She had money enough; the things in that house were replaceable, and she didn't want the memories anymore anyway.

Annie had left the house and moved into a hotel, the most extravagant thing she'd done in all her life in spite of her money. She'd unpacked her car, moved into the hotel and written another book from her suite, just as if the divorce had never happened. Emotionally, she'd protected herself by shutting down and ignoring the situation to the best of her ability. Sinking into her work had helped for a while but over time, pretending had become impossible. Auto pilot had failed her; she'd finally seen the worry and the concern on her friends' faces. That was when she just knew it wasn't working, that she simply could not ignore the changes in her life or the injuries to her spirit.

It was time now, she'd decided, to turn off auto pilot. She had run to a new place, a place of emotional safety, a place where she could create a new self, a new life, and new memories. She had run to a place where she could begin to feel peaceful. It was time now to face up to her own flaws, to forgive Chase for his, and to begin the business of moving on.

Heaving a sigh, Annie stood from the rocks. The tide was coming in again; before long, the sandbar would be temporarily gone. It was time to go home.

***

Rolling over in her bed, Annie was blinded by the sun. She cursed and dragged her pillow over her face, instantly regretting the move when the pressure of her hand revived the soreness of her tear swollen green eyes. It had been a long night, the kind she referred to as one of "those" nights; the nights when every song that came on the radio felt emotionally soaked in her personal pain and every movie on television was a happy love story where no one got divorced.

She'd taken a pen and an empty spiral notebook to the kitchen table and forced herself to sit down and write out everything that she was feeling. She'd forced herself to let the music play on the stereo, to let it reach inside her heart. For the first time since she'd caught her husband sleeping with her best friend, she had stopped running and forced herself to sit there. And for the first time since the divorce, she'd managed to just be still and *feel*.

As the mournful notes of a piano had breathed sadness out of the stereo speakers, Annie had cried herself dry. She had penned over seven pages of hurt and rage and pain, taking the time to give a written voice to the effects of Chase's betrayal. When flutes and cellos and the solemn clarinet had joined in to round out the heartbreak that poured throughout the house, Annie had emptied herself of self-pity, fear of the future, and resentment of Chase for his choices. When the music had washed over her soul in waves of grief and despair, she had forgiven herself for the things she now knew she'd done wrong. She had forgiven both herself and her ex-husband for being human, for being imperfect, and for seeming weak and childish and pathetic in each other's eyes.

The hard part had been writing a letter to Chase afterward. She knew she would never send it; he would never see it because she had already burned it to unrecognizable ash in the fire pit on the back patio. Still, Annie would never forget the words that had not come easily, words that cut her deeply even as she forced them out, words that had only come at the cost of a still aching hand and a heart that bore the fresh, raw scars of rejection. Knowing he'd never see the letter had given her a new freedom to speak her heart, and she had forced herself to do it honestly.

Annie had forgiven Chase in her letter. She had, honestly and with all of her heart, taken him down from the level of a sex-crazed, spiteful and careless demon of a man. She had turned her vision of the man she had once adored into what it should have been all along; that of a simple human man, a flesh and blood creature filled with the same basic desires and weaknesses that she also possessed. She had released her anger, released them both from the dragging emotional weight of it, and struggled to free herself from the inner turmoil that had driven her at thirty-two years of age to run away from the only real home that she had ever known.

She had ended her letter with well wishes for Chase, pulling from somewhere deep inside of her a heartfelt desire that he should find whatever it was that he was seeking in his life. She had bid him goodbye, finally able to dry her eyes and stop her nose from leaking. Standing there on the patio, Annie had crumpled the pages filled with her aching, heartbroken handwriting, and she had touched them gently with a match from the box in the kitchen drawer. Watching the flames eat away the bitter expression of a pain she'd been lost in for months, Annie had felt free for the first time since the divorce. She had smiled just a little, watching the moon shimmer behind the clouds as the last symbol of her past disintegrated in the little rocky fire pit behind the home she'd decided to make her own.

Finally letting all of that go had been so good for her, and she did feel better when she woke, other than the relentless pounding in her head and the swollen, throbbing sensation that was her eyes. Swallowing a painkiller from her purse, Annie crawled from the bed; she flinched a little as the morning chill whispered over her bed-rumpled skin.

Later, she shopped. It was too early for the tide pools yet, those peaceful little miniature worlds that swayed and breathed beneath little pockets of ocean and fascinated her endlessly. But, it was never too early for shopping and Annie was a master shopper.

She bought little boring things she'd needed; new socks, a watch battery, shampoo and new lip gloss. She bought throw pillows to soften the living room, a rug for the floor. In the decor section of the department store, Annie found her most treasured purchase of the morning; the most perfect, most simple representation of her fresh new inner peace.

It was a rustic shadow box built of driftwood, covered over with what felt like sand, but couldn't be because it didn't brush away under her fingers. It had a light stain that left the wood looking completely bare and unfinished; it was rustic and had the simple impression of being darkened with age instead of being brand new. Mounted on the back wall of the box, there was a beautifully preserved giant starfish the color of tangerines, perfectly perfect except for the fact that it had six legs. Annie loved it, deciding that it would look perfect on the wall in the foyer, just above the little table where she dropped her keys in a little crystal bowl shaped like the scooped shell of a mussel.

On the clearance table, she found a crystal statue of a seal, frosted so that it looked white and textured to mimic the fur of a seal pelt. It was maybe eight inches tall, nearly a foot long, and was a perfectly beautiful model of the creatures she had come to love at the tide pools on the sandbar. The realistic sculpture was completed with frosted crystal whiskers and smooth glass eyes the color of rich dark espresso; it was a stunning piece of glasswork she couldn't wait to take home.

Walking gingerly back to the car, Annie was almost sorry she'd bought the giant crystal seal. Along with the other things she carried, it seemed terrifyingly weighty and she was horrified at the possibility of dropping him, or accidentally snapping off one of the fragile, thin whiskers. Never so happy to find something for fifty percent off, she settled him gently in her trunk and lovingly surrounded him with her other purchases, tucking the blanket from her emergency kit around him as a buffer from any shifting weight as she drove.

Satisfied with his relative safety, she gently settled her starfish shadow box beside her bags and sent out a quick prayer that her beautiful new things made it home safely at the end of the day. Then she strapped herself into her car and drove out to West Street.

***

Annie was lucky again to find the sandbar mostly abandoned. She loved the tide pools on any day; she loved watching parents show their children the life of the ocean, encouraging them to look without touching, to admire but not disturb the creatures living within the waters. She loved watching people walk their dogs back and forth; she loved watching hikers come and go on their way to explore the terrain of Bar Island.

Bittersweet as it was, she even loved the lovers who came hand in hand to gently woo each other, surrounded by the chaos and the rich life of the ocean. What she loved best though, were the quiet days when other travelers chose to see the Bar Harbor Pier or the Village Green instead of the sandbar, when it seemed like she was the only person in the world, alone there among the lapping of the waves and the barking chatter of the seals.

Looking out among the rocks, Annie slipped her camera from her tote bag. She smiled and crept out slowly, closer to the ocean that she both loved and feared. About twenty yards away, a lone seal sunned itself among the rocks, its eyes closed and its body still, its doggy face resting on a rise in the stone. It was mostly white, speckled all over with black and gray spots that varied in size and shape; his spots also varied in darkness. Along one side, he bore a short hairless scar that slid across and down beneath his massive body, close to where his front flipper joined with the rest of him.

Annie continued to move slowly toward the sleeping animal, marveling at the sheer mass of the beautiful creature. She had always thought of seals as fun loving, curious and playful beasts. Still, this giant looked to be at least five feet long and she guessed he outweighed her by over a hundred pounds. Careful not to get too close, Annie found a safe perch nearby and sat quietly watching him. He looked so alone; but somehow, he looked equally at peace, oblivious to her presence and sleeping gently in the warm light of the sun. Alone, she mused, but not lonely at all. Occasionally, his whiskers would twitch, but for a long time he was so utterly motionless that Annie began to photograph the others in his group also.

The other seals were much farther out, and she found herself playing often with the settings of her camera. She hoped desperately that her photos would be better on her oversized laptop screen than they appeared in the tiny digital LCD screen on her camera. Eventually, Annie's stomach growled and she realized she was hungry. As the magnificent seal slept on nearby, she situated herself more comfortably and ate the simple lunch she'd packed in her tote, waiting for the seal to awaken. She'd been hoping that he would be more active.

Eventually, he did come slowly alive, waking from his sleep to find her there, watching her silently with eyes so like the ones now hidden in the depths of her car trunk. His eyes shimmered at her in the sunlight, and his whiskers moved as he scented the air. Occasionally, he would readjust his massive bulk on the rock, seeming almost to pose in front of her camera. Once, he seemed to speak to her; he gave a long low roaring sound that was both bark and growl. The sound surprised her into stillness but scared her into pressing her camera shutter one last time. His mouth was open in the photo, whiskers standing chaotically out from his face, one eye closed in a playful wink.

As he slipped into the sea with a splash and a glitter of water droplets, Annie decided firmly that the last photo, the one of him giving his farewell before he plunged into the sea, was her favorite of the entire batch. The tide was coming in and her shoes were getting wet; she tucked her camera back into her bag and walked contentedly back to her car, thinking still of her wet and furry new friend.

***

Several days later, Annie turned into the parking lot of a car dealership, having finally reached the end of her tolerance with her own beaten old car. She'd had it before she met Chase, before her writing had taken off. It had lasted her well through the years, but Annie needed a change. Besides, it was getting downright torturous for her; she hated driving around in a car with no music. Checking her lip gloss in the mirror, she swung her purse up onto her shoulder and pocketed the car keys. Locking the door, Annie looked around and started walking.

She had planned to walk around the car lot for a little while before seeking out a salesman, but she had only just bent to look into the windows of a sweet little red four door when a man spoke from behind her. She was surprised at how quickly she'd been discovered; she had anticipated a quiet walk alone, seeking out whatever might strike her fancy.

"Would you like to drive it?" The voice was low and rich, with a little rumbling quality that reminded her of her father. Turning around, she was struck dumb by the clear deep blue of his eyes, gleaming brightly out of a chiseled face tanned from the sun. His hair was black and very shiny; it was just wavy enough to give him a tousled and wildly sexy appearance. His white button down over dark slacks only served to make his muscular arms look completely delicious, though he wasn't really a large man. Only a few inches taller than Annie herself, he was fit and well built, like a swimmer or some other such athlete. Pinned to his chest, he wore a plastic tag with his name on it.

"Jason," Annie murmured, fighting her tendency toward shyness. "I'm Annie Jacobs. I'm actually here to trade in my old car for something new. I haven't really looked around very much though. Is it alright if I just wander a bit?"

"Sure," he replied. "If you tell me what you're looking for in a car, I can maybe speed up your trip. Car shopping can be fun, but surely a pretty girl like you has something else you'd rather be doing." At this point, he waggled his eyebrows at her and grinned rakishly.

"Well, I really would rather get it over with. I'm embarrassed to say that I'm a terrible judge of cars, because I know next to nothing about what's under the hood; I tend to shop for a car by what it looks like. You know women, there has to be a certain visual appeal." Annie heard herself talking as if she were eavesdropping on someone else's conversation. She couldn't believe she'd just said that!

"Oh my goodness, am I flirting? I can't be flirting," she thought. "I don't flirt! What is wrong with me?!"

"-- and then I can show you what you want," Jason was saying. "So what exactly are you looking for?" His eyes were smiling. Annie realized in shock that he was flirting with her too, and she had to scramble for some coherent thing to say before he realized she was about as experienced as a second grader. She'd never been the flirting type because she'd simply never had the confidence for it, and she hadn't really dated much before meeting and marrying Chase.

"Music," she blurted. "Ahem, that is, I love music, so a good system in the car is a major point for me. My car radio actually just died on me last month, and it's been awful driving around in the silence. I'm one of those people who can't live without music, so ... what?" she asked, looking up and noticing the way he was looking at her.

"Nothing," he laughed. "You just get really animated when you're talking. It makes me want to keep you going just so I can watch."

Annie was blushing furiously, struggling to think of something to say, some witty response to his obvious attraction to her. Unfortunately, her mind was a blank, and she tucked her hair behind her ear in a desperate struggle not to accidentally say something stupid. All she could think of was that even if he was interested, he couldn't possibly stay that way. Clearly, she lacked what it took to hold a man.

"Do you have a color preference?" Surprised at his voice breaking into her thoughts, Annie's eyes shot up to his face. She shook her head and smiled, grateful to him for breaking the awkward silence. He cleared his throat and continued, "Everything here automatically comes with power everything, heated seats, and all digital gauges. Almost everything here has pretty close to a top-notch system in it, but you can upgrade any component you like. Are you looking to stay in a car, or are you interested in something bigger? Maybe you want to try an SUV?"

"No, no," Annie stammered. "Just a basic car for me, and I don't really need top of the line on the radio system, just pretty good is good for me."

"Well, then," Jason said. "All that's left is to decide what looks good to you. Shall we walk?"

Annie nodded, and they fell into a mostly comfortable silence for a while. Occasionally, Annie would stop to lean into the windows of one car or another, and Jason would ask her what she liked about that car, what she didn't like, or what would make it perfect. After each car, he led her to yet another, each one closer and closer to what Annie wanted. Eventually, they found the car that Annie felt was right.

It was basic black, but it looked sleek and professional to Annie. With four doors, it was nice and roomy; it also had a surprisingly large trunk. The fabric and accents were all the color of burgundy, a sharp but lovely contrast to the black, and Annie loved it.

"I can test drive it, right?" She turned to look up at him, smiling nervously.

"You sure can," he answered. "Just as long as you don't mind a tag-along salesman." He raised one clean dark eyebrow, questioning.

"No problem," Annie replied, choking on self-doubt. She knew she had no reason to be so nervous, but ever since she'd caught Chase cheating on her, her confidence had taken a real dive. Jason turned, leading Annie into the building to fill out paperwork before leaving the lot, and then they climbed together into the little black car. As Annie drove, soft music played while she and Jason fell into an easy conversation. She asked how he liked working in sales; he asked what she did for a living. When she asked if he'd been in sales very long, he answered briefly and then changed the tone of the conversation, asking if he could take her to dinner.

"Um, sorry," Annie muttered, having hit the brakes a bit too hard at the stop sign. She looked over at him and found him watching her, nervous and amused. "Do you do this often?" she asked.

"No," he said, sounding a little offended behind his chuckle. "I generally have a rule not to ever date anyone I encounter at work. I'm not a dater, really. But you're just --" he swallowed and licked his lips, dropping his eyes to his lap and continued, his voice in a rush to spill out his words. "I think you're beautiful, and you're smart, and you seem to know exactly what you want. I'd like very much to sit over dinner with you and watch you sip wine over conversation. Are you interested?" he asked, a glimmer of hope making his eyes dance.

Annie's vocal cords felt frozen, strangled in disbelief. First the two boys in the bookstore and now the car salesman! Hearing Chase's horrible insults in her memory, she struggled to believe that a man could be this interested in her. Annie knew she was pretty enough, but she also knew she hadn't been woman enough, not for Chase. There was a moment when she wondered if Jason had only asked her out in order to flatter her into buying the car.

Fortunately for him, she liked the car, and she was planning to buy it with or without a date. Unfortunately for him, she was still feeling raw from all the things she'd been through in the past months. She didn't think dating anyone at the moment was a good idea.

"I'm sorry," she said, "but I can't go out with you. I really just got out of a marriage, and I just don't think I'm there yet. I like you, but I'm honest enough with myself to know that if we went out, I'd be going for the wrong reasons."

"Well, doesn't that just figure," Jason laughed, embarrassed as his eyes met hers briefly. "A woman walks right onto my lot, sweet and thoughtful and lovely. And you just had to be one of the few with your head on straight. I'm sorry if my asking you out offended you," he said.

"Of course it didn't, Jason. Really, I'm flattered that you asked me. Had I been on the market, I'd have accepted. But I'm just not ready to date again yet, and that's not fair to either of us. Now let's go make a deal on this car," she continued with a smile, trying to ease the mood and smooth over his obvious embarrassment. "I plan to haggle you down to half price with just a flutter of my lashes, now that I know your weakness," she teased, glancing over to send a wink his way.

"Good luck," he shot back, laughing. "You've broken this old weathered heart, and if I'm ever to recover, I need a good sale!"

Annie was thankful for his being such a good sport about her awkwardness. It felt good to know a man was attracted to her, no matter what his reasons were; it felt just as good to know in her heart that she'd done the right thing in turning down the date. Annie hated to reject him; she could just imagine those beautiful eyes over candles and wine, but she knew herself well enough to know she didn't want a relationship yet, not even a rebound. It was freeing, knowing that she could trust herself again to follow her heart, and that it had led her in the right direction for once. The sense that she could once again trust her own instincts made her feel more confident, even if those instincts were self-protective and lonely.

A short time later, Annie drove out of the car lot with considerably less money in her bank account. She had music in her ears and Jason's card in her purse, under strict orders to call him the second she was ready to take him up on that date. In the meantime, she and her camera had a date with a certain gentle giant seal down at the sandbar. She had a lot of thinking to do.

***

Annie had to remind herself that it would not start her off well in her new town if she jumped up and down, squealing with glee right there in the coffee shop. The other patrons probably wouldn't care that she'd just had a meeting with the owner, soon to be previous owner, of the home she was now in the process of buying. Over the last few weeks of living in Bar Harbor, Annie had fallen in love with the history and the feel of the town. She loved the Bar Harbor Pier, and she'd spent many afternoons reading in the Village Green.

She loved the coffee shop; the baristas had learned her coffee order so well that it was usually sitting on the counter waiting by the time she made it there to pay. More than that, she loved Well Worn Books, the little used bookstore adjacent to the coffee shop. She'd struck up a minor friendship with Stephanie, the cute little girl who worked there. But above all that, Annie loved the house she'd originally planned to use only as a temporary retreat.

Now that the deal was in motion, Annie couldn't wait to go back to the house with a fresh look. It would be her house, her first real home on her own, and she couldn't wait to really make it hers. Here and there, she'd added little things that made the house feel more like home to her, like the starfish shadow box hanging there above the proud and majestic crystal seal. Those things were truly her favorite things in the entire house, but they were portable little things that could be packed up and moved without much difficulty. Annie still didn't feel rooted yet, but now that the house was on its way to being hers, she was going to take root.

Sitting there in the booth and slowly savoring the rest of her coffee, Annie felt swollen with pride and excitement. She was really doing it; she was really moving on, and it felt better than she had imagined it would feel. From the pit of depression immediately after the divorce, Annie had not seen the light ahead. She had not seen the possibility that being single could mean feeling free. She had only known the deafening loneliness of the quiet, the oppressive weight of trying to hold up under the pressure when her insides were cracking from the strain of it. Now, she truly felt she could do anything.

Glancing toward her purse, tucked into the booth beside her, Annie remembered the card tucked inside. She thought of Jason, the cute salesman who had asked her out when she'd bought her new car. Briefly, she thought of calling him and taking him up on his dinner offer. Annie wanted to celebrate; she wanted to feel genuine laughter shivering up through her ribs and bubbling out of her throat. She wanted good food and a great atmosphere; she wanted someone who thought they saw something good in her. But when she looked inside herself and thought of actually finding those things someday, when she thought of finding the perfect man who would compliment her in all the right ways, that man was not Jason. His card remained, untouched but not forgotten in the zipper pocket at the back of her wallet.

Lifting her purse and placing it on the table, she unzipped it and pulled out her tablet computer. She propped it up and checked to be sure the little SD card hadn't fallen out of place, and pressed the button to activate the screen. In the weeks before, Annie had spent time nearly every day at the tide pools, and she had hundreds of photos of the crabs, the minor sea life, the starfish, and the seals.

The seal she had first encountered among the rocks there had seemingly grown to trust her a little, and now he seemed to bark a greeting to her whenever she arrived, slipping in and out of the water at random times as if to play a game of hide and seek with her. She had pictures of him sunning, sleeping, and barking; she had several of him standing up on his flippers as if to pose. Once, she'd been laughing so hard at his antics that she'd nearly dropped her camera into the tide pool. She had completely soaked her shoe, almost falling in to save the camera. Several of the pictures from that day had been too unfocused to keep because she'd been shaking with laughter.

Now she understood why the Native American tribes of generations past had been so steeped in legends and traditions involving a spiritual connection with one animal or another. At first, Annie had felt downright silly, looking forward as she did to her trips to the sandbar. She'd felt almost childish to admit to herself that she felt a certain level of friendship with the seal who'd given her so much cheer over the past weeks. Now, she'd grown accustomed to her new attachment to him, and had learned to simply take joy where she could find it, at least for now. Scanning through the photos, she couldn't help smiling to herself.

"Wow, those photos are really beautiful!" A female voice came over Annie's shoulder, making her jump and gasp, her heart leaping into her throat. Her hand followed her heart, flying up to her throat in surprise. Recovering, she turned slightly to glance behind her, which brought her gaze to meet warm, pale blue eyes under a fringe of red eyelashes. The woman's skin was fair, almost actually pale, and her nose was sprinkled with freckles reminiscent of a child at the end of the summer. Her hair was aflame in shades of bronze and copper, soft and smooth and shimmering. Innocent as she looked, she had an inherent sexuality that Annie immediately liked and envied.

"Did you take them all? The photos?" the woman asked.

"I did, thank you," Annie answered. "I go out to the tide pools at the sandbar near Bridge Street pretty often, and this guy and I," she gestured to a photo of the seal on her screen, "seem to have made a sort of friendship. He always seems to be there, barking and posing for me. He's a real showoff," she finished. Embarrassed, Annie sipped her coffee.

"Well, I love the photos, and it's really beautiful that you've been able to get that close to him. Sometimes the males can be pretty territorial and they even bite occasionally, so you remember to be careful out there," the redhead said with a gentle laugh. Extending her hand over the back of the booth toward Annie, she continued. "I'm Brenna, Brenna O'Connor. I just moved into the lighthouse down the street from here."

"Annie Jacobs," Annie answered, awkwardly grasping Brenna's hand. "I actually just moved here myself."

"Really," Brenna said. "What a small world! I haven't been here more than a few years myself. What brought you to Bar Harbor?"

"Divorce," Annie grimaced. "I needed a fresh start, I guess. So here I am, taking pictures in my spare time, starting over. You?"

Annie and Brenna sat talking for over an hour, eventually ending up tucked into Brenna's booth together as they browsed Annie's photos and got to know each other. Brenna was an Irish immigrant who'd met her husband in Ireland. He was an American but had been in Ireland on some sort of medical conference. He had been a pediatrician, and Brenna had admired his dedication. Their courtship had been romantic but wildly fast, like a tornado wind that had lifted her spirit right out of Ireland and whisked her away to America. Brenna had fallen in love with Bar Harbor immediately, and she'd lived there happily with her husband for three very short but happy years.

She'd been so proud of him! He was a man who gave of his medical gift as often as possible, traveling all over the world to serve in clinics and villages with a local missionary group. Two years ago, he'd been in Cambodia on his way to work in a poverty-stricken village suffering horrible plagues of illness. In the children's clinic he'd been running, Thomas had contracted dengue fever, and by the time anyone was able to reach Brenna by phone, her husband had already died.

The women bonded over their mutual loneliness, each struggling to understand and relate to the suffering of the other.

It had been Thomas O'Connor's dream to settle down with a wife one day, to buy and restore an old lighthouse, to raise a family of his own. His dream of having a child had died with him, but Brenna was determined to build for him the home he'd always wanted, and Annie couldn't help getting swept up in the romance of it all.

"If there's ever anything you need or if you need any help, if you just need someone to talk to," Annie said, "feel free to call me." She took a business card from her wallet and slid it across the table to Brenna. "I'm not writing much these days, so until my agent starts calling me night and day to kick me into gear, I'd love to make myself useful in other ways."

"That's really great," Brenna smiled, "I'd love someone to help or even just to keep me company while I'm working in the lighthouse. I really appreciate the offer, and you should know that it goes both ways. The phone isn't set up until next week, but you should feel free to show up and come knocking at any time."

They talked a little longer, slowly growing more and more comfortable with each other as the minutes passed. As the women grew more at ease with each other, they made tentative plans to meet at the sandbar early one morning for a hike up into Bar Island. Their plan was to meet up in two days, crossing the sandbar as the tide was going out. On Bar Island, they would picnic and then make the return walk from the summit before the tide rose up and covered the sandbar. Eventually, Brenna caught a glimpse of the clock on the screen of Annie's tablet, and scrambled out of the booth in a rush.

"Oh no, oh no," she said, embarrassed as she gathered her things, "I hate to but I have to run, Annie! If I don't get home to feed my dog, he may just eat the house while I'm gone! He gets wild when he's alone for long. Come see me at the lighthouse tomorrow if you can," she said, dropping her hand on Annie's shoulder in farewell. "I'll be home all day."

With that, Brenna blew out of the coffee shop like a breeze, and as Annie headed home, she felt refreshed by the promise of feminine company. She'd missed having a woman friend to talk to, and she had often wondered if she would ever really trust another woman again. Meeting Brenna had seemed so easy though, and their conversation had been smooth and effortless. As she drove home, Annie idly wondered what would make an appropriate housewarming gift for an Irish lighthouse owner.

***

The next morning, Annie woke up smiling. During the night, she'd dreamed that she was running in a giant barren desert. There was nothing but sand all around, nothing grew anywhere around her. The air was hot and dry; it felt stale, as if there had never once been a breeze to blow through and lift the staleness from the area. She didn't know where she was going or why, but she was walking there with no hope of escaping. She just walked on with a quiet but somehow desperate acceptance of her circumstance.

The dream began to change; as Annie walked she heard a noise behind her, and she turned to glance over her shoulder, gasping in shock. Where her feet had fallen upon the ground, her toes sinking softly into the sand, grass had begun to grow. She walked a few more steps and turned back again to look, and it was as if the grass was following her. She smiled, now walking backward so as not to look away from the spreading green of life.

As the smile reached her eyes and swelled her up with joy, a dandelion appeared in the place where her foot had just been. She picked it, feeling like a schoolgirl, and blew the fluff into the sudden wind. As the seeds of the dandelion blew all around her, more dandelions appeared as if sprinkled suddenly into the grass. Annie laughed and kept walking backward, watching a new world spring up before her. Finally, she sat down in the now beautiful field in amazement.

Even in the dream, she was present enough within herself to know that she was only dreaming; which led to her understanding how the dream represented her own life. Only the day before, Annie had realized that it was only when she truly began to accept her life as it was, that it began ever so slowly to become better. The thought process made her burst into giggles; her laughter in the dream finally awakened her.

The happy mood lasted all morning as Annie went about her business in the house. She received and answered faxes regarding her purchase of the house; she took phone calls from her bank and her lawyer. She showered, had breakfast and went about the monotonous morning schedule of a single woman living alone. For the first time in ages, Annie was able to make it through the morning with a true sense of contentment.

Knowing as she did how fleeting those moments were, Annie made a point of enjoying each and every second of that morning. She sang in the shower, she danced around the kitchen with her music blaring while she made and ate breakfast, and she made faces when she caught herself walking by the mirror in the hall.

Annie was so thrilled to finally be having a really good morning that she was almost afraid to stay home, afraid that if she acknowledged her sense of happiness too fully, it would dissipate like fog and be gone. Deciding to go out, she dressed and grabbed her purse, intent on finding the perfect house-warming gift for Brenna.

Annie had been heartbroken before and she had felt the sting of betrayal, not just from the man she had loved, but also from a woman she had trusted. Still, she had to acknowledge that every woman wasn't the same as Teresa, and Annie refused to live a life of distrust. She couldn't predict the future of her blossoming friendship with Brenna, and she couldn't deny her fear of what could happen, but she also couldn't deny her desire to see it through.

Leaving the house and heading to the mall, Annie mentally walked herself through the conversation she'd had with Brenna the afternoon before in the coffee shop. She thought about the few things she'd learned about Brenna, trying to put herself in Brenna's shoes. Annie tried to think of what would help make a home for a still-aching widow who'd left her home country for the sake of love, only to lose her new husband to a horrifying illness.

Annie wandered around the mall for a long time, rejecting this idea or that one. There were the generally chosen easy options: flowers, wine, a plant, a decorative vase or bowl. None of that really spoke out to Annie though. She'd nearly lost hope of finding a truly perfect gift when she found a plaque that explained the history and meaning behind the traditional Irish home blessing. It was lovely but simple, in a mix of bold blues and relaxing shades of gray. The blessing was written out like a poem with each line represented by a tiny little jeweled charm fastened to the wood. Like a charm bracelet, the charms were all strung together down the side of the plaque on a fragile but shining silver chain.

"May love and laughter light your days," Annie read to herself, lightly touching the little red heart fastened there. She continued, smiling as she touched each little charm in turn. "May good and faithful friends be yours, wherever you may roam. May peace and plenty bless your world, with joy that long endures. May all life's passing seasons bring the best to you and yours."

Annie carried the plaque to the nearest cashier and swiped her credit card.

***

A frenzy of barking startled Annie when she knocked on the heavy door of the lighthouse. She'd stopped at the coffee shop on the way for a drink and had asked the barista if they knew what Brenna liked. They had, so Annie had ordered coffee for Brenna as well. She stood now with her hands full of coffee and Brenna's new plaque, mildly afraid of the booming sound of the dog on the other side of the door. Usually she loved dogs, but the idea of wearing two cups of piping hot coffee was not cheerful.

The door burst open and Brenna was there, one hand struggling to hold back a wild-eyed golden retriever. The dog was jumping around madly, his claws clicking on the dark hard wood of the floor as he rumpled the teal rug that was rapidly sliding away under his efforts. "Go lay down, you wretched hyper beast," she laughed, looking up at Annie with a grin.

"I stopped by the coffee shop and they knew what you like so I ordered for both of us," Annie said. "The dog thinks he's a real man-eater, huh?"

"Not so much a man-eater," Brenna laughed. "More like just a nut job with no manners. Lugus thinks the entire human race was created so that they can all come along eventually and pet him. He doesn't jump up on people though; he just sniffs madly around your legs until he decides that you've administered sufficient pats and scratches. Here, let me take that coffee and you can come on in." Brenna swung the door open and stepped carefully over her bunched rug to reach for the coffee carrier Annie held out to her. With the coffee safe inside, Brenna released her dog and Annie braced herself for his onslaught.

Snuffling and quietly yipping to himself, Lugus circled Annie's legs. True to prediction, he did not jump; he just danced around as his tail wagged wildly, looking expectantly up at Annie. His eyes closed in pleasure and his tongue flopped over the side of his teeth as Annie bent to scratch his head, her fingernails digging softly behind his golden ear.

"Come on, now Lugus," Brenna said. "Let her in."

Hearing his name, Lugus popped his eyes open and leapt through the door into the house. He scrambled for traction, slipping a few times hilariously before he was able to move off down the hallway. As the dog disappeared back into the house, Annie handed the gift-wrapped plaque to Brenna.

"House-warming," she said with a grin, lifting the coffee carrier from the entry table and following Brenna down the short hallway to the kitchen. At the table, Brenna pushed aside a sheaf of papers and dropped into a seat. She gestured for Annie to sit, and as Annie lifted the cups of coffee from the carrier, Brenna ripped into the paper on her gift.

"Oh wow, Annie," she whispered. "This is lovely. You didn't have to bring anything but yourself, but oh I love this!" She looked up at Annie with a wide grin. "Mom had this same poem printed in our house when I was growing up, just a little thing in a frame inside the front door. I remember it because when she died, dad took it down and put it in her dresser. I can't wait to tell him about this; thank you Annie."

Annie blushed. "Sure it's not too cheesy to get an old Irish poem for an Irish girl?"

Brenna snorted. "Yeah, not unless you think living in a lighthouse in Maine is too cheesy. No, I love this. Really." Brenna cleaned the scraps of paper from the table, tossing them into a giant trash can in the corner of the kitchen. Bits of wood and paper stuck out from the top of the garbage at all angles.

"Sorry about the mess," Brenna said. "I'm still settling in. Want a tour?"

"Sure! I've never been in a lighthouse," Annie answered, rising from the table. "Bring the coffee?"

"Absolutely," Brenna said, taking her cup and walking through an archway into the living room. She showed Annie how she'd refinished part of the archway trim, staining the fresh wood with a natural but polished look.

In Ireland, Brenna had worked with her father in his business, building cabinetry and other furniture. When Brenna had been a teenager, they'd even built a house from the ground up, just the two of them. She had an old black and white canvas print of the house on the wall in her bedroom, part of a horizontal collage. There were several canvas prints displayed there, each one hanging from a wide yellow ribbon attached to a wooden dowel mounted far above the head of the wide bed. The bed was dressed in a quilt that was mostly the same yellow as the ribbons, with large white polka dots sprinkled here and there. The pillows were a fluffy mix of white and varying shades of sunshine, cheerful and bright.

The bathroom was done in seashells, shades of light blue mixed with white and accented in soft cream. Along the wall opposite the claw foot-tub, there was a bench with storage underneath and a shelf above the bench was littered with nail polish bottles.

Eventually, they made it back to the living room where Annie admired the gallery wall Brenna had designed on her own. Without the distraction of hooks, ribbons or shelves of any kind, dozens of framed photographs and prints were a wild mix of visual attraction above and around the fireplace mantel. The frames were all natural wood, but the photos themselves were as varied in color as they were in size, subject and location.

On the right edge of the mantel, there stood the largest of all the photographs, a sunset image of a giant temple. With the evening sun blazing orange over the back of the temple, it truly was a majestic scene.

"Angkor Wat," Brenna said softly, running the tip of a finger down one side of the frame. "This photo was on Tommy's camera when they sent me his things. Later, they sent his ashes; he'd always said he couldn't stand to rot underground, so I had him cremated. That's him, there," she finished, pointing.

Beside the Angkor Wat photo, there stood a simple urn, with a shiny finish and a beautiful Asian pattern carved along the edges. Slightly beside and to the front of the urn, there was a small photo of Thomas O'Connor in a sparkling silver four by six frame. In basic blue jeans and a fitted white tank top, he was beautiful. In his arms there lay a small boy with dusty brown skin and solemn dark eyes. He wore a faded red shirt that was too large; it was much too long on his undernourished body, and his feet were bare.

"I have better pictures of him," Brenna whispered, her eyes dry but bleak in the midst of her bright fair skin. "I have lots of them. But I wanted to use one where he was doing what he loved. That shot was in his camera too."

"It hasn't gotten much easier for you yet, has it?" Annie asked, quietly, respectfully. "I have suffered a lot of loneliness after my divorce with Chase, but I know it isn't at all the same."

"Maybe not," Brenna said, visibly forcing herself back into her usual bright cheerfulness. "But he wouldn't have wanted me to drown in my own tears. I'm not even sure Tommy would have wanted this," she said, spreading her arms and waving at the house around her. "This lighthouse; the way I've worked on it. I mean, the mantel alone is like a tribute to his goodness. But he was a hero to me, and I just can't seem to let it go. Not yet."

"You don't really have to, Brenna," Annie said, "Grief comes and goes sometimes, always in a different pattern, and always a different speed. Each time and each circumstance is individual. You can't control it; you can't force it to go faster or in any way other than what it will. You just go through it. You learn to accept it and live with it. It heals like a skinned knee, all on its own."

Hours later, Annie left Brenna's lighthouse. Both women seemed to feel lighter, freer, somehow less injured than before. They had not shared the same tragedy; they had not shared precisely the same circumstance. They had, however, shared a common emotion; a common grief and a common sense of understanding. Now, it seemed, they would also always share a bond of friendship.

Driving home, Annie sang along with the radio, cheerful pop music that eased her soul and raised her spirits. Walking into the house that would soon be her very own, she dropped her keys into the scoop of the crystal mussel. She shut and locked the door; she met the eyes of the giant crystal seal and then raised her vision to the starfish on the wall. In her mind, she saw the memory of satisfaction on Brenna's face as she drove a nail into the wall and proudly hung the Irish poem near the door. Feeling that same satisfaction within herself, Annie kicked her shoes off and headed to the kitchen. She needed to pack for her hike with Brenna and Lugus in the morning.

***

Annie had just finished packing her tote bag with extra sandwiches for her hike with Brenna, when her cell phone rang from the living room. She ran to catch it before it went to voicemail and snatched it up without looking at the screen.

"Hello?" she asked.

"Hey, it's Brenna."

"Oh, hey! I was just packing us some sandwiches for today. Want me to swing over and get you guys? We can ride together in my car if you want," Annie said, dropping onto the couch to retie her shoe.

"Annie, I can't come, I dropped my coffee cup this morning and it broke. I cut my foot pretty bad. It finally isn't bleeding anymore, but I probably shouldn't be on it too much for a couple days. I'm really sorry Annie."

"Don't be sorry, I'll be just fine. Really, Bar Island isn't going anywhere unless we have a tidal wave, so we can just reschedule our hike. Want me to bring you anything, or maybe come sit with you? Keep you company?"

"No way," Brenna said, laughing. "Don't skip the hike just because I'm a klutz. Go and have fun. Take pretty pictures to show me while I'm stuck here on my butt for the next few days."

"Count on it," Annie laughed. "Well I guess I'd better go then, before I miss the tide change. I want to cross the sandbar as soon as it opens so I can get back before the tide changes and leaves me stranded. I can't swim, so I don't want to get caught up in the tide."

"Yeah that gentle swell of the tide can be brutal," Brenna teased. "But you go on. And if you're bored when you get back, I'll be here. On my butt. You can come by if you want." Brenna laughed again, and the women said their goodbyes. Ready to go, Annie unplugged her cell phone from the charger, slipped her tote bag over her shoulder and headed for the car.

***

Listening to the gravel crunch under her shoes as she walked across the sandbar, Annie knew she'd have to finish her hike pretty quickly. The tide was already beyond its low point, which meant she had maybe a ninety-minute time limit to get back to the bar before the ocean swallowed it up for the rest of the afternoon. She marveled at how open the place was, loving the lack of crowds.

"Yeah they probably all sleep in like normal people instead of rolling over and waking with the sun like you, nerd," she muttered to herself. "Who ever said the early bird wanted a worm anyway?"

She made quick work of crossing the sandbar, stopping for only a moment to listen for the seals, to glance around and see if her seal friend was hanging around the rocks. He wasn't there so she moved on, walking carefully over the rocky area at the start of the Bar Island pathway.

Once she was through the entrance to the trail, Annie stopped long enough to lift her camera from her tote bag and take one last look at the sandbar. As a woman who couldn't swim, Annie's comment to Brenna about tidal waves had only been about fifty percent joke. In truth, she dreamed often of drowning, of desperately clawing for air and being unable to breathe as the water pressed in around her. She was fully aware that the power of the ocean was a whole lot different from the glassy swimming pool she'd nearly died in as a child.

"Well, you just can't live in fear," she told herself, "so grow a pair." Taking a deep breath, Annie ventured deeper onto the trail, her camera in hand. The trail climbed gently uphill for a short while, but then forked into two different paths. The narrow path was thought of as a shortcut to the summit of Bar Island, but with or without her concern for the tidal schedule, Annie wanted the whole experience. With a little nod to herself, she took the wider, well-worn path through the forest.

Annie walked a while, stopping often to take pictures, admiring a flower here, a mushroom there. She loved the way the tree branches tangled and crossed over her head, the sunlight spilling through the leaves at odd times and odd angles. Through the branches and trunks around her, Annie could see little glimpses of the surrounding ocean. On one such stop, Annie was squatting on the ground, taking a close shot of a bee buried in the neck of a flower. When she stood and turned, there was a deer right beside her, almost close enough for her to touch him. He stood looking at her, silent and still, waiting as she slowly raised her camera. He remained frozen in the flash when she pressed the shutter button, and then as suddenly as he had appeared, he was gone.

The island was a beautiful place, and for a while, she forgot her unease. She worried more about the right light and the right camera angle, not nearly as much anymore about the time or the ongoing threat of the ocean. The quiet all around was like a blanket of peace, wrapping her in solitude and reminding her of the comfort of her own company. Finally reaching the summit of the island, Annie was amazed at the view.

It was only after she reached the summit of Bar Island and had spent a while taking pictures, that she remembered the tide and looked at her watch. She'd been wandering, admiring the beauty of the island for seventy minutes.

"Shoot," Annie said, louder than she had intended, the sound of her own voice somewhat startling after a period of such peaceful quiet. "Oh crap. Crap, crap, crap." Annie turned her camera off, stuffed it down into her tote bag, and held it against her side as she trotted cautiously back down the trail.

It didn't take long before she was running full speed, one arm hindered as she still gripped her bag to her side. Her breath was a strangled rush of air, trying somehow to enter and exit her chest at the same time; the trees whizzed by, and the path was a blur under her feet. Birds took flight, abandoning their perches as she went crashing clumsily down the trail as if she'd forgotten how to run. Her mind had become a tangled, jumbled mass of irrational terror; she felt as if the predictable cycle of the ocean's tides had ground to a halt, as if this were to be the last chance to ever get off the island.

In that moment of blind panic, Annie felt trapped, completely cut off from the world. She'd left her cell phone in the car by accident so she was quite literally alone. The quality of her running had dropped off as panic wracked her, her stride became shorter, jerkier, and her lungs were burning. Her muscles were screaming. The trail was less than a mile long, but she felt like she'd been running for hours.

With both arms moving, maybe her balance would have been better. With better timing, she wouldn't have been running down the trail in such a panic. Without her fear in front of her, she might have seen the uplifted tree root on the edge of the trail. As it was, her balance was off and she was definitely in a panic. Annie didn't see the root, though it was standing proud in a raised loop just in front of her foot. She hit the ground hard, all the air crushed out of her lungs by the fall. Her bag slipped off her shoulders and she lost her grip on it, skidding a few feet down the trail. Her palms burned where she'd tried to catch herself, the left knee of her jeans had ripped open on a rock, and there was a horrible pain in her side when she was finally able to breathe again.

Moving gingerly, she lifted her face from the trail and slowly sat up. Relief flooded her as the pain in her ribs receded, followed instantly by the weight of disappointment when she realized what she'd been laying on. Lifting the lens cap from the dust, she pressed it gingerly onto the crushed lens of her camera, knowing it was already too late. The body of the camera lay cradled in her hands, but the little red shutter button was still there on the ground, lying next to Annie's right foot.

"Oh no," she whispered, fighting tears. "Oh no, not my camera, I broke my camera." Gently, she packed the broken bits of her camera back into her tote bag, consoling herself with the promise of a new camera. Just as she had many times during the past few months, Annie looked skyward and sent up a silent prayer to whoever might be listening, a silent thanks for the financial freedom that her writing had earned her, for the money to replace the beloved camera that had been such a big part of her ability to find peace. She sat there a while, knowing she must have missed the tide by now and that the sandbar must be covered.

"No more rushing," she said into the quiet, pulling out her water bottle and drinking deeply. The tide wouldn't go out again for maybe twelve more hours, and Annie was trapped, held hostage by the patterns of the sea on an island with no shops, no people, and no bathrooms. Thankful for her own preparedness, Annie ate the sandwiches she'd packed. Scooting around until her back rested against the trunk of the tree she'd tripped over, Annie pulled her book from her bag and settled in to wait.

***

After spending a couple of hours reading by the tree, Annie had grown bored enough to scream. With maybe ten hours left before the next low tide, she had wandered aimlessly around the island, even venturing off the trails several times. She liked the adventure, figuring that since she was stuck on the island anyway, she had plenty of time to find the trail again if she lost it. She examined flowers, searched for deer, and admired the birds of the island.

Still, she was always checking her watch, watching the sea and occasionally walking back and forth along the trail to check the status of the sandbar. She read more of her book, pointlessly tried to get her broken camera working. She'd written out her frustrations in her journal. She'd wished for her phone; the latest smart phone, it was her lifeline.

She couldn't believe she'd left it in the car. It was a gadget full of amusement; it had come preloaded with a camera, music, games and digital books, only enhanced by the things she'd downloaded on her own. It would certainly have made it easier to pass the hours. Not to mention the probability of being able to call Brenna for a chat. Eventually, Annie had wandered back to the summit of Bar Island, sitting there in relative peace, watching the waves wash the shores as the sun passed overhead.

Making the best of her time alone on the island, Annie stripped her t-shirt and jeans off, until she was down to her lacy blue underwear and matching bra. She lay there at the top of the Bar Island trail, sunbathing nearly naked in the salty air and the soft grass as if she hadn't a care in the world.

Finally, a sufficient amount of time had passed, and Annie dressed to head back to the foot of the trail. Walking out of the trees at the end of the day, Annie was irritated. She was thirsty and had run out of water. She was hungry from all the mindless walking. Her feet were sore, her palms were aching, and her knee throbbed under the tear in her jeans. She mourned the loss of her camera, which had been like an extension of her own hand for so long. Tripping as she crossed the rocks onto the sandbar was the last thing she expected, and was the last straw in a stressful and emotional day.

"Shit," she swore, looking around to be sure no one had heard. "Shit," she said again when she lifted her hand from the rock she'd braced her fall on, only to see the rock spotted with her blood.

"Aw, shit," she growled, struggling to get up as she realized her ankle was stuck between two of the rocks and she couldn't twist around properly to free herself. Thankfully, she hadn't dropped her tote bag this time.

"Yeah," she muttered bitterly, checking inside the bag. "Because that would have been just freaking fabulous, to have dropped the damn thing in the sea and lost all my pictures along with my stupid camera, not to mention the damn car keys." Hot tears of frustration filled her eyes as she grunted, jerking at her leg in spite of the pain, trying to free herself.

Looking up, Annie glanced around the sandbar, struggling to see in the dim late afternoon light. She'd been hoping there would be people to call out to, but it seemed just as abandoned as it usually was when she was there. Somehow, she seemed to always be there when the tourists and locals had chosen to be elsewhere.

"Oh, it figures. This freaking sandbar is a freaking tourist trap, and the one time I really need a damn crowd, there isn't a soul in sight." Annie swore again, her frustrations mounting, coupling with her earlier panic as she realized that not only was she stuck again, she was stuck this time in the danger zone.

Hard as she tried, she couldn't remember ever hearing how deep the water could get when the sandbar was covered. Would it be deep enough to float in? Could she stand in it? Would her own foot be the anchor that drowned her, here in the sea where she'd made friends with a wild barking seal who posed for her camera and gazed at her gently with his liquid chocolate eyes?

"I guess there's only one way to find out," Annie whispered to herself, resigned for the moment to what seemed to be her fate. Most people she knew were terrified of death, but not Annie; she'd faced death many times in her life, at least twice by nearly drowning. As an adult, she had a more relaxed view about it; if it was her time, she figured, then it was her time. She took her book back out of her tote bag and spent the next hour reading to stay distracted, lounging uncomfortably among the rocks. Her ankle felt swollen, and when she'd tried to slip her foot out of her shoe to free herself, the shoe had been too tight to get off.

Watching over the top of her book as the moments drifted by and the evening tide rolled in, Annie felt her panic level rising, but she forced herself to keep reading. In that moment, the book she held in her hands was the only protection she had from full-blown panic; memories slowly came back to her, memories of news stories about hikers who'd been forced to amputate their own limbs in a desperate struggle for survival. Annie carried no weapon with her, nothing more than the pen she carried to write in her journal. Her earlier resolve began to dissipate, and she was forced to come to terms once again with the prospect of death.

As the first rush of cold, salty ocean water swirled around her trapped ankle and then receded, Annie finished the last sentence of the novel she'd been reading. Knowing it to be a worthless gesture in the face of death, she neatly tucked the book back into her bag and tried to ignore the quick mental image of her book floating in to shore on the current, her body lost underwater. She curled herself up as high above the water as she could get, and balled her tote bag on her lap. Wrapping her arms around herself, Annie helplessly watched her foot vanish beneath the sea and waited to see what the underwater world had in store for her.

It wasn't long before the sun was setting and Annie was transfixed by the painted colors of the sky. She watched as shades of blue and pink played chaos with yellow and orange among the fluffy clouds that floated by on the chilled breeze. Annie wished for a sweater, laughing at how she waited for death but still wished for the comforts of life. The water was licking at the backs of her thighs now, a scratchy salty tickle that soon ceased as the ocean rose above her hips and made its way toward her waist. By this time, she had tied the straps of her tote bag in knots to make them shorter, draping them over her shoulder to keep the bag lifted from the damage of the ocean.

She felt mostly calm; too emotionally tired to fight the idea of dying as the water washed up around the waistband of her jeans, licking up under the hem of her t-shirt. She thought of her failed marriage, her lack of children, her parents already long dead. She had no one to wish for, no one to say a mental goodbye to. In spite of it all, though, Annie continually scanned the narrow passage of the sandbar, praying for a hero, hoping someone might come along, see her and come to her rescue.

"What I wouldn't give for a mermaid friendship right now," she whispered, terror washing over her with every new wave of the ocean. Her lower half was covered now by the water, her breasts washed in foam from the waves. Her cut knee and skinned palm burned in the salt wash. Annie tried to ignore the sudden idea that sharks could smell blood in the water for miles, telling herself that surely they didn't venture this close to land, where the water was deep enough to drown in but not deep enough for giant human-eating water beasts. Her tote bag was hopeless, soaked in a rogue wave that had washed her all the way up to her chin, yet she held onto it firmly.

The emotional numbness was beginning to wear off as Annie realized that she was well and truly stuck, trapped among the rocks of a sandbar she had visited safely so many times. Panic washed freshly over her with the sea, covering her as surely with the stench of fear as with the saltiness of the water. She jerked at her foot mindlessly, scrambling to stay on top of the rock she'd been perched on. She stood, trying to stay above the water, but as the waves reached above her chest, Annie finally could take no more. She panicked and burst into tears.

***

Annie was going to drown; she knew it as surely as she knew her own name. As the waves rolled gently in around her, her grief poured out as her tears fell into the sea. One after the other, the salty drops of her fear and sadness blended in with the salt spray of the ocean. She found herself wishing again, helplessly, for a hero.

Her breathing had become panicked; she was struggling against the rocks in a desperate effort to disentangle her foot, trying to keep her lungs full of air and not water as the tide rose higher and higher. Trying to calm herself, Annie counted along with the tears as she felt them drop from her chin.

"Four," she whispered, drawing breath before the current washed over her again. "Five. Six." Her throat was getting sore; she'd swallowed a good amount of water by then and her eyes were burning with the ocean salt. "Seven," she gasped. She was looking skyward now, her face just barely above the water.

One last time, the water backed away until her head was exposed. She could feel the seawater clogging her ears; her hair was matted around her face. Her tote bag was gone, but she'd stuffed her keys and wallet down her jeans pockets before letting go of the straps of her bag. She wanted her body to be identifiable. Brushing her hair quickly from her eyes, Annie tried to look around, afraid the sea would wash over her forever at any moment. She turned her head, thinking she'd heard the barking of a seal nearby. Something brushed her leg under the water; she screamed, nearly choking on the water as a high wave closed over her head.

She hadn't had time to draw a breath. Annie didn't know how long until the water might uncover her face again, or if she would be given one last breath before she drowned. Suddenly, she realized that there was something around her ankle, down where she was trapped in the rocks; it felt hard and solid. She kicked against it with her free leg; it went away but came again, and then she was free.

Annie kicked her legs in a panic, desperate to reach the surface of the ocean, desperate to draw just one more breath of air. Around her waist was a belt of steel; she had no clue where it had come from and didn't have time to care. Her lungs were burning, screaming for her to inhale. It could be either water or air; her lungs didn't see the difference just then.

It seemed to take forever before her face broke the surface of the water. When it did, she still refused to inhale, terrified that she would reach her freedom only to inhale a wave as it washed over her. She opened her eyes, salt water pouring in and burning them. Squeezing them shut, she tried again; instantly, she stopped struggling in the water.

There before her was the face of an angel, the hero she had so desperately wished for, seawater dripping from his dark hair; his skin was dark in the meager light of evening, his teeth gleaming white as he spoke. Annie couldn't hear him over the water and the deafening rush of her own confusion. Her eyebrows came together; she felt the salt-tightened skin of her forehead wrinkle, but when she inhaled and tried to speak, fear had paralyzed her voice, stealing her ability to communicate.

He shook his head and wrapped one arm tightly around her waist, dragging her back against the warm solid flesh of his chest. Annie struggled briefly, but he held her snugly against his body. Turning his attention to the swim, he made his way through the current to the shore. His body was strong behind her, as if he alone could beat back the power of the sea, and Annie felt oddly reassured, safe in his arms. He was wrapped around her like a safety net, and Annie had grown certain as he swam that she was completely safe.

Knowing this, feeling that sense of instant trust, made it easy for her to give in finally to the exhaustion of the day, the hard result of the fear and the panic she'd been drowning in. Her eyes fluttered closed; the last thing she heard was his swearing as her body went limp.

When Annie woke, she was tangled in a pile of towels on the couch in her living room with no memory of how she'd gotten there. Her clothes had dried into a salt stiffened cast of fabric around her. As she moved, her jeans crackled softly, and she looked around nervously. She did have a faint memory of salt-burned eyes, clogged ears unable to hear the voice of the man who'd saved her from her rocky trap.

Her wallet was lying open on a towel beside her. She wiggled her toes; her shoes and socks were gone. Lifting her wallet, Annie checked to see if anything was gone, thankful she never carried cash. All her cards were there, her driver's license, even her discount card from the coffee shop.

Gingerly moving her sore and tired body, she looked around. He was there, in the wingback chair near the fireplace. He was also resting on several towels, and she smiled to think he'd thought of her furniture. This quick gratitude was followed closely by suspicion. Obviously, he'd gotten her address from her driver's license, but how had they gotten here?

She watched him sleeping; his hair was black, cut short and very clean around the ears and neck. His hair shone in the morning light streaming through the window. His eyes were closed and his breathing was a soft sound, like that of the ocean on a calm and easy afternoon. With his head tilted back against the chair in slumber, his throat looked long and strong; occasionally he would swallow in his sleep and she could watch the bobbing Adam's apple beneath his sun-bronzed skin.

He wore no shirt. She gazed at his bare chest, her eyes admiring the tone of his body as her mind continued to contemplate the man who had saved her. He was muscular but not terribly large; his arms were toned and strong even at rest, and as Annie watched him, she realized with a shock that she wanted to touch him. His flat stomach rose and fell with his breath, and she wondered if his skin felt as smooth and soft as it looked. He wore royal blue surfing shorts that had a sparkling white drawstring. His legs were powerful, stretched out long before him toward the warmth of the softly burning fire. His feet were bare, neat and clean. Looking back at the shorts, she wondered hazily what he might do if he awoke to find her pulling the neat bow from the drawstring.

Blushing, she sat up as silently as possible and stood to walk quietly into the kitchen. She'd never been a bold woman, but this man had an odd effect on her, making her want to open up to him, talk to him, reach out and pull him to her. It left her feeling loose and scandalous; this man was a stranger!

Looking out the window, Annie checked to see if her car was there, wondering where her cell phone was. Apparently, he'd brought it inside; it was there on the entry table next to the seal, and her keys were there in the crystal mussel where she always left them. It just barely occurred to her to wonder what else he might have done to her while he was searching her pants for her wallet and keys. She did wonder, though, as nausea rolled through the pit of her stomach, how he'd managed to move her into her car, into her home, and all without waking her. Turning, she walked back to the kitchen, struggling to remember the night before. On the table was a note, written on the back of an envelope; the writing was sure and strong, neat and unhurried.

"Annie," it read. "I know your name because I searched your wallet. You were unconscious and I couldn't wake you; maybe you were in shock. We got lucky with your car; it was the second one I tried after setting off someone else's alarm system with your key. Anyway, I thought about the hospital, but you seemed okay, only sleeping, so I used your license to find the address. I was awake watching you until I thought you must be okay, but I'm wearing down so in case you wake before I do, I promise I didn't do anything creepy. I just stayed to watch over you, you looked so helpless. It was a hard swim; don't be surprised if I sleep for days unless you wake me. But if you need me, give a shout and I'll be there." The note was signed simply, "Malik."

It was still early, and Annie couldn't help thinking that maybe some of her stuff might have washed up on the beach by now. She flipped the envelope over and scribbled on the front.

"Malik," she wrote, "Thank you. I'm sure you saved my life last night. As to the creepy, we shall see as the day wears on. I have to run out for some things, but I will be back as soon as I can. If you wake while I'm gone, don't worry, I'm fine. But stay here, please. Make yourself at home, and I'll be back soon. Annie."

Reading over the short note, she realized the truth in her words. He had saved her life, and she was filled with gratitude. But why tell him to stay? She really should wake him, thank him, and send him on his way. Still, she couldn't bring herself to want him gone. She wanted to come back and find him still sleeping in her living room; she wanted – maybe -- to ask him to teach her to swim. She wanted to run her fingers through his dark hair, and … "Well, now, that's enough of that," she muttered.

Leaving her socks abandoned by the door, Annie slipped her ruined shoes back on and grabbed her keys, running down the driveway to her car. Getting in, she marveled that somehow the seats were not wet, the carpet and interior were not salty or even dirty. Her car was as it had been, as if no one had been in it at all. Driving back to the parking lot where she usually left her car parked, she locked the doors and walked slowly toward the sandbar.

"Stupid ankle," she muttered as she walked, twinges of pain creeping up her leg from the ankle that had been trapped in the rocks.

Too early for low tide, the sandbar was still covered with a shallow layer of ocean water. But there at the water's edge, she could see a little speck of pink that she knew was her water bottle. Moving closer to the water, she snatched the bottle up, looking around to see if anything else had washed up. She didn't see anything else, not even the blanket she tripped over. Dropping to her rear in the gravel, she scrambled over to pick it up, realizing it was not a blanket after all. It was soft, furry on one side and completely smooth on the other. Warm and heavy with short thick fur, it was white but was speckled with black and gray just like her seal friend. Her breath caught in her throat when she saw the scar toward the edge of the pelt. It was like the scar on the seal she'd been photographing for weeks.

"Oh my goodness," she whispered, her gaze going out to sea. She didn't know where it had come from, but somewhere inside her, she knew that she held the skin of the animal she'd grown so attached to, and yet there was no carcass anywhere, no blood on the ground or on the pelt. It was actually clean, almost as if someone had washed it and then simply forgotten it here. Her heart aching at the thought that something might have happened to the seal she now thought of privately as her own, Annie clutched the pelt to her chest. She couldn't leave it; she bundled the weight of it in her arms, and stuffed it into her trunk.

She had no idea what she would do with the pelt or why she'd felt the need to keep it. All she knew just then was that she definitely didn't want the faintly fishy perfume of it permeating her car. Once she arrived home, she took the pelt from the trunk, carried it to her outdoor shed in the backyard, and set it safely aside while she pulled her wedding gown from its old cedar trunk. Stuffing the gown into a plastic storage bin instead, she emptied the trunk and made space for the pelt.

***

Annie couldn't put her finger on why, but she felt somehow guilty for bringing the seal pelt home from the sandbar. More than that, she had a distinct sense of how important it was to keep the beautiful silky pelt hidden away, although this feeling made her stomach rise up and her heart flutter nervously.

Stuffing her strange feelings away to be dealt with later, Annie piled the pelt into the chest that had once safely held her wedding gown, double-checking to be sure that it was locked. She placed several other boxes around it, stacking some of them directly on top of it as if to keep the pelt from somehow slithering out onto the floor. Swiping the dust from her hands, Annie walked back to the house, curious about the man she'd left there.

Stepping softly through the house and into the living room, Annie peeked around the corner at Malik. The fire had died down. He still slept, but he had crossed his arms over his stomach and had bent his knees as if pulling in against the chill of the room. Leaving the fire to die completely, she turned on the heating system and brought a spare blanket from her closet. Annie held her breath and tried not to wake him as she gently draped the blanket over his sleeping body.

Standing back, she watched him sleep. Malik had beautiful skin, golden and clear. His jaw was strong, his body toned and sleek, muscular and well defined. As she looked down at him, Annie wondered, what miracle had called him to the beach just when she needed rescue? How had he been thinking clearly enough to find his way to her house? Already, she loved his obvious respect for her personal space; he had not stripped the wet clothes from her body, nor did it appear that he'd entered her bedroom or any other private area of the house. The towels he'd spread for her on the couch had come from the closet in the hallway.

Still, she couldn't help looking around her home for signs of his presence. She could find no shoes other than her own; he'd left no wallet, phone or keys lying about. No shirt, pants, or jacket; there was no backpack or any other thing that might have belonged to this man.

"Well, it's not like he could have just risen from the ocean. He has to be from somewhere," Annie muttered to herself, scanning the house a second time. "He's got to have stuff someplace, doesn't he? Since there doesn't seem to be anything here though, it's not like I can just leave him half-naked like that and with no shoes. Not the best form of gratitude, hmm?"

With her decision made, Annie glanced toward the hallway, wishing for a shower. "Not fair to shower if he can't even get dressed when he wakes up," she muttered, snatching up her keys again. Sighing, she glanced over at him one last time before leaving the house. He was a bit larger in build than Chase had been, but she could still remember all of Chase's sizes. With a little effort, maybe she could guess Malik's sizes and find him something decent to wear on his way out of her life and back to wherever he came from.

***

Standing in the men's section of the closest department store, Annie fought off a wave of nausea. She was terribly nervous to be picking out a man's clothes again, since she hadn't done this sort of thing in so long. It brought back too many memories. Even before the divorce, it had been months since she'd shopped for Chase, always afraid that he wouldn't like what she'd chosen for him. It had been a rare thing for her to do even when she'd been someone's wife, and now? Shopping for Malik was a completely new thing; he was a completely new man.

He was a total stranger to her and she didn't have a clue what he liked. Was he wearing surf shorts because he was some sort of swimming athlete? That might explain his presence in the ocean the night before.

Or did he just like them, as Chase had, because they were comfortable? She hadn't noticed any tan lines to indicate what kind of shirts he wore. To be honest, she hadn't noticed much at all, other than how attractive he was, glowing as he did under his bronzed tan.

Finally, deciding that she could just return whatever he didn't like or couldn't wear, Annie tossed off her worries and bought a range of different clothes. She had the money to spend, so she tried to just have fun with it. Because he obviously liked surf shorts at least a little and for whatever reason, she bought more of them in a range of colors and styles. She also bought tank tops, t-shirts, shoes and socks before seeking out boxers and boxer briefs in addition to regular brief underwear. All of this Annie bought in a range of sizes, blushing furiously as she went through the checkout line. As she'd solidified her plan to bring Malik something fresh to wear, it hadn't occurred to her how strange she might look, buying new clothes that would fit a range of men in different sizes. Still, it couldn't be helped; she couldn't simply wake him and ask what size his shorts were. She'd also thrown grooming and hygiene products into her cart, trying to buy products that came close to what he already smelled like, a wash of ocean and sea salt, musk and manliness.

Stopping for breakfast on the way home, she ordered a range of things because she didn't know what he would like to eat. By this time, she was quite afraid that she was going overboard, but her gratitude for his saving her life won the battle with her pride. Fully aware that she was alive because of his efforts, she wanted him to know she was thankful. Feeling nauseated and already exhausted certainly didn't ease her decision-making, though; she ended up with far more than she needed because she just wanted to be done shopping, to get home and eventually, hopefully take a shower.

It took several trips before she was done carrying everything into the house, and on the last trip, Annie slipped as quietly as possible through the door, kicking her shoes off into the basket beneath her little entry table. She kept her keys in her pocket to avoid jingling them accidentally, hoping to get things organized before waking Malik to help her eat the feast she'd brought home. Sighing, she turned to enter the kitchen, and bumped against the solid wall that was Malik's naked chest. Electricity sizzled through her; she'd always thought that instant chemistry was a myth, but here she stood, suddenly more alive than before as she came into close contact with Malik's body. Gasping, she dropped one of the bags on the floor and momentarily lost her ability to speak.

Squatting down easily, Malik retrieved the bag Annie had dropped, looking her over as he lifted the bag from the floor. He took a few others from her hands, smiling as he met her nervous eyes.

"You're not gonna faint again, are you?" he asked, his low voice trailing lazily through her, his eyes laughing.

"Um, well, I'll try," Annie muttered. "That is, I mean I'll try not to. I, um, I brought food."

"That's all food?" he asked, gesturing to the overflowing kitchen table. "I hope you don't want me to eat it all!" He was teasing, his laughter a pleasant sound as he watched her. His gaze was steady enough to cut through the humor and make her stomach tremble and shiver.

Annie forced a smile in spite of her nerves. Being attracted to the half-naked strange man standing there in her kitchen had certainly had a quick effect on her mental abilities, but she didn't want to seem standoffish.

Swallowing the nervous lump in her throat, Annie squeaked, "I went shopping. There wasn't anything of yours anywhere, but you, um; you'll need more clothes than those shorts eventually. And I thought you might want a shower after the swim you took to save me. So I got you some things to wear while I was out. I don't know what you like, obviously, so I just guessed at sizes and stuff," she finished, nervously catching her bottom lip between her teeth.

Now that she'd done it, she felt pretty stupid. Why had she assumed he didn't have any clothes anywhere? Bar Harbor was a small enough place to allow for a lot of walking, and for all she knew, he'd only been hiking near the sandbar when he'd found her among the waves. For all she knew, this hero man in front of her had a car still parked and waiting near the sandbar, maybe even a wife and family somewhere.

Mortified, Annie realized the possibility that she had just gifted some woman's handsome and sexy husband with underwear. More than that, wherever he lived, he hadn't gone home last night! What must his family think?! She hadn't seen any ring on him, but she did know that some men simply chose not to wear them. She'd only just moved here, and now it was likely that she'd have her first local enemy – whoever this man belonged to. He couldn't possibly be unattached, handsome as he was, and she was now wishing quite firmly that some natural disaster would occur, that fate would intervene before she could embarrass herself any further.

"Wow," Malik was saying. While Annie had been frozen, mortified, he'd been digging into one of the bags on the table, pulling out a red pair of shorts with a black drawstring and black tribal patterns starting at the waist and flowing down the outer thigh on both sides. "What is all this?" His dark eyes rose to hers, warm and somehow gently comforting.

"Well," Annie started, and then trailed off as the nausea rose up again. She closed her eyes, one hand on her stomach. Swallowing firmly in a steadfast refusal to vomit nervously in front of him, she continued. "I noticed there wasn't anything around that was yours, not in here or in my car. So I don't know if you left your own car somewhere, or if you left any things near the sandbar when you saw me. I went there this morning to see if any of my stuff had washed up, and there was nothing around that I could see. And I can't very well send you back to wherever you came from with no clothes and no food and no shower, so I went shopping. I wanted to thank you, Malik. You saved my life last night."

His eyebrow rose, a dark arch above surprised eyes. "You went to the sandbar," he asked. The fingers of one hand crept up to drag through his hair, but then he seemed to regain his composure. "Busy woman this morning, huh?"

His apparent nervousness about her return to the sandbar confused her, but she nodded silently answer his question, leaving her own questions for another time.

"Hmm," he said. "Ok. So the sandbar was empty, and you wanted to thank me for saving you with new shorts."

"Well, it sounds stupid, I guess." Annie muttered. "I just needed to be doing something, I guess. I can return anything you don't like or can't wear. Or I can return all of it, it doesn't matter. I just tried to get everything I could think of that you might need because there wasn't anything here so..." She trailed off, her nerves in an uproar and her embarrassment reaching new highs.

"No, it's cute," Malik said, dropping a black tank top on top of the pile of bags. "Thank you. Really. Annie, this is sweet. I think most women would have kindly but suspiciously booted me out the door by now, but not you. You bring me something clean to wear and something good to eat. It's very endearing."

"I just, I want you to know that I really appreciate what you did. Even if I hadn't been trapped in the rocks," Annie said, walking over to the table, "I can't swim, so I was pretty much gonna die last night if you hadn't found me there."

Malik stood silent, watching her speak, taking in the still-salty clothes he'd rescued her in, her hair slightly mussed from sleeping where he'd settled her on the couch.

"Lucky you," he said. He went back to digging in the bags, pulling out a package of white boxer briefs. His eyes darted to hers, and she immediately dropped her gaze to the floor, her face and ears going red under his scrutiny. She peeked up at him through her lashes; his cheeks flushed first, then his lips trembled and soon he was laughing outright, with one slender hand on his chest as his teeth flashed in the light from the window. His laugh was a sexy vibrating rumble that was at once comfortably loud and deliciously contagious.

Eventually, Annie was laughing with him. "You just wait," she giggled. "Just wait till you see what else I have in those bags." She stalked over to him and pulled two other packages of boxer briefs from the bag he'd been digging in, each a different size than the first. "I did this with regular briefs too, and boxers because I didn't know what to get."

"Well I still think it's cute," he said, the laughter finally edging away so that he could speak. "You're very thoughtful, Annie, I'm glad to have been the one who found you in the waves."

His eyes held hers, and Annie felt altogether mesmerized. Suddenly she couldn't look away, and she could think of no witty remark to make. She'd never really been a natural flirt; she'd certainly never reacted so strongly to a man before, but she was suddenly struggling to restrain herself from stepping forward into his arms, lost in the eyes that held her, further embarrassing herself with this beautiful man who stood laughing at her with his twinkling eyes.

Just as suddenly, she was turning away as the nausea that had haunted her morning rose up uncontrollably. She was running for the bathroom, the meager contents of her stomach bubbling up as fast as she could run. When the heaving stopped and she finally lifted her sweaty forehead from her arms, she realized she hadn't needed to push the cloud of her hair away from her face. Annie closed her eyes, licked her lips and swallowed, as sheer humiliation made her stomach rise up again.

"Oh no, you're not still here," she finally muttered, having turned and heaved until her very insides threatened to abandon her. As if it wasn't bad enough to find herself on the bathroom floor with sweat on her face and slobber on her chin, of course it would be her luck that an incredibly sexy, apparently very good Samaritan had witnessed the entire show.

"Yes," he answered, gently lifting her from the floor. "You are obviously unwell, and I am still here for as long as you need me to be. What kind of man would I be, if I lifted you from the rocks, swam with you to the shore, brought you to your home, watched over you through the night, and then left you to die of dehydration? It's common for people who take in too much seawater to become ill, Annie, and I can't save you from drowning just to leave you to e. coli. I'm here now, and I'll stay with you until you're okay."

***

In the next few days, Malik had gotten to know Annie better than anyone ever had, better than Annie had ever wanted anyone to know her. He held her hair while she vomited; he washed her forehead while she sweated out fevers in her bed. He brought her endless quantities of soup and water and juice in a valiant struggle to keep her hydrated, though she'd begged him after a particularly violent episode of sickness to simply leave her to die.

Annie spent the first few days running back and forth to the bathroom, each time opening the door to find Malik standing there patiently. Each time, he quietly took her hands and gently guided her back to bed. At first she had protested, saying he must surely have somewhere he'd rather be, somewhere better than in the company of a sick woman he barely knew. Malik had responded gently as always, telling her that he loved taking care of people and that he wouldn't leave her sick and alone. He'd winked and said that her general sweetness as a patient made his effort worthwhile.

Eventually, she had been sick enough to stop caring about his motives, slowly beginning to lean on him out of necessity, and learning to enjoy his company in the process. Annie was thankful to have someone to depend on while she was ill, thankful that for some reason the universe seemed to have sent her a hero.

Initially afraid to accept the sudden gift of his friendship, Annie began to accept his presence, quietly dreading the day he would decide to walk out of her life and go back to his own. She had to stop herself from constantly comparing his actions to what she would have expected from Chase, waiting for him to betray or abandon her, trying to send him away before he could leave on his own. Still, he stayed, kindly nursing her, keeping her company. Despite her fears, Annie grew increasingly attached to Malik, which terrified her. She lectured herself frequently, reminding her injured heart that Malik would not stay, that he had no responsibility or commitment to her, that he had no reason to stay with her beyond that of his own kindness.

He never mentioned the sounds that emanated from the bathroom and for this simple kindness, Annie's pride was incredibly grateful. It didn't take long before she was weak and dehydrated enough that Malik didn't allow her out of bed even to be sick. Instead, he brought a bucket to her bedside and kept it clean, no matter how often it was used.

He was an attentive caretaker, always beside her as she drifted in and out of a weak and restless sleep. Somehow, he always seemed to be there when she woke, always talking to her, keeping her updated on the news and telling her where he had placed her mail.

By the end of the second week, Annie was on the mend but her house was a complete mess. Malik had kept up the laundry; he'd washed the clothes, towels, rags and blankets, all of which bore the effects of Annie's illness. Annie had been unable to put them away, weak as she was from sickness, and he had not bothered asking where things belonged. He had simply folded what he'd washed and stacked it on her couch for later. This had been his strategy with the kitchen also; dishes and gadgets had been washed and neatly stacked along the counter, except for things that obviously went in one place or another.

When Annie could finally hold down fluids, Malik had walked with her to the living room, gently guiding her as one would guide a child. Annie's laughing protests amounted to nothing, and soon she was enthroned in the wing back chair by the fireplace, the one he had slept in during his first night at her house. This time it was Annie who was gently covered and tucked in; though she insisted that she was fine. Malik would lift a stack of clothes or towels, and Annie would tell him where to put things. Next, they worked on the kitchen; Malik swept and chattered busily, while Annie watched him over the mug of broth he had placed before her.

He asked a lot of questions, and Annie was flattered by his interest. For the first time in years, someone seemed genuinely interested in her, and she was able to talk to him honestly about how hard it had been for things to fall apart with Chase.

"It just wasn't my plan. I had this perfect plan, this perfect life," she said. "I had a successful husband and good friends, a blossoming career; I thought I had it all. It was my plan, the old-fashioned American dream. And now it's just gone. I know this must all sound silly to you," she trailed off, her face flushing.

"It isn't silly," Malik said. "We all have our dreams, Annie. Everyone wants that spectacular love, that kind of love that explodes in this passionate fire and never burns out, and a plan for life that goes just as we always thought that it would. But life, it's all about adjusting, isn't it? It's about finding a new plan, building up a new life if you find yourself in a place where everything you ever thought turns out to be a lie."

"Wow, sounds like you speak from experience," Annie said.

"I do. But enough about me, I'm boring," Malik said with a smile. "Tell me what your parents are like." He checked the mug in her hands, poured more broth in, and tucked a lock of hair behind her ears before starting to mop Annie's kitchen. By this point, she had learned that arguing with him was futile, so she sipped her broth and answered his questions.

"My parents are dead," she said. "They were killed in a car accident not long after I left home. They were always my top encouragement when I was little; always right there to support me. It was the same way when I first said that I wanted to write. I have never gotten over knowing that it took me too long to write anything successful. My parents were gone before I wrote my first book. What about your parents?"

Malik sighed, finished with the floor. He came to sit beside her at the table. "My dad lives here still, but I haven't seen him in years. I was actually on my way to see him when I found you in the waves, and I've been mostly here since then. Time well spent, from what I can see," he laughed, ripping a chunk from the loaf of bread he was munching. Winking, he offered it to her. "You look much more alive now. It suits you."

Annie lowered her eyes, embarrassed at his comment. Accepting the bread and cautiously nibbling at it, she chose to ignore the comment and asked him, "And your mom?"

"Gone," he muttered, turning his gaze to the ocean view out the window. Clearing his throat, he said, "Your grass has been growing wild. You have a mower out in that shed that I can use?"

"You want to mow my grass?" Annie asked, incredulous. She had an immediate vision, a memory of the lawn mower resting against the wall in the back yard shed. Knowing that the pelt was hidden there, Annie felt a twinge of unease. Ignoring it, she told herself that he was just trying to be nice and wouldn't be prowling through her things.

"I doubt you're up to it," he answered smoothly.

"But, my grass?" Annie was struggling not to show how very attracted she was to him. Getting to know him had certainly made it seem easy to be so drawn to him. But after the emotional trauma of her divorce from Chase, she was finding it hard to believe that Malik could truly be interested in her, that he could honestly be this much of a nice guy. He was incredibly sexy, gentle and easy to talk to, and she was a mess who had spent most of the last week quivering and vomiting all over him. She couldn't help wondering what made him stick around, what he might be running – or hiding – from.

"Well, I've fished you out of the ocean, Annie," Malik said dryly, leaning one broad shoulder against the patio door, oblivious to the way his actions made her thoughts fly away like ash on the breeze. "I've held your hair while you struggled with the results of too much stress and too much seawater. I've cleaned your face, your laundry, your car and your kitchen floor. And now, I will absolutely mow your grass." He grinned, watching as Annie's mouth dropped open in surprise, embarrassment coloring her face.

"Any other things I can do to be of service, you just feel free to let me know." With that final teasing statement and a wink that left Annie trembling, Malik slipped out the door and into the backyard.

***

By the end of the next day, Annie was mostly back to her old self. The problem was that she had gotten far too used to having Malik around. He was like an old friend she'd known all her life, always a source of cheer and laughter for Annie. He had his serious side, but for the most part, he was always smiling. He loved to laugh, and he found Annie to be an endless source of amusement.

At first, Annie had been nervous about Malik, always watching her with his dark eyes, always radiating strength and sex and good humor. She wasn't used to being the center of anyone's attention. It wasn't long before his charm simply won her over, and she was happy each morning to wake up and leave the warm comfort of her bed, to brush her hair before pulling on a nightgown and robe to pad barefoot into the kitchen, seeking him out.

She loved the mornings when she woke before he did, hearing the blankets rustle in the guest room he'd taken, the sound of him moving quietly around as he woke and readied himself for the day. She loved the simple act of placing two heavy mugs next to the coffee pot instead of her lonely one. This was nothing special in itself, but for her it was a reminder of how happy she was in his company, an emotional break from the loneliness she'd begun to feel trapped in.

There were benefits to sleeping in, though. She had especially loved waking up late one day, to find her coffee mug already filled and prepared exactly to her liking. Malik had not needed to ask what she wanted; he'd simply made an effort to watch her throughout their time together and discover for himself what she liked. For Annie, this was an uncommon gesture of attentiveness; it was wholly new to her. Chase had never specifically remembered things that she liked or didn't like. He'd usually guessed well enough, but simple daily things like her coffee preferences had never mattered to him.

Malik had made a point over the short time that they'd known each other to really get to know Annie. He'd asked her lots of questions about her parents; he'd expressed genuine interest in hearing her chatter on about her childhood. He'd listened to her ramble about childhood friends she'd lost touch with, and he had understood when she'd told about long-term friends she'd purposely left behind with the ruins of her marriage. To her knowledge, he had hardly even left her house since he'd arrived, burdened with her unconscious body after dragging her from the hands of death in the ocean.

There were times when she found herself sitting back, silently watching him, and wondering at his motives. She couldn't deny the unusual nature of their relationship, but the chemistry between them also couldn't be denied. Whether they stayed friends or someday developed into more, she wanted to see where it was going. Strange or not, something about being with Malik felt right to her, and she felt that after the emotional struggle of divorce, she owed it to herself to try to love again. If she were to love again, she wanted an easy fit, a simple way of falling naturally into someone, and that's how it felt with Malik; being around him was simple, easy.

She grew used to the illusion that Malik could be hers; that they could simply keep going just as they had been, sharing coffee and breakfast each morning seasoned with genuine laughter and good conversation. She'd wanted to believe she could keep watching him glisten with sweat in the sun as they worked together in her flowerbeds, that they'd always be throwing ideas back and forth about things she could do with the house once the purchase was finalized.

Having him walk into the kitchen one morning fully dressed with a backpack slung over one shoulder had shattered the illusion entirely. *"Could he be leaving?"* she wondered, hoping she hadn't grown attached to him only to watch him walk away.

She found him breathtaking, wearing what she called his 'trademark surf shorts'. They were teal green, with a crisp white tribal pattern foaming down the outer thighs like the waves of the sea. He had paired them with a simple white t-shirt and the white running shoes Annie had chosen for him. The white of his clothes emphasized the darkness of his tan and the sleek black of his hair; Annie had to struggle to pretend that she wasn't suddenly breathless and fluttery, aching to touch him, to invite him to stay with her. She clutched her coffee under her chin, both hands wrapped around the mug in her effort not to reach out to him.

"Keep it together, Annie," she thought. "He is just a nice guy who was here because you were pathetically ill. He's been here for months already! And you can't get all clingy if he wants to go on with his life. That's normal, people walk in and out of each other's lives all the time so just deal. Remember how much you liked being single." For some reason, she couldn't remember liking single life at all in that moment.

"Good morning," she said aloud, forcing a smile.

"I can see it, you know," he said, raising his eyebrows as he stepped close. He moved into her personal space and her breath caught. Reaching one toned, tanned arm around Annie's waist, he gripped the mug of coffee she'd left for him on the counter and lifted it to his lips.

"You can see the coffee?" Annie asked, trying to hide her inner struggle behind a joke.

"No, I can see the insecurity, Annie. It just seeps out of you," Malik answered her, scooping one crooked finger under her chin and lifting her face to his. "You have a whole different stance this morning, a different look on your face. You think I'm all finished with you now that you don't seem in any danger of killing yourself somehow. As if I could ever believe you'd be safe now that I've seen you near death in one way or another for almost the entire time I've known you."

"Finished with me? Malik, I hardly think anything like that," Annie lied, lowering her eyes as much as possible without actually pulling away from him. She'd never been an overly confident woman, and having her husband choose another woman over her had shattered what self-esteem she'd had to begin with. The idea of another man growing this close to her just to disappear was painful. Still, she refused to show her weakness. She moved her chin from his hands, sipping her coffee before she said, "I just, you know, it's ok for you to be on your way. We've gotten to be friends, but you can't drop your life just because you met me. I'm sure you have places to be."

"I see," he said. Ducking down so that his eyes met hers again, he continued. "So you're telling me that you'd be just fine if I walk out that door and go on with whatever life you think I have? And you wouldn't miss me at all, hmm? Total understanding?"

"Malik! Don't be silly, of course I would miss you!" Annie's eyes darted away, and she took a step back. She needed to break the contact with him, to separate herself from his physical space. Since she'd first laid eyes on him, all she'd been able to think was what it would be like to share space with him; to share true and honest intimacy with this beautiful and gentle stranger who'd appeared as if by magic in her life.

"I would miss our talks," Annie said honestly, struggling against her pride to say what she needed to say, knowing that if he walked out, he might never walk back in. She was determined to know she'd said her piece, that she'd given her best to the effort. She wanted to know that if he walked away from her, it wasn't because she hadn't asked him to stay. But could she ask him to stay? Could she bare herself in that way to him?

"I'd miss hanging out with you," she continued, struggling to find the right words. "And I'd miss the easy way we get along, you know? But it's not as though your life began the second I started drowning. The world doesn't revolve around me, and I'm not silly enough to have expected you just to stick around here forever. I've sort of been expecting you to go, at some point. You know, back to your own life."

"Well, of course I'd still like to see you, Annie," Malik said. "I've enjoyed our friendship too."

Friendship? Annie's heart sank. This beautiful perfect man was gentle and kind, considerate and caring; she'd wanted him from the first day, and he offered *friendship*. She felt like an unguarded and immature schoolgirl with a crush. Her own husband hadn't been able to remain faithful to her, had been overjoyed in the end to throw all of her faults right in her face. Chase had been cruel in the divorce, watching her tears fall as he'd told her all the reasons he'd had for having an affair with her best friend, all the ways he'd found her lacking over the years. She felt like an idiot to have hoped that Malik could want her.

"Friendship," she said, gulping her coffee, feeling it burn a trail of humiliation all the way to the pit of her stomach. "Right. So, you're venturing out today, hmm? What have you got planned for the day?"

"To start out with," Malik said, "I was going to give you this." He stepped forward, closing the space between them again, and handing her a small folded paper. "It's my dad's phone number," he continued, tipping his head to indicate the paper. "I haven't seen him yet, so I have to go see him, let him know I'm around."

"And after that?" Annie kept her eyes down, her hands busy unfolding the paper so that she could read the number written there. She folded it small again, not looking at him as she stuffed the slip of paper into the side pocket of her purse on the counter.

"After that, I was planning to come back here."

Her eyes shot back to his face, so serious around those laughing eyes. "Here?"

"Yes, I fully intend to come back and charm you silly now that you aren't sick anymore." Now he was laughing for real, his smile breaking her composure.

"Oh please. Malik, you can't possibly be interested in me like that. You have been nothing but respectful to me, which I love, but in all this time, we've basically been living together. And you haven't said or done anything to make me think you want anything more than my friendship." Embarrassed, Annie's face flushed. Wishing she could run and hide, she turned and went through the motions of making a second mug of coffee.

"You never drink two cups." Malik's hand was on her elbow, his breath on the back of her neck. The warmth of his chest was seeping through her nightgown, and her lungs were refusing to expand. "Are you hiding from me?"

"No. Sometimes, I like a second coffee," she lied. "Sometimes, I --" His lips cut off her protest, gentle and feathery on her shoulder.

"You really think I could be this close to you all the time and not be interested?" He had her hair in his hand, sliding it across her back as he kissed her shoulder again, edging closer to the curve of her throat.

"You think I could start and end every day with your perfume all around me and your laughter in my ears but not be interested?" This time he was gently whispering his way up the column of her neck, and she was dangerously close to spilling the coffee she hadn't really wanted in the first place.

"How could you think that I could spend a full week with my fingers in this beautiful hair while you were sick, and not be thinking of what it will be like to touch you when you grew well again? And now, it's been some time, and you are well again." He kissed her again, a wispy touch just in the hollow behind her ear, and the mug in her hand clattered to the countertop, her fingers clutching the edges of the counter. Her eyes closed, her breath came in a strangled gasp.

"You think I'm not interested?" His voice was a whisper as his left hand released her hair in a scented wave of strawberries and summertime, his right hand slipping down her arm to settle the coffee she held before her trembling hand could spill it.

"I'll be back," he said. "And then you'll see. I waited to be sure you weren't going to get sick again, but now? Oh, Annie, just you wait." He laughed to himself, the sound bouncing away from her as he lifted his backpack and turned to the door. Unable to move or respond, Annie heard the back door open and close. For the moment, he was gone.

"He likes me, too," she whispered. "Huh. Now I didn't see that coming."

***

Annie was so completely rattled by Malik's attention that she actually drank the second cup of coffee. She carried it around the house with her as she dressed for the day, grinning at herself in the mirror on the way to her room. She relived his kisses as she chose her clothes for the day, and she sang to herself in the shower, marveling at the sudden boost in her confidence.

Clean and content, Annie dried her hair with more enthusiasm than usual before going back to the kitchen, planning to have a late breakfast alone since Malik wasn't there to keep her company. She spent the afternoon enjoying being alone with her thoughts, but by late afternoon, she was in need of a good conversation. Annie didn't have an awful lot of women friends these days, but there was one woman she was just dying to talk to. Dialing Brenna's number, Annie dropped into a chair at the kitchen table, propping her feet on the table opposite her.

"Hello, stranger," Brenna said, answering the phone.

Annie laughed. "I can't believe I got that sick for that long," she said. "Probably a good thing I can't swim. I guess I'm just outright allergic to seawater or something. I've been much better for a while, though. I'm sorry I haven't called."

"Mmmhmm," Brenna teased. "I'm sure it had nothing to do with a certain hunk who's been hanging around."

"Oh, ha ha ha," Annie said. "You know, though, I just have no idea how all this seemed to happen, honestly. I went on the hike that day, and I missed the tide so I was stuck on Bar Island. And wow, I was so freaking bored."

"You should have called me," Brenna answered. "I was sitting here trying not to bleed everywhere. My foot would settle down and the bleeding would get slower, but then I'd have to pee or something, or Lugus would want something, and I couldn't figure out the right way to walk on it without opening the cut again. I think it's actually going to leave a little scar. Anyway, being stuck must have been rough, huh? What did you do while you were on the island?"

Annie laughed. "I sunbathed in my underwear, what else?"

"Shut up! Seriously?!" Brenna was laughing too, as if scandalized by the idea of such public boldness.

"Well, I was the only one there, and the tide was in," Annie said. "I felt pretty sure no one was gonna bust me in my silkies. It was kind of nice, really. I was all alone in the quiet, with the sun shining down on me. That part was good. Other parts, not so much. I fell when I was coming back down from the island, right before I realized that I'd missed the tide, so that part wasn't so fun. I tripped over a root and totally broke my camera."

"Oh, Annie, that's awful! Sounds like Bar Island is not for you, huh?" Brenna said.

"Yeah. And to top it off, I was pretty achy and I guess I wasn't really paying attention coming back. So I ended up with my foot stuck in the rocks crossing back onto the sandbar."

"Ouch," Brenna said.

"Yeah, the tide was coming back in for the night too, and no one was around. I was really scared."

"That's right," Brenna exclaimed. "Because you can't swim, I remember you telling me that. You couldn't get your foot out?"

"Nope, I was totally stuck," Annie said. "Honestly, I wondered if I hadn't broken my ankle or something because my shoe got really tight. So I was feeling pretty dramatic, stuck there with the tide coming up and the sun going down. I really think I would have died. And then Malik was there, and I wasn't stuck anymore. He scared the heck out of me, too, trying to free my foot. You know, I didn't hear him coming, or see him. Nothing. He was just there suddenly."

"Yeah, he sounds like he's really something. I called you that night, and he answered your phone. He told me what happened and I offered to come over so he could go do whatever he needed to be doing. I've lived here a while, but I don't know him, so I didn't know if he was just in town or something, or if he had somewhere to be, but he said not to worry and that he'd watch out for you. With my foot cut like it was, I was kind of stuck anyway so I just called every day to check in. But you were pretty sick so you weren't talking, and Malik kept me updated," Brenna finished.

"Well thanks for checking in on me, Brenna," Annie said. "I hate to think what could have happened to me. I mean, he could be any kind of guy, you know? And I'm lucky enough to have a genuine nice guy find me?"

"I came over once, a while back. It was before you started getting up and about again, but my foot was healing up pretty well and Malik had said your kitchen was low on a few things. He wanted to run out for supplies but he didn't want to leave you alone, so he called and asked me to come over. It was nice to meet him, and to check in on you in person, you know? By that point, I was getting a little worried so it was nice to have him reach out and show me that he's not some kind of creep. You don't find that old-fashioned Good Samaritan anymore, you know? But Tommy was like that, so Malik's good-natured personality is familiar to me. You really don't remember me being there?" Brenna asked.

"I was so out of it for that last couple of days," Annie laughed. "I really don't remember much at all. Thank goodness he's not some kind of weirdo. I'm still a little curious about his motives though, I'll admit. I mean, he drags me out of the ocean, hunts down my car to bring me to my house, and then nurses me while I'm all sick and gross. And as far as I can tell, he hasn't done anything gross or freaky or untrustworthy. But why? I mean, it just doesn't make much sense, right? I mean, I seriously didn't think people like that existed anymore. But then I find myself wanting to trust him because there's just this ... something. You know?"

"I get it," Brenna said. "That's kind of how it was with Tommy and me; it was like this instant connection between us. I swear, my poor father nearly died of shock when I told him I was leaving Ireland to marry Tom. And Malik really seems to like you; he kept tucking your hair back from your face when he was telling me how sick you'd been." Brenna laughed, and then continued. "Little cute stuff like that, and he kept giving me nursing instructions before he left. It was sort of cute, like he'd always been around or something."

"Really?" Annie asked. "What a shame that I don't remember any of that. Still, it's weird with this strange guy kind of living here like this isn't it? I feel like it's totally weird and kind of sad that I hate the idea of him leaving."

"Nah," Brenna said. "I don't think so. When you connect with someone, I believe it can happen just like that, just in a second where you feel like this other person is an extension of your own self. A lot of people don't feel that, or don't notice it right away, but that's what it was like for me when Tommy and I met. Didn't you feel that with Chase?"

"Not really," Annie said, remembering. "Honestly, I think Chase and I got married just because we'd been together for so long, and after a while we just sort of felt like we had to. I mean, I loved my husband, don't get me wrong, and I tried to be a good wife. But he didn't get me, and there were times when I knew I wasn't getting him either, you know? Like, I loved him, but it wasn't this dramatic thing that we all wish for. He didn't make the sun come up for me or make the stars extra shiny or any of that, and I didn't get all excited to wake up and see him there. He was just there. I guess he was more of a habit. Not like an addiction where I couldn't get enough, but more like the way people bite their nails just because they always have?"

"I get it," Brenna answered. "I totally get it. And after a relationship like that, one that was lukewarm, feeling a sizzle like I hear when you talk about Malik can definitely be odd. It's just new, and new is always exciting. Has he said anything to you about really getting together or anything?"

"This morning he left," Annie said, deliberately holding back, waiting to see what Brenna might say.

"Oh my gosh, what?"

Annie laughed. "He left me with a phone number; he said it's his dad's. And he said he'd be back later. But I'm not sure I get what the number is for," Annie said.

"Aw, that's cute! He left you with a connection, so you can reach him if you need him. I think he's offering proof that he's not planning to stay gone," Brenna explained. "If he knows about Chase, then I think it's sweet for him to offer something like that, you know? Like he's saying he's there if you need him; he's making himself accessible. What else did he say?"

"Um, I think he was trying to get a message across without saying things," Annie muttered, her face flushing with the memory of her reaction to him.

"Ok, time to start talking, Annie. Come on, I need juicy delicious details. I need to live vicariously, so spill it!" Brenna was teasing, her laughter coming through the line, making Annie laugh with her.

"I don't know, I guess he knew I was feeling weird or something. So he made a point of telling me he'd be back and that he had been enjoying our friendship."

"Friendship? Friendship?!" Brenna was nearly shouting. "Friendship doesn't make a man look at a woman like he looks at you. Jeez, I only met him once, but I could tell he is not looking for a friend. What else happened? Tell me the rest!"

Annie pulled herself together, drying up her giggles so she could give her friend the whole story. "I had turned around, and I was making coffee because I'm just awkward sometimes and I needed my hands to be busy, you know? I needed to be doing something other than melting into a weak puddle around his feet at the thought of him leaving."

"Uh huh," Brenna said, her words coming in an excited rush. "Uh huh, I get it. So tell, tell. What next? You're killing me, Annie."

"He kissed me," Annie laughed. "It was nothing fancy, but oh man. Brenna, I seriously almost exploded. And it wasn't even anything hot, but at the same time it was just so hot. I'm not even making sense am I?"

"You make perfect sense. So? Tell me more," Brenna coaxed.

"He was behind me; I'd turned my back to mess with my coffee. So he kind of kissed my shoulder and he was whispering stuff. By the time he was up to my ear, I couldn't remember anything he'd said, and I was biting my tongue so I wouldn't start squealing like a trapped pig at Christmas."

Brenna laughed. "Good job on that," she giggled. "I don't think piglet noises make men googly eyed, but wow! I'd have probably been doing the same thing. I always had problems like that when Tommy was around, too. I always had such strong reactions to him; it was like I was on hyper alert or something."

"Exactly!" Annie exclaimed. "That's exactly it. I felt like I had to be perfectly still and quiet because if I moved, he'd just vanish or something. And then I'd explode of frustration instead of deliciousness."

"Sounds like a hot ticket to me," Brenna said. "I can't wait to hear what happens next."

Annie laughed. "Honestly, I think I can't wait to see what happens next either."

"I can't either," Malik said, his laughter rumbling out of his chest when Annie whipped around, her ponytail coming over her shoulder to slap against her cheek. He was leaning against the open patio door, shaking with laughter as he took in Annie's shocked expression. In one hand, he balanced a short stack of movies. In the other, he held a single orange lily that mirrored the colors of sunset, surrounded by baby's breath and cheerful green ferns.

"Um," Annie stuttered into the phone, her eyes wide and her voice strangled. "I gotta go, Brenna."

***

"So I guess you're probably thinking I'm kind of a gossip, huh?" Annie asked. Her face had gone hot, and she was completely embarrassed that Malik had heard her on the phone with Brenna. She closed the phone and placed it on the table beside her, standing and walking shyly over to him.

"Not really," Malik grinned, reaching out to place the lily in her hands. "I actually think it's cute. I must be some kind of big news, to have made you call up a girlfriend and chat about me while I was away. How's her foot? Healed up yet?"

Further embarrassed by the fact that she hadn't remembered to ask, and yet he had, Annie turned to find a vase under the kitchen sink. "Well, you know, we didn't really talk about her foot much."

"I see." Malik was laughing. "Have I made the news, then?"

"Well, you're news to me," Annie said. She glanced up from the vase, a faint tinkling sound rising up as she mixed water with the little packet of flower food that had come with the simple bouquet. Tossing a smile over her shoulder at him, she slipped the flowers into the water and dried her hands on her jeans. "It's not every day a strange man saves me from certain death, then sticks around to do it a second time, and somehow finds all my digestive tricks and wretchedness to be cute."

"I find everything about you to be cute," Malik said, stacking the movies on the counter and heading for the still open patio door. When he reappeared, he held a giant paper bag with braided paper handles. The bag was red, with black Chinese lettering down the front. He turned the bag, allowing Annie to see the back of the bag. A black medallion surrounded a red silhouette of chopsticks, crossed over each other and rising up from a small bowl.

"I brought dinner for later," he said, lifting the bag in salute to her before placing it gently on the table. He unpacked a variety of egg rolls and wontons, a covered container of cheng du chicken, followed by cartons of chow mien and fried rice. There were also containers of kung pao chicken, moo shu pork, and salt-and-pepper-squid.

Finally, Malik placed a miniature version of the take out bag on the table, overflowing with fortune cookies. "These should be fun," he said, gesturing toward the cookies before starting to pack the other food into Annie's refrigerator. "I know it's not really authentic Chinese, but I didn't know if you'd like that kind of thing. And really, who doesn't love American Chinese?"

"I don't," Annie said, struggling to make her face look serious.

Malik froze, the dish of squid hovering in his hand above the stack of other food. "Well," he cleared his throat. "I, uh, it's no big deal, I can eat most of this. I think. Let me go out and bring you something else," he said, his hand nervously passing over his hair.

Annie smirked. "I was kidding."

His dark eyes met her gaze, his mouth dropping open in surprise. "Really?" he asked. "That's great, because I was probably going to explode if I tried to eat all that. Not to mention, I was starting to get a little afraid of my movie choices." He gestured to the stack of DVD's sitting on the kitchen table.

Wandering over, Annie browsed through the titles. They were a mix of action flicks, romantic comedies and basic family dramas. "Avatar, Titanic, The Da Vinci Code," Annie muttered to herself. She kept flipping and then held up the next three cases, fanned in her fingers. "The Matrix! I loved these!"

Malik laughed, closing the refrigerator on the impressive stack of takeout containers as he turned to look at Annie. "I actually haven't seen them," he said.

"That's just wrong in pretty much every possible way. You can't just go around saying that to people. And we have to watch them, now," Annie said. Without thinking, she reached for his hand and pulled him to the living room.

***

Later, Malik sat back on the couch, having pressed stop on the television remote. "I can't believe I'd never seen those," he said. "The moves were awesome, and the plot line is just, whoa. And the black suit crew? Wow, I'm glad I picked those."

"Well, now that you've seen the Matrix trilogy, I guess you're not such an oddball," Annie laughed, unfolding her legs from the couch and standing up to stretch. She reached her arms to the ceiling, her head thrown back and her hair falling down to sway over her hips. Groaning, she dropped her arms. She looked down at Malik with a smile and said, "Man, I'm starved."

In the kitchen, they made a mess of the counter, stacking cartons and containers everywhere as they piled cooled Chinese food onto Annie's square white plates. Taking turns with the microwave, they heated their meals and went comfortably to the kitchen table, sitting across from each other as if they'd been eating that way all their lives.

"Wow, I hadn't had squid before," Annie said. "But it's good, I like it." She took another bite, watching Malik's teeth neatly sever the end of an egg roll. They ate in a comfortable bubble of quiet. One or the other spoke occasionally, but they ate companionably to the simple sounds of silverware moving and the beep of the microwave as they got up in turn to refill their plates.

"Oh, wow," Malik groaned, swallowing the last bite of what had been his third heaping plate. He leaned back in his chair, turning his head to examine what was left on the counter. "We make a good team," he laughed. "I can't believe we almost ate it all! But I'm seriously about to burst."

"Oh no you don't," Annie laughed. She shoved the bag of fortune cookies toward him with a grin. "You just can't eat American Chinese without a fortune cookie. It's the most American of all American Chinese! The fortune cookie is like a requirement. You gotta pick one." Annie reached into the bag herself, choosing a cookie and ripping into the cellophane package.

"You know what they say about these cookies?" Malik asked, opening his cookie and placing the rattling package on his plate.

"I don't know," Annie answered. "What do they say?" She held her cookie in one hand, a glass of water in the other; her eyes met his laughing expression across the table.

"I heard once that if the cookie comes already broken, then the fortune inside will be reversed," Malik winked, breaking his cookie and reading the tiny slip of paper inside. "The world is round," he said, his eyes on the fortune in his hand. "Any place which seems like the end is really only the beginning."

"Nice," Annie said, breaking open her own cookie and straightening the paper between her fingers. "Mine says ..." she trailed off, blushing.

"Never mind, it's silly. Maybe the cookie meant for me is still in the bag." Annie folded the paper neatly in half and placed it on her plate. "What movie are we watching next?"

"Oh no," Malik laughed. "I read mine, it's only fair!" He plucked the sticky little slip from Annie's plate before she could stop him, and read aloud. "You are entering a time of great romance. Hmm," he teased, waggling his dark eyebrows at her. "This looks like a fun one, not at all silly. In fact, I think it could be true. After all, the cookie was intact, you know."

Annie laughed. "Mmhmm, I'm sure. But really, do you believe anyone can ever know the future?" She looked up at him, standing above her as he gathered their dishes from the table. He turned, taking them to the sink. Annie followed, stacking the empty containers and taking them to the garbage.

"I don't know, really," Malik answered, with his head in the fridge as he placed the container of leftover egg rolls on the shelf. "Maybe, maybe not. I think we can know a small portion of the future though."

"Is that so?" Annie stood beside him, closing the paper flaps on the carton of fried rice and handing it to him. He left it beside the egg rolls and closed the door, turning to face Annie.

He settled his hands on her shoulders, his eyes twinkling with laughter as he lowered his face. Annie's breath caught in her throat, choking her as she realized what he was going to do. As the dawning knowledge settled in her eyes, Malik touched her lips with his, sliding his hands down her arms to grasp her hands in his.

"For instance, we both knew I was going to do that, just then, right before I did it. And I tell you with certainty," he whispered against her lips, "that it will happen again. Soon." Dropping another kiss on Annie's forehead, he released her and returned to the table, retrieving their glasses from the table.

Annie gulped; she watched his graceful fingers as he placed the glasses in the sink with their plates. She struggled to find her voice, both dreading and anticipating the truth of what he'd said. She knew with absolute surety that Malik had meant what he'd said. He would kiss her again, but when? She dreaded his next kiss, knowing that each time he touched her, he left her breathless and speechless, uncomfortable with her need to be near him, uncomfortable knowing that each touch of his skin against hers gave her an opportunity to make a fool of herself. Simultaneously, she anticipated his next kiss, loving the knowledge that each time he touched her, he left her electrified and deliciously wanting; she hadn't felt that kind of electricity even with Chase.

***

Waking the next morning, Annie was filled with a mixture of extremely pleasurable comfort and incredible discomfort. Her right foot was twisted up, asleep; her arm was tangled up underneath her and her neck was twisted at a rather odd angle.

That's when she realized she was on the couch, with her head pillowed on Malik's lap and the naked expanse of his golden chest ranging up above her face. She didn't remember lying down, didn't remember falling asleep. She definitely didn't remember him taking his shirt off!

And yet, there she lay with her head on his lap, with her soft hair spilling over the surface of his shorts. The arm she wasn't laying on was curled up beside her, the hand curled under her cheek. The heat of his thigh warmed her palm as her fingers curled lazily over him. He slept peacefully, with one arm dangling over the side of the couch and the other draped casually over Annie's hip. His fingertips were in the pocket of her jeans; his thumb stretched up, just barely underneath the hem of her t-shirt.

That one small area of skin on skin contact burned Annie as surely as a match, and she had to remind herself to be still. Eventually, she couldn't help waking him; her effort to remain still slowly tightened the muscles of her body until she was so tense it woke him.

Malik awoke with the sensation that he was holding a strong and sturdy log under his hands instead of a warm, soft woman. His eyes drifted open just as Annie's screwed shut, and she sneaked a peek at him as his thumb began to move like a torch in gently searing circles along the upper edge of her hip bone. He was looking down at her, and when he saw her eye sneak open, he chuckled and she felt his other hand tangle in her hair.

"Good morning," he said. "I've taken a mental note. Clearly Braveheart isn't your kind of movie."

Annie smiled, suddenly shy. "I liked it fine," she said. "But we'd watched so many and I just couldn't stay awake I guess. Why didn't you wake me? I would have gone to bed; you couldn't have been comfortable sitting up like this."

"Oh, believe me," he smiled down at her. "I was happy as a clam."

Later, after they'd both gotten up and taken turns in the shower, they met in the kitchen for their usual coffee, conversation and breakfast.

"I have to go out today," Annie said.

"I remember," Malik smiled. "You're closing on the house today, right?"

"I am." Annie grinned, a little embarrassed. A few days ago when she'd gotten the call for the final appointment, she'd been so excited that she'd chattered at Malik all the way through dinner, telling him this thing or that thing she couldn't wait to do.

"What are you doing today?" Annie asked.

"Well so far, my plan is to see a pretty lady off to an exciting appointment, and then go to my father and tell him all about the aforementioned pretty lady. I may even squeeze in some time for mowing when I get back," he winked.

"Hmm, a pretty lady, hmm? Sounds like you've got a little crush on someone, Malik," Annie teased, dunking a grape into her yogurt and popping it into her mouth.

"A crush," he scoffed. "Oh no, my dear, I am entranced. I am enchanted. I am just completely downright --"

"Silly?" Annie laughed. "You make your pretty lady seem rather intimidating. She sounds like quite a woman."

"Oh, she is," Malik said, his face sober and serious. "She's funny and pretty and smart."

"Well, I shall have to meet her one day," Annie said.

"Let's go then, there's time enough before you have to get to that meeting." Ignoring the shocked expression on Annie's face, Malik gripped her elbow lightly and hauled her out of her chair. She giggled when he led her down the hallway, and set up a token struggle as he steered her into the bathroom. Her back pressed against his chest as he wrapped his arms around her, pinning her arms to her waist and propelling her into the bathroom. Like a man steering a skittish horse, he herded her right up to the vanity counter. Flipping the light switch, he pointed to the mirror.

"There," he said, directing Annie to meet her own eyes in the reflection of the mirror. "There's my new lady. Isn't she something?"

***

After her meeting at the bank, Annie felt absolutely exhilarated. She was now the proud owner of a plot of land, the proud owner of the house that stood proudly and quaintly on that slice of land. She'd loved the little house from the first night, and now she had made it her home. She had made various changes since deciding to buy the house, things like hanging the shadow box starfish and buying the crystal seal for the entryway, but she hadn't done anything big yet. She'd held off, waiting until the house was truly hers before making any real changes.

Now was the time; the house was hers to do with as she pleased. And right that moment, Annie couldn't wait to go shopping. Walking out of the bank with a giant smile on her face, she unlocked her car, threw her purse into the passenger seat, and slipped behind the wheel. She pressed her key into the ignition, gave it the usual twist, and put her seat belt on. The radio blared the newest pop sensation, some teenaged girl crooning a ballad about her true love. Singing along cheerfully, Annie drove off to the local furniture store.

Annie sat on couches; she lounged in recliners. She rocked in an overstuffed chair set on gliders so soothing that Annie immediately ordered one for the corner of her bedroom, complete with a matching footstool that had gliders of its own. The chair and footstool were a shade of blue that reminded her of the ocean, with little flecks of foamy green scattered randomly over the fabric. A soft throw pillow that was the same foamy green completed the set.

Sitting there, testing out the chair and imagining it in her room, Annie glanced around. She would of course, want a little side table for books, so she rose from the chair and found a salesman.

Before Annie left, she had found more than the perfect table for her chair. It had perfectly matched the most magnificent bedroom suite, so Annie had purchased a giant new bed with a mattress that felt like clouds. It matched perfectly to the dressing table, the chest of drawers, and the night tables that doubled as bookshelves for either side of the massive bed. All of the furniture was old world elegant and the warm brown color of mocha, all to be delivered in a week. Annie arranged for the delivery truck to also haul away the old furniture in her room, and then she went to her next stop, in search of new accents to match her new bedroom.

At the department store, Annie chose a set of sheets in the same shade of blue that had graced the gliding chair she had purchased. She found a quilt in shades of blue and green, and throw pillows for the bed that perfectly matched the comfortable chaos of the quilt.

Searching for art to complement her new room, Annie scanned a table full of knick-knacks, passing her fingertips over a miniature version of the seal she had bought weeks ago in this same store. The seal brought her memories alive and to the surface, memories of afternoons spent in solitude on the sandbar, talking quietly to a seal that had not known or understood her. Still, he had nearly always been there, as if lying in wait for her company. He'd been like a friend to her, in the way someone is friends with their dog or cat; she'd felt a sense of comfortable kinship with the seal, though she knew he couldn't possibly relate or understand.

She hadn't been back to the sandbar since the morning after her near death, the morning when she'd found the seal pelt. Annie had frequently thought about going back, thought about spending some time sitting among the tide pools again. She hadn't gone, though; she wasn't sure she could take the idea that her seal would not be there. She didn't like thinking that his brown eyes would not shimmer at her over the rocks anymore, or that he would no longer frolic in the sea to make her laugh at his antics. In her heart, Annie knew that her seal could not play for her amusement anymore. She knew that he would no longer sun himself among the rocks, because she had his rich and beautiful fur in a storage trunk in her shed.

What she didn't know, and couldn't fathom, was how it had happened. Annie had been out to the shed many times, sitting quietly with the pelt as if the answers might be written in the fur. Some part of her knew that what she had found was very mysterious, very special. Always, she crept to the shed in secret. Always, she lifted the pelt of the seal, seeking answers. She examined it for cuts, for blood, for any flaw that would answer her questions, anything she might have missed before. So far, there were no answers to be found, and the soft pelt of the seal was still hidden away in that trunk in the shed, buried under several other boxes.

Stroking the tiny face of the seal in the store, Annie was determined to find some answers. He may only have been another seal sunning himself on the rocks, the same as all the others. Still, she couldn't deny how odd it was for the seal to vanish. He was an animal, after all. It might be normal for him to migrate to another area. Still, it certainly wasn't normal for him to have left his pelt behind. Grinning to herself, she added the little miniature to her cart, and went on with her shopping. There was probably a completely logical explanation to the whole thing, anyway, right?

***

Finished shopping for the day, Annie was not ready to go home just yet. Instead, she drove to Brenna's lighthouse. She was thrilled with her new furniture, and equally thrilled with the new decor she'd bought to go with the lovely bedroom suite. She couldn't wait to see it all put together, and the idea of waiting the rest of the week made her anxious. The thought of the seal pelt nagged continually at the back of her mind; not only did she feel unable to let it go, she also couldn't figure out exactly why it suddenly seemed so important. What she did know was that a visit with Brenna would provide the perfect distraction.

Knocking on the heavy door of Brenna's house was like a flashback for Annie, so strong was the memory of Lugus barking and rushing at the door. A thud and a yelp indicated that he'd lost his traction on the hardwood and skidded right into the door. Brenna's muffled laughter confirmed her suspicions, then the door opened and Lugus came bursting out, circling Annie's legs in a mad frenzy. Reaching down to pet him while he sniffed wildly at her feet, Annie shook with laughter.

"All right, all right, let her in, Lugus," Brenna laughed, holding the door open. "Hey, Annie, come on in! What you been up to?"

"I've been shopping all morning," Annie said. "The purchase on my house is now officially final, so I went looking at furniture."

"Oh, wow! Annie, you should have told me, and I'd have come with you! We could have gone to lunch to celebrate or something!"

Annie grinned, "Well, I wasn't planning to get a lot of stuff at first. But I found a chair I really liked for my bedroom and somehow, I ended up with an entire suite of bedroom furniture. And then, of course I had to go find linens and decor to match. But all day, there's just been one weird thing really on my mind, and I'm just bursting to tell someone."

"Is it something to do with Malik?" Brenna's perfectly arched eyebrow rose.

"Not really," Annie said. "I don't think, anyway."

"But you haven't said anything about it to him? Whatever it is?"

"No. I don't know why I feel like I shouldn't mention it to him, but I just feel like you're the person for this."

Brenna settled into her couch, tucking her legs under her, while Annie perched on the edge of the chair opposite. "So you came here to me, for good old fashioned chick talk," Brenna said. Then her eyes widened comically and she leaned forward in her seat. "It's nothing uterine, is it? Because I'm squeamish."

Annie burst out laughing. "No, it's nothing like that! I'm not that good at that kind of chick talk," Annie reassured. "But remember the day of the hike, when I was trapped and Malik saved me from drowning?"

"Yeah," Brenna said. "The dramatic and heroic save of the year. For someone with such bad luck, you have really great luck."

"Well, I went back to the sandbar the next morning," Annie told her. "I'd lost my tote bag and everything, so I wanted to see if any of my stuff had washed up. Or you know, maybe if there was anything there that Malik may have dropped or something. I didn't find anything, just my water bottle. But I did find something totally weird, and I have been completely unable to get it off my mind."

"Okay," Brenna said. "What was it?"

"I, um, I kinda found a seal-skin." Annie watched Brenna's mouth fall open in surprise, nodded her head, and continued. "I thought it was a blanket lying there, and it took me a minute to realize what I had. But I'm pretty sure it's a seal-skin. And it might be crazy, but I'm pretty sure it's the skin of my seal."

"How do you know which one it was?"

"It has a scar." Annie said. "My seal had a scar, and this skin has the same scar, same place as far as I can tell."

"Wow." Brenna stood, walking over to the bookshelf along the wall. Scanning the titles, she asked, "Was it bloody? Torn, anything?"

"See that was my thought too, that maybe there was a poacher or maybe a fight, something like that. But there was no carcass, Brenna. There was no blood, nothing there. I just found the skin. Not even bones. And it was clean, like someone had washed it. I seriously thought it was a forgotten blanket."

"Hmm," Brenna murmured, coming back with a book that she handed to Annie. She dropped on the floor next to Annie's feet, folding her legs easily into a lotus position. She looked like an ancient yogi, apart from the fire of her hair and the smooth icy blue of her eyes in the midst of such fair skin.

"Selkies?" Annie looked up from the book, confused. "What's a selkie?"

"Being Irish, I was raised on myths and legends, songs and stories. You know? Old faeries, saints and stories about the children of Lir. Selkies are another thing I grew up hearing about. The selkie is like a shape shifter, a seal that comes up out of the sea and sheds the seal-skin to become human for a time."

"A time?" Annie asked dryly, mocking Brenna's serious talk of legends and fairy tales. "What kind of a time?"

"The amount of time varies a lot. With the stories about the women, it's almost always the same basic premise. A selkie female comes upon the land; she sheds her pelt and reveals herself to be a beautiful maiden who has a voice straight from heaven. She sings and any man who can hear is basically mesmerized. If a man can find and hide the pelt of the female selkie, then she is trapped on the land and can never return to the sea until she can find her pelt again."

"Because she's stuck as a beautiful human woman who enraptures men all around," Annie said dryly.

Brenna winked. "Well, of course. Unfortunate for her, isn't it?"

"Ok, so this seal woman rises up out of the sea, takes her skin off and somehow this makes her both lovely and fascinating. Not to mention, she sings like an angel, right? Don't all mythical women sing like angels? Of course. But with no family, no connections, no job, no home, and forced to stay a human, what is she supposed to do now?"

"Well, Annie, you are just ever so practical, aren't you?" Brenna laughed. "The legend says the female selkie makes a wonderful wife, and she typically marries the man who has stolen her seal-skin. Generally they have children in the marriage, and the woman dutifully serves her husband, always longing for the sea."

"I'd kill him so I could search the house," Annie smirked. "What if she finds her pelt again?"

"The stories almost always agree that one of her children finds it by accident and brings it to her, asking what it is. Having found it, the selkie woman abandons her children and husband and immediately returns to the sea."

"Some wife," Annie muttered as she flipped through the book Brenna had given her.

"At least she didn't kill him," Brenna retorted. "Some stories say she comes back to visit her children, but that varies a bit, too. Some say she comes to her children as their mother, some say she just plays with them among the waves of the ocean. A seal friend, like you had."

"Oh, but my mother was human," Annie laughed. "What about the men? Do men come out too?"

"There are a lot less stories about male selkies, really. I'm not really sure why, but the stories generally agree that the males can be summoned directly, usually to a kind of emotionally injured woman. Typically, it's a lonely wife, like a fisherman's wife who is lonely because her husband has been away. Or heartbroken women count too, I suppose. So they go onto the rocks of the sea and summon the selkie for an affair."

"And how does she do that?"

"I'm not sure. I knew at one time, I guess I read it somewhere or something. It might be in there somewhere, though," Brenna answered, waving a long fingered hand at the book in Annie's lap. "You can borrow it if you want."

"Thanks," Annie said. "I'll stick it in my purse to read when I'm out; I've needed a new book for a few days now. But why did you give me this? What makes you think of selkies?"

"A cleanly discarded seal-skin and the simultaneous magic appearance of a hero? I'm pretty sure that would raise the neck hairs of any self-respecting person of Celtic descent," Brenna scoffed. "Had he been poached, I'd say you wouldn't have found much, because they are hunted for lots of purposes, including the skin. I don't think they're really hunted in America though. You know, because of animal activists and stuff."

"So that puts out the idea of hunting. Which really just leaves what? Like a fight or something? Maybe with another seal? But that would at least have left a carcass, a mess, something. The pelt would be damaged, I guess. But what would leave a clean seal-skin just lying there?"

"A selkie," Brenna laughed.

"No way," Annie said, laughing too. "You said yourself; it's just an old Celtic story. Not an American legend. Aren't we on the wrong side of the ocean?"

"Seals can swim, you know. Who knows, maybe yours was a traveler," Brenna teased, nudging Annie's knees with her elbow.

"Right. I couldn't keep a human man entertained," Annie muttered. "An exotic seal man that's basically a living transformer isn't going to swim the ocean from Ireland, just to get a hook up with me."

"I don't know. Being Irish, I'm thinking something smells fishy about you finding an empty seal-skin after having a lousy divorce, followed by a super really crappy day, and then almost drowning in the ocean. Only to find a seal-skin on the sandbar where you were saved."

"But it was Malik who saved me."

"Mmhmm."

"He's not a selkie man," Annie laughed.

"Yeah, ok," Brenna said, nudging Annie's knees again. "If you say so."

***

During the drive home, Annie's conversation with Brenna kept replaying itself in her mind. She kept thinking of Brenna's absurd idea, the idea that Malik could be a selkie. She had, of course, tossed the thought away immediately as a funny joke: a charming and exotic but utterly impossible fantasy. Still, other parts of the conversation did apply to

Malik in real life, making some aspects of life with him stand in sharp contrast to any relationship she'd ever been in before.

She had so many questions: *Where did he come from? How did he find her at so perfect a time? Where did he belong?* But of all the questions she carried inside her, there was one she simply couldn't ignore. How had Malik been able to stay with her for as long as he had? Surely, he must have some other obligations, other connections elsewhere in his life. Didn't he?

There was another thing she couldn't ignore; in spite of her questions, Annie really did love having him around. In fact, she was rather in danger of falling in love with him entirely. In spite of her past hurts, his gentle nature and ever-present sense of humor were winning her over, certainly and without doubt. Still, his life before they'd met was a complete mystery to her. Other than hearing him speak in passing of his father and what she knew of his personality just from spending so much time with him, she knew next to nothing about the man she had somehow come to value so highly. She knew nothing of his history; she didn't know anything about his life, what he'd been, who he'd been. She knew nothing of who or what he wanted to be, or what he wanted from the future.

Driving home in the quiet of her car, Annie had to accept that simply loving Malik's company was not going to be enough to last them forever. She needed more than just his company, and if she was going to drift into a relationship with someone, she wanted someone she could share with, someone who would know her and allow her to know him completely. She was terrified of what he might say, or not say, but she had made the decision to sit him down for a serious talk that evening over dinner. Whatever happened or however it went, she needed to know where she stood with him.

As she neared her house, Annie tried to plan what she would say. She had been excited that morning, anxious to show him the things she'd purchased and to absorb his usual encouragement, excited to spend another evening of peaceful chatter with him before bed. The excitement had faded; instead, she now struggled with how to ask the questions she needed answers to. Turning into the driveway, she tried to imagine Malik's possible responses to her questions, her mind working to envision the way the evening might go. The harder she tried the more blank her mind became, the more scattered her thoughts, the more nervous her stomach. Finally turning her car off and locking the doors, Annie took a breath and readied herself for the conversation to come. Leaving her bags in the trunk for the moment, she squared her shoulders and entered the house.

Inside, the kitchen was warm and fragrant, the muscles of Malik's shoulders rippling with movement under a simple grey t-shirt as he worked over the stove. He was at once plainly ordinary and extraordinarily sexy, cooking dinner while steam rose up around him like fat fluffy clouds.

Just as Annie thought he hadn't heard her come in, Malik grinned at her over his shoulder. "Hi," he said. "You're early, I was just making - what's wrong?" Giving the pot on the stove one last stir, he covered it and turned the heat down. He approached Annie, his eyes searching her face.

"Malik," Annie said. "We need to talk. Or, really, I need you to talk."

"Okay. What shall I talk about?"

"Talk about yourself. I have spent so much time enjoying your company and our --" Annie broke off, searching for the right words. "Our, whatever this is, that I didn't think to ask you how you can manage to be here like this. With me, all the time. We've talked and talked about me; we've talked about my divorce, my life, my career, what I want. But you don't say anything much about yourself."

"I can be here with you because this is where I want to be and I stay because you didn't ask me not to. Because I don't have anywhere else I'd rather be, or any other place that I have to be," Malik said, his warm hand gently turning Annie's face up to his. He met her eyes, his expression lacking the usual trace of humor. Looking into his face, Annie saw his intensity, his honesty. In her heart though, she saw the painful memory of another man who had not wanted her enough, who had not been able to stay faithful to her, who had lied to her. Resolving to ignore the memory of Chase's betrayal, Annie focused on the man before her, listening as he finally opened up.

"I have money because my father was incredibly fortunate when I was growing up," he told her, his eyes clouding with some unknown emotion. "After my mom ran off, my dad ran a fleet of fishing boats, and he was very successful. I have a place to go because his house is mine and I know that it will always be open to me. But I stay with you because I prefer your pretty face to his scruffy one. And I haven't talked much about me because I just find everything about you fascinating. I guess after hanging around myself all these years, I'm rather bored with me," Malik chuckled. Leaning forward, he kissed Annie's forehead.

"So you have no job, no other commitments to anyone?" She stepped back, breaking the physical connection between them, needing space to think clearly. His honesty relieved her; she'd always trusted her gut, and it had never led her wrong. It had been her gut instinct that had sent her home from her office the day she'd caught Chase cheating on her, and right now, her gut believed in the honest openness on Malik's face. His sense of calm spread through her like the warming, smooth influence of the best quality wine, like the cleansing wash of a hot shower. As always, his nearness took her breath, making her stomach flip over itself and her heart race like the invisible flight of a hummingbird.

He smiled. "I have no other commitments right now. I occasionally take work offshore with diving boats. Most often, they're just low scale treasure hunters. You know, seeking downed ships and stuff. They pay pretty well usually, and I never sign on with anyone unless I get a share of the findings."

"That's what you do for work?"

"When I can do it, it's what I do. I love the water. I love the adventure, and I can't deny that I love the risk. Because of my dad, I don't really need money, but I just love doing it," he explained, meeting her eyes as he spoke. "I've actually collected a bunch of really cool stuff over the years. Gems, coins, jewels, lots of stuff."

"Oh." Annie didn't know what else to ask him. She felt secure that he would answer her; secure that if she wanted to completely unravel his life and examine it, he would allow her to. Still, would a hundred questions make her feel any better about her ability to hold his interest? Would a thousand questions ease her fear of trusting someone new? Would a million questions stop the panic that filled her as she realized that she was too late, that she already trusted him? Even now, her trust that he would answer her questions made those questions fly from her mind as if they'd never existed.

"We've gotten to know each other well over the last weeks, Annie. We know each other as we are, right here and now, in this place in our lives. Every morning when I wake up, the first thought I have is for you. And each night when I go to my bed, all I can think about is you lying in yours. I feel a real connection between us, something rare. But whatever questions you ask me, I know there's something else, something you're thinking but not asking out loud. So just come out with it. What is it that you really want to ask, Annie?"

With his questioning, Annie's insecurities became too hard to keep to herself, too heavy to carry, and she asked the questions that had been burning in her throat for so long. In the past weeks, she had been enjoying the idea of having a man around again, but she had to admit -- at least to herself -- that she was always waiting for the moment when he would realize, as Chase had, that he could do better. She had been waiting for him to change his mind about her, to pack up and walk out of her life as suddenly as he'd walked into it.

"Why are you here?" she asked, her eyes rapidly filling with tears. She hated asking him that, hated taking the chance that her questions might drive him out. She hated herself for needing the answers; still, she had to ask. "Why did you stay here with me? And how long until you get tired of me and decide to leave?"

"Oh, Annie," Malik whispered. "My Annie." His hands were on her face, gentle thumbs swiping tears from her thick lashes. He stepped forward, lowering his face until his lips touched hers, so softly that she might have thought she'd imagined it, if not for his breath still upon her lips. Kissing her again, his fingers slipped into her hair, her hands rising up between them to flatten on his chest. Releasing her lips, he kept her close to him and pressed his forehead to hers.

"Question number one. I'm here because it only took these few short weeks for me to grow so wildly attached to you that I cannot imagine spending my days with anyone else. Question number two. Same as number one; I stayed here because I simply can't bear the idea of leaving. Question three. For as long as you want me, I'll be here. I'm not going anywhere. I know Chase hurt you, and I know he damaged the very core of your confidence. You've told me as much. But Annie, whatever it was that Chase did or didn't see in you? It doesn't matter to me, because I see what you are right now."

Kissing the corner of her lips, he whispered, "I see beautiful Annie Jacobs."

Gently turning her face and kissing the opposite corner of her mouth, he whispered, "I see fascinating Annie Jacobs."

Lifting her chin and nibbling his way along her jaw, he whispered, "I see irresistible Annie Jacobs."

Chuckling to himself when her breath caught in her throat and her trembling fingers fluttered against his chest, he stepped back and waited until her eyes slowly floated open. Tapping the tip of her nose with one long finger, he said, "I see the future, right here. No fortune cookies needed. And now I need to check on dinner."

Spinning on one heel, he turned and stalked to the stove, lifting the lid from their dinner and sniffing appreciatively. Annie stood frozen, watching him, the trembling fingers of one hand pressed to her tingling lips in an effort to keep her heart from leaping out of her body.

"Any more questions for me?" He asked, his teeth gleaming out of his smile as he turned to look at her.

Annie gulped. "Um, not right now," she answered weakly.

***

The next few days flew by in a rush for Annie. Malik stepped up his courtship, spending much of each day touching her unexpectedly, dropping his hands warmly on her shoulders as he walked by or nudging her gently as he teased her over one thing or another. It kept her mind in a desperate scramble, one part of her screaming with joy and the other part full of doubt. Much as she loved the attention, much as it soothed her injured ego, she still fought against the ravages of self-doubt every day, struggling with the idea of being woman enough to keep a man attracted.

Still, she caught herself watching him as they worked in the garden together or secretly observing him under her eyelashes when she sat reading in front of the living room fire. He was even there in her dreams, dreams where Annie felt confident and attractive, dreams where she felt free.

They talked almost constantly and Malik was always calm, always gently reassuring when Annie brought up things she was afraid of or insecure about. They watched movies or occasionally blasted Annie's radio and danced in the living room together. They went out too; most afternoons, they were walking the Bar Harbor Pier, speculating about the people they saw or simply sharing a picnic lunch on one of the benches overlooking the sea.

Through all of it, there was one thing Annie kept from him. She never mentioned the seal pelt in her shed. Annie couldn't pinpoint why, but the idea of showing the pelt to Malik had filled her with dread so forceful that she'd become nauseated. She'd immediately discarded the idea of sharing the pelt with Malik, resolutely ignoring the guilt of her omitted honesty. Brenna's stories of vanishing selkie-folk haunted her, though she refused to admit this even to herself.

Every few days Malik went to visit his father, always telling Annie to rest, reassuring her of his return. She loved his easy acceptance of her flaws, his instinctive reassurances. Still, each time he left, Annie waited until she was sure he was gone, and then she would run out to the shed to dig out the pelt, to examine it again as if it might have suddenly changed when she wasn't looking.

She'd gone through her photos of the seal countless times, looking at the patterns of his fur, the size and shape of his scar, the way it wrapped around him just underneath one flipper. Several times, she'd held up the pelt too, literally slinging it over her shoulders and wrapping herself in it, her thoughts traveling to Brenna's talk of mythical creatures that could magically shed their skins and walk on land as humans.

Each time Annie was in the shed, the pelt would be thoroughly re-examined and stroked as if it were the soft fur of a pet. In the end, it was always quickly folded and packed away, back into the locked trunk which had become its hiding place. For Annie, the pelt was her own buried treasure. Annie would shake off the dust and go back into the house long before she expected Malik to come back; she'd spend the rest of her time finding things to keep her busy while she awaited his return. One such day, Annie was in the kitchen chopping salad vegetables when Malik arrived. He came into the house, kissing her cheek and asking how her day had been while he was away.

Annie gave him the same response as always, "Oh I did a little of this, a little of that." The desire to tell him the truth was there as always, and as always, she stamped it down, hiding it the way she had hidden the skin of the seal.

"What are you making?" he asked, bending down from behind her to drop a kiss on the back of her neck, on the tender skin bared by her ponytail.

"Just a salad," Annie said, narrowly missing her fingers as she sliced a cucumber, the usual jolt of his kiss shooting down through her. Warmth ran from his lips like the quick rush of a forest fire, down through her body to pool deliciously in her core, chasing all other thoughts from her mind. Forcing herself to speak normally, she said, "I thought we'd do something light for dinner. Salad, grilled chicken, baked potatoes?"

"Sounds great," Malik said, his breath caressing her ear as he moved forward to lean over her shoulder, kissing her cheek. "Do I have time to mow the grass again? I don't know how that stuff grows so fast."

"Sure," Annie breathed, forcing herself to concentrate on the blade of the knife as she diced the tomato in her hand. "Go ahead, I'll call you if dinner finishes before you do."

Malik chuckled softly in her ear, still leaning over her shoulder to watch her work. Whispering that he adored her, he left Annie with one last gesture of affection, the tip of his tongue gently tracing the curve of her ear followed by a soft kiss in the sensitive hollow below. Annie held her breath and waited until she heard the door close behind him as he went outside. Then she dropped the knife among the bloody tomato bits on the counter, and went to bandage the finger she'd just stabbed.

***

With her finger properly seen to and her hormones back under control, Annie was able to clean up her mess and finish making dinner without trouble. She plated the chicken, dressed and settled the potatoes and carried the salad to the dinner table. After checking to be sure the bandage on her finger was as invisible as possible, she poured a drink and took it with her as she walked to the patio door to call Malik.

The mower had been silent for some time, so Annie knew that he had finished with the grass. Still, it surprised her to walk outside and find him shirtless in her yard. It always surprised her to see him comfortable around her, as if she expected at any moment for him to vanish as cleanly as if he'd never existed. Standing bare-chested in her back yard, he was like a bronze statue; he was muscle and sinew, standing there basking in the sun with his face turned up and his eyes gently closed. As Annie watched, the heat of her attraction to him deadened the frigid cold of the glass in her hand. A smile widened her lips as she played with the idea that he wanted to be hers.

He hadn't heard her open the door and come out. Raising his hands skyward, joining his fingers above his head, he twisted and stretched, leaning first to one side and then the other. Sweat rolled down his back, and droplets clung to his chest; he was a stunning specimen. Some part of her mind was taking it all in, drinking in his beauty to revel in later. It was in that moment that Annie noticed something new.

He had a scar, one that she hadn't noticed before. One that was completely new to her and yet it was somehow utterly familiar. Beginning at the edge of his back, just under the shoulder blade, it stretched and rolled around the side of his rib cage underneath his arm. She guessed it was as long as her fingers and maybe a full inch wide, angry against his beautiful skin. It was a hideous scar, making Annie wonder what had happened to him to mark his body that way. She wanted to touch it, to soothe him, to question him.

With the sense that her sympathy was because the scar felt so familiar to her, Annie suddenly felt as if it was Malik himself that was so familiar, in a way completely separate from the fact that they'd been living together. Silly as it was, she felt as if she'd known Malik before, perhaps in another time or even another life. Her brows came together, her lips pursing as she thought. Her head tilted, and as he turned and noticed her standing there he took in her beauty, his own smile widening as he watched her.

Looking into those deep dark eyes, Annie realized why his scar seemed so familiar to her, and the glass in her hands crashed to the patio floor.

Shards flew as the glass shattered, ice and water sliding unhindered toward the edge of the patio.

It was then that Annie knew she wasn't just being fanciful; she knew with certainty that she had seen that scar before. She knew that scar. She was familiar with it, and she was familiar with it because she'd already spent so much time wondering about it, worrying about it, looking at it. On another body, a very different body.

She'd seen it on her seal, the seal whose pelt now lay hidden in her backyard shed.

Forcing herself to act normally, she put the scar out of her mind. Of course, it was nothing more than a coincidence, she told herself, and she was obviously spending way too much time reading Brenna's history book of the selkie legends. Making apologies to Malik, she dropped to her knees and began cleaning up the bits of broken glass that littered her patio.

He knelt easily beside her and as they cleaned up the mess together, Annie reassured Malik that she was fine; she insisted that the sweat of the glass had made it slick enough to slither from her fingers. After all, she couldn't tell him that her crazy friend thought he was a selkie. And she certainly couldn't tell him that she herself was beginning to wonder.

***

Waking up the next morning, Annie dragged her pillow over her face. The sun was streaming in because she'd been so frazzled by the course of her thoughts that she'd forgotten to close her curtains before bed.

He'd followed her into her sleep again, walking through her dreams and speaking out of the seal she'd grown to love on the sandbar. In one of her dreams, Annie perched on a rock with her bare feet dangling over the edge and swinging in the water. A sense of safety surrounded her, and as she looked into the depths of the water, she saw him.

Malik.

She knew it was him, though he wore the seal-skin as he swam and frolicked around her feet. He vanished continually into the darkness of the sea, always reappearing to splash her with his flippers, leaving the ocean water to dry on her cheeks.

In another dream, Annie sat alone on an unfamiliar beach and the seal came up out of the waves, his flippers morphing into human hands as he opened an invisible zipper in his pelt. Removing it, he came to her slowly, speaking silently. Annie couldn't hear him; she asked him to repeat himself, but always his speech was silent. He walked and walked with his hand outstretched, beseeching, but he never reached her. Finally, the sea rose up behind him angry and boiling, and it closed over him, reclaiming him for itself.

The night had been filled with a chaotic mix of dreams. Blending with the more confusing images, there were dreams of the two of them happily laughing and playing together. Sometimes he appeared in her dreams as if he were a pet, a furry seal with a sweet doggy face. Other times he appeared passionate and sexy, as a man who wanted nothing other than a life with her. In one dream, there had been a little seal pup, playing with floating blocks in the bathtub of a house Annie had never seen before.

"Ok, that's it. No more books," Annie told herself. "No more reading. No more mythology. No more weirdness. Only cold stone reality. Unless it's your own fiction." Throwing off her blankets, she slipped into a robe and padded to the bathroom for her morning shower, trying desperately to toss off the weight of the selkie legends.

The shower was like a mental cleansing, the dreams of the night before washing away and running down the drain like the suds of her berry scented shampoo. Her mood restored and the fog of a long night removed, Annie finally left the shower, going back to her room to dress for the day. Taking a long deep breath, she walked to the kitchen hoping with all her heart that if Malik was there, he at least had his shirt on so that she could ignore the scar.

Stepping into the kitchen, Annie heaved a sigh of relief. Malik was there, as decently covered and irresistibly attractive as always. He wore a cream-colored t-shirt that offset his tan, over surf shorts the color of chocolate with cream-colored leaves sprinkled all over them. His back was to her; he was bent over the coffee pot, humming to himself as he prepared their favorite morning beverage. Annie grinned, deciding in that moment that it was time she had a turn as the flirt.

Creeping up behind him, she slipped one arm around his waist. Feeling his stomach muscles tense as she invaded his space, Annie's grin widened but she had only meant to rattle him, so she did nothing more. She grasped the mug he'd filled for her, pressed a hand to his back as she stepped away, and then feigned innocence as she sipped the strong coffee. Looking up at Malik's flashing eyes, she had a hard time keeping a straight face as she lowered the mug.

"Thank you Malik, for the coffee." Winking, she turned and placed the mug on the counter, opening the refrigerator and bending over to stick her head in. "Want some breakfast?" she called over her shoulder. Gathering her typical yogurt and fruit, she stood and turned to face him.

As calm as always, Malik stepped closer and unloaded her hands, placing the makings of her breakfast on the counter next to her coffee. His next movement was so swift Annie had no time to brace herself. Suddenly, she was in his arms and his lips were hot on hers. Her hands rose to his chest in an instinctive protest, but then slid up over the solid strength of his broad shoulders. With one hand in her still damp hair and the other slipping firmly around the curve of her hip, he held her captive.

The kiss was fierce and passionate, but somehow also gentle and tender as Malik unleashed physically, his body making her believe all of the things he'd been saying to her recently. Annie's mind was a storm of thoughts; her breath was ragged and her breasts tingled where they pressed flat against his chest as he pulled her up onto her toes.

Finally, he released her, tenderly tipping her head back and placing a gentle kiss on the sputtering pulse in her throat.

"You are just the cutest, sweetest little tease I've ever seen," he said, swiping the pad of his thumb over her tingling bottom lip. "And I am wildly infatuated. Makes me almost annoyed that I have to go see my old dad," he laughed.

"Silly, no it doesn't. He's your dad!"

"Well, maybe only a little annoyed then. But I can fix it," he said, his arms around her again as his hands rested low on her waist. "Come with me today, Annie. I'm so tired of going to my father and trying to tell him how beautiful you are and how much you fascinate me. I keep trying to explain how things happened so fast between us, but I never seem to be saying it right."

"Meet your dad? You want me to meet your dad?" Annie stood stiff, nervous. His warmth was distracting, the tip of her thumbnail finding its way between her teeth as she debated with herself.

"If you want to," he answered quietly.

"Well, meeting a dad is a big deal right?" Annie asked. "For you, I mean?"

"Maybe a little," he said. "I don't usually bring girls home; I'm not really the serial dating type. But you? You're different, Annie. You're not just any girl to me. And he can tell just from listening to me talk about how special you are. Come on Annie. Come with me so I can show you off, before he starts thinking I've made you up completely."

"I guess I could," Annie said. "What should I wear?"

Malik laughed, releasing Annie and picking up her breakfast. She carried her coffee and followed him to the table, noticing for the first time that he'd already made his breakfast; a thick blueberry bagel slathered with cream cheese sat half eaten on a paper towel. He arranged her breakfast on the table, and went back to his own chair, reassuring Annie that she looked fine in whatever she chose to wear.

"My dad is a simple guy," he said. "He lives in the same little house I grew up in, just a regular guy growing old, trying to get by like the rest of us. No need to be nervous. He'll love anyone who means something to me."

"Well, ok," Annie said. "If you're sure."

"I'm sure," Malik answered, lifting his bagel and biting into it decisively.

***

Sitting in the passenger seat of her car, Annie watched Malik turn into the driveway of a two story Victorian model home. The house was sparkling white; rising up over a long gravel driveway, it was accented with window shutters the pale blue of a clear sky. On the front porch, which appeared to wrap entirely around the house, a man rocked in one of several chairs the same color as the window shutters. The house was as simple as the man appeared to be, standing and moving to the porch rail as he waved to his son.

Malik parked, squeezed Annie's thigh in reassurance, and said, "Let me open your door or you'll get me in trouble for bad manners." He winked, making her laugh as she waited for him to walk around the front of the car, waving back to his father as he walked.

Like an old-fashioned gentleman, Malik extended his hand when he opened Annie's car door and she laughed again, causing him to grin back at her. Taking his hand, she stepped from the car, surprised when he actually tucked her fingers into the curve of his elbow and escorted her up the driveway to the porch.

When they reached the top of the stairs Malik's father was there, smiling welcomingly. His hair was thick and short, a salt and pepper mix of colors that Annie had always thought of as the human hair equivalent to age and wisdom. His eyes were a faded shade of blue, his face weathered by his years on the sea. He was still fit and trim, only slightly soft around the middle, but he stood tall and proud in khaki pants and a plain white t-shirt.

"I'm Nathaniel," he said warmly, his hands firm and strong when Malik passed Annie over to him. Nathaniel held Annie's hands in his, examining her face. "And you must be Annie. Well, you really are something aren't you?" he said.

Releasing her hands when she nodded silently, he turned to his son. "And here I thought you'd been hallucinating. I have never seen a woman as enchanting as your mother, but this girl? Those green eyes will bring you right to your knees." He winked at Annie, tilting his head in amusement as her face flamed.

Malik laughed. "Oh, believe me, I've noticed them," he said, taking Annie's hand and leading her into the house. Inside, Annie was immediately comfortable, reminded of the comfort of her own home. On the table in the foyer, there was a poster print in a driftwood frame, a stark white seal with long whiskers and liquid amber eyes. Throughout the house there were more photos, most of which appeared to be the same seal. Statues and figurines littered shelves and tables, interspersed with photos of a dark haired woman, who looked into the camera with Malik's eyes. Everywhere Annie looked, there was some image, some likeness of a seal. There were even photographs of a little seal pup, playing in the waves of the ocean.

Finding Nathaniel's aged eyes with her own, she asked, "Are you a collector, then?"

At this, both Nathaniel and Malik weakly dropped into chairs, dissolved with laughter. "I suppose you could say something like that," Nathaniel sputtered, trying to sober himself. He mopped his eyes with a worn handkerchief he pulled from his pocket. "Yes, I suppose you could." He looked to Malik, who cleared his throat and promptly changed the subject.

"Hmm," Annie said quietly, curious about the laughter of the men. In her mind, she could hear Brenna's voice, whispering selkie tales that couldn't possibly be true. *Could they?*

***

Over the next few days, Annie couldn't stop thinking of the selkie stories she'd read. It was getting harder and harder to ignore the similarities between those stories and the way she'd met Malik. Looking through the book Brenna had loaned her, Annie stumbled upon a section explaining the possibility of summoning a selkie.

According to the legends, a woman desiring the attention of the selkie could call him out of the waters by shedding seven tears into the sea. There were few clear memories of those final moments Annie had spent waiting to drown, but she did clearly remember accepting her coming death, counting her falling tears in an effort to remain calm. Seven salted tears, dripping from her chin and blending with the spray of the tide as it closed over her.

The chaos of that night became increasingly vivid in her mind despite the loss of her panicked memories. Allowing herself to imagine for a moment that Brenna was right, and that she was now living with a real life example of these legendary stories, Annie tried to picture what it would have been like for Malik. Called up out of the sea by her tears, he'd have shed the pelt that allowed him to exist under the water. As a man, he'd have looked around, seeking the woman who'd summoned him.

Finding her among the waves, would his inner humanity have caused him to forget the selkie pelt in his effort to rescue her? Could carrying her unconscious body out of the waters have caused him to leave his seal-skin unattended, unprotected there along the shore?

Annie thought back to that first morning, waking up to find him sleeping in her living room, watching over her. Had he gone back that night and been unable to find the pelt in the dark? Had he perhaps used her cell phone to call someone who knew about him, like his father? It seemed the most likely suggestion, that if Malik had found himself unable to retrieve the beautiful furry skin on his own, he might have called his father for help. A quick check of her cell phone history revealed this to be true; the number Malik had given her the first time he'd left her alone was there on the screen, listed as an outgoing call in the late hours of that first night.

She remembered waking up that morning, finding the pelt on the shore, shopping for Malik. She'd also fallen ill so soon afterward that he hadn't had a chance to leave her at first, perhaps to retrieve his seal covering. Still, how was it that a selkie man had a human father?

She'd done a little research online as well, curious about the strange amount of seal things in Nathaniel's house, the way he'd looked to Malik when Annie had tried to ask him about his collection. It had bothered her that Malik had changed the course of the conversation so quickly; it had left her feeling that Malik and his father were hiding something.

It hadn't taken Annie long to find answers to her questions on the internet. A selkie child could be born to a couple who was half selkie and half human, generally a human man and a selkie woman. Memories flashed in her mind, the myriad photographs of a sparkling white seal, blended with framed pictures of a beautiful woman Annie had assumed to be Malik's mother. The photos on the wall of the little seal pup played in her memories; she now knew in the secret places of her heart that they were baby pictures of Malik.

Annie now believed she understood Nathaniel's unusual decor -- he wasn't just a seal collector. It seemed to her, taking in all that she had learned, that Nathaniel was an abandoned man living out a quiet life alone. He was a man who had lost his selkie lover, a man who'd helped to create a selkie son.

His collection seemed less eclectic to her now, knowing what his home possessed. He hadn't filled his home with visual trinkets of some strange obsession. Like any other husband and father, his home was full of his memories, unusual as they may be.

So many questions remained; was the stunning dark haired woman dead, or had she taken up her beautiful white pelt and returned to the sea? And if so, had she abandoned her young son to grow up and choose the sea on his own, or had she taken him with her, forcing him to shed his own pelt in order to visit the father he'd left behind?

Sitting in the shed whenever she had the chance, Annie struggled to bend her mind around the chaotic thoughts that left her feeling slightly insane. For a short while, she entertained the idea of checking herself into a mental facility, but there in her hands she had held the proof of what she now believed. The seal-skin warmly covering her lap had once closed over the body of the man she now loved, sheltering him from the cold rages of the sea.

Finally, playing with the idea of telling Malik what she thought she knew, Annie decided to put him to a test. When he came home, she would talk to him over dinner. She wasn't ready to tell him everything yet, but she would show him the book Brenna had loaned her. Annie's plan was to play it off as a silly book of stories, watching Malik for any hint of truth to her suspicions. Based on his behavior at his father's house, she knew his reactions would tell her if she was crazy or not.

***

That night, Annie served simple deli sandwiches and chips for dinner, unable to concentrate on anything more complicated.

"This is nice," Malik said. "Dad wasn't much of a cook when I was growing up, after my mom left. We had a lot of sandwich dinners, sitting together on the porch in the evenings."

Annie hurriedly took another bite to relieve herself of the responsibility to respond. He'd just answered a few of her questions then; if she was right about the selkie part, then it sounded like his mother had abandoned her family to return to the sea.

"Annie?" Malik was watching her, his hand hovering just above the glass he'd been drinking from.

"Yeah?"

"You were zoned out for a second, just staring off at nothing. Are you okay?"

"Oh," Annie laughed, trying not to blurt out everything. "I'm fine, just daydreaming I guess. I've been reading a book I borrowed from Brenna that's had me thinking of weird myths and stuff."

"Myths? What kinds of myths? Like, you mean elves and stuff?" His shoulders tensed slightly. The difference was so minute that if Annie hadn't been living with him, she might not have noticed the change. He lifted his sandwich, placed it back on the plate, and took a drink from his glass instead.

"Well, the book Brenna loaned me is about selkies, actually."

Malik jerked, water sloshing over the top of his glass onto his hand. Gathering himself, he cleared his throat. "Selkies?" he asked.

"Yes," Annie said, pretending not to notice his reaction. She turned her face to the windows, looking out beyond the shed in her backyard. "Apparently," she continued slowly, "they're like some kind of shape shifters, able to live in the sea as seals and on land as humans."

"Interesting." His one word answer was unusual enough to force Annie to look at him.

Turning back to meet his eyes, she forced her voice to remain as normal as possible. His eyes were narrowed slightly as she told more about what she'd read. "I read that they shed their skins and hide them, the women do. And they come onto the beaches, and they sing to enchant human men. In the legends, the selkie women made excellent wives, if a man were able to find her pelt and hide it from her."

"Is that so?" Feigning disinterest, Malik was now swallowing bite after bite of his dinner as if he'd been months without food.

"Apparently. The book also says that lonely wives would sometimes call up a male selkie too, in order to have affairs while their husbands were away."

"Hmph," Malik grunted. By this time, he'd finished his sandwich and was now working his way through the bag of chips on the table. Annie bit off a chunk of her own sandwich in an effort to slow down the conversation and stop herself from asking him what he was by accident. Chewing, she watched him swallow a mouthful of chip crumbs and guzzle the rest of his drink. He avoided looking at her, taking the now empty bag to the garbage and placing his glass heavily in the kitchen sink.

"I, uh, need some stuff from the store," he said. "I'll see you later, Annie."

Watching him walk out, Annie's fingers started to tremble. Her throat felt swollen, and tears clung to the ends of her eyelashes. Malik's stiff demeanor and the absence of his usual good cheer had just answered all of her questions.

***

Malik didn't come back that evening. Eventually, Annie grew tired of waiting for him to return, and she went to bed, leaving the back door unlocked so that he could come in if he came back. In the morning, he was there; he acted as though nothing had changed, as though the previous evening and his strange behavior had never happened. Annie, however, felt as if everything had changed irrevocably. His behavior when she'd started talking about selkies had been so odd; it all but confirmed what Brenna had been saying all along.

She needed time away, time to think, so she'd chosen to spend the day outside the house, telling Malik that she had planned a shopping day. It was true enough; she had gone to the pier and wandered through the area before choosing an empty bench to rest on, letting her thoughts flow as she watched the ocean. She still couldn't believe how out of character he had behaved! His behavior and quick departure from the conversation and indeed the house, had confirmed everything Annie had been suspicious of. The man she was living with was not human. He was the stuff of myth, the stuff of legend. He was the reality of old Celtic stories that were so unbelievable as to be nearly forgotten.

Watching the moments roll by with each wave of the ocean against the pier, Annie thought about what her revelations meant. Some things were certainly different, seeing him now as she did. Some things had not changed at all. What hadn't changed was that she still felt as she had before, that he honestly enjoyed her company. She knew as surely now as she had known before, that they had good chemistry between them. She also had to admit that in spite of everything, their attraction was undeniable. None of that had changed at all.

What had changed was Annie's fantasy of simply falling into the habit of being with him, the fantasy of allowing their easy companionship to become something more. No, she couldn't allow things to go on as they had been, because the consequence of that happening -- without them both being 100% honest with each other – would be that he was forced to remain on land. Pelt or no pelt, Malik didn't have to stay with her; he could certainly stay with his father and live out his life as a human. He could meet another woman; he could choose to take a regular job. He could even buy a boat and choose to live his life on the sea as his father had. But with his pelt locked away in Annie's shed, Malik was forced to remain human, and his choice had been taken away from him.

Annie knew that at some point in his life, Malik had lived as a human boy, growing as all boys did into a human man. Annie didn't know the circumstances behind his eventual choice to go to the ocean, but she did know that he had been living among the seals on the sandbar. There had obviously been a time when his choice had been clear to him, and he had chosen the sea. He had taken up the pelt of the seal and for whatever reason, he'd gone to live beneath the surface of the ocean.

Eventually, Annie had come to terms with the idea that he was not exactly what she had thought him to be, that he was quite special and incredibly rare. She had even accepted the fearful idea that she loved him, as surely as she loved Bar Harbor, as surely as she had learned again to love herself. What she could not accept was living out her life with a man who was tied to her by the furry pelt she had hidden in her shed. She could not accept the idea that one day he might stumble upon it and think she had tried to trick him or trap him.

Worse than that, she couldn't look herself in the eyes in her mirror each morning knowing that she held control over his choice, not to mention the idea that if he should somehow discover the pelt, he might just take it up and abandon her without any word or warning. No, she'd rather that if he should leave her and return to his life in the sea, it should be in front of her; it should be with a real goodbye. This thought made her eyes water, tears spilling silently down her cheeks as she swiped them angrily away. As hard as it was to think of Malik choosing to leave her, she simply could not abide the idea of having him vanish with no explanation. He deserved a choice, and if he would choose to leave, she felt that she deserved a goodbye. It was a conversation she knew they simply had to have.

The decision Annie had come to filled her with dread, and yet she was proud of herself. She was in a situation where a beautiful man had stumbled upon her and they had fallen in love. He couldn't stop touching her, his fingers in her hair, his hands on her shoulders, his occasional kiss. She loved him too, loved talking to him over meals, working beside him in the yard, his easy laugh and gentle humor. She loved the way his muscular arms worked as he built the fire in her living room fireplace, or fixed little things around the house. All of this, she held within her hands. She could throw the pelt away, bury it forever, and never mention it. She had the power to hold him, without his even knowing.

"But I don't want that. I can't hold him that way, it just isn't fair to him. Or me. I deserve to be chosen," she whispered to herself, readjusting her weight on the bench. She dug in her purse and pulled out her water bottle and the muffin she'd stopped at the coffee shop for. It was a simple meal, but it was all she had the stomach for.

As she ate, Annie watched boats float away on the horizon and wondered where Malik was, what he was doing with his day. She wondered if he was worried about her, if he was angry. She wondered if he knew that she knew what he was.

The one thing she was really certain of, as she whiled away the hours of the afternoon, was that she had to tell Malik what she knew and she had to offer him the pelt. She had to offer him his freedom and she had to do it soon. The hardest part was trying to decide when, not knowing what would happen. In her heart she hoped Malik would choose her, but everything she'd read told her that he wouldn't. Everything she'd read told her that he simply could not resist the pull of the sea.

The part of her that believed in their budding love made her want to tell him immediately, to keep the quiet honesty they had built, to put the choice in front of him and let the cards fall where they may. But there was another part of her, a damaged and betrayed part that believed Malik could never choose her, would never choose her. This part couldn't let him go just yet. And so, while Annie knew with all of her heart that the conversation was coming, she also knew with all of her heart that the time for it had not yet arrived.

***

That evening, Annie walked into the house windblown from the pier, tired from the sun and emotionally raw from the decisions she had come to. She responded quietly to Malik's effort at conversation, not rejecting him but not really participating. Laying his big hands on her shoulders as she finished cleaning the dinner dishes, he turned her to face him.

"Annie, is something wrong? Look, I'm really sorry about last night, I don't know what got into me, really. Please tell me we're okay. Tell me that you're okay." His dark eyes searched hers, his palms on her face, the warmth of him disturbingly close.

"We're okay," Annie said obediently, hoping that someday it would be true, hoping that her choice to tell him soon about the pelt wouldn't backfire and explode in her face.

"Are you sure? You didn't even buy anything today on your shopping trip. You found nothing you liked?" He hadn't yet released her face, his thumbs tracing the dark places under her eyes, while his fingertips gently stroked behind her ears.

"I'm sure," Annie told him. "Maybe I'm just tired or coming down with something, I don't know."

"Well hey, let's watch a movie then." Malik slipped his arm around Annie's shoulders, pulling her gently to his side. "We'll watch whatever you choose. And I'll rub your feet and tell you you're beautiful until you feel all better."

Annie couldn't help the little smile that played on her lips, an instant response to his incessant flirting. But inside her secret heart, she was crying, sobbing, screaming. It just wasn't fair, finding a love that felt real and true and safe, only to have to let it go. Still, she wanted to make the best of whatever time she had with him. She forced a frown to her lips, and wrinkled her eyebrows before looking up at him.

"And what if that doesn't work?" Annie challenged.

"I bet I can figure out something," Malik laughed, slipping his fingers into the back pocket of her jeans and guiding her into the living room.

***

Watching the movie, Annie reclined across the couch with her bare feet in Malik's lap. One foot resting on his thighs and the other being worked rather deliciously through his able hands, her mood was improving steadily. The idea of Malik leaving her never eased, but she was able to bury it somewhat under her determination to enjoy him.

Thoroughly enjoying his efforts with her head thrown back against the armrest of the couch, her eyes closed as his hands worked the soreness and tension from her feet. Her easy relaxation fled when he shocked her senses, moving the heat and strength of his hands up past her ankle and under the leg of her jeans. Thankful she'd chosen to shave that morning, her eyes flew open and she pulled gently at her leg before she realized what she was doing.

"Sorry," she muttered. "You surprised me."

Malik laughed. "Lucky for you then, you aren't wearing shorts."

"Is that so?" Folding her legs in front of her, Annie sat up and watched him run his fingers through his hair.

"Oh, it's definitely so," he said. "I confess; I'm kind of a leg man. And if it takes a little massage to finally get my hands on those legs, so be it. I think I'd give my entire gem cache from my diving days."

Annie laughed, wondering just what form he'd been in when he'd hunted the sea for treasures. Fighting the urge to ask, she reminded herself again to make the best of it, to soak up memories of her time with him in case he chose not to stay with her.

"Well, alright then," she said, dropping her feet on the floor and standing. "I shall be right back, to test your qualifications." Leaving him with a shocked expression on his face, Annie sauntered to her room to change.

When she returned, Annie wore pink and white plaid cotton shorts and a basic pink tank top. They were what she usually wore in Boston when she and Chase had gone jogging together, but they were the only clean shorts she owned that were not lingerie style pajamas. They were rather short, barely going halfway down slender but muscular thighs. In her hands, she held a bottle of pink lotion that matched the berry smell of her shampoo; on her face was a daring grin.

"Short enough?" she asked. Taking a spin to show off the change of clothes, Annie spread an oversized towel on the floor and lowered herself neatly to sit in the middle of it. Holding out the lotion, she raised an eyebrow at him in challenge.

Rubbing his hands together in front of him, Malik grinned. "Oh, honey girl, you just fell into the fire." He slipped off the couch and crawled to her, laughing as she dissolved into nervous giggles. She obeyed when she was instructed to turn over and lie flat.

Stretched out on her stomach, Annie pillowed her head on her arms and tried not to think that this might be the only massage she ever got from Malik. He started with her toes again, working his hands into the arch of her foot, warmly covering the heel and ankle as he passed to the lower end of her calf.

"Wow, you are awesome at this," Annie whispered, grieving in advance for the day when he would not be there to talk to.

Mistaking her tone for simple relaxation, Malik laughed. "Well, we all have our talents, I suppose."

Annie felt the coldness of the lotion as he drew a line up the back of her calf, followed again by the warmth of his hands. She had nearly fallen into a relaxed sleep when he passed the sensitive backs of her knees, springing suddenly awake and aware of his touch. She tried to stay relaxed and easy as he spread the lotion over the muscles at the backs of her thighs, but her inner sexy schoolgirl was screaming with glee.

"Okay, turn over," Malik said, clearing his throat and giving the back of one thigh an easy tap with his fingertips.

"Turn over?" Annie had faked her courage in changing her clothes. She had faked an easygoing attitude when she'd dropped to the towel and challenged Malik to a massage. At the idea of lying there watching him as his hands worked over her skin, Annie's bravado crumbled. "Really?"

"What?" he laughed. "Is the great Annie a great big chicken? Come on," he continued. Then his voice took on a threatening note as he said, "Turn over. Otherwise, you'll have crusty knees and uneven skin. Disastrous, I assure you." Leaning down to wink at her, he waved the lotion bottle at her and waited for her to sigh dramatically before flopping onto her back.

"I think I am chicken," she said, her nerves winning out over her insecurity.

"Well, I like chicken. But not when it's dry, so be still," he said, his voice serious in spite of his laughing eyes. Annie forced herself to roll onto her back and lay still, her eyes closed, her fingers laced over her stomach. She pretended he wasn't there for as long as possible, but soon the sensation of his fingertips pressing into the renewed self-conscious tension of her feet was more than she could endure.

"Mmm," she murmured. "It's too bad my ex left me with so many issues, otherwise I'd be feeling pretty magical right now."

"Believe me," Malik said huskily. "You are magical. More than magical. If you were any more magical, you'd be somebody's fairy godmother."

Annie struggled to maintain her control, the feeling of Malik's attraction to her warring with the memories of the things Chase had said to her during their ugly divorce. Right that moment, if she could force her mind to stay in that moment, she felt delicious; she felt attractive. She felt sexy in a way she'd never felt before. But the past kept rearing up in her memories, reminding her of how easy it had been to lose her self confidence in a moment, a glimpse of her husband's body working over the naked form of a woman who'd been her best friend.

Her eyes watered; she couldn't believe how disappointed she was in herself. The past months had been all about relearning to love and appreciate herself as a woman, about finding her confidence again, from within herself. Why then was her confidence so quickly rooted in the need for this man to find her sexy? Her lips trembled and she forced her mouth into a straight line, struggling to hold her face motionless lest the facade of confidence truly break away. Her eyes dampened and then flooded. As a tear slipped down the side of her face and ran into her ear, Malik's hands were there, running up her arms to her face.

"What's this?" he asked, leaning over Annie's face.

Shaking her head, Annie refused to open her eyes, hoping he would sense her need for quiet, that in a moment of quiet she would regain her composure.

Gently, he held her face, refusing to let her hide from him. His thumbs traced over her closed eyes, and his voice was in her ear. "Leave the past out of this, I'm not anyone else but me. Don't I have a good track record? Mostly, at least?" He kissed her cheek tenderly, steering her face to his with his palms.

Unable to speak but unwilling to ignore his questions, Annie answered in a way that felt more natural to her than breathing. She lifted her lips to his, one hand rising up to settle feather-light on his shoulder. A low groan escaped him. Stretching out beside her and bracing himself on one elbow to protect her from his weight, he deepened the kiss.

As Annie's hands rose up his shoulders, Malik cradled her gently, whispering to her between kisses that she was unbearably beautiful, infinitely incredible. He insisted that she was nothing short of perfect. Before long, Annie was simply mindless in his arms, their clothing a mess on the floor and his bare body pressing close to hers. They spoke with physical touch, with simple naked closeness, long into the night.

Limp and liquid after Malik's thorough lovemaking, Annie hardly noticed when he left her, reaching up to the couch and retrieving the blanket she kept there. She was unaware as he arranged her on her side and slid in behind her, drawing her close to the heat of his body.

Well-loved and peacefully resting, Annie didn't hear him whisper into the night, "I do believe I have fallen in love with you, Annie."

***

"I get it," Brenna was saying. "This must be so hard on you, trying to figure out the right thing to do."

"It is," Annie mumbled. It had been a week, and Annie still hadn't told Malik what she knew. She hadn't offered him the pelt; she hadn't freed him. Every day, the choice was more difficult as she fell more deeply in love with him. They'd spent so much time together, talking, touching and learning about each other. They'd spent time with Malik's father also, and Annie was growing to love him as well, his gentle nature and knowing eyes.

She had not asked him again about his collection of seal memories, but she continuously found herself struggling not to stare into the dark liquid eyes of the seal pup on the living room wall. Once, Nathaniel had caught her staring at the photo and had looked at her rather oddly, asking her if she and Malik would like it for her home, saying that he had plenty of others to replace it with. Malik had thrown his head back, laughter rumbling out of him until his eyes had watered and run over. Flustered, Annie had muttered a quick denial, and then excused herself before either of them could see the quick upwelling of tears in her eyes, or how much Nathaniel's gesture had meant to her.

Over the past week, Annie had spent countless hours on the phone with Brenna. They talked whenever Annie wasn't with Malik, discussing Annie's feelings about him and the way her insecurities from her marriage still affected her, discussing the way those separate feelings seemed to crash together within her uncontrollably.

Annie had also talked to Brenna about the selkie legends and the book she'd been reading. That afternoon, she had stuffed the pelt into her trunk and taken it to Brenna's house; they'd spent the afternoon drinking spiked coffee and trying to figure out how Annie could tell Malik what she knew.

"I just don't know how to tell him that, you know? Like, if I'm right, it means I've found someone who loves me," Annie said wistfully. "And I feel beautiful with him. I feel precious to him when I'm talking and I know he's really listening. I feel fascinating because he never fails to respond to me. But I can never rest secure, knowing that I hold him hostage with this." She buried her fingers in the fur of the seal pelt, tracing the oblong roundness of a dark grey spot.

"Maybe he won't choose to go back," Brenna said gently. "You don't know if you don't try. And if he really feels that way about you, how could he leave?"

"I had thought Chase felt that way about me though, too. You know? When he'd tell me he loved me, I believed." A solitary tear slipped slowly down Annie's face and she blinked quickly, swiping at her cheek with one hand.

"Is this the same? Does it feel the same with Malik?" Brenna pulled a tissue from a box on the table and offered it to Annie, slipping under the pelt so that they both wore it as a blanket, fur spilling over their legs and pooling at their feet.

"No," Annie said. "It isn't the same at all. It isn't, but I mean, I believed with all my heart when I was with Chase too, and I was so crushed to find out that what we had wasn't real anymore, not for him anyway. But with Malik it feels like a whole different experience. I'm not sure I believe it though. I just have this sense of disbelief that he could really want me. I guess the only way to describe it is like, I don't really trust myself with a man. With my own judgment. And I'm terrified that I'll try, and I'll tell him I know, and I'll tell him how I feel and he'll walk out on me anyhow. Like he'd be proving all my personal self-doubt to be cold hard fact."

"Oh, Annie," Brenna said quietly. She draped an arm over Annie's shoulders in a quick hug.

"But that's only if I'm right," Annie continued. "What if I'm totally seeing things that aren't there and he is completely turned off because I sound like I've had a mental breakdown? I mean, selkies? Can I really sit down with this perfect dream man who is sexy and charming and gentle and understanding, this man who has made me feel so special again, and tell him I think he's a transforming seal man? If I'm wrong, he won't be able to run fast enough to get away from me, the crazy fruitcake nut job who believes in shape shifters."

"I don't think you're wrong," Brenna said gently. "Crazy as it sounds, even to me and I'm born Irish, raised on this as surely as I was raised on colcannon and black pudding. If you'd only found the pelt on the morning after he saved you? Maybe odd, but not necessarily indicative of a selkie man risen from the waves. The seven tears thing? That's another factor of very odd coincidence. The scar he has? I saw it that day when he helped with the delivery guys moving the new bedroom furniture, and it's like this almost exactly." Brenna traced a fingertip over the scar on the pelt, running down the side of her lap.

"I know, and it all just makes me feel like I'm crazy. And then I went to his father's house with him, and there are all those pictures. He has little figurines and stuff too, but there are seal pictures everywhere, mixed in with photos of Malik's mom. Nathaniel said her name was Muirin, and I looked it up. It's an old Gaelic name that means--"

"Born of the sea," Brenna broke in. "How about that? Was she a selkie too?"

"I think so, and the book you gave me seems to agree. The way to get a baby selkie is for a human man to have children with a selkie woman. You know, or a selkie and a selkie, of course. And all those pictures in Nathaniel's house? I just keep thinking of the baby seal in that frame on the wall, I can't get it out of my head that it's a baby picture of Malik."

"You're not wrong Annie. It all just fits. Crazy as it sounds, I think you've found yourself a real live selkie."

"I have to give him this," Annie muttered miserably, bunching the pelt in her lap and then smoothing it again. "I have to tell him."

"Do you?" Brenna said, lifting an eyebrow and turning to better face Annie.

"I have to," Annie said. "I can't walk around knowing that he can never go back to his life. I mean, he obviously chose that, you know? I don't know if he went to be with his mother. Maybe she left them. Or she died somehow but living as a seal was his way of getting to know her, I don't know. But whatever the reason was, his choice was to live under the sea, on the rocks of the sandbar where he's still close to his home and his father. And I can't take that choice from him. I just can't. I don't want to be a trap, Brenna."

"I understand," Brenna said. "I'd feel the same way, I suppose. But I don't guess that makes this any easier, hmm?"

"No. Having someone I can talk to means the world to me, but no it isn't any easier. I wish it could be, you know? I wish I was so self-confident and so self-assured that I could just show this to him and not be afraid. But I just know, I just know how hurt I'll be if he chooses the sea. I can't help how my heart feels, even if I know in my head that he may not be able to choose otherwise. Everything I've read talks about the pull of the sea, and how the selkie always goes back to the water. But I want him to want to stay."

"Well, you know what they say, Annie. If you love something, you let it go. And if it comes back, then you know it's really yours."

"Yeah," Annie mumbled. "But if it doesn't, you're an idiot who just tossed away your treasured possession."

"What are you going to do?"

"I'm going to tell him, of course. I have to, in order to be able to live with myself, I just have to. But just because I have to tell him, it doesn't mean I have to like it, right?"

"Exactly. And Annie, for what it's worth? I'm here, either way."

"Thanks Brenna," Annie said, dripping tears in a steady flow onto the furry seal-skin as her composure finally crumbled.

***

Pulling into the driveway of her house, Annie took a deep breath and looked over at the seal pelt. Instead of stashed in the trunk as it had been before, it lay piled softly on the passenger seat of her car, spilling into the floor like a speckled puddle of magic.

For Annie, it represented the friendship she'd felt for the seal on the sandbar. It represented the love she had found with a strange and gentle man who'd refused to leave her ill and alone, a love she hadn't expected but had been so thrilled to find. It represented new beginnings. But did it represent the new beginnings of love and family? Or did it represent yet another new beginning alone, back to wishing for strong arms in the middle of the night and a man's low voice with the first rays of the morning sun?

Sitting there in the silence of her parked car, Annie remembered the first time she'd pulled into this very driveway. Then, she'd come as a renter, a freshly broken divorcee with an injured sense of hope for the future. Just as she had then, she took another deep breath, gathered her things and anxiously exited her car. She struggled to hold the heavy pelt in her arms, lifting her hands high to keep it bundled, to keep it from dragging along the dusty walkway.

Annie opened the door to her house, chastising herself for being so fearful. She kicked her shoes off next to the door and walked into the kitchen, full of dread at the idea of finding Malik there. Finding the kitchen empty, Annie quickly attempted to fold the soft pelt, placing it gently on the table. Looking through the window to the backyard, she found him; he lay bare-chested in the sun, lounging on a chaise on the patio.

His skin shone, sleek with the tanning oil that lay on the table beside him. His hair was slightly longer than usual; her fingers twitched with the memory of its softness. He lay with his eyes closed; one arm was draped over his flat stomach while the other was raised lazily overhead, his fingers tucked under the curve of his neck. Annie stood motionless, watching his chest rise and fall with his breath. His lips curved gently in a smile, then receded to their natural position.

She wanted to remember him exactly this way, sleeping peacefully on her patio in the sun, a beautiful man who had been her hero from the moment they'd met. Racing for her new camera, she tiptoed back to the patio, pressing the power button to open the lens. She crept around him, choosing different angles and different levels of focus, her finger dipping gently to activate the shutter and capture his image once, twice, a dozen times.

Even without the aid of the camera, this was a moment frozen in time for Annie, just as permanent as the first time they'd made love. She knew now the shape of his body, the feel of his hands, the firm but gentle curves and angles of him. She knew the freckle on the side of his wrist, the shape of the hairline on the back of his neck, the silken smooth line of the scarred tissue that wrapped under one arm.

Still, the phrase that a picture holds a thousand words proved itself afresh for Annie just then. In her mind, each image her camera captured wasn't just a still, two-dimensional likeness of his handsome face, his perfect body. Every image was engraved in Technicolor with words and phrases, memories of things he'd said to her, silent thoughts she'd been too afraid to share with him yet.

Eventually, she started feeling a little silly, and the anxiety of the conversation to come began to nauseate her. Annie took her camera back into the house and put it away, determined to wake him and finally get it over with.

"Malik?" Annie said quietly, sitting on the edge of the chaise. She laid a familiar hand on his chest, his eyes opened gently. Tears formed in her eyes as he smiled sleepily up at her.

"Hey, you," he said, his hand drifting over her cheek, gently pulling her face to his.

"Hey," she whispered when he released her. She couldn't help wondering if this would be the last time she saw him, lying beautiful under her hands, pressing warm lips into her throat in the heat of the afternoon sun.

"You ok?" Malik had pulled back, leaving Annie cold. The gap between them was small, only enough to allow him to look into her face, but Annie felt suddenly as if they were from different worlds. In her heart, she hoped that he would choose to live in her world, with her. Her mind was a cynical soundtrack playing over and over, telling her he could never choose to leave the sea.

"No," she said. "Malik, we need to talk. Can you come inside?"

Sensing her seriousness, seeing the shimmer of unshed tears in her eyes, Malik's joking nature fell away, his eyebrows drawing together in concern. He took his shirt from the table beside him, draping it easily over one shoulder.

"Come on," he said. He took her hand, standing to lead her inside.

***

"What is that?" Malik whispered. He had just walked into the kitchen; seeing the pelt on the table had frozen him so suddenly that Annie had nearly run into him. His voice was like the voice of a stranger, all trace of his usual gentleness suddenly gone. He dropped Annie's hand, spinning to stare into her face. His dark eyes were usually so warm, liquid and tender. Instead, they now seemed as hard as stone, as hard as the marble eyes of the seal statue gracing her entry table. His gaze was hot, his posture rigid.

"What the hell is that?" he repeated.

Annie stood frozen, speechless. The change in him was terrifying, and as she stared at him, she realized for the first time how big he really was, how strong he was. How little she really knew him. Taking an instinctive step backward, Annie struggled to force words from her lips.

"I, I, Malik --"

"You're backing away from me?" he asked in disbelief. "Annie, really? After all this time? God, woman, you kill me!" He ran his hands through his hair, stalking further into the kitchen and flopping into one of the chairs. "I'll stay here, okay? Way over here. Now what the hell is this?" He gestured to the pelt, one hand waving angrily.

"You know what it is, Malik." Taking a shaky breath, Annie forced her legs to move. Her hands had come up without her permission, her arms wrapping themselves around her waist as if for protection from the unexplained rage in his eyes.

"Of course I do. What are you doing with this?"

"I found it. Malik, I found it that first morning, when I went to the sandbar to see if I could find any of my stuff or anything that you might have forgotten there. I didn't expect that," she said, her eyes darting to the seal pelt on the table. "I didn't. I almost tripped over it. I thought it was a blanket," she whispered.

"A blanket? A blanket!" He shot up from the chair, the sudden motion jarring the table. The pelt slipped to the floor; he stood over it, glaring at her.

"I didn't know what it was, at first." Annie was choking on her words, trying desperately to stop the conversation from spiraling out of control. His hands were shaking; so were hers.

"At first," he muttered. "When?" He looked to her, his face transformed into a mask of unexplained emotion.

"Remember when I told you about the book? The one I borrowed from Brenna?"

"You knew then? You knew? And you kept this from me?" He snatched his shirt from the floor; it had slipped from his shoulder. With jerky motions, he put it on, his hands meeting each other over the fabric covering his chest.

"I wasn't keeping it from you, Malik! I didn't know what it was at first, and then I didn't know what to do. I didn't know if I was right, I --"

"You know now, though?" His eyes had cooled; his face had turned anguished. His posture was stiff, his hands still before him as if he held his heart in them.

"I know," Annie whispered.

"Why did you give this back to me?"

Annie looked to him in shock, unable to believe his asking. "I couldn't be a trap. When I thought of the pictures in your father's house, your mother, all those things he's kept. His memories? Malik, that baby seal, the pup in the picture he offered me? It's you. Isn't it?"

"You know that it is," he said, dropping back into the chair he'd vacated, propping his elbows on the table as he cradled his head in his hands. He looked up, confusion in his eyes.

"You couldn't be a trap?" he asked, as if only just realizing what she'd said.

"I know you can't go back, not if I have this. If I kept it, Malik, you have to understand, after what I've been through; I'd never have believed you really wanted me, not if I kept that pelt hidden away. I'd have always wondered, did you miss the sea? Did you only choose to be with me because you couldn't go back? Were you with me because you had no choice?"

"I can't believe you," he growled, enraged again, his hands fisting before him on the table. Annie stepped back again, her shoulder bumping into the edge of the door she'd forgotten to close.

"Damn it!" he shouted, making her jump. "Stop backing away from me like I'm a scary beast from the streets! I've held you Annie, right here," his hands curled toward his chest. "I've touched you, with these hands," he said, holding them out to her. "I've loved you, night after night. I've nursed you. For Pete's sake, I love you! How could you think I could hurt you?"

"I don't know," Annie whispered, a tear spilling down her cheek. Her stomach was in knots, her head ached, and her throat threatened to close up entirely. "I just didn't want to wonder, Malik, I don't want to live like that, in doubt."

"Doubt? You can doubt me? After everything?" This time his voice was quiet, his anger spent. His face had melted into the soft obvious pain of heartache, his hands reaching out to her instinctively before he curled them up and shoved them in his pockets.

"I'm not him," he said, gently. "You can't put Chase's screw-up on my shoulders; I can't wear a scarf made of his mistakes. I'll choke to death. Any man would."

"That isn't what I meant, Malik. I --"

"I gotta get out of here," he interrupted, his voice barely more than a whisper as he turned away. Not even stopping to put on his shoes, he simply snatched them from the floor as he left.

Silent, Annie followed him to the door, tears streaming down her face. Her hand hovered in front of her chest as if to stop her heart from breaking, or to catch the pieces as it shattered. Wanting to scream but unable to make any sound, she watched the man she loved stomp angrily down her driveway and turn the corner in his bare feet, his shoulders strong and proud, carrying his shoes in one hand. When he turned the corner and left her sight, Annie slowly closed the door and slid down the wall to the floor. Malik had left her.

***

Some time later, Annie rose from her place on the floor, dried her face with the hem of her t-shirt, and went through the motions of finishing her evening. She made dinner, leaving a covered plate for Malik in the refrigerator. She showered, she dried her hair and she went to bed. The first night was long, each sound of the house around her waking her to listen anxiously, struggling to hear Malik among the usual night noises.

He didn't come back.

The next morning, Annie woke as usual, the sun streaming in through curtains she was always forgetting to close. She dressed for the day, made her breakfast and forced herself to eat though she was in no mood for it. She folded the seal pelt Malik had abandoned, placing it again on the kitchen table. She sat beside it, running her fingers through the soft fur and trying to figure out what he would want her to do with it.

Why had he left it? Would he simply watch for the moment she was gone, and then come in and take it without saying goodbye? Or had he left simply out of some emotion he couldn't express, simply needing time to think and to make his choices? If that was the case, did his leaving the pelt mean that he would come back to her?

Eventually, she couldn't sit there anymore. She wrote her goodbye to him, pinning it to the pelt in case he should come back for it while she was out, using it as a way to explain the things he hadn't given her enough time to say. Then she got up and went about her days, always listening to his return, always watching for his face in the streets. Each time her phone rang, her heart lifted with hope that it was him, then plummeted with the realization that it wasn't. She was happy enough to hear from old friends, from her publisher, from Brenna. Still, none of those people spoke with his voice; none of them could look at her with his eyes.

Days went by, passing before her in a haze of growing confusion and anxiety. The pelt remained, but Malik did not come back. He didn't call, he didn't text, he didn't email. Countless times Annie scrolled through her phone and sat staring at the call button next to Nathaniel's phone number. Countless times her trembling fingertip hovered there above the little green icon of a ringing phone, before she'd sigh and close out the screen, slipping her phone back into her pocket until the next time she repeated the ritual.

After a while, she'd simply had enough and she started forcing herself to really go out. Spending time with Brenna cheered her, as did the hours she spent shopping for new things to put in her house. Trying to distract herself on other days, she hiked Bar Island; she spent hours on the sandbar with her camera, pretending that she wasn't looking for Malik. She started a new novel in her series, delighting her agents and her publishers.

Still, he did not return. Every morning, the pelt still lay on her kitchen table, untouched. Every night, she left a fresh covered plate for him in the refrigerator, unable to believe that he would never return. Even if he'd decided to walk away from her, he'd want the pelt with him.

After the first week, Annie had found a new routine, beginning to adjust slowly again to life on her own. She made her meals, and she went back to reading while she ate alone. She kept her house clean, adding little things to it here and there. Each day she spent time writing, telling herself that she had to work in spite of her personal crisis, telling herself that in all things, life must still go on. If there was anything Annie learned from her divorce, she'd learned to pick herself up and go on.

As Annie forced herself to adjust to the idea that Malik might not come back, the pelt remained on the edge of her thoughts. Always there, it was a constant reminder of him. Though she was adjusting, again, to the silence around her, she began to feel as if she'd frozen in time, unable to move on fully while the pelt remained, waiting for Malik. She couldn't give it back to him if he didn't come back. And she certainly couldn't get rid of it, in case he came back looking for it.

Sure, she could have locked it back in the shed. She could have delivered it to his father. But she waited, perhaps unwilling to admit her real reasons for keeping the pelt so close to herself. How could she admit to herself just how unwilling she was to move on fully from her time with Malik? By the second week, she had decided there was no sense in leaving it to gather dust, and she'd taken the pelt with her into the living room to use instead of the throw blanket she kept on the couch.

Annie struggled to maintain the confidence she'd begun to build after her divorce, struggled to control her desire to wallow in the fresh grief of new loss. Still, it didn't take long for the anxiety and the worry to take its toll on her, for the headaches to come and the occasional bouts of vomiting to begin. It had been this way during the divorce, struggling to process the facts of her life, struggling with how she defined herself as a divorced woman. Annie could be strong in the face of others and she could pretend she was just fine, but she couldn't deny even to herself that she was a complete mess of nerves and emotion when she was alone.

During that time, she'd been more nauseatingly ill than ever in her life, her bunched nerves so tense that her body began to ache. She'd had a headache for three full days, and she had no appetite for anything. Her grief and the overwhelming stress she'd been feeling had even begun to affect her female cycles.

She'd spent hours looking through the last set of photographs she'd taken of Malik, those last peaceful moments before their budding relationship had flared up and burned out so quickly. Alternately, she cursed his image and begged it to come alive again. "You just had to prove me right, didn't you?" she'd sneer into his beautiful sleeping face when she was bitter. "You can walk away without a word, just like any other man, without a care or a thought for me, and silly girl that I am, I offered you my honesty, myself. I gave you my heart, and this is what a get. Nothing more than a few stolen images of perfection that can never be mine."

In moments of tenderness, she'd gaze upon him, his eyes closed in peaceful slumber, his limbs relaxed, his mind at rest. She'd imagine the way his chest had risen with his breath, she'd remember how warm he was; she'd remember the easy way he'd flirted with her as if he'd held her confidence in his hands, feeding it back to her morsel by delicious sexy morsel. She'd remind herself of the things he'd said to her; that she was beautiful, charming, funny, smart.

Each morning, Annie woke wishing to find him as always in her kitchen, with twinkling eyes and a flirtatious grin, a mug of coffee in his hands for her. Each morning, she woke and made her own coffee, alone in the empty house that reverberated with memories of his laughter.

"Alone again," Annie muttered to herself, trying to settle comfortably under her covers. It had been fourteen days since Malik had walked out on her, fourteen days of trying to pretend she wasn't wondering where he was. For fourteen days, she had been trapped on an emotional roller coaster of anger and grief and horrible gut wrenching sadness. She knew she would survive his leaving, and she knew she could find a way to rebuild herself again, just as she had after her divorce from Chase. Still, she wished for the contentment she'd held in the time spent with Malik, the easy companionship they'd found together.

Drifting off to sleep, Annie wondered if she'd ever hold contentment again.

***

Waking with a start, Annie lay still, with the scent of her hair floating around her face. It was dark in her room; turning her head slightly brought the clock into her vision. Two in the morning. Usually a solid sleeper, Annie wondered what had woken her.

It took her a while to rise up fully from sleep, to become more aware of her surroundings. When she did, her body tensed as she rose to full alert. Unsure of herself, she closed her eyes and lay motionless, listening. She heard, as always, the steady quiet drip of the faucet in the bathtub, the occasional passing of cars on the street and the ticking of the clock in the living room. Everything sounded as it should, and a glance through the door of her room revealed the darkness in the rest of the house, only broken by the miniature lamp Annie always left on in the bathroom.

Annie toyed with the idea of getting up, knowing herself well enough to know that she wouldn't fall asleep again anytime soon. Everything seemed normal; the regular sounds of the night were all around her. But underneath the noises, underneath the reassurance that the house must be as usual, there was a sense that something was not quite right.

Finally, deciding that she simply couldn't rest without looking around, Annie drew an irritated breath and threw her covers aside. Thankful that she'd chosen to wear one of Malik's t-shirts to sleep, she rolled to the edge of the bed, planning to go check the locks on the doors. Scooting to the edge, she raised her eyes and finally noticed the shadow, tall and dark, silent in the corner of her room. Before she could scream, he spoke.

"I wondered if you'd wake up anytime soon," he said, his voice quiet, the darkness moving around him as he crossed his arms.

"What are you doing here?" Annie said, quickly pulling the blankets back up to cover herself nervously.

"I came to see you." The shadow dropped into the new chair Annie had spent her evening reading in before going to bed.

"And? That doesn't tell me what you came for, Malik. More than two weeks ago, you walked out on me with no explanation or goodbye, nothing. And in all that time, not one word from you. So I'll ask again, what are you doing here?"

"I needed time to think, Annie. I've never had anyone in my life who knows what I am before." he whispered, leaning forward to rest his elbows on his knees. This position brought his face into the moonlight, reminding Annie of how beautiful he was, how much she had missed him.

"Okay. And?" Fighting the urge to leap into his lap and welcome him with a spray of kisses, she kept herself rigid, her posture straight and almost regal. If he wanted a welcome back after leaving her sick with worry, she was determined to make him work for it.

"I missed you. As soon as I walked out the door, I missed you. I couldn't even stop to put my stupid shoes on, knowing I'd just turn around and walk right back inside, back to you. I walked all the way to the pier and I sat there in the dark, by myself. I sat there watching the night come down around me, and everything was beautiful but all I could think of was you."

"You might have deigned to let me in on that," Annie said in a small voice, her fingers folding and unfolding the edge of the quilt on her bed as her resentment began to crumble.

"I sat there half the night, and then I walked back here and I stood out in your driveway. I debated coming in but the house was dark. Then I debated waking you up to talk to you. I debated taking the pelt and leaving," his voice trailed off as he watched her, struggling to hold herself together.

"You didn't." Annie searched for his eyes in the dark, but he'd dropped his face into his hands, his fingertips tangling in his hair.

"No. It wasn't what I'd come for," he said.

"Okay," Annie said. "So what did you come for, after all this time?"

"You," he said, lifting his face to look at her. He smiled, shy after so long. "I came for you. I came to tell you that it terrified me when you said that you know about me. When you offered me that pelt, it was like I knew you were going to be afraid. Afraid of what I am, afraid of what it could mean for us. Afraid of me, you know? And then you were afraid and I was furious with myself for scaring you, and then you were really afraid. Of me, Annie. And I couldn't take the thought of scaring you or hurting you. I just couldn't stay, right then."

"Now what?" Annie asked. She folded her legs under her, tucking the quilt around her legs, self-consciously smoothing his shirt over her body. She wondered if he'd noticed what she was wearing, how much she longed to reach out to him.

"Now I am here. I didn't mean to wake you; I just wanted to look at you."

"Before leaving?" Annie's hands fisted nervously in her lap, and terror coursed through her as she waited for his answer.

"No. I came to see you, Annie," he sighed. "I came to see what you'd done with the pelt, where you left it. I came to see if you missed me, if my stuff was still here. Mostly, I came to watch the sun come up in your face like it has every morning since the night we met. I came to see if you'd let me make coffee, if you'd let me watch you smile over breakfast. I came to see if you'd still want me here when you've come fresh out of the shower and your hair does this little wet curling thing everywhere." His voice was rushing now, as if in a desperate effort to spit out words that did not come to him easily.

"I came to reassure you when you're feeling less than beautiful," he went on, "and to wipe that little smudge you always end up with on your cheek when we're in your garden. I came to mow your grass, and to eat your sandwiches, and to watch movies with your feet in my lap."

Annie sighed. "Huh. So, what does all that mean? What does it mean for you? I mean, I know well enough from reading that you can only really stay human by means of a trap, that a selkie simply can't resist the pull of the ocean. Have you come to tell me goodbye?"

"Haven't you been listening, Annie?" he asked, coming over and easing onto the edge of her bed. Lifting one of her hands from her lap, he folded her fingers in his and lifted them to kiss her knuckles. "I left because you're right. It is a choice between human life, and this completely free, completely non-human life. I may not be just your average human man, but I do have the power to choose. It won't be easy, but I can choose."

Her hand lay wrapped in his, resting in his lap as he stroked her wrist gently with his thumb. "And what do you choose Malik?" Annie tugged her hand away from him, folding her fingers together and burying her fisted hands in the quilt. She looked away from him, desperately trying not to choke on the lump in her throat. Her stomach flipped, tripped, fluttered.

"I choose you. I have chosen you from the beginning." He laughed when Annie's mouth flopped open in disbelief, her eyes flying to meet his. He lifted a hand to her chin, gently bringing her lips together and tracing them with his thumb. "The sea has its pull," he said. "But you have an entirely alien gravity, and I am helplessly tangled in it."

"Is that true? You can choose to stay?"

"It isn't easy, but I can," he said. "If you choose to allow me. If you still want me here with you."

"How long? How long are you going to be able to resist?"

"I don't intend to have any choice in the matter," Malik said seriously, lowering his eyes.

"What does that mean?" Annie asked, her eyebrows coming together.

"Right now, it means I'm here for as long as you want me here," he answered, pulling her close to him and fitting his lips to hers.

"Hmmm." His lips were so soft, so tender, traveling from her mouth to her throat, down to her collarbones and back again. Annie suddenly felt as if she hadn't breathed in weeks. Finally, drawing a full but shivering breath, drawing in the scent of him and the sheer warmth of his presence, she found him completely irresistible. Her arms crept around his neck, a forgotten fire suddenly bursting to life in her core. Her determination to remain rigid was forgotten also, and all she knew in that moment was the hot band of his arms around her.

"It means you're here for right now? What about next week? Next year?" she whispered, her words fading away as her mind shattered under his efforts.

"We can work out the details later," he whispered back. His voice was like a low growl, his hands working their way up the back of the t-shirt she wore, smoothing over her bare skin.

"But you'll stay? You can choose to stay?" Annie asked, pausing.

"I choose to stay," he answered. "I am not a creature only of the sea, and I belong to you now." Groaning as her hands found his chest, Malik pressed her back into the mattress and together they celebrated their reunion.

***

The next morning found them in the kitchen, chatting over coffee and breakfast as if Malik had never left. It felt natural for the two of them to be moving around the kitchen together, preparing breakfast and coffee. Occasionally Malik reached out for Annie, touching her arm or twirling a tendril of her hair as if he were afraid to lose physical contact with her.

Annie fought to keep the little remaining resentment hidden away inside her, telling herself that if she had been Malik she'd probably have needed time to process things, too. In the few seconds when he'd first seen the pelt on the kitchen table, his face had lost all color and he'd frozen as solid as if he'd never been made of flesh at all. Struggling to be understanding, she forced herself to think through how she might have reacted if it had been she who'd spent her entire life as something other than regular, with a monumental secret to keep, only to be found out so unexpectedly. Grudgingly, she admitted to herself the likelihood that she'd have done as he had done. After all, hadn't she already done what he had done, running away from home to find peace and time to think?

She reminded herself that he had come back to apologize and explain, to ease her fears and her worries. She tried to put herself in his shoes, wondered if maybe he'd been afraid to come back. He'd said he had been afraid that she would fear him, knowing him for what he was. What she suspected, though he hadn't said it, was that he'd been afraid she would reject him as too odd, too different, too unreal. And here she'd been afraid that he would think she was crazy!

She'd have been crazy to send him away, this gentle complex man who was from another world, a world she had never entered, a world in which she could not survive. Remembering how it had felt to wake up beside him, to turn over and watch him reach for her in his sleep, Annie smiled to herself.

"What's that sneaky grin for?" Malik said, reaching over the table to tap the tip of Annie's nose.

"Nothing," she said, ducking away. "It's just nice to have you here again. Gosh," she teased, "after so long, I'd just almost forgotten what you looked like."

"Right, like you could forget this," he laughed, running a steady hand down his chest mockingly. He winked, flexing his arms above his head in a playful attempt to look overconfident, and then sighed dramatically, throwing his head back as he ran his fingers through his silky dark hair. "I'm spectacular. You said so yourself, remember?"

Remembering that moment in the middle of the night when her ability to control her speech had failed, Annie flushed crimson. She remembered well what had been said, and what he'd been doing when she'd said it. Her stomach fluttering, she bent her head over her breakfast and took a hearty spoonful, making a point of chewing thoroughly to avoid having to answer him.

"Well, I definitely remember," Malik said, answering for her as he struggled to sober his amusement. "I remember exactly, every single breathy little word. You know, Annie, you can probably swallow that now without choking, since it's just yogurt." He jerked back as Annie threw a grape at him, his mouth wide. Annie giggled when the grape soared right into his open mouth. Taking up a second grape, she aimed and threw it, impressed when he caught it too.

"There was a chunk of strawberry in that bite, I'll have you know," she said. "Which happens to be hazardous if not properly chewed."

Laughing, he scooped up a bite of egg on his fork and dropped it onto his toast, folding it over before taking a bite. "Uh huh," he muttered. "I've never choked on a strawberry."

"Not fair! That's because seals live on fish," Annie laughed.

Malik snorted, flicking a breadcrumb across the table. He gulped the rest of his coffee and lifted an eyebrow at her. "Not fair," he retorted. "Animals need protein."

"Cute. But seriously though. Malik, what do we do about the pelt? Should I just put it back in the shed? We can just let it be, out there. Then, um, if you ever want it," her voice trailed off, her eyes lowering to her plate.

Sobering, Malik shook his head. He swallowed; his eyes were steady as he met Annie's eyes with his own. "No, it needs to be gone. Eventually, the ocean will be calling me, but that's not what I want, I don't want the option just sitting there in front of me. That's like a drug addict keeping his pipe and his stash around for the memories. I want swimming in these shorts to be my only option, Annie. When I said I was here to stay, I meant it. For good."

"What do we do then?"

"I will need to destroy it completely," he said, his gaze flickering to the entrance to the living room. "I'll have to burn it."

"Burn it! Malik, you can't be serious!" Annie pushed her breakfast away, her stomach rising up into her throat threateningly.

"I am serious," Malik answered.

"But it's your pelt; it's your way back to the sea. It's your connection to - -"

"My mother," Malik interrupted. "It was a connection to my mother, and I took it up to go and see where she came from, who she was. I left my father, trying to understand why my mother left me," he muttered.

"I know her now," he continued, "and even though she was dead by the time I went to the water, I know why she left my dad and me when I was little. I have been with her family; I have lived that side of this life. I even know why she didn't have a choice. I get it. And the way I protect this," he said, taking Annie's hands in his, "the way I protect what we have, is to make sure that I don't have a choice either. I have to destroy it, or it will take me back, and this -- what we have here between us -- it'll be gone, Annie. And that's not what I want."

"So we burn it? What will happen then?" Annie's eyes searched his, the gravity of what he was offering settling heavily on her shoulders. "Will you grow to resent me, Malik? To hate this life when you realize you can't escape it?"

"I have chosen. And I have thought it through." He spoke with finality, but his eyes were tender, his thumbs tracing circles on her wrists.

"Okay," Annie said. "But it's a part of you, your pelt. Will anything happen to you?"

"It'll be fine," Malik said, his eyes dropping to their joined hands. "It'll all be just fine."

"Are you really sure?" Annie couldn't help wondering if he could really do it and she had a sudden fear that destroying the pelt would also destroy the man in front of her. She wanted to talk him out of it, to lock the pelt away and protect it from him. Her conscience won the battle; she would respect his choices.

"I'm really sure," he answered. "I have to burn it. We have to burn it."

"If you're sure," she said, forcing a smile that didn't dispel the uneasiness in her eyes.

"I'm sure."

***

A month later, Annie and Malik had discussed every aspect of their plan for the future. Malik had formally proposed; it was an incredibly beautiful event that Annie was unlikely ever to forget. They had not yet broken the news to Nathaniel; Malik wanted to be rid of the seal pelt first, and he'd balked when Annie had suggested that they tell him their plans.

Sitting there in the sand on a beach down the coast, Annie reveled in a breeze that lifted her hair from her shoulders. Looking down, she admired the sparkling antique blue diamond ring that so elegantly encircled her finger. Set in platinum, six striking blue diamonds encircled a white center diamond. The band was carved and engraved with vines and leaves that wrapped around Annie's finger. Malik had told her he'd found it on a dive, a shimmering and beautiful underwater flower that would never wilt in the sun, a perfect thing that would never die.

"Like us," Malik had said to her, slipping the ring onto her finger and wiping away her joyful tears. "We are forever, my darling. And no wind, no sea or fire or stretch of land shall ever come between us. And you will never fear for your safety, or your security or your future, because I have chosen you. Because you are mine, I am always yours; I will always be your protector, your lover, your friend. And you shall always be well-loved and well cared for."

Unable to speak, Annie had only nodded her head, falling into his arms.

Now, she watched him work only a few feet away. She rested with her back leaning against a giant piece of driftwood, and the sea roared close beside her. The sky was just beginning to darken, to take on the painted colors of the sunset.

Annie's focus, however, was on Malik, the bronze and beautiful man she called her own. He'd taken his shirt off; it was tucked carelessly into the hip of his shorts, dangling down his leg and pooling beside his foot as he squatted to build the fire. Malik's back and shoulders worked at the effort of building the fire, but Annie could see in the tension of his neck and the angle of his head that his mind was working too; maintaining his composure, steadfastly following a plan that was wholly against his personal instincts. But he would only be melancholy for a short while longer. She had some news for him, news she'd been saving for when he'd finally made his choice.

"I'm almost finished," he said, glancing quickly over his shoulder. "Do you want to go ahead and start unpacking?"

Annie smiled, watching his gaze linger on her outstretched legs before passing over to the basket of food she'd braced her elbow on. "Sure," she said, lifting the basket lid and pulling out the blanket she'd packed. Flinging it out and watching it spread and slowly float to the ground, Annie struggled to ignore the other thing they'd brought to the beach with them, packed into an open wicker basket; Malik's pelt. She felt the warmth of the fire begin to climb her back as she knelt on the blanket, warming her as the breeze turned cold, reminding her that this was not only to be a sad night for him.

By the time Annie had finished unpacking the dinner they'd brought along, Malik had built a raging fire on the beach, and they curled together in its warmth. Annie had packed miniature ham and Swiss cheese sandwiches, toasted and slathered with her mother's specially seasoned mayonnaise recipe. They'd stopped at a local deli and picked up a variety of other finger foods, and Malik had surprised Annie with a bottle of light and fragrant Moscato wine.

Laughing, Annie poured the wine into one of the two cheap plastic goblets Malik had handed to her. "I'll have some in a while," she said. "Honestly, I can't even figure out how you did this. Where did you manage to hide this while I was packing boring old regular water?"

"Well," Malik answered, mocking as he draped his arm around her and pulled her close to him. "I happen to be a man of many talents, you see."

Leaning closer to touch his lips with her own, Annie giggled, surprised at the happiness bubbling up within her. "Why yes, I think I remember. You have quite an amazing talent for --" Annie broke off, pursing her lips and dragging her eyebrows together, pretending to think. She watched Malik raise his own eyebrow, questioning, and then brought her palm to her forehead in a mocking slap.

"That's right, I remember!" she exclaimed. "A talent for --"

"This?" Malik whispered, slipping his palm under her cheek to lift her lips to his.

"Oh," Annie breathed, later. "I was going to say you were talented with mowing grass, but yeah, I think you're pretty talented at that kissing thing, too." She broke into giggles as he growled low in his throat, her arms circling his neck as he lunged over and pinned her to the ground with his weight, tickling her mercilessly. His wine spilled, a pink stain soaking into the ground, though neither of them noticed.

Eventually, the tickling gave way to more kissing, and it was some time before they finally found themselves upright again, leaning against the driftwood as they ate.

"I know you said this was the only way to handle this, Malik. But is it really what you want, for sure?" Annie whispered, finally acknowledging the seal pelt, pulling it over carefully beside her. She felt him stiffen, and she knew his answer before he gave voice to it.

"That's how it has to be, Annie, whether it's what I want or not. For the first part of my life, I was just a regular little boy, growing up in a regular house with regular parents. I didn't know my mother was trapped, I didn't know dad had hidden her pelt in the attic. He sent me up there one day to find something, and I guess he'd forgotten, because he didn't tell me where to look. Or where not to look. I went digging through things, random like kids do, and I found this giant wooden chest. I opened it up and there inside was a fur blanket," he murmured, talking more to himself than to Annie. He smiled a little to himself, remembering how Annie, too, had mistaken the pelt of a selkie for a simple blanket.

"I pulled it out to look at," he continued, "and the next thing I knew, my mother was there and she was crying. She held it up to her chest, and then held it out so she could shake the dust away, and she just cried and cried. She made me swear not to tell dad what I'd found and I didn't tell, not until after she was gone. But before she left, she sat me down and she gave me my own pelt, the pelt I'd been born with as a selkie baby. It started then, the moment the truth was out."

He tucked Annie again into the curve of his elbow as he spoke, stroking her hair softly as she pillowed her head on his chest. "I'd always been a champion swimmer, even before that. Everyone called me a water baby. Mom said I was like a fish out of water, and dad would always laugh like a crazy person. Once she told me what I really was, that's when it started calling to me more strongly, the sea. She was gone and I didn't want to leave dad like she had, but I started diving, taking jobs on expeditions. I was still pretty young back then, and I was already known as the one to be hired for the big jobs."

"When did you leave?" Annie raised her face to meet his eyes, watching his memories flicker by in the darkness of his face in the twilight.

"I don't really remember what age I was, honestly," he said, running the fingers of one hand through his hair. "I'd graduated high school, so maybe I was twenty or so. One day I just couldn't take it anymore, the ocean was pulling at me constantly. I was taking longer and longer dives. Dad was upset, but I couldn't stand being in the house with his memories of my mother all around me and I was so angry that she'd left. I was angry that she'd made me, that she'd given birth to me, knowing what I would be, and I was angry that she'd left me. I was so confused. I just needed the freedom of a new existence, you know?"

Remembering why she'd come to Maine, Annie nodded, the fine curling hairs of his chest tickling her cheek. "I get it," she said.

"I went out, and I just ... I just stayed gone a while. I'd come back sometimes, and I'd stay a bit and visit with my dad but then I couldn't stay anymore. I'd leave again, and he'd always look so wretched, watching me take up the pelt and leave him the way she had."

"And so it has to be this way," Annie murmured, her fingers buried in the fur of the pelt beside her. Chilled, she moved to pull it from the basket and over her legs; as the softness of the fur touched him, Malik sprang suddenly alive. Taking the weight of the pelt in the strong grip of a life of practice, he flicked his arm, and as suddenly as it had touched him, the pelt was flying.

"It has to be this way," he murmured. "My life is here now."

Annie gasped as it hit the flames, wriggling animatedly among the fire. A tear slipped down her cheek and vanished into the hair of his chest as the pelt sizzled and fizzed in the heat, slowly turning the bright red orange of the flickering flame. He held her as she cried, mourning his loss but rejoicing in his finality as the pelt slowly died down and lost itself in the embers.

***

"Didn't you believe me?" Malik whispered, while his fingers buried in her hair as he held her.

Annie nodded, and then shook her head, conflicted. "I thought I did, but I guess some part of me wasn't so sure," she whispered, wiping the tip of her nose with the back of her hand. She kissed his chest lightly, where a tear shimmered in the moonlight against his skin. The fire had died down some and it wasn't as warm or as bright, though it did lend them a glow of warmth and faintly flickering light.

"I really meant it, Annie," he said, his arms tightening around her briefly. "I chose you. I choose you. And now the sea cannot call to me in the same way ever again."

"Malik, I'm just so afraid that you'll resent me. Am I so silly for that?"

"Never silly, my love," he answered, the tips of his fingers traveling lightly up and down her back. "But I can't blame you for a choice I made readily and willingly. I am not one for putting my choices on the shoulders of others, whether I regret those choices or not."

"And do you?" Annie asked, unbearably afraid that he would answer and equally afraid that he wouldn't. "Do you regret what you've done?"

"Not for a second. Besides," he said, in a desperate attempt to lighten her mood. "Seal women are kind of ... blubbery."

Annie laughed, curling her fingers on his chest only to open them again and spread them wide. His breath caught as her fingertip grazed a nipple, and his arm tightened again before he relaxed and resumed stroking her back.

"I meant what I said, Annie," he whispered, his lips against her forehead as she turned to gaze up at him. "I want you; I want to be here with you. I've had that freedom to roam and do as I please, and now I want something I can count on, something steady and trustworthy that I believe in."

"And you believe in this?" Annie asked, quietly, thinking of the thing she needed to tell him.

"I do," he answered. "This is my choice, and I am not sorry." Lowering his face to hers, he kissed her wrinkled forehead, her tender, worried eyes, and the tip of her grief-swollen nose. Turning her face in his hands, he kissed both cheeks, and traced her jaw with kisses. By the time he reached her mouth, Annie had lost track of her worries and all she knew was the gentle touch of the selkie man she'd caught up from the waves of the ocean.

As the fire beside them continued to flicker and slowly die, the fire between them rose up, raging and emotional. They grieved together, the loss of the pelt and the permanence of Malik's decision. They celebrated together, the freedom his choice had given them, a freedom to be together as simple humans, a man and a woman in love.

His shirt worked its way loose and came untucked from the waist of his shorts, slipping unnoticed to the edge of the blanket they lay on. Soon, Annie's shirt was lost in the dim light of the fire and the moon as well; she lay wanton under the sky, hidden only by the fragile lace of her bra and the covering of Malik's body.

"I am so happy to have met you," he whispered, his lips traveling the column of her throat. "I love you, endlessly. I love your face, I love your body." He punctuated his speech by kissing his way down the left strap of her bra, his breath a warm burst against her skin, relief from the growing chill of the evening. "I love your sense of humor, and the way you find me hilarious. I love the way you take on what I offer you, I love the way your eyes tell me that you understand my choices and my past, that you see value and not just oddity in me." Her bra was gone by then; she hadn't even been aware of it until a sudden gust of wind washed over her and she felt its absence for a moment, before he was there to warm her again.

Then she knew nothing, only his hands and his body, her hands slipping up and down his back, her breath coming in quick panting gasps, her voice a breathless murmur in the wind.

Finally sated, Annie lay curled beside Malik. He'd removed the weight of his body from hers, but she was kept warm by his closeness. One heavy thigh lay between hers, his arm pleasantly weighty on her stomach, his fingers splayed over the globe of one round breast. Nearly asleep, it took her a moment to realize she was being rained on.

"Oh my gosh! Malik, it's raining!" Annie scrambled out from under him gathering things and stuffing them hurriedly into the picnic basket. She yanked his t-shirt from the ground and hauled it over her head, throwing the rest of her clothes into the basket they'd carried his pelt in.

"Mmmm," he groaned, still lying contentedly on the blanket. Propping his head on one hand, he watched her rush around, frantically trying to gather everything as the rain poured over her.

"I think you're getting wet," he said.

Dropping his shorts over the side of his hip, Annie laughed. "Come on, we have to get out of here, we can't just sit here in a storm!"

"Well, alright," he growled, standing to stretch, reaching skyward as the rainwater flowed over his nakedness and soaked the blanket under his feet. Lifting his wet shorts, he struggled into them, drawing the strings together and tying them deftly. He snatched the blanket from the ground and tossed it into the wicker basket with the other things Annie had thrown in. Lifting it, he cocked an eyebrow at her, somehow also managing to narrow his dark eyes against the rain.

"Race ya?" he asked.

Without answering, Annie gripped the picnic basket in front of her and let loose, all her years as a young track runner fueling the speed which carried her toward her car. Laughing, they raced down the beach, toes digging into the ground for traction as the rainwater ran into their eyes. Malik was a powerful sprinter and he could quickly close the distance between them, but as a distance runner Annie regained and held her place in the lead.

Reaching the car first, Annie hugged the picnic basket in one arm while she yanked the door open with the other. Stepping on the floor lever that opened the trunk, she slammed the door against the rain and raced around to the trunk, her hair a wet and heavy mass down her back.

They hit the trunk together, Malik lifting the lid so that Annie could tuck the picnic basket into the corner of the trunk. Slipping the bigger basket in beside it, he took her in his arms and kissed her, laughing. It was only after they'd both settled into the car that they realized neither of them had the keys.

"Are they in either of the baskets?" Malik asked, his hair dripping into his face as he tried to meet Annie's eyes in the dark of the car.

"I don't remember picking them up," Annie said. "I was just shocked it was raining, and I don't even know why but I guess I panicked a little. I hope I didn't leave them on the beach, we'll never find them in this."

"I will," Malik said. "Just hang on, pop the trunk. If they aren't there, I'll go look where we were sitting. You have a flashlight back there?"

At Annie's nod, Malik took a deep breath, slicked his wet hair back from his face, and then he was gone. Only moments later, the trunk slammed and Annie watched Malik jog back down the beach, his body strong and agile, his bare feet meeting the ground with confidence. The beam of the flashlight jerked crazily as he ran, bouncing among the flickering blindness of the first lightning.

It met the ground right near the edge of the sea, the waves rolling back to escape its heat, a billowing cloud of steam rising up as darkness fell again. Annie searched the night for the beam of her flashlight and found it, sweeping along the driftwood they'd lain against. The light grew faint as he swept the ground, searching for her keys, going one way and then the other.

She knew the second he'd discovered them, flicking the flashlight over and then going back at once to find them. Thunder rolled as he turned the flashlight on himself, illuminating his hand as he held the keys in the air to let her see that he'd found them.

The next crack of thunder made her jump, followed so close by the blinding flash of the lightning. She watched shock come over him, saw the beam of the flashlight tremble and go out, and a scream tore from her throat as he crumpled to the ground.

***

Shock filled her, her hands clutching her stomach in panic. Water flowed freely now, the sky having opened fully in what seemed to be a public show of Annie's emotions. Her fingers scraped along the door, finding purchase and hooking over the latch release. Throwing the door open, Annie fell from the car, her knees hitting the ground as Malik's t-shirt soaked up rainwater and began again to cling to her body.

"No, not now, not him, not now," she whimpered, scrambling to her feet, looking again to where he had fallen, to the place where he continued to lay motionless, in an uncomfortable pose in the downpour on the beach. Annie ran, a low keening sound pouring out of her, rising and falling with her breath as the muscles of her legs carried her. Pained seared her chest, stifled breath coupling with fear of what her mind insisted must be happening. Reaching him, she fell again to her knees, heedless of the scrape of her skin on the surface of the ground beneath her.

She lay forward, gulping air and forcing herself to silence. It was dark now; she laid her head on his chest to see if it would rise, disbelieving when he failed to breathe. In a panic now, she rose above him, screaming his name. She shook his shoulder; she slapped his face, still warm in the rain. Pressing two fingers to the artery in his throat, she searched for a pulse and found only stillness. Straightening the angle of his head and tilting his face to open his throat, Annie tried to block the rain with her body as she layered her hands on his naked chest, linking her fingers and pressing the way she'd been taught years ago.

Praying desperately as she pumped his chest, Annie struggled to bring life to the man she loved, wondering if CPR was even effective in the anatomy of a selkie. She knew nothing else to try. Laying her lips upon his, denying what her heart was screaming, she pinched his nose and held his chin, breathing air from her own lungs into his. From breathing into his lungs to manually pumping his heart, again and again in a pattern of sheer survival, Annie offered her dedication to Malik's body, begging him to come alive again.

It was a desperate process and Annie went on until she'd exhausted herself, lying limp on his lifeless chest, staring weakly at the ring he'd given her. It had been alive when he was, a symbol of their time together, a symbol of the promises they'd made to each other. Even now, it remained beautiful, and yet it was now as dead as any flower sliced away from its source of life. It was only metal now, cut and shaped by human hands, enhanced by sparkling rocks borrowed from the earth. Without his promise, it was only a ring.

Lifting his arm, Annie pulled it around her one last time and curled close to the lingering warmth of his body. Reaching for his other hand, Annie dislodged her car keys, examining the hot, burned flesh of his fingers, the darkness of damaged flesh from the lightning strike traveling up his arm. She lay there for what seemed like forever, begging him silently to take a breath and come alive again, to reassure her that all was well.

Grief took over her, thoughts of what might have been plaguing her mind, rending the fabric of her heart. As she slowly came to terms with the fact that Malik was lost to her now, the life driven from his body, his heart stopped forever by the electrical force of the storm, her grief raged in her, and she sat up beside him, not caring or noticing how ineffectively his shirt covered her nakedness. Pounding his chest, she screamed at him, raged at him for leaving her, for breaking his promises to always be with her.

The screaming didn't wake him, and he lay still in the sand, the rain pouring down on him. All too soon, logic set in and Annie was forced to decide what to do with his body. Could she call his father, tell his father what had happened to him? Could she tell him that she knew everything and that he'd finally lost his only son for good? That it had been because of his choice to throw off the sea? What would be revealed to the human world upon examination of his body? Was he normal on the inside, with convincingly human organs? Annie didn't know, and the only person who could tell her was Nathaniel.

Remembering, Annie groaned. Wanting to be alone for the burning of the seal pelt, she and Malik had not brought a cell phone with them to the beach. There was no way to call anyone, and she couldn't drag him all the way to the car alone. Neither could she leave his body alone in the elements. Sitting silently beside him, Annie stroked his chest, his shoulders, and his face. She spoke to him as if he was still alive, trying to imagine his answers, what he would tell her to do.

"I can't believe this is happening," she mumbled, her voice a strangled noise among the rush of the ocean, the crack of thunder and the sounds of the falling rain. She pressed her hair back from her face with shaking hands, looking into Malik's lifeless eyes as rainwater dripped from her face with her tears. Pressing a hand to his face, she lowered his eyelids, gasping as the closure of those once tender and now empty eyes left him looking peaceful. Now he looked alive again, as if he only slept there in the rain and would awaken at any moment. It made him easier to talk to.

"How could this happen to me? To us? This was supposed to be magical; we were supposed to go on! Malik, we had plans, please come back! I don't know what to do. Don't go, Malik." Sitting there beside him, Annie listened to the storm raging around her. Water poured over her face, running in rivers over the curves of her body and pooling around her in a flood. The waves of the sea crashed and foamed, battling with the thunder for volume. Watching the waves come charging in, Annie was swept up in the constancy of the water, the steady rushing in to shore, the chaotic pull back to deeper waters.

It occurred to her that if Malik had chosen the sea as his home for most of his life, he might find it an appropriate place to be laid to rest. Knowing she was illogical with grief but unable to control the course of her thoughts, Annie screamed into the face of the sea, into the ear of the storm.

"Did you want him this bad?" she screamed, rage filling her again as she climbed to her feet, her hands fisted beside her as if ready to strike. "Was he so important to you? Damn it, he was important to me!" Rage took hold of her, and she scooped up rocks, shells, stones, everything she could reach, throwing everything into the approaching waters of the tide.

"Take him then!" In a desperate rage, her body wracked with grief as she cried, Annie reached for Malik. Squatting near his head, she looped her hands under his arms, dragging him closer to the waves as sobs wracked her body. The tide was coming in with the storm; the water was now beginning to swirl around her ankles in an ugly remembrance of the night they'd met.

Before long, Annie had dragged Malik as far as her body would allow, and she dropped to the ground again beside him, spent. She took his hands and pressed them to her heart, looking into his face as the waters rose and fell around them, gently tugging him with each cycle of the waves, toward the depths of the ocean. Time escaped her, and soon she realized that the sea had taken hold of both of them, moving them ever so slightly deeper and deeper into the water. Shivering with shock and cold, she held fast to his hands.

Eventually, a wave crashing over her head broke the trance, shocking Annie back to the present. In her grief, she had acted impulsively; unaware of what was around her as she gazed at the man who'd once risen from the sea to save her, only to be taken again so viciously. Malik's body was now floating in the water, and Annie tried to remember how she'd gotten so caught up in the current with him. When had she stood? When had she walked, still holding him in her grip? How had she ended up in water that licked around her upper waist, in the danger of the waves and the current, with the malevolent threat of the undertow dragging persistently at her feet?

Another wave foamed up in the distance, growing ever taller as it approached her. It rolled closer, standing higher and higher, beaten by the rain and raging forward with shocking speed. Annie drew a breath, anticipating the wash of the salted water, the disorientation of being swept from her feet, and the fear of not knowing which way was up.

Malik had begun to drift slightly below the surface of the water, but still Annie clung desperately to him. She knew she should let go and try to reach the shore, but her body refused to obey her commands. As another giant wave swept over her, tossing and twirling her through the waters, Malik was ripped from her temporarily, and she grasped desperately in the dark for him. Finding one hand, her fear and her grief gave her desperate strength; she clung to him as her lungs began to burn for oxygen.

It was in that moment that Annie realized how dangerous her situation had become, but she didn't know which way to kick, or if she could even force herself to let Malik go. She knew then, still desperately holding her breath, that she'd spent her last day on earth. Even if the ocean should calm itself suddenly, she couldn't swim back to shore and would have to rely on a stormy current. In that moment, hope left her.

ANNIE'S INTERLUDE

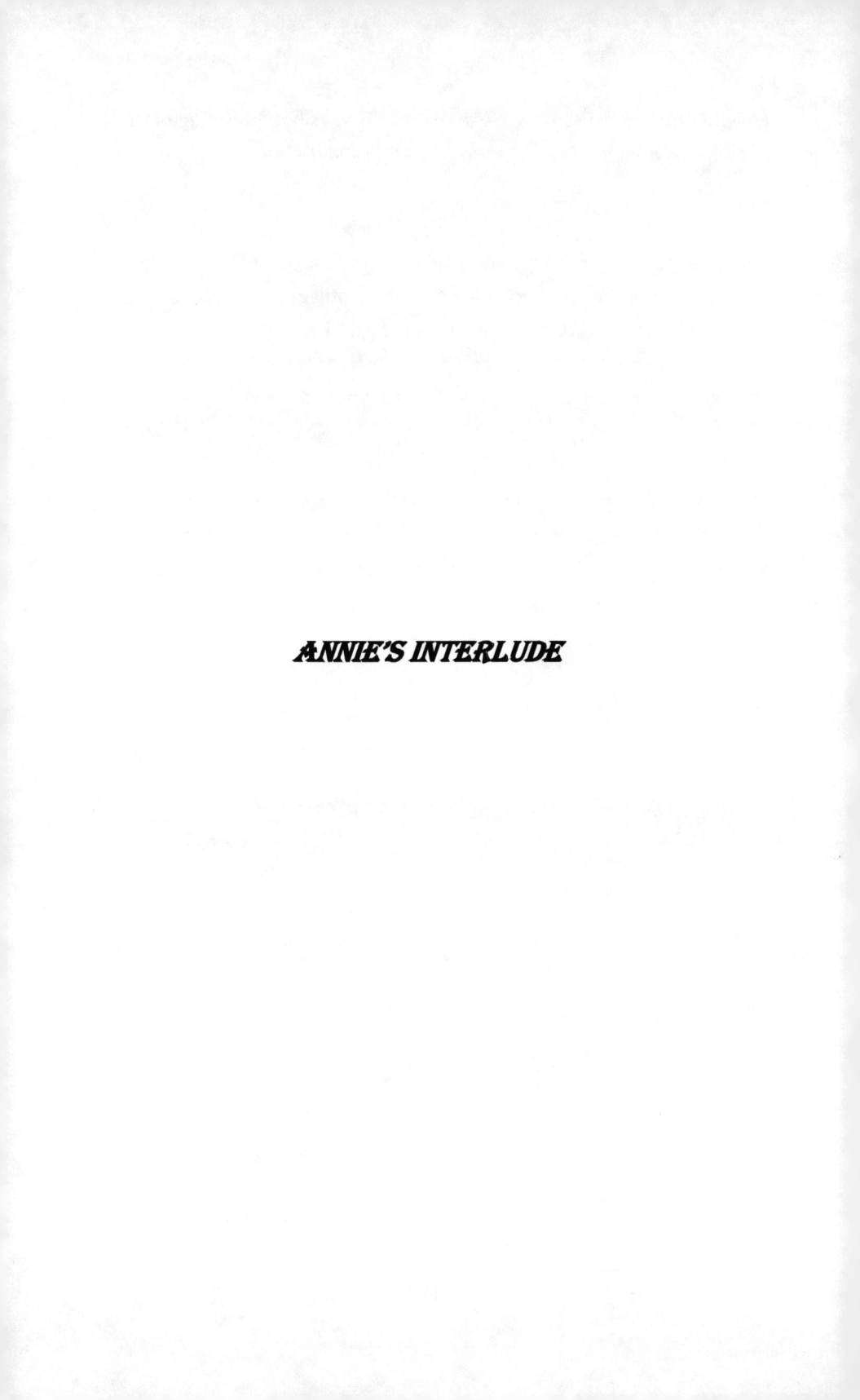

This time, when the waves rushed against me, I wasn't afraid. When the water was suddenly surrounding me and lifting me, taking my feet from under me, I wasn't afraid. I didn't cry; I knew that no number of tears would bring him back, and the strength of my grief had weakened me immeasurably. I felt like one of those women on television that receives bad news and crumples to the floor. But this was the ultimate 'bad news,' and there was just no point in crying anymore.

All of my life, maybe even during my marriage to Chase, I think some part of me had always been searching for Malik, for the easy love that I shared with him. There had always been something inside of me that was craving his kiss, his touch, the joy of simply resting in the way he loved me. With Malik, I had that easy love that all women crave, that effortless feeling of being 'someone' to someone.

But without him ...

In those first few moments of his death, I heaved and dragged his body back to the ocean that had loaned him to me. Irrational? Maybe. I felt like I'd fought for him and he'd chosen me, but the world of darkness and wetness and ocean waves had stormed up the beach to take him from me anyway. It didn't matter how I'd lost him; the fact was, he was gone and I was alone to raise our child, drowning in the weight of my grief.

Never again would I hear his laughter, never would he twinkle his eyes at me the way he used to when I'd amused him. I would never know the pleasure of being his wife; I would never hear his voice again. I'd never cook with him again or burrow down for movie nights in front of the fireplace in my living room. I would never give birth to the child growing silently inside of me, the child I hadn't been able to tell him about. I'd waited to tell him, waiting to be sure of his choice. And then suddenly, I was left without him, without my selkie man to hold me and help me raise our child. Without the love I'd only ever felt with him.

I was caught up in the storm with his body before I realized what was happening, caught up in the rushing waves of the sea, the rain pouring down on me when the waves would settle. In the dark, I couldn't even see the shore anymore; had I tried to swim, I wouldn't even have known which direction to go in.

Finally, I had no choice but to let go of my dreams for us. A fresh wave rolled toward me and I heaved what I knew would be my one last breath. The water settled over me in a rush; I exhaled slowly, watching the air bubble up from my lungs and through my lips. As the bubbles blended and floated toward the surface of the water, my heart ached for the baby I would never hold. With one hand, I held Malik's hand, watching his hair float in the current of the ocean. With the other, I held the belly that would never swell with the growth of my child, imaging hair that I would never brush, giggles that I would never hear. A child that would never be.

I knew it was over. Even if some part of me had wanted to fight and live on without him, I couldn't swim and the storm had heated the anger of the sea to boiling. I was given one more breath and then the ocean closed over me, tossing me against Malik and then pulling us away from each other. Still, I held on. When I'd exhaled again, I waited as long as possible for the sea to settle, to open up and give me a chance. It didn't, and eventually my lungs began to burn, screaming for air that was out of reach.

The time had come. My end had come. I opened my eyes to the sea, embraced my death beside Malik in the waters and inhaled.

It was my fate.

I had escaped watery death twice by then, once as a child and then again on the night that Malik had found me trapped in the rocks on the Bar Harbor sandbar. Finally, I had learned to accept it, learn to accept my watery destiny, though the thought of my child never knowing my face broke my spirit as Malik's death had broken my heart.

But then, I heard it. A quiet, child-like voice from somewhere inside my mind.

Mommy?? Mommy?!

And that was the end of me. I lost consciousness. I lost my battle with the raging waters.

MALIK'S INTERLUDE

Immortality has a way of making a man feel safe. I knew there would be consequences, though. Burning a selkie pelt is not just frowned upon; it's illegal in the selkie community, and most selkies are either cast out or executed for rejecting the ways of our kind. Some are occasionally given a chance to prove their renewed loyalty, thereby regaining their place among our people. I suppose as a relative of the clan leaders, I will be given a chance to redeem myself, but at the moment, that's the least of my worries. Annie is dying, and I'm hearing things.

I keep hearing this voice. I don't know who it is; it isn't Annie, though. I can feel her touching me, her hands trembling and her fear seeping out of her to surround me in the water.

But there's something there, someone there, and I don't who or what it is. All I know is that someone important is in grave danger, someone other than Annie and me, someone much more significant than either of us. And I am rendered useless, unable to help.

Wake up ... wake up, help me ...

I can't shake off the voice, but I struggle to ignore it. The biggest concern I have right now is Annie. I'd known there would be some way I'd have to pay for my choices, some price for going against the way of things. I'd known all along that there would be a price. But I'd thought there would be time to protect Annie. I'd thought there would be more time. And yet, here I am, stunned, unbelievably stunned by the lightning strike. Stunned by the forces of the sea and unable to save her as she clutches me in fear, unable to even move as the water washes over us again.

Please, we're running out of time ... I can't hold her forever ...

It's still hazy in my mind, though I can feel the skin where the lightning struck me repairing itself. It's good; it means that I haven't lost my immortality with my pelt in the fire. Maybe I still stand a chance then. But suddenly, the water covers me again and Annie's hands are ripped away from my body. I can feel her nearness though, her fingertips coming back, groping along my arm in the chaos. I want to reach out and clutch her, save her. All I want is to reach out and pull her close to me, to take her back to her safe little house on the harbor, where I can love her for all of her days.

I want to save her, but wanting simply isn't enough. I'm weak from the strike and not healing fast enough to be able to move much. Screwing my face up tight, I manage to stretch my arm, keeping it close to her so that she can take hold of me again.

Someone please! Help me!! Help us!!

The voice is familiar to me somehow, though I have never heard it before. There is a pull in my chest, a longing that I've never felt before, and my healing grows faster as Annie's breath slowly rushes out of her, bubbles floating over my skin on their way to the surface. I open my eyes and am able to turn; she has her eyes closed, one hand resting lightly across her abdomen.

Help me, help me ... I'm running out of time ...

It hit me from behind as Annie grew limp, a gentle crashing against my back that brought me up through the water. Watching Annie, I saw them come up behind her, lifting her too, though her body had gone completely limp. The sound of barking jarred me, and I looked around more closely, realizing that I knew the seals swimming along with Annie's body floating between them. Cursing my inability to speak, I struggled against the heaviness of my limbs, only to have one of the seals surrounding me nip angrily at my arm. Instantly, I fell still, waiting.

Floating to the coast, the seals pressed me up into the sand beside Annie, and I realized that the storm had passed. Panic filled me as they surrounded us, rolling wildly in the sand, barking occasionally to each other. Eventually, they began to change, leaving their pelts lying in the sand to come back and inspect me.

"Shit, it's Malik," my cousin Doyle groaned. "Ah, I was really hoping it wasn't him. The ones who reported this said it was a clan Killian pelt burning, but damn it, Malik, damn it man." He shook me wildly, asking, "Who's gonna dive with me now?" Blinking, I tried to clear the fog from my eyes. As I healed, my mind was clearing and I could hear the others hunting for the fire site. Someone must have seen us; somehow, the clan already knew about my choice to burn the pelt.

"Well he's not dead yet," Doyle's brother Bryce grunted, leaning down over me and allowing his long dark hair to drip into my face. Fighting the stiffness in my neck, I turned my face away, out from under the constant drip of salty ocean water.

"Poor stupid fool, now he'll have to endure the test," their father muttered bitterly, coming over to squat beside them. "They found the burn site, Malik. You know this will not be taken lightly," he said, resting a hand on my chest. I nodded at him, my mother's brother-in-law, the leader of my clan. Shaking his head with a sigh, he stood and left me, walking the few short feet to squat beside Annie.

"She's human," someone whispered to him. "But not dead. She didn't die, Angus. And she is with child, I can feel the presence of the child. Could it be? Is she the one?"

"The one?" I thought. *"What are they talking about?"*

"I don't know if she is or not," Uncle Angus answered. "We'll have to get them down to clan Killian caves. Tiernan will want to see them, and Malise can look over the woman."

"They'll need the scuba tanks from the stash, right?"

Uncle Angus snorted, frustrated with the weight of the situation. I listened helplessly as my future – and Annie's – were decided as Angus spoke. "Of course they'll need tanks, you idiot. Unless you have an extra couple of pelts up your ass for them to borrow, they'll need air from somewhere. And she's human; no pelt will help her. Yet." Hearing this, I heaved a sigh, finally able to lift my chest enough to take a deep breath. I'd burned my pelt for the sake of my love for Annie, and now we both would be returned to face the leaders of clan Killian, to accept their judgment for my choices.

Only a miracle could save us now.

PART TWO: TO BECOME A SELKIE

"She must be changed if she is to survive," Annie heard a woman speaking, her mind slowly leaving the fog of unconsciousness behind. "If she is the woman spoken of in the prophecies, she must be saved. The child must be saved."

"I can't change her, I can't," came the response. This second voice was familiar, but Annie's disorientation kept her thoroughly confused.

"She's fading, damn it! Can't you see that you've sentenced her to death? You must be the one. Change her!! Do it now! There is no other way, don't you see?" screamed the feminine voice, her words coming in a loud harsh whisper, trembling with rage and fear. Instinctively, Annie knew that she was the topic of the heated conversation, though she couldn't figure out what they wanted to change her into. If only her eyes would open, if only she could speak to question them …

"No, Aunt, I won't!" the familiar-sounding man shouted back. "We can't, it would kill her! She's human, don't you understand? Her body won't be able to take it! I won't kill her."

"Do it, damn you!" the woman shouted, the sudden volume causing Annie's body to jerk, hidden beneath the heavy coverings that weighted her in place.

"I can't!" the man roared, his voice calling to Annie even as his ferocity frightened her.

"You can! And you will," the woman commanded.

"You don't understand, Aunt; they bleed much faster, much worse. Her body won't take it. Can't you see? She'll die!"

"Imbecile!" the woman hissed furiously. "They'll both die anyway, right there on my cot if you don't try it! Just do it! The only way to save either of them is to change her, now. This is not just about the prophecies, Malik! Won't you even try to save your own child?"

The shouting was loud and nearing a frantic pitch as Annie's foggy mind tried to process where she was and what was happening. She didn't know the woman; she felt sure of that. The familiarity of the man rang through her mind like a gong as the woman pronounced his name; Malik. She smiled softly, her eyes still closed, her body still motionless. She knew Malik; she loved him.

"But didn't we die? Didn't we die in the storm? No, something's off. Something's wrong ..."

She remembered drowning; she remembered clutching Malik's hand until the last moment, when he was finally wrenched away in the waves. She remembered the storm; she remembered giving in, inhaling the water to stop her lungs from burning. She remembered aching for her baby, the baby she'd never been able to share with Malik, the baby who had never had a chance to live. Shying away from the pain of those memories of death, Annie allowed the fog to take over and as the darkness fell around her, the shouting faded away.

Later, she woke to the same voices, now lowered and no longer angry.

"I know it's hard for you, Malik. But it must be done. If you don't change her, you'll lose them both," the woman said quietly. The answer was lost as Annie's mind raced. *"Malik?"* His name raced through her mind. *"He was here earlier too, but how could he be here? He was dead! Wasn't he? Wasn't I?"*

Annie's thoughts turned toward fear, toward panic. She felt heavy, her arms and legs weighted down by heavy coverings that prevented her weakened body from moving. Her eyes fluttered but refused to open; her brow wrinkled as her heart began to race, followed by the frantic sound of beeping from the other side of the room.

"It's the baby, Malik. You can hear the monitors, how they flare up and then go quiet again. She is losing the struggle; she is losing the fight for life. Go, try to save the child while you can," the woman murmured. "This may save the woman, too, or it may not. But you must do as you must. You cannot simply leave them there to die without trying to help. You are strong, the son of my sister, the blood of clan Killian runs through you. You cannot give up, Malik. Go, try."

There was a heavy sigh and the scrape of chair legs on the floor. He roared again, an inhuman sound, a low quiet growl of frustration. Something crashed, the sound of shattering glass tinkling prettily through the room. Heavy footsteps approached and Annie forced her eyelids to lift, wanting to see if Malik was really alive, if it could really be him. He bent over her as she blinked to focus on his face, smiling sadly.

"You're awake," he whispered, barely audible over the shrill beeping. His fingers floated over her forehead, slipping down into her hair.

"Malik," the woman said from behind him, her voice fierce with warning. "Time is short. Do it now!"

He swallowed, his eyes pooling as he stroked her cheek. "I'm sorry. This will hurt, and I'm sorry," he whispered. She felt his hand close on hers, lifting it from whatever she was laying on. "I would never hurt you but for this, Annie. The pain won't be terrible, but it's going to hurt some and for that, I'm so sorry," he said. And then she felt the slice, stinging across the inner surface of her wrist. Her brow lowered, her eyes clouding with confusion, her head tilting slightly to give her a better view of him. He lifted her hand further, swiping his tongue over the welling blood that spilled down her arm before he quickly sliced into his own flesh. Holding his bleeding wrist to her mouth, he allowed the bitter tang of his blood to drip onto her lips, slipping between them to trail thickly down her throat.

"Swallow, my love. Drink," he commanded, and she locked her eyes with his as she fastened her mouth to his wrist. Sucking gently, she swallowed once and then released him. He nodded slightly, whispering to himself as he took her wrist again, pressing their slashed flesh together and holding their wrists tightly. Their blood mingled, and he continued to whisper quietly to her as he pressed their wounds together. Annie felt her arm start to tingle, her eyes widening with the sensation, sparkling dimly in the low light.

"What's h-happening?" she asked, her voice rough and scratchy from disuse, her throat burning as she spoke.

"I will explain when you are well again," he answered, forcing a smile that didn't reach his eyes.

"But I died. I'm dead," Annie croaked, the tingle moving from her arm to spread slowly throughout her body. The sensation was like that of renewed circulation, the pins-and-needles feeling that was at once gently unpleasant and excruciatingly painful.

"No, Annie. You are alive, you will live uncountable days with my blood. Remember when I told you that we are forever?" He waited for her nod weakly letting him know that she was trying to understand what he was saying, and then he went on. "I meant what I said to you. Now more than ever, I will always be yours, and you will always be truly mine. We are one now Annie, by the bonds of the heart and by the mixing of our blood. My heart beats in your chest now, as yours beats in mine. Now we are handfast, not by rope but by the ancient blood vows of my people."

Helplessly, Annie nodded, the simple movement bringing the tingling pain back to life. She gasped as the tingling grew worse, watching Malik as his forehead wrinkled with concern. "Malik?" she asked, the pain bringing a shrill tone to her voice. He didn't answer; instead, he kissed her lips, gently peeling their wrists apart and placing her hand lightly on a folded towel he rested on her stomach.

"She didn't bleed the way I expected," he said, turning to call over his shoulder. "I think she'll be okay, and it's done. What now?"

A woman appeared beside him, short and portly with fluffy graying hair. "This has not been done in many years, Nephew," she said. "Now, we can only wait."

"Wait," he scoffed, his voice harsh, though his hands were still gently stroking Annie's face and arms. "All I have done is wait. Wait to see if she wakes. Wait to see if the baby would give her life. Wait to see if the baby would live at all. And now wait to see if the change takes hold to save them? Why, Aunt? Why is everything waiting?"

She laughed, leaning down over his shoulder to inspect Annie's drawn face. "I forget sometimes, how young you are," she answered. "But look, my boy; see her tremble. See the pain cross her face. See the color rising in her cheeks. See the life glowing inside her. She is changing, Nephew. She will be like us. And the child's birth will come to pass."

"Child?" Annie whispered. Her mind raced. *"Could it be possible,"* she wondered, *"that my baby is still alive, that I will be a mother after all, as I am now to be Malik's wife?"*

"The child lives," the woman said, smiling as she rested her hand on Annie's stomach. "Do not worry, young mother; the child lives." She moved away and took a few steps back, her hand moving to rest on Malik's bare shoulder as she looked down at the two of them together. "I'll leave you now, and I will be back to bring you food in a while."

Malik nodded silently, his hand rising up to touch the woman's hand before she took it away, and then they could hear her feet shuffling as she crossed the room, followed by the quick click of the closing door. "Why do I hurt?" Annie asked. "What is in your blood? What did you give to me, Malik? Am I dying?"

"You will never die now, apart from certain dangers. I have given you immortality," he answered.

Annie struggled to rise, her coverings too heavy for her. Malik pressed his hand flat to her chest, urging her to settle again into the softness of the pillows beneath her. "The woman," she said, turning her head and gazing toward the door of the room. "Who is she?"

"Malise. She is my aunt, my mother's sister. She is a high member of the selkie council, and —"

"Council?" she asked, her breath coming in pants as the magic of Malik's blood coursed through her body. "Malik, where are we? How did we get here?"

"Shhh, you have to stay calm. Try to relax and I'll explain if I can."

Annie nodded, her agreement relaxing Malik's face. He rewarded her with a tender smile, his fingers working through her hair again. "My uncle and his friends were out hunting in the storm and they found us in the water," he told her. "They lifted us to the surface, and my cousin Doyle recognized me. Malise, the woman who was here, she is his mother. My aunt, remember? The men brought us here, trying to revive you."

"Not you?" Annie questioned sadly, her hands reaching up, her fingertips feathering over the roughness of his cheeks. "Why not you?"

He laughed slightly, a thick lock of his dark hair falling over one eyebrow. It had grown since she'd last seen his face. "I didn't need help," he answered.

"You died," she said, shaking her head as confusion clouded her thoughts. The pain was growing beyond simple pins-and-needles now, and she was struggling to hold herself still, struggling to follow and comprehend his words. Her hands tightened slightly on his face, and he took them in his own, clutching her gently.

"Annie, I can't die," he whispered. "Immortality, remember? I age, and I will age as humans do – to a point -- because I am half-human. But I will age slowly, and someday I will simply stop aging at all because I am half-selkie. I wasn't dead."

"But the lightning," she murmured, her brows creasing with her efforts as she turned their hands to look at his arms. "You were burned, you were –"

"Stunned," he interrupted. "Only stunned."

"And I was drowning," she whispered, tears pooling in her eyes, flooding over to slide down her temples and into her hair. If what he was saying was true, it was her fault they were with the selkies now, her fault they weren't safe on the beach, her fault for dragging him back to the water. "I was drowning," she repeated.

"The baby kept you," he answered. Watching her face cloud again, he continued. "I don't know how it happened ... I've never heard of it happening before. We didn't even know a human woman could carry a selkie child, Annie, that's why I wasn't worried before. About protection, you know." He settled his hand heavily on the flat of her lower abdomen. "I didn't think this could happen."

"Is the baby like you? Is it selkie? Or will it be human?"

"We don't know yet. No one in the council has heard of this before."

"The council?" Annie grunted, forcing the words through gritted teeth. There was that word again, council. *"Immortality? What council?"* she wondered, her thoughts growing clumsy and disconnected as the pain took over. She wanted to ask him to explain, but the pain kept growing worse, throbbing throughout her body in waves, slowly growing to a fiery roar. Sweat had broken out on her brow, and her hands were beginning to shake, her breathing becoming heavier.

Malik watched her, concerned, leaning close as she whispered her questions haltingly into his ear. "The council?" he repeated, waiting for her to nod before going on. "Selkie council is kind of like what you would think of as -- uh, maybe like you'd imagine the Native American council. The Indians?"

"Uunnh," Annie groaned, her teeth sinking into her bottom lip as a wave of pain overtook her. "I don't suppose ... that ... you need ... rain dance," she muttered, trying desperately to lighten her sinking mood.

"Ah, she still has her sense of humor after all. I know you're hurting but soon, the pain will pass," Malik answered with a chuckle, stroking her face with a cold cloth. "It will be over soon."

"And then?" she whimpered. She'd begun to writhe unwillingly on the hard cot, her hips rolling, her toes curling and uncurling as her legs worked back and forth. As the pain continued to worsen, her teeth began to chatter and she eventually lost the ability to speak coherently.

"Shhh," Malik whispered, stroking her face, her hair, her hands. "It'll be over soon, my love. Just let it take you, Annie. Then you'll rest, and when you wake, we can talk again."

Nodding painfully, Annie closed her eyes and let the blackness around the edges of her vision move in, clouding and covering his face. Then he was gone; her consciousness slipped away and her body slowly began to relax as she stopped fighting the changes in her blood.

***

"She stirs," a male voice said. Annie had regained consciousness but she had yet to move, fearful that movement would bring back the pain, hoping that if she remained still, she would learn more about where she was. "See. She stirs."

"Angus, give her time," a woman answered, her voice somehow familiar. Annie's brows bunched together. *"Was it the woman from earlier, the one Malik had called 'Aunt'?"*

"She'll awake when she's ready," the woman continued. "She's been through a hard time, you know. And her troubles have only begun," she finished softly.

"And where is your nephew?" the man replied, his voice a low grumble, though there was a hint of a smile in the sound. "Should he not be serving as her sitter now, instead of me? I am Head Councilman. I am not a babysitter, Malise."

"I know," Malise answered, the light sound of flesh patting against flesh as the woman calmed the man. "But he is my sister's son and I am obligated to him, bound by the blood of my sister Muirin and the love that I carry for him as my family. And this woman is his love; he burned his pelt so that he could stay with her. If she is that important to my nephew, I owe her my care, for his sake. But then, you owe her also, for my sake, do you not?"

The man grunted; the woman laughed softly at him. "Don't you remember love, Angus?" she asked. "In the early days when we were young and the weight of the clan was not upon your shoulders? Angus, she carries a child. A human woman, able to birth and shelter a selkie child that will rise to bring the clans together again? You know the prophecies, Angus. She could be the one."

A sharp thud forced Annie to startle, her body jerking involuntarily at the heavy noise. She kept her eyes closed and slowly allowed her body to relax again, hoping to hear more, hoping Malise would be able to calm her husband, that they would talk more and she could gain some understanding. "I know the damn prophecies, Malise," Angus growled. "We all know the prophecies. But we all hope for the prophet to be wrong, at least in his timing. If the prophesied child is here and it is time, how can we protect the clan? The council is still weakened from the battles of the past, and our clan is not as strong as it was before. There are yet too many who will seek to stop the reunion of the clans, by war, by death. And we, a weakened clan, are we to struggle under the weight, under the burden of her life? If that woman carries our prophesy within her fragile body, may the forces of the sea help us all."

Chair legs scraped quietly against the floor, followed by the heavy footsteps of the man as he stalked to the door.

Waiting quietly until her angry husband had gone, Malise heaved a sigh into the quiet. "The forces of all the seas may not be enough," she murmured to herself, the quiet strength in her voice reassuring Annie even as the presence of fear terrified her. Struggling to keep her breathing even, she listened as Malise continued her mutterings. "He's right. There are too many clans who wish to fight the joining, too many clans who would see the child dead to stop the prophecies. And Angus is right. We are not strong enough. And will our kind be destined then to live separately, at war for all time?" Her voice broke as she spoke, and the sound of weeping filtered softly through the room.

Annie held herself still, though compassion made her wish that she could simply rise from the stiff cot to comfort the sobbing woman. Instead, she began to test herself, moving only one finger experimentally. Surprised to discover no pain at all, she slowly tested all of her fingers. Still no pain. Flexing her hands into fists, Annie felt more than just the absence of pain; she felt unknown strength flowing through her hands. Her fists were tighter than before; they were firmer and her movements were smoother, more precise. She felt as strong and sure as she had as a teenager, when she'd been a track runner in high school.

Exhilarated, she opened her eyes, blinking in the dim light of the room, surprised at how well she could see in the near-darkness. The walls around her were smooth and hard, shining gray-black stone. The air in the room was still and cool, comfortable with only the slightest chill. Wiggling her toes, Annie progressed slowly to rolling her ankles and then bending her knees, which brought Malise over to check on her.

"How do you feel?" Malise asked, her palm landing softly on Annie's forehead as her teary voice echoed slightly in the room. She sniffled, forcing the corners of her mouth to lift in a smile.

Annie smiled nervously back at the older woman, taking in the simple cotton t-shirt Malise wore over denim capris. She wanted to laugh crazily at the idea of seal women wearing comfortable human clothes, but then she figured they had to wear something when they weren't wearing the seal pelts. "I feel confused," she said quietly. "Where is this place?" Sitting slowly and swinging her feet over the edge of the cot, she realized that she had been dressed too, in a simple sundress that was slightly too large.

"This is my home," Malise answered. "My quarters. You've been sleeping there in my cot for three days."

"Three days!" Annie exclaimed. "Only three days?"

"Three days," Malise repeated with a laugh. "But that's better than the last human who took a blood vow with a selkie. That one died. And three days is nothing compared to the week you slept when you were first brought here."

"I slept a week? Why didn't I die?" Annie asked, tilting her head, pressing her hands into the cushioned cot as if to stand, testing her weight on her feet. Malise didn't answer but instead stood with her, taking her elbow and leading her a few short steps away from the bed before leading her back again. It made Annie glad to have the woman's company, her sympathetic support. She could walk fine; her energy was high and she felt strong, though her body protested so much movement after resting so long. Turning back to Malise once she was seated again on the edge of the cot, she repeated her question.

"We think it was your child," she answered with a sigh, the slight heave of her chest lifting the blue cotton of her shirt. "You were not improving, but not getting worse either. Finally, you began to worsen, and then we had to do what we had to do." She tucked a strand of blonde hair behind her ear, and Annie was startled to realize how much Malise looked like her sister, Muirin, Malik's mother.

"And then Malik … did what he did," Annie murmured.

"Yes. To save you both."

Annie nodded, thinking a while before she spoke again. "But, this place, the walls … is this a cave?" she asked, settling back onto the cot, folding her legs under herself and scooting to sit in the middle of the cushioned top.

Malise laughed. "I should have realized that was what you were asking before. Yes, it's a cave, one of largest underwater caverns on the American coast, though it is officially undiscovered. We span almost the entire length and breadth of Bar Island, though most humans don't even know we're here. The entrance is well hidden, and with the high tide, there is no visible entrance at all. This is the home of clan Killian, as it has been for many years."

"Clan Killian?" Annie echoed.

"Malik's people. My people. I am his mother's sister, Malise." Lowering herself carefully, she settled on the edge of the cot, turning her body so that she faced Annie comfortably.

"You are a selkie, then? Like Malik?"

"I am," Malise laughed again. "My husband, Angus is the Head Councilman. We are the leaders of the clan Killian."

"And what defines a selkie clan?"

"Our culture has been compared many times to that of the Native American tribes that ruled North America in its early days. Our Council is similar; the way we live and lead our people is similar. Now, we live in separate clans, much the way Native Americans lived in their tribes, I suppose. But long ago, we lived as one people. I suppose that is a story for another time, though," she finished, lowering her eyes to her hands, folded in her lap.

"Selkie. Is that what I am now? What my baby will be?" Annie asked, allowing the woman to keep her stories to herself, more in favor of immediate information. *"Plenty of time for history lessons later,"* she thought, her hands finding their way to the barely noticeable round of her stomach.

"We don't know exactly. Malik has given you immortality, in order to save you and the child from death. But we will not know if you are a true selkie or not until you grow the pelt. We will not know about the child until it is born."

"How do I grow a pelt? And where is Malik?"

"He is gone off," Malise said, laying her hand gently along Annie's arm. "He is accepting the discipline for what he has done. And he will be tested, Annie. Unpleasant as it may be, it is the way of our clan. He burned his pelt, and his loyalty to the clan is now in question. I cannot step in to save him from this."

"Gone off? He's gone off? What will happen to him; what is this discipline?" Annie asked, brushing Malise's hand away and standing again to pace along the floor, concern aiding her new strength even as her weakened body protested the effort. In her worry, she began to pace faster, her skin heating to an itch, as her emotions grew stronger, as her blood began to flow faster.

"Come with me," Malise said, watching Annie carefully, her tone thoughtful. "I will show you where he is taken, and we shall see if your change is true or not." Standing, she took Annie's hand and tucked it swiftly into her elbow, leading her through the door of the stone room. The sound of water dripping followed them down a long corridor lit with natural gas flames, and as the water sounds grew louder, Annie filled with fear.

"We're underwater," she whispered, her heart tripping in her chest.

"Mmhmm. Not entirely," Malise responded, tightening her grip on Annie's hand.

"I can't swim," Annie told her, her voice taking on the edge of panic, her body stiffening in protest of the perceived danger.

"We shall see," was the only response, as Malise continued to propel her forward with surprising strength.

Rounding a bend in the corridor, Annie saw him, her feet jerking to a stop as her hand flew up to cover her mouth. Her eyes widened, the color left her face as she let out a gasp. Malik was suspended from a jutting shelf in the wall, his wrists held high in circular bronze manacles fastened to the bottom of the stone shelf, his arms spread above his head. He'd been stripped from the waist up; he wore no shoes, but he still wore his trademark surf shorts.

A muscular black man was dancing around him, his loose cotton pants swirling slightly around his feet as he chanted in a language that Annie didn't recognize. Annie was terrified; as she looked closer, it appeared that Malik was sweating blood. His face was twisted in a painful grimace, and he groaned helplessly as the man continued to dance.

"Tiernan," Malise said, her voice soft but firm. The dancer froze immediately, turning to face Malise. His eyes lit as he caught sight of Annie and he glided forward to take her hands into his own, his energy spilling through his fingers to tingle up her arms. His bare chest heaved with his breath, though peace emanated from him in such a way that Annie suddenly felt less afraid.

His skin was cool, as smooth and brown as ancient bronze in the firelight. He gleamed in the meager light of the giant room, shining with oil. Tattoos ran over his body in intricate patterns and shapes; a fuzzy goatee graced his chin and his dreadlocked hair stood wild in all directions. Fierce as he looked though, with the whites of his eyes glowing from his face, the gentle ease of his touch on Annie's hands soon filled her with calm.

"Are you Annie?" he asked, his black eyes staring into her green ones. "The one who was changed by this man?"

Annie nodded, her eyes flicking to Malik's face before coming back to Tiernan. With no idea what would help or hurt Malik, she answered simply but with honesty. "I am Annie," she said. Gesturing toward Malik as he uttered another helpless groan, she asked, "What's happening to him?"

"He must be tested; his loyalty to our clan is not assured. But it is painful for him, for any selkie, to have their hearts examined. The manacles are only to restrain him, to keep him still. But your presence will help me," Tiernan said solemnly. He took Annie's hands, drawing her close to him, and she heard Malik utter a low growl. Tiernan brought her flush against his chest, closing his eyes and breathing her in. "Yes, you will help me," he said, still breathing deeply. "But do not be afraid. You must put your trust in me."

"I don't even know you," Annie protested, wanting to step away but strangely unable to move her feet.

"Listen, my girl, you must listen. Do not underestimate the situation he is in. Only you can help him, but you must trust that I love him too, and that I wish to see him succeed. But he has sacrificed his pelt; he has turned his back on this life. This gives him only a half-life, immortal but frozen in human form. He cannot protect you; he cannot serve as a proper husband to you in this way, and he will be useless to the clan in times of war. He must force a new change to prove his loyalty, to prove his connection to us, to prove that his heart has not abandoned the clan. He must call forth a new pelt."

"A new pelt? How can I help him? I don't understand any of this ... what do I do?" Annie asked, terrified of saying or doing something wrong but unable to step back and leave Malik on his own. His blood flowed through her body, his child grew in her womb; she could not leave him alone.

"Believe me. Trust me," Tiernan said, his voice low and hypnotic. "You must call to his selkie. You must call him to change, call him to come to you in his selkie form. Call him back to our ways, to our people. It will save him from having me read his heart, if he can call his inner selkie to come out again. He would have to do it anyway, even if I read him, though he would be exhausted then."

"But how?"

"First, I must read your heart," he said, taking Annie's hand as terror filled her. "And then you must complete your own change. You must become one of us to solidify his loyalty to our kind. You must be one with us, and he will be one with you."

"I don't know what to do," Annie whispered. He smiled, taking her hands and leading her to a raised disk on the other side of the room. Guiding Annie to climb onto the disk, Tiernan urged her to sit. "Will it hurt my baby?" Annie asked, reaching one hand out to Tiernan beseechingly.

Stepping back, he smiled, shaking his head. His dreadlocks swayed as he moved into a writhing dance; he began to chant, and smoke billowed out from the under the disk. Annie waited, frozen in fear as his chanting grew louder and she felt her skin start to itch again. Turning, she met Malik's eyes with her own, taking in the anguish on his face, the way he struggled against the manacles as the smoke rose to shade them from each other.

Pain filled Annie's chest as Tiernan's chant grew louder. Malik's chains rattled and clinked as he struggled to break free, struggled to reach her. "Annie," Malik growled, his call not reaching her through the pain of Tiernan's work. He never touched her, only walking around the disk as he chanted, but soon, Annie's whole body was filled again with pain, pain that first rivaled and then seemed to diminish the pain she had felt after Malik had given her the blood vow. She had no need of manacles or chains; she simply dropped to her knees, crying out, her skin crawling with the now-familiar itching sensation.

The itch grew worse and Annie's fingers and hands began to ache, her toes curling, her calves cramping. Helpless against the chaos of sensations, she dropped weakly to her stomach on the disk, lying there as cold sweat broke out over her exhausted body. Hearing screams, she filled with panic, writhing in pain on the raised disk as the smoke continued to thicken around her. Tiernan chanted on, and soon she could hear Malise in the background, adding the somber power of her own voice to the chant as Annie realized that the screams were her own.

"Don't fight! Annie, don't fight!" Malik shouted, his chains creaking and groaning under the pressure of his struggles; there was a thud and he groaned pitifully, fading into silence. Wishing to go to him but unable to move or see through the haze, Annie tried to do as he had instructed, taking deep breaths and trying to force her body to relax. Finally, the pain overtook her, the animal instinct coming to life against the force of the pain; Annie's eyes rolled back, her body convulsing powerfully as she underwent the change. The last thing she heard was a short, deep bark, the bark of a seal.

***

The smoke cleared slowly, the pain receding with it into the background of her mind. In her peripheral vision, she could see whiskers trembling. *"Are those mine?"* Looking down, she took in the new shape of her body. She was as large as any seal she'd ever seen, her coat soft and smooth in shades of grey and white that matched Malik's pelt, the one that they'd burned together. She propped her flippers beneath her chest and lifted her body, raising herself up to look around. Still on the disk, she was able to see well as the smoke continued to clear from the room.

Spying Malik, she opened her mouth, surprised to hear the barking roar of a seal in place of her own voice. He struggled mightily as Tiernan danced and chanted around him, the chains above him rattling with his movements. Annie waited, occasionally giving the same barking roar in his direction, each time watching the sound refresh his struggles. Malise watched approvingly as Tiernan continued to chant, his words coming faster and faster each time Annie sounded her call.

Finally, the moment came when Annie called out steadily, again and again, and Tiernan seemed to be only humming loudly, his lips flying through the chant, his wild dreadlocks swinging with his movements. It was then that Malik threw his head back with a roar, his eyes bulging, the manacles exploding from his wrists as he fell to the ground. Despite herself, Annie closed her eyes and tipped her face away, her whiskers trembling with the force of her fear.

When she looked again, he was there, her seal friend from the beach. He'd done it; he'd forced a new pelt. Fresh and glorious, his spotted pelt gleamed. His body was large and round, as it had been in the days when they'd played on the sandbar of Bar Harbor. He roared, his whiskers shivering, his teeth showing. Annie opened her mouth, releasing her call again, and he came to her as she slipped down from the disk.

"Go then," Malise said, stepping close to lock arms with Tiernan. "You have earned your pelt, Nephew. You have earned your place." Turning to look down at Annie, she continued, "And now we shall see if you swim or not."

Fearful, Annie growled, a roaring sound that rumbled low as she backed away from Malise. Malik was there though, nudging her with his nose as he guided her closer to the edge of the cave. Approaching the edge with him, Annie looked down, her deep and soulful brown seal eyes taking in the sparkling depths of the water before her. She backed away, balking from the idea of the jump as her human self remembered her fearful death in the waters, but Malik was pushing her. He nudged her one last time, shoving hard against her with his body, pressing her over the edge. She uttered one frightened bark as she fell, and then she was in the water.

It wasn't what the human in her expected at all. Her ears and nostrils closed against the water before she slipped beneath the surface, and her inner selkie knew just what to do as if by life-long instinct. Her hind-flippers worked powerfully together, waving from side to side so strongly that it seemed her entire body was working smoothly through the coolness of the water. She rejoiced in the sense of freedom, giddy with the release of her fear, flipping and rolling through the water.

She felt the wave of pressure as Malik slipped into the water beside her, his body bumping firmly against hers. He swam around her, caressing the round firm flesh of her seal body with one of his fore-flippers as if to beckon her. She followed as he left her, diving deeper beneath the surface of the water purposefully. Catching him, Annie followed him through the entrance of another cave, slipping behind him onto the rocky ledge before them.

Malik rolled heavily along the rocks and his seal pelt seemed to suddenly break open, splitting neatly along the length of his belly and revealing the human within. He lay for a moment, breathing heavily as water slid down and away from his naked form. Watching Annie as she watched him, Malik caught his breath before he spoke.

"Your turn," he said, smiling. His hair dripping along the sides of his face as Annie raked soulful animal eyes down his naked human form. "Just roll, and tell it to come off," he said. "You'll need to know how to do it quickly, so you want to practice."

Annie's whiskers trembled. The cave they were in hardly seemed more than an air bubble in the rocks beneath the island. What if the cave collapsed or filled in? Would they drown together – again -- or would they have time to change back? Why had he brought her here? She barked to him, and he laughed.

"Just do it. Come on Annie, trust me; I want to show you something."

Heaving her body over, Annie rolled along the rocks, waiting for her pelt to open and release her human body. But after three rolls, she was still a seal, grayish-white fur speckled with deeper shades of grey and black. Rising up on her flippers, she called again to Malik, a touch of fear in the rumbling roar she sent his way. What if she couldn't change back?

"Try it again," he answered, sitting calmly amidst the pile of his pelt. "It'll come off; it just takes practice."

Annie heaved again and rolled her body, frustration aiding her as she desperately commanded the pelt to fall away and release her. She felt the cool air of the cave along the skin of her human body as the pelt opened and fell away, her body transforming almost instantly. Sitting up, she reached for the pelt, intending to cover her nakedness with it.

"Don't put it around your head or neck," Malik said, his laugh breaking the quiet of the cave again. "It'll close back up then, if you wrap it around yourself like that."

"Okay," Annie said hoarsely, wrapping the pelt around her back and under her arms, crossing it over her chest to hold in the warmth. It opened down the front of her hips and legs as she walked to him, dragging gently behind her on the rocks. "You wanted to show me something?" she asked.

He stood, bending down to gather his own pelt in his hands. Folding it in half, he wrapped it lightly around his waist, tucking it into itself to make it stay and then throwing the end up and over one shoulder. Turning then, he reached for Annie. "Come on."

"You look like a weird cross between a successful hunter and a toga-sporting Greek," Annie laughed. As they walked together through the darkness of a tunnel behind the opening of the cave, Annie moved her feet cautiously, occasionally catching the sides of her feet on stray bits of rock. "What is this place?" she asked, pacing herself to keep up with his longer strides.

"My cave," he answered. "Well, it was. I'm married now though, by selkie custom; I'm handfast to you, so we'll be living up in the other caves with the other married couples."

"Oh. Is it crowded? What if they don't like me? I'm not ... I'm not one of them."

He laughed, tugging her arm to pull her closer in the cool dark of the tunnel. "You are. You are as much a selkie as any other, born or changed. They think you're very special, Annie."

"Because of the prophecies?" she asked, allowing him to pull her against his body.

He ran a hand over the back of her head, gathering her dripping hair in one hand. "Maybe because of the prophecies, but maybe because there is another woman in the community now who can tame a selkie man. It doesn't happen often in our culture. There are women with children, and the men protect the clan, but marriage – commitment – is rare." He gripped her hair tightly as he spoke, clutching her head against his chest as he jerked his other arm sharply against the wall. Fire sprang to life in his fingers, the match he'd slipped from a little box on a shelf coming to light. He touched the match to the blackness of a gouge that circled the wall and as the light of the fire spread around them, Annie was able to see the room he'd led her to. They were now surrounded by the warm light of the fire, lighting the room as it filled the little niche that circled the walls.

"Natural gas, like in the other caves. It's one of the reasons we chose to settle here," Malik said, answering the questioning look she sent him.

Stepping away, Annie walked the perimeter of the room, watching the fire before turning to inspect the room. The walls were bare, shimmering with moisture; in the middle of the room was a stone circle that was big enough to sit in. It was raised about two feet from the floor and filled with small black pebbles. Stepping closer, Annie could see short small sticks mixed into the pebbles, and as she wondered what they were, Malik silently answered her question. He threw another lit match into the pebbles, and a flame sprouted from the center of the circle.

"Hmm. Natural gas again?" Annie asked.

Malik took her hand, laughing as he led her to one side of the room. Seating her at the table against the wall, he turned to open a little cabinet next to the table. Lifting out a water-warped wooden box, he set it before her. "My collection," he explained, waiting for her to open the box.

Annie gasped as she gently lifted the top of the box. The contents sparkled brilliantly, gems and old jewelry mixed carelessly together with ancient coins and lumpy bits of different crystals and metal. Lifting a handful of items from the box, Annie sorted through them, admiring a sapphire the size of her thumbnail, a rosy quartz that filled the whole of her palm, and what looked suspiciously like a quarter-sized diamond.

"This is what you dive for?" Annie asked, still pulling out bits and pieces of jewelry, her eyes wide as she inspected Malik's riches.

"It is. Some I found accidentally, other bits I found on human dives, treasure hunts. But you're my wife; it's all yours now," he finished, taking her hand and urging her to her feet. Tugging her close, he took her face in his hands and pressed his lips lightly to hers, smiling as her breath caught in her throat. "I'm so glad we were found. They told me you'd drowned, Annie. I don't know how I could have survived without you, if I'd woken up and found you … just … gone."

"You'd have done alright," Annie joked, running her hands down his chest, around his ribs, closing them behind his back. "You're immortal, remember?"

"And now so are you. But immortality doesn't make me completely indestructible, my love. There are three things that kill the selkie folk." He waited, letting what he'd said float in the air. "Iron can kill us; if it's left against the skin long enough, it can poison us to death. It can cause mortal wounds. Our weapons are all made with iron tips, iron blades. Loss of the sea for long enough will cause us to weaken and age as humans do, allowing us to die of old age along with other humans." As he spoke, he cradled Annie's head against the hollow between his chest muscles, his fingers combing the wild ends of her hair.

"And the third thing?" Annie asked, her hands flattening against his broad chest as she lifted her face to meet his eyes.

"Heartbreak," he answered, looking tenderly down into her face, his arms tightening slightly around her back. "That's why marriage is so rare among us, and why we're known in the legends to be faithless lovers. Falling in love endangers us, Annie; we feel, but we stay away from love because the loss of that love weakens our will to survive. Eventually, broken lovers simply waste away."

"And that would have happened to you?" Annie asked, her eyes darkening with curiosity. "It would have killed you, really?

He sighed, pulling her tightly against him, his arms slipping around her to hold her close to him. "It would kill me to lose you, and that's without even knowing about the baby," he said, his hands lowering to her hips as he spoke, pulling her snugly against him as his lips trailed warmly down her throat as he spoke. "I love you, Annie. And when I say that, you need to know how deeply I mean it. I loved you enough to burn my pelt, to turn away from the selkie life. I loved you enough to age with you, enough to die beside you. And I'd do it again, if you needed me to."

"Well now you don't need to worry about that. I'm here with you, and our baby is growing stronger. It's the three of us now, a family," Annie gasped, tipping her head to the side as Malik found the sensitive place behind her ear. He turned her so that she stood with her back pressed to his chest, his palms flattening, spreading over the slowly firming round of her lower stomach.

"Good," he whispered, bringing his chin to rest on her head, his breath blowing her hair slightly as she leaned against him.

"But we can really die of heartbreak?" she asked quietly. "That's just tragic; to die of a broken heart." Still, she could feel the truth in his statement; her divorce had broken her terribly, and regaining her sense of self had taken a great deal of time. The possibility of losing Malik – again – brought a searing ache into her chest that tightened her gut and flooded her eyes.

"My mother did," he answered softly, his hands moving lightly up and down the length of her torso, his hands warming the pelt she was still wrapped in.

"I'm sorry you lost her," Annie said, turning to circle his waist again with her arms, drawing close to the firm strength of his body.

"Me too," he said. "But I understand her better now. I have love of my own now; I know how hard her choices must have been for her." Watching Annie's face soften in compassion, he stepped closer to bring their bodies together, lowering his lips to hers. Smiling against her mouth, he tugged her hips flush against his own, his need for her pressing firmly against her belly. His hands slid down to cover her hips, lifting her closer against the hard line of his arousal, insistently seeking satisfaction.

Annie shivered, moaning softly as her lips opened and his tongue slipped against hers, twirling in an erotic dance that lit her blood and shivered over her skin. She tangled her tongue with his, helplessly whispering his name, drawing a low groan from him that rumbled up from his chest. Her head fell back as Malik left her lips, kissing the corner of her mouth and the curve of her jaw, following the slender column of her throat.

He walked her slowly backward, each step an erotic dance as their bodies collided, separated, collided again, the backs of her thighs finally hitting the edge of the table. With a grunt of satisfaction, he gripped her hips, lifting her enough to settle her on the table, the open box of shimmering gems beside her. He left her to latch the top on the box, tucking it back into the cabinet before returning to open the covering of her pelt, baring her to his sight. He drew in his breath with a hiss, the warmth of his palms covering her breasts, skimming down her body to grasp her hips again.

"God, Annie, you're so perfect, so beautiful," he murmured, stepping between her thighs as his lips wandered from her throat to her collarbone, searing a trail over the sensitive curve of her shoulder. Annie closed her thighs around his hips and locked her ankles; the hair of his seal pelt tickled her bare legs, causing her to giggle helplessly. Malik growled in mock frustration, stepping back to flick the pelt away from his body and allowing it to drift to the floor of the cave before he moved close to her again, the strength of his body finding the softness of hers, the hard velvet shaft of his arousal seeking the inner warmth of her body.

Annie moaned as she took him in, feeling him move against her as she rocked on the table, her cries mingling with Malik's groans as his body filled hers. Her blood raged, pulsing faster as he whispered her name, burying his face in her neck as she scraped her nails down the sweat-slick flesh of his back.

"Malik!" Annie cried, feeling him quicken his pace inside her. Her thighs trembled against his hips, the walls of her body clenching, massaging him as goosebumps began to spring up over his back and shoulders. He whispered her name, nipping lightly at her shoulder as he drove into her, clutching her hips to his as he climaxed.

***

Later, Annie sat at the edge of the cave entrance, her pelt discarded beside her. Malik frolicked in human form in the water, flicking droplets up at her as she laughed, sitting naked in the center of his pelt. Water beaded and dripped down her chest, tickling down the length of her stomach.

"Obviously, my clothes didn't survive my changing," she asked, looking down at her body. "Will it be that way every time?"

"It will," Malik answered, sliding through the water to pluck at her toes. "You get good at hiding clothes in every possible place up and down the coast and throughout the caves. You noticed the lockers, before? When Tiernan helped you change?"

"I did," Annie said. "What are they?"

"The locker is a false front," he laughed. "It does open, but go to it in seal form, press the little button over to the side on the floor, and it'll swing out. There's a little room behind it, and every member of clan Killian has sort of a mini-locker in there. Like what humans think of as a changing room, but bigger. I guess maybe more like a locker room. Everyone has storage in there, clothes and stuff."

"Ha!" Annie retorted. "And there's room enough to change in there? Forms, I mean?"

"Sure, want me to show you? We can go back, if you want. I can show you our suite in the married caves. There're clothes for you in the locker already, too, some stuff I borrowed from a few of the other women for now. Later on, we'll get you some of your own stuff, if you want."

"Okay. Yeah, I'd like that," Annie said quietly. "Malik?"

"Yeah?"

"Will I be okay here? I mean, will they —"

"Will they like you?" he interrupted with a grin. "Of course they will. My cousin Bryce has this friend, Finnigan, who has already been talking trash about snatching you from my cot and keeping you for his own."

"Your cousin? You have cousins?" Annie asked, tilting her head curiously.

"Yeah. Malise and Angus have two boys; Doyle's a little older than I am. And Bryce is a good deal younger, though he doesn't look all that much younger."

"And Bryce has a friend? Finnigan?"

Malik laughed. "He does. Finn's a little smartie, but he loves the ladies."

"And he wants a piece of the not-human-anymore girl, huh?" Annie continued, teasing.

Malik growled a warning from his place in the water, narrowing his eyes. "He wants a piece of every woman. Human, selkie, he's not picky. He had an affair with a faerie once, too."

"Oh. Well, then," Annie answered, giggling. "As long as I have options." Shrieking, she yanked her feet back from the edge as Malik slapped his hands onto the ledge and pulled himself up beside her. He rolled her backward, dripping cold water over her as his weight landed along the length of her body, his hard arousal sliding inside her.

"Options?" he growled, nibbling along the curve of her ear. He filled her core, the water cooling from his body as the sheath of Annie's core warmed him. "You need options?"

"Uh huh. Options," she breathed, rolling her head to the side as he moved from her ear to her throat.

"You've got two options now, wife, and only two," Malik answered, his arms trembling as he held himself above her, straining against the urge to begin moving.

"What are they?" Annie gasped, arching her back to rock herself against Malik's still form. Reaching up between them, she ran her hands over his body, smiling as he sucked in his breath.

"Option one," he whispered, sliding slowly deeper into her body. "You get to be with me. And option two," he continued, backing out inch by torturous inch before slowly sliding deeper again. "You get to be with me."

"Oh," Annie moaned softly, her breath quickening as he began to rock within her center again. "I guess I'll stick with you, then."

***

"Come on," Malik murmured later, lifting his head from where he'd been resting between Annie's breasts. They'd spent a good while discussing Malik's talent as a swimming instructor, and at that point, Annie was ready to give in. She smiled down at him, running her fingers through his hair to pull it back from his forehead as he went on, "Pease Annie, come into the water with me. I'll be right here. And we can wash up before we change to go back to the clan." Nuzzling her throat softly, he wedged one knee between her thighs, pressing slightly, smiling as she gasped. "If you're a good student, I'll give you a prize."

"Mmm, well alright," Annie mumbled, pushing lightly against his chest. He moved away, giving her room to sit up, watching her in surprise. Clearly, he hadn't expected Annie to agree, which made her laugh. "It's the idea of bathing; you know I can't resist. But if I drown again …" Annie's voice trailed away to helpless giggles as Malik's eyes widened in surprise.

Malik laughed as Annie trailed off, her threat diminished by the giggles that took over her. "Silly," she said, jabbing her fingertip into his chest. Sliding to the edge of the rock, Annie took a deep breath and slid beneath the water, her hair trailing along the surface. Watching, Malik grinned and slid to the side of the ledge, leaning over to watch as Annie floated on her back.

"How am I able to do this?" she asked softly, her breasts shimmering with droplets of water. Her hips were just below the surface of the water, her shins and feet sticking out slightly above. She'd curled her arms around her head, pillowing her head with her laced fingers. "I could never float before," she said. "I don't even know why, but I'd always sink like a rock."

"Maybe because you were afraid before. Maybe it's instinct. Young selkies swim instinctively; no one teaches them," he answered, lowering himself to his belly on the rock ledge, one hand dropping down to swirl through the water beside her elbow. "Maybe it's the baby, maybe it's your change. I don't know. We could probably ask Tiernan, though."

Annie shivered, her pebbled nipples waving at him from the water. "I don't know, he creeps me out. All wild and sinewy and … he doesn't look old but he feels old. Does that even make any sense?"

Malik laughed, flicking his fingers through the water to splash a slight wave over her stomach. "He feels old because he is old. Something like three hundred years I think, but I'm not really sure exactly how old he is."

"Wow. Will we live that long?" Annie asked, bending her knees in turn, her toes dipping and floating, dipping and floating, her motion surrounding her with circular ripples on the surface of the water. "Will we live hundreds of years?"

"I hope so," he answered, heaving a sigh she didn't understand. "But there's no telling, Annie. Like I said, there are ways for us to die. And we aren't exactly safe."

Annie's eyes darted up to his face, her hands reaching for the ledge as her body dropped below the surface of the water. She sputtered, and Malik reached for her hands to keep her afloat as he rose to his knees. Helping her pull herself from the water, he settled her beside him. "What does that mean?" she asked. "These are your clan, your family. Why are we not safe, Malik?"

"There are things I can't fully explain to you yet, some things I don't really understand yet. But it has to do with the old selkie prophecies, and … Annie, it has to do with you, and me. With the baby."

Flinching beside him, Annie covered her stomach with her hands. "The baby?" she whispered. "The baby is in danger? From what?"

"Like I said, I don't know," he answered. "But there's been a lot of talk about you. Human women can't have selkie babies. It's never happened, but it's in some ancient prophesy that a human woman will come into the water, into our people. That she will bear a selkie child. And here you are, a human woman pregnant with a selkie child. Not human anymore, maybe, but you were when we conceived."

"And then? Am I expected to live? Is the baby?" Her voice grew shrill as she spoke, her fingers crossing over her stomach protectively.

"I don't know. The prophecy is long and there are a lot of parts that are unclear, Annie. Even to the prophet."

"Damn it, Malik. I am not a child. I get that you don't know everything, but you can tell me what you do know! Talk to me!" Annie commanded. He blinked at her, watching the panic rise in her face, trying to decide how much to tell her. Anger bloomed pink in her cheeks, her fingertips clenching unconsciously on the still-naked flesh that protected their child.

"The prophesies give life to both of you," he answered finally. "It is said that the child will bring the clans together as one united group. But the selkie people are independent, happy to live among our own clans. There is occasionally some intermarriage, but mostly we are very separate communities. And there are some clans who would wish to keep it that way."

"How would they accomplish that? How would someone stop the prophecy?" Annie asked warily, knowing but refusing to accept the answer in her heart.

Malik cleared his throat, drawing her in close, wrapping his arms around her. Curling around her protectively, he whispered, "The child. Our child. If the baby can be eliminated, then the prophesies obviously cannot come to pass."

"Eliminated?!" Annie yelped, gasping. She pulled away to look into Malik's face. Seeing the truth in his eyes, she held herself tightly again, her arms wrapping around her waist, her breath coming in frightened gasps. "What do we do, Malik? How do we protect the baby?"

"Telling you was step one. You can't fight what you don't know about, and that's part of why I brought you here, to tell you. But now, we need to get back to the clan. My aunt is the keeper of the prophecies, and Tiernan is the only one who can read them. We'll need to have a little conference with the council, get their advice."

Annie nodded. "Will they be able to help us?"

"Clan Killian has wanted peace among the selkie people for generations. They will help us, and there are other clans who can be called in as well." Averting his eyes slightly, he continued, "I believe Tiernan will know what to do."

"Alright then." Annie stood, bending to lift her pelt from the floor. Malik lifted his as well, slinging it over his back and closing it around himself. Watching, Annie mimicked his movements and gave her body to the mysteries of the change.

***

Back in the caves of clan Killian, Annie exited the change room in the wall of the cave and stood watching as the lockers slid back into place, covering the entrance of the alcove. The shirt she'd been given was too long, swishing around the middle of her thighs over shorts that were much too short. Turning, she caught the eyes of Malik's aunt and uncle, who were seated along the wall with Malik and Tiernan, who Annie had come to see as the clan shaman.

"Come," Tiernan said, his voice smooth and low, rumbling pleasantly from the depths of his chest. "Sit."

Nodding, Annie stepped forward, cautious of her bare feet along the rough surface of the cave floor. When she reached the table, she sidled quietly around the edge, her bottom sliding softly along the smooth cool rock of the wall behind her. She slid until she reached Malik, who reached out and took her hand, urging her onto the wooden bench beside him.

"You wanted to know more about the prophecies?" Malik's uncle Angus asked. He waited until Annie nodded firmly in his direction, her fingers clenching tight around Malik's hand. "Very well, then," Angus turned his head, nodding quickly to Malise, who opened a battered leather book and slid it across the table to Tiernan.

Tiernan rose to his full height in the corner of the bench that edged the table. He sighed, allowing his eyes to flutter closed. No one spoke; the air was tense as they waited for him. Only Malise reacted to his dramatic behavior, smiling quietly to herself as she lowered her eyes to her lap. Finally, Tiernan spoke, his eyes still closed, his fingertips gliding along the yellowed pages as if they were written in Braille. Annie leaned closer as he spoke to see if it was Braille, but it wasn't; the paper was smooth, covered in smeared drawings and letters. She lifted her eyes to his face and saw that his eyes were still closed; as she looked around the table, she realized that everyone else had closed their eyes as well. Guiltily, she closed her eyes also, settling back and resting her shoulders against the wall as she listened.

"The selkie people have been in existence since the beginning of time," Tiernan intoned. "In the beginning, legions of angels fell from the heavens and were sent to live out their lives in this lower world. There are those who fell upon the land and are known as the faeries, the wee folk of ancient Celtic lore. Others fell to the depths of the sea. In their struggle for life, they began to take up the pelt of the seal, and to live among the waves of the sea, surviving by the blessings of the waters. This pelt allows us to live in the waters we have settled, but also reminds us to rise to the surface, to visit with our faerie brethren and to observe the humans who came to existence after us."

Annie peeked through her eyelashes as the book shifted on the table. With his eyes still tightly closed, Tiernan slid the book closer to himself, turning the pages blindly and running his fingers over the strange print as he continued to speak. "First, the selkies were one people, living together in peace and harmony but soon, the selkie people began to separate and to feud among each other. They fought bitterly for leadership, for respect, for mates, for food. Over the course of the centuries, families moved away from the original community and built their own homes elsewhere. Now, it seems as if it has always been that way, because the ancient ones who remember the original ways are now gone. But there was one, a young selkie who was cursed with the sight. He spent his early life in useless ramblings, speaking in nonsense and telling outrageous tales. This curse has passed on through history, through blood, and --"

"Hmm," Annie murmured quietly. Tiernan froze, and Malik's clenching fingers on her hand caused her to open her eyes. Around the table, the eyes of the Killian leaders were open, fastened on her in shock. Her face hot with humiliation, she lowered her eyes to her fingers, joined with Malik's. Closing her eyes again, she bit her lip as waves of embarrassment washed over her, keeping her head down until Tiernan cleared his throat and spoke again.

"As the boy grew older, his tales became rooted in truth, and the events he had spoken of came to pass. The people of his clan urged him to write down his visions, to take note of them so that they might remember. He began to mark them in a book, in both text and drawing, and notations were made as the events he predicted came to pass. The tradition has been passed on also, one prophet among the people writing down what his visions tell him. There have been many visions: visions of peace, visions of war. But there is one long awaited event that will bring back the true peace of the old days." Opening his eyes, he waited for Annie to open her eyes, their gazes colliding across the table.

"It is you," he said. "It is you who hold the prophecies. You are the human mother."

"How do you know?" Annie asked, her voice nothing more than a horrified whisper. She'd pulled back without realizing it, pressing herself against the wall in her effort to lean away from Tiernan's steady focus. "How do you know it's me?" Her heart pounded in her chest, her mind flying with the chaos of her thoughts.

"I have seen," he answered simply, closing the heavy book with a thump and pressing it toward her. Taking its weight in her hands, Annie lifted the book, adjusting the grasp of her fingers so that she could examine the Celtic design that covered the thick back cover. She turned it over, gently gripping the edges of the book as she resettled it on the table. And that's when she saw it:

The Tales of Tiernan, the Seer

Swallowing the lump in her throat, she brought her eyes to his again, the sparkling green of her irises shimmering in the low light of the room. "You? You have seen?"

He nodded solemnly, the depth of his dark eyes making her feel as if he could see right into her mind. He smiled slightly and gooseflesh rippled down her back. "I have seen," he repeated. "You were human, and yet you carry within you the seed of the selkie. And the child is selkie, the blood of its father. I know that it is so, because otherwise you would not have survived the change; no human ever has before. And soon," he said, gesturing toward Malik, "You will bring forth the fruit of your love with this young one, and then shall everything change for our people."

Malik's fingers had been clenching more and more tightly on Annie's hand until finally she was forced to tear her eyes away from Tiernan, looking over to notice the distress in his face. Turning back, she spoke to Tiernan. "How?" she asked. "What will happen? How can we be ready?"

"There are many clans to rival the clan Killian, many who would not wish to join with us. Many who would not wish to return to the days of peace and community, who would prefer to be alone, doing as they choose. There are warmongers among the selkie clans, young mother. And they will come."

"For me?"

"No," he said, shaking his head as he took the leather-bound book from Annie and slid it back to Malise. "They will not come for you, unless it is to kill you. They will not wish the child to be born, and their interest in you will be limited to your protection of the child."

"And if the child is born before the war comes?" Angus murmured, his fists clenched on top of the table.

"Then we will need to shelter the child until it has achieved its purpose. The child will need training as it grows, it will need advisors, protectors. But Angus, we must not wait. I tell you, this child will bring war upon us before there is peace. We must make ready."

"Um," Annie mumbled nervously, her voice taking on a shyly quiet tone as she stared resolutely into her lap. Her fingers worked the fabric of her shirt, fierce red color rising up from the collar of the shirt to cover her neck, spreading over her face and ears. "I – I was wondering," she said.

"Yes, my daughter?" Tiernan questioned, tilting his head, his eyes gleaming with some unknown amusement.

"Do you, um, do you know what it is?" Annie stammered. And all around her, the selkies burst into laughter. Angus roared with it, pounding the table with his fists while his wife sat quietly beside him, tittering into her hands as her eyes streamed. Malik lowered his face into his hands, his shoulders trembling as he laughed silently. Only Tiernan did not laugh; instead he watched her closely until she met his eyes again.

Smiling gleefully, he rose from his seat. "Of course I do," he answered, turning and striding away.

***

"I can't believe he wouldn't tell me!" Annie grumbled later, pulling her face into a scowl as Malik laughed. They'd taken a while, settling in their new cave, down the tunnel from Angus and Malise. Annie had wandered around the quiet stillness of the cave, her fingertips guiding her along the wall as Malik closed the simple wooden door and lit the fires. The fire here was similar to the one that circled his bachelor cave, though the groove in the wall here was taller, giving off more light and more warmth. It was higher up in the wall also, for greater safety, and the fire pit in the center of the room was smaller. Annie had exclaimed over the way the pebbles in the pit were multi-colored, somehow refusing to stain black from the heat of the fire.

There was a large cot propped into the corner of the room, low to the ground, safely below the bottom of the fire grooves. Covered in soft furs, the bed was warm and cozy – not that they'd spent much time resting. The remainder of the room was much like any of the others Annie had seen, somewhat barren if not outright cold.

"I wonder if he really knows but even if he does, he won't tell. It is unusual here for people to do that, to want to know. Most selkies don't really care," Malik murmured. "With males and females mostly equal and not really interested in permanent relationships anyway, no one seems to care if there's much difference in the population counts. And neither sex is given greater worth among the selkie population; not the way humans always fight to see whether men or women are better, anyway."

"Actually, I just wanted to know what I'd dress it in. I mean, boys need different things than girls, even if it's a selkie child, right? And anyway, how do we get those things here in the first place? Clothes, things like that?"

"Most of the clan members don't really like going up on land unless they have some need to. And generally, they prefer their land adventures to be the old fashioned way, swimming up and all that. For the older ones, that's maybe like being about to touch history, you know? There's something … primitive maybe, about rising up out of the sea and hiding the pelt, finding clothes you may or may not have remembered to leave behind. But for things for the children, furniture and stuff, there's a tunnel we can use to transport things down here. Human things we might want, like the wood to build these cots, for instance," Malik explained, lazily tracing circles on Annie's stomach with his fingers. "Can it hear us?" he asked. "In there, I mean?"

"I don't know," Annie answered with a grin, her voice smooth and quiet in the warmth of the cave. "I'm pretty sure everyone could hear us earlier. They say babies can hear from inside, but I don't know how early."

"Hmm," he murmured softly, bending down to place a feathery kiss just below Annie's belly button.

"Malik? How does the tunnel work? What about the pelt? If you use the tunnel, do you take it with you?" Annie rose up onto her elbows, waiting for him to answer.

"If you'll be gone long, usually you take it. Having it with you allows you more options, more ways to get back home. But the tunnel actually lets out right behind a hotel in Bar Harbor. There are a couple of cars there, and the clan keeps a room in the hotel. I've stayed there a time or two, when I was on land to see my dad."

"Oh my gosh, Malik!" Annie shot up in the bed, her hands flying up and into her hair as her wide eyes sought his face in the dark. Realizing how long she'd been away from home, how long they'd both been away from the life they'd been building, she scrambled around in the bed, searching for her shirt as she spoke. "Your dad! And Brenna, my house! We have to –"

"They know," he interrupted, his hands reaching for her, pulling her back into the cozy warmth of the skins.

"How?" Annie asked.

"I've been up there. Just once, before we were able to wake you. I talked to my dad, and I talked to Brenna."

"What did they say? And what about my house?"

"Well, we need to go back, and soon. They don't know you made it completely, but they knew you weren't dead when I went up there. I talked to Brenna a bit, and I took the liberty of leaving a message for your attorneys – I hope you don't mind, I had to search pretty hard to find the right numbers," he said, raising his brow in question as he looked at Annie. She shook her head and he went on, "But I was able to get in touch with them, tell them that you'd had an emergency and needed them to handle your affairs until you could get back."

"Oh." Annie quieted, sinking back into the cool feather-stuffed pillows. "So that's settled for now, I guess, but I'm not sure it makes me feel much better, really. I want to see my house; I want to see Brenna. For a little while, maybe, I want my own life back. Just for a little while."

Malik nodded, his dark eyes invisible in the shadows of the corner, the ends of his hair tickling Annie's cheek as he settled beside her with a sigh. "And I need to update my father, tell him how much has changed. I think I can make arrangements for us to go in the next few days, if you're sure you're feeling up to it."

"I'm up to it. I like it here, but I miss my life, too. I know we should be here though, and I'm okay with that. Besides, if the prophecies are true, my being pregnant puts all these people in danger, the entire clan. Right?"

"It does," he said, his voice solemn.

"I don't want to just leave them. If they're in danger because of us, we should be here shouldn't we?" Annie turned, squinting in the darkness to meet his gaze.

"I don't know if they'd be safer with us here or with us gone, honestly," Malik sighed, his hands finding Annie's shoulders, bringing her down to rest in the curve of his shoulder. On the other side of their door, children ran shouting through the tunnels.

"I don't want to put everyone at risk," Annie whispered. "Do we bring our pelts when we leave?"

Malik slipped away from Annie and rose from the bed, slipping into his shorts and tying the strings, checking the glowing surface of his watch before he turned back to speak again. "I think we should bring them, just in case we need them or want them. I'm going to go talk to my aunt, okay? I need to make sure one of the cars will be available, but I'll be back in a little bit."

"Malik?" Annie asked.

Headed toward the door, he'd turned back to look into the pile of furs on the cot. "Yeah?"

"Am I losing my life up there?"

He smiled slightly, walking back to sit beside her. "You don't have to, but the selkie life is pretty secret. We don't just run around telling everyone, you understand. So you could still write, but you'd be reclusive. You can maintain your house and car if you want, but it's unlikely that you'd be there much."

"Don't the books say we're limited to how much time we can spend on land? Living as a human, I mean? I read some things about --"

Malik laughed. "That's a myth, love. The only truth in that stuff is that if we spend too much time up there, we can age and we can die. We need the water. Even here, you'll notice most of the time the people aren't here, and that's because they spend their days and sometimes their nights in the sea. Some of them rarely even come here. Even within the clans, there's a variance to how we live. Some prefer to live in the caves, mostly as humans but within reach and sound and feel of the water and its peace. Others choose to live in the water itself, and there's a place for both types. Those who live in the water help to protect the underwater ends of the caves, keeping us from being discovered by divers and such. You'd be surprised how thrilled a diver is to come across a playful seal. Those of us who live here protect this end, keeping humans from venturing into the tunnels and finding the caves."

"So I can move freely, then? Back and forth? We could even live on land as humans?"

"Do you want to?" He asked warily, tilting his head, one hand rising slowly to flatten on the warm skin of his chest.

"I'm really not sure. I just wanted to know what my options are, I guess. What if I did want to?"

He sighed, thinking of what he'd endured in his efforts to regrow his pelt. "I guess we'd have to think of something, if that's what you want. We'd both be fighting the call of the sea. But we've got time to figure all that out ... if you want to be up there anytime soon, I need to go talk to my aunt."

"Go ahead," Annie said. She stood, reaching to touch his face as his arms circled her waist, sorry for the wrinkle she'd brought to his brow. "Go. I'll be here when you get back," she told him.

***

Once Malik was gone, Annie allowed herself to fall back, sinking into the furs that surrounded her on the cot. The idea of going back to her life on land terrified her. How could she explain her absence to everyone? What would she say to Brenna? And how would she manage two separate lives?

Would it be better to just allow herself to fade from life on land, to sink into her new selkie life with Malik? After all, if Tiernan was right, Annie had duties to clan Killian, duties to her child. She owed it to all of them to protect the child, and beyond the prophesies, every part of her soul screamed that this was where she belonged. Malik had looked devastated at the idea of giving up clan life again; obviously, this was home for him. Looking around into the dim light of the cave, she thought about leaving her human life behind.

She would gain so much; she was a lone woman in the human world, without family or connection. But here in the midst of clan Killian, she'd found a sense of purpose and an instantaneous familial acceptance. Malik's people wanted her here, they'd protected her, rescued her, changed her. They'd taken her in and made her one of their own.

Had it only been because of the baby?

"They love you, you know," she whispered into the dark, her hand finding the slight curve of her already changing body. Fear gripped her as she realized that she didn't know what to expect. She didn't know the gestation time of a selkie child! She didn't even know the gestation time of a normal seal! How long would she be pregnant? A month? Ten months? Forever? And what would the baby look like? Would she love it? Would it be too different, too unexpected? Would it live? Would she be able to protect it?

And more importantly, how big would it be?

"Can you hear me in there?" she whispered, wishing she could connect in a more real way to the child. It lived within her body, grew with the nourishment she gave, but there were moments when nothing felt real. Her life – her world – was in turmoil and everything was changing. The only constant was her love for Malik, and her certain knowledge of the growing child. Stroking the lower smoothness of her stomach, she spoke to the child. "Are you awake, my baby? Are you worried, afraid? You don't need to be, not at all, because you've a mama and a daddy that will love you so much. And I know that you'll be just fine. You've got a whole family waiting to love you already."

Mama ...

Annie jerked as the voice whispered in her mind, her hand tightening over her stomach. "Baby?" she asked.

Mama? Don't worry, mama ...

"Holy crap. Are you – can you talk to me?" As Annie spoke in to the quiet, a sense of peace stole over her and her worries quieted.

Don't worry, mama ...

Thoughts rose and fell in her mind, crashing like waves before drawing away and fading into the distance. She felt her body relaxing further, her eyes drooping slightly as she rolled to the side and curled herself around the baby that grew within her.

Don't worry, mama ...

Her baby was talking to her ... her thoughts continued to fade as she helplessly obeyed the peaceful voice drifting up in her mind. Her fingers stroked slow circles over her abdomen; she drifted off to sleep, smiling, whispering, "And I can't wait to tell your father about you."

***

"Annie," Malik whispered, gently shaking her shoulder to wake her. Her eyes fluttered open, and she smiled as she realized he was there, her hand floating up from the fur coverings to stroke along his cheek. "Wake up, sleepy selkie-girl," he said. "We're set to travel. We're going up to your house."

"We are?" she said, shooting up out of the pillows in her excitement. "When do we leave?"

"Actually," he said with a grin, tucking a strand of her hair behind her ear. "Uncle Angus and Aunt Malise seem to think now is good. So far, we think you're still a clan secret, but there's no telling how long that'll last. Tiernan says the best way to protect you and the baby is to hide you. Keeping you away from clan Killian and other selkies as much as possible will help keep the word about you from spreading to other clans, hopefully. He's hoping that'll buy us some time to store up things we'll need here for the birth and for the baby, and things the clan will need to shore up our securities."

"Securities?" Annie asked.

"Protection for you and the baby. It isn't just possibility we're worried about here, it's a certainty that the other clans will come, Annie. It's only a matter of time; the clans will hear about you eventually, a human woman able to carry and birth a selkie child, saved already by the life-force of the child and able to accept the magic of our change into your blood. You're no average happenstance, Annie."

"You mean there was a chance it wouldn't work? The change?" she questioned, turning to look more closely into his face.

"There was," he said quietly, nodding his head, a shock of dark hair falling into his eyes. Brushing it away, he took her hands in his own. "But I had to try, right? If you'd died, the baby would have died too. I had to try." At Annie's silent nod, he continued. "But you can't be kept secret forever. The other clans will hear about you and they'll come. Sure, some will come to celebrate, to unite and join forces with us in favor of the prophecies. But the others …" He trailed off, shaking his head.

"Others?" Annie asked scooting to the edge of the cot, allowing her feet to dangle toward the floor.

Malik took her hand in his, sitting beside her as he linked their fingers. "Others will not be so happy. More independent clans prefer to stay that way, apart and alone, acting as their own governments, their own people. They won't want the joining."

"How do you know this?" Annie said, scooting to the edge of the bed.

"It's prophesied," he said simply. "That is simply how it will be. Tiernan has never had a vision that didn't come to pass."

"When do we leave?" Annie asked again.

Malik sighed, his shoulders heavy as he looked around their new cave for what could be the last time. Staying put the entire clan in danger, but leaving meant they might never make it back alive. He hadn't told Annie the complete truth – there were other clans, rival clans that already knew about her. He also hadn't told her that they already had an ally, though he'd have to tell her that soon. "We should leave now. I've given directions to your house to my cousin Doyle, and to some of the others, so that they can find us if we're needed, or if we need warning. I've given him directions to Brenna's house, also. Once the rebels know who you are, they'll seek out your connections."

"Is Brenna in danger because of me?" Annie asked.

"It's not because of you," Malik said, trying to be reassuring, trying to keep her from worrying. "And she's likely not in any danger yet. But she could be, eventually."

"And what then?" Annie asked. "What can we do for her?"

Malik ran his hands over his face, his body language expressing his lack of answers before he could form the words. "I don't really know yet," he said. "But we should go now."

"What should we bring up with us? To my house, I mean?"

"Well, to begin with, I'm going to go get our pelts from the locker," Malik answered. "Pack whatever you like or whatever you might want to take from here, just in case we don't get to come back right away. I wish I'd brought my dive collection up from my other place, we might have needed some of it for money."

Annie shook her head, laughing. "Silly. Gardening and watching movies isn't that expensive, and I have money. Or at least, I had money ... I have to hope if you told my law firm that I'm still alive, I'll still have money, right?"

He laughed with her, his shoulders shaking. "You'll have your money, whatever you had before. I told them you'd be coming back to check in as soon as you could," he said. "Still, maybe I can get Doyle to go down and get my stash for me before we go."

"Do you think we'll be gone that long?" Annie asked nervously.

"I honestly don't know. We could go to your house and be safe for months, or it could be hours. I don't know what will happen."

"Hey, Malik, can I ask a question?" Her eyes widened in surprise, sparkling green in the firelight as he laughed again, clutching his stomach helplessly. "What is your problem?" she asked.

"You've done nothing but ask questions since you woke up," he roared, still laughing. "What questions could you have left?"

"What do we do about the baby? I mean, about a doctor?"

"We'd better steer clear of doctors if possible," he answered. "In the general way, a selkie baby is born in the form of a human, the pelt coming later, something like the way humans think of the afterbirth. But that's with a selkie mother. No one has ever heard of a human mother before, so I don't know how the baby is or what it looks like. We don't want to risk doctors seeing anything unusual."

"Hmm," Annie murmured, her hands moving to cover her abdomen protectively as visions flashed in her mind of her child being used by science, investigated, dissected. "Hmm," she said again, "Yes, I think we'd better avoid that."

Annie waited until Malik was gone before fully leaving the comfortable warmth of the fur-laden cot, wandering slowly through the room, seeking something from this new life that she might want to carry with her into the human world she'd soon be leaving behind. There was nothing to take though, beyond her new pelt and the child that slumbered innocently within her womb. She hadn't been in the caves long enough to acquire real possessions of her own.

Sitting back on the edge of the cot, Annie's eyes continued to wander around the small cave room, wondering if she and Malik would ever be able to come back, if they would have the chance to raise their child. "Oh!" she gasped, thoughts of the baby reminding her that she'd forgotten to tell Malik about her interaction with the baby. Wide-awake now, and much more logical in her wakened state, Annie was more prepared to pass off the interaction as a dream. After all, how could a mother interact with a child in the womb, a child that was still not even developed enough to kick?

But then she heard the child giggling in her mind.

***

"It's really dark in here," Annie was muttering, only a few short hours later. Her fingers were laced tightly with Malik's, her uncertain hand held in his strong grip as he led her away from the caves, a giant pack strapped to his back. Inside the pack were several pieces from his dive collection – there'd been plenty of time for Doyle to go and fetch a few pieces – and their new pelts, folded and rolled carefully so that both would fit inside the pack.

The tunnel leading from the selkie caves to the Bar Harbor hotel was short but dark; it was clean but it wore the chill of underground air and the weight of the land on top of them. The tunnel was wide enough to allow them to walk side-by-side with just a little room to spare, though 'spacious' would be far too generous a word.

"I know," Malik answered, laughing slightly as he pulled Annie close to him and nuzzled her throat. "Nice and private, hmm? A man could get lost in here with a woman like you. A sweet little woman, a deep dark tunnel …"

"Malik!" Annie giggled, wriggling away from him in the dark, keeping their linked hands together to maintain contact with him. "You behave yourself, mister! There will be no 'getting lost' in this tunnel at all!" She twisted her face into a wry grimace in her effort not to laugh at his silliness, though he couldn't see her well enough in the dark to make out her expression.

Malik laughed helplessly at her choice of words, pulling her along by the joining of their hands. "Not in this tunnel, huh? That's okay, maybe I can try another tunnel later," he laughed, jerking out of reach as Annie reached to swat his arm. "I'm just kidding. Seriously, though, we should be out of here soon; it's not that much farther now."

When they broke through the mouth of the tunnel and into the daylight, Annie shielded her eyes with her free hand and took in the scene around her. Doyle's younger brother Bryce, and Bryce's best friend, Finnigan were quietly sitting off to the side, shielded from the sun. "Hey Finn, Bryce," Malik called, waving as he and Annie passed them.

"Heading out then?" Bryce asked, watching Annie's hand as it nervously fluttered up to tuck her hair behind her ear.

Malik laughed. "No luck, Bryce. But let Uncle Angus know we made it out, yeah?"

"Yeah," Bryce laughed, tilting his head to Annie, who tipped her face, blushing.

"Alright, we're on the way then," Malik answered, waving to his friends as he led Annie away.

"Take care," Finn replied, waving back.

"Oh, wait! The keys!! I almost forgot to give them to you. The truck's way out in the front," Bryce said, walking over to give a jingling key ring to Malik. Looking over to Annie, he nodded slightly to her, his ears turning red as she smiled and nodded back. "Be careful. We'll be there to pick up the truck later on." At Malik's nod, Bryce turned to go back and join Finn at the watch.

"Well, he really does like me, huh?" Annie whispered, angling her face up toward Malik's ear as they walked.

"I told you," he laughed, wedging his elbow playfully into her side as they walked. "But he'll survive."

"Hmmm. He's a little young to be on guard duty though, isn't he? Bryce, I mean?" Annie asked, struggling to keep up with Malik's longer strides as she turned back to watch Bryce and Finn joking together in the shade. Malik slowed his pace to match hers, smiling down at her as amusement lit his dark eyes.

"We're immortal, remember? Bryce is seventy-five years old, Annie," he said, his lips twitching with a restrained smile.

"Oh, wow," Annie said, glancing back at the two youthful-looking boys guarding the entrance to the selkie tunnel. "He looks like he's barely old enough to buy his own beer. And Finnigan?"

"Finn's the same," Malik answered, guiding Annie around the front of the hotel and over to a shining red truck. "They were born in the same season. Like Doyle and me."

"Are there many other young ones?" Annie asked curiously, thinking of their child. "Really young? Like, children? I mean, I saw a few, but are there many?"

"Sure, there are some," Malik answered, slipping the key into the door of the truck and popping the locks. He dropped Annie's hand and worked the pack free from his shoulders, settling it carefully into the backseat of the truck's giant cab. Turning, he met her eyes with a smile. "Ready to go back home?"

Annie nodded, laughing as she strode around the front of the truck and climbed up into the cab. "I keep imagining that we'll go back and find the house turned into a little old shack," she said as they settled into their seats. "Like I know it hasn't been that long since we were there, but so much has changed. I feel like it's been years since I've been above sea level. Like I'd get back up here just to find that everything had changed."

"And has it?"

Annie sighed. "It has. Everything is different now, just because I am. I think it would have been anyway though, because I'm pregnant now, and I've already started to see things a little differently just because I'll be a mother someday. I saw pebbles in the parking lot that would poke little toes, things like that. But leaving my humanity behind, becoming something else, becoming a selkie ... it's different."

"Are you sure you don't want to just stay up here?" Malik asked, his voice tense with unexpressed nervousness. Looking over at him, Annie knew that if she chose to continue living on land, Malik would support her choice. He would be with her, and they would raise their child as a human child if that was what she chose. He'd been willing to choose that life anyway, the human life. But was that really for the best? It might protect them, if they left the selkie world behind. But it would also allow them to age and die, and it would deprive their child of a centuries-old heritage. It would deprive their child of what appeared to be its destiny.

And would living on land really protect the child from the dangers of the underwater prophecy of the selkies? Would not knowing about the selkie prophecies protect the child from enemies who did know about them?

Probably not.

"No," Annie sighed. "I'll want to come back often, to feel the human still living inside me for a while. I'll want to visit Brenna. And I'd like to visit your dad. But other than that, there's nothing for me here, not really. I want to be where you are. Where you go, I will go, like it says in the bible. And your people shall be my people."

Raising Annie's hand to his lips, Malik pressed a kiss to the inside of her wrist, a relieved smile lifting the corners of his mouth. Seeing his joy and feeling what must be the inexplicable joy of the child, Annie knew she'd made the right choice, and having made that choice, a weight she hadn't even been aware of lifted from her shoulders. Smiling to herself, as Malik turned his attention to driving, she settled in to wait until they reached her house in Bar Harbor.

It was a short drive, and before she knew it, Malik was steering the truck down her street, turning into her driveway. "Oh, my house," Annie murmured, tears springing to her eyes at the sight of her little house. She hadn't realized until that moment, how much she'd missed her house, her simple human life, and the basic excitement over discovering that she was pregnant. Now, sitting in the driveway with Malik's eyes sweeping her face, Annie couldn't wait to go inside. There was just one problem.

"I don't even know how we'll get in. Where are my keys?" she asked. "And how did my car get here?"

"Doyle brought them," Malik said quietly. "He went back to the beach while I waited with Malise to see how you'd take the blood, if the change would work with you. He found your keys in the sand, brought your car back here. He says we'll find the keys under the step in front of the shed, which is handy because I was thinking we could store the pelts there."

"No," Annie said, reaching to take his hand. "This was my life before, and I can't say that I won't miss it. But I meant what I said about going with you Malik. I know that it means something big that the change worked in me. I know that the prophecies mean something; I've seen how Tiernan watches me, how Angus watches me. I loved my life here, my time as a human, and I know that I'll miss parts of that. But I'm also embracing a new life, my life with you. I'm not human anymore, am I? And I can't expect to live as one?"

"Not entirely," Malik said. "We can walk among them, but we are not human. You are not human anymore."

"And I don't want to live a pretend human life. The pelt is a part of me now; even now, I feel it calling to me. I want it with me. And I can't live here like that, not happily."

Malik smiled again, the last of his tension leaving his face. "I was really terrified that we'd get here, and you'd look at that house and decide that it's where you'd want to be. Now that I've been given a fresh chance to prove myself to the clan, I ... well, I'd have done it. I'd have stayed here with you Annie, but living here would have been harder, harder than when I'd decided on it before, even."

"I understand, I promise," Annie reassured him gently. She heaved a breath, one hand running lazily over the surface of her lower abdomen as if to caress the child hidden within. "Ready to go inside? Or did sitting here looking at the house give you a sudden craving to mow grass and wash my car?"

"Haha, funny girl," he answered, tweaking her nose before turning to exit the truck. "I just did all that before because you were disgustingly sick and still incredibly cute. I had to find a way to keep from reaching out to you, and your car was filthy." Reaching into the backseat, he dragged the giant pack from the truck and strapped it back to his shoulders. Annie laughed, jumped down from the cab and headed for the shed in the backyard.

They met back at the front door, the quiet reminding Annie of the first time she'd entered this house. She'd come here as a runaway, a broken woman seeking a quiet place to hide from the pain of her divorce. Now she entered the house again, healed from that pain and excited at the prospect of her new life, a life she'd never even known to hope for. Opening the door, she was surprised at how little had changed. There was the starfish in the shadowbox on the wall, a little dusty but otherwise just as it had been. The crystal seal was still resting proudly on the table, bringing back memories of the way Annie and Malik had met. She smiled, touching a fingertip to the nose of the seal as she dropped her keys into the crystal mussel she'd always used as a "catch-all," kicking her sandals off in the basket under the table.

"It's funny how different everything is even though it's all exactly the same, you know?" she asked, moving aside and allowing Malik room to enter the house. He sighed as he settled the pack on the floor, turning to press the door shut as he took Annie in his arms.

"Everything changes, Annie, but some things will always be the same," he murmured, stepping closer, aligning their bodies as he laced his fingers together just above the swell of her hips.

"Oh yeah? Like what?" Annie asked on a sigh, her head falling back as his lips found the sensitive hollow behind her ear.

"You're just as intoxicating as ever before," he answered. "And that's just the beginning."

"Hmm, just the beginning, huh? What else is the same as before?" she murmured, allowing him to steer her toward the couch in the living room, a trail of clothes lying abandoned along the way.

***

The next morning saw them back to their old routine, sitting together in the kitchen, drinking black coffee because they hadn't thought to run out for milk and other groceries yet. After an improvised breakfast of Pillsbury biscuits spread with butter and strawberry jam, Malik was planning to visit his father and Annie readied herself for a visit with Brenna.

"You sure you're ready for this? I can come with you, help you explain things to her," Malik had offered, sitting beside Annie on the couch to tie his shoes.

"No, I think we'll be okay. She's actually the one who kind of helped me figure out what you were. I mean, I had the pelt already, and I knew that it was from my seal on the beach because of the scar, but she was the one who made the connections for me. She was the one who thought to connect your mysterious appearance and the seal vanishing."

Malik raised an eyebrow, wondering how revealing Brenna and Annie's conversations had been. "She knows about the selkie people?" he asked. "How?"

"Well, she's Irish," Annie answered, shrugging as if that explained everything. Taking in Malik's surprised expression, she laughed and explained further. "Apparently the selkie folk are legendary in her history. You know the myths and legends surrounding the Celtic people. You know, the fairies and the wee folk and whatnot? I mean, your clan came from Ireland anyway, right?"

"Of course," he said quietly, thinking about Tiernan, about the woman who had once left him brokenhearted and aging. "So she knew about selkies. All along, she has known."

"Mmhmm," Annie answered, misunderstanding his tension as she brushed her fingers idly through the dark waves of her hair. "She knew before I did; she gave me the selkie book that I was reading. But that's why I'm okay with telling her. I feel that I can trust her, Malik. She's a friend."

"She should be told," he answered. "I agree that you should tell her; she needs to know that she may be in danger, and also, we may need her help someday. For the child," he said.

"To protect it?"

His mouth had flattened into a stern line as they spoke, his expression tense. "I don't know. But if she's a friend, you're to going to need to tell her everything that's happened." Glancing over at the clock on the wall, he stood, palming the keys to the truck. Reaching out with his free hand, he ran the tips of his fingers along the smooth round curve of Annie's cheek. "You'll be fine on your own?" he asked.

"Absolutely. Angus and the others have said they don't think anyone knows about me yet, so I should be okay." At least, that's what she hoped, anyway. Malik had been unusually quiet in the last few days, and Annie had begun to wonder if he wasn't keeping something from her.

"You should be alright," he answered, bending to kiss her gently before turning to leave. Annie watched Malik's shoulders working through the fabric of his tee shirt as he headed for the door, walking to the window and watching his easy pace as he walked to the truck outside. Her hands fell to the newly-firm place in her lower abdomen where she knew her child waited to be born. "There's goes your daddy for the day," she whispered to the baby.

Daddy ...

"Don't worry, he'll be back," Annie answered, dropping back to the couch to put her own shoes on. She'd felt silly at first, talking to the baby as if it could understand; but as time went on and the threats against her baby began to feel more real, she was just happy to have someone to talk to at all. Still, it felt odd to share her fears with an unborn child. "But you know what little one? We're going on a ride of our own. We're going to spend some time with Brenna."

Brenna ...

"She's a friend of mine," Annie explained, bending forward to tie the laces of her shoes. Images formed in her mind, bringing a smile to her lips, images of a day when she would not be able to tie her shoes due to the swelling belly of her pregnancy. Finishing, she stood and walked to the door, exiting the house to the cool morning air. "And you know what, baby? She's sure going to be interested in hearing about you."

***

Pulling into the driveway in front of Brenna's lighthouse, Annie took a long, shaky breath, wondering how she would be able to explain everything to her friend. She still didn't really understand everything herself; it was easy enough to fall in love with a stranger, and it had been fun to fantasize that maybe he was some mythical creature that had come up from the depths of the ocean. But now it was all real.

Malik really was a selkie and now, so was Annie. How could she explain the handfasting, the blood exchange, the way her pelt had simply burst forth while the smoke had surrounded her and Tiernan had given his chant? And how would she explain the prophesies, the child? How could anyone explain a baby that somehow managed to communicate from within the womb?

Brenna was a slightly superstitious Irish woman, raised on myth and legend. But would she believe that legends really could come to life in this way?

Annie didn't have to wait long to find out. Brenna's dog, Lugus, came bounding around the side of the house, barking and bouncing in his usual psychotic style. Behind him, Brenna appeared, her feet freezing to the ground as she looked up and noticed Annie's car in the driveway. Her mouth fell open; she broke into a grin and let out a shriek, running over to the car. As she approached, Annie opened her door and stepped out, nervously smoothing her hands over her clothes.

"Oh my gosh, you're alive," Brenna whispered, her voice trembling with emotion.

"I'm alive," Annie said, smiling, tears stinging her eyes. "And I'm thinking I'll be alive now for ... a while."

"That's good," Brenna said with a laugh, her eyebrows coming together over blue eyes that sparkled in the morning sun. She tucked flaming red hair behind her ears, her lips pursing slightly. "I talked to Malik before, but he didn't say much. Wanna come inside and tell me what happened with you two?"

"Definintely, and boy do I have a lot to say," Annie said quietly, reaching out to touch Brenna's arm briefly. "I'm sorry … I wish I could've come sooner."

"You're here now," Brenna said, smiling slightly as Lugus lunged and frolicked around Annie's feet. "Come on in."

Annie followed Brenna into the lighthouse, grinning at the Irish poem still hanging on the wall by the front door. It had been Annie's housewarming gift to Brenna, just after they'd met. Waiting for Brenna to call Lugus into the house and shut the door, she followed the bounding animal into the living room, sinking into the soft cushions of the couch.

"Okay," Brenna said with a sigh, settling into the chair opposite Annie, pulling her feet up and tucking them beneath her. "Tell me everything."

"Hmm. Where to begin," Annie sighed, laying her head back on the cushions behind her and dropping her forearm over her face.

"Chronological order is always nice," Brenna laughed, shoving the mass of her hair behind her shoulders and settling further into her own seat.

"Okay, then," Annie said with a grin, bringing her head back up so that she could meet Brenna's eyes. "I'm pregnant." She broke into giggles as Brenna's mouth fell open for the second time that day. "And we burned Malik's seal pelt."

"What?! Oh my gosh, you're pregnant?? And how did you burn the pelt? Doesn't that kill them?" Brenna asked, nearly shouting in her excitement. She sat up straighter, smiling slightly to herself as she waited for the rest of Annie's story.

"Um, well. Yes, I am, and we threw it in a fire. And no, apparently not. Well, I mean it does, but not right away," Annie answered, her eyes watering as she laughed.

"Well, sure then," Brenna said, waving her hand dismissively. "But you're pregnant? Oh my gosh, do you know what it is?"

"It's a selkie child," Annie answered wryly.

"No, I meant if it's a boy or a girl, silly." Brenna laughed. "Of course it would be a selkie child. Wouldn't it?"

"Actually, we won't get to know what it is until it's born, I guess. Apparently, this isn't supposed to be able to happen. Malik says there's never been a human mother pregnant with a selkie child before."

"Really," Brenna murmured quietly, her fingers digging through Lugus's fur as he curled himself into the chair beside her.

"Really," she answered. "From what I'm told, selkies can be born to human parents but only if the father is human. They all say no one knows of a human woman carrying a selkie child before, or even for sure if the pregnancy will last."

"Will you survive?" Brenna asked, narrowing her eyes slightly as she waited for Annie to answer.

Shrugging, Annie laughed and said, "That's what they tell me. There's some kind of prophesy they keep talking about, but I didn't learn any of that until after Malik died, so I'd better go back some."

"What?!" Brenna asked, shouting for real that time. Lugus jerked in her arms at the sudden noise, licking his front paw before he settled back into Brenna's lap. "You're killing me with this story, Annie! Tell me faster!"

"Okay, okay," Annie giggled. "So I was going to tell Malik that I was pregnant, but I wanted to wait until he'd decided what he was going to do about me. And you know about that part, but just not about the baby because I wanted to tell him first. I found out I was pregnant when he'd left, right after I showed him his pelt."

"Right, I remember that," Brenna said.

"Well, then when he came back, he said he wanted to be with me. But you know, we both knew the sea would always call to him."

"Yeah, I remember that too, when he came back. Waking you up in the middle of the night like a weirdo," she laughed.

Annie laughed too, remembering the mix of joy and anger that had filled her, waking up to find that Malik had returned, that he was watching her sleep in the dark of her bedroom. "So we talked about the way the sea would pull him, and I told him I didn't want him to resent me, but that I also didn't want to wake up one day and just find him gone. He said we had to burn the pelt, and that getting rid of it entirely was the only way to stop it from calling to him." As she spoke of the way the pelt would call a selkie to the sea, Annie herself could almost feel the waves of the ocean washing gently over her skin. She shivered, closing her eyes as she took a steadying breath.

Brenna watched her, rubbing lightly along the length of Lugus's back. He flipped over in her lap, nearly toppling onto the floor in his effort to expose his belly. She laughed, raising her eyes again to meet Annie's gaze. "So you burned it. You two really burned the pelt."

"We did," Annie nodded. "We went down the coast a little way, had a picnic. It was very romantic, his choosing to stay with me that way. But then, at the same time, I could almost feel the sadness on him, it was so strong. He was giving up his life, you know, and the choice to burn the pelt wasn't easy for him. We sat there in front of the fire and I could see the conflict in his thoughts, almost like I could reach out and touch his tension."

"I'm sure it was very hard for him to do that," Brenna said quietly. "If he was living in the water then, being a selkie was obviously a big part of who he was. I've read that some selkies live on land as humans, but I'm sure burning the pelt is a big decision. There's probably not any going back from that, is there?"

"Sometimes there is, but with him feeling like that, I couldn't tell him about the pregnancy. Not like that, you know? I didn't want to be a noose around his neck; I didn't want him to feel trapped with me for the sake of our child. But he chose on his own, without even knowing about the baby. He chose me; he chose us," Annie continued, her hands covering her stomach lightly as she spoke, "And after we ate, he threw the pelt into the fire."

At this, Annie felt the first physical awareness of the baby in her womb, a sort of momentary flicker, there and then suddenly gone.

Chosen ... Annie smiled as the word slipped through her mind, her heart swelling with the memory. In her first marriage, her husband had chosen to betray her; having Malik choose to be with her in such a dramatic way validated her as a woman, in a way that she hadn't even known she'd needed.

"And then what?" Brenna asked, breaking the spell of the moment.

"There was this huge storm, which was so odd because we'd checked the weather before going out there. But it came on really suddenly, and the sky just opened up. Thunder, lightning, the works. We went running back to my car in the rain, but we didn't notice we'd lost the car keys 'til we got there. So we're sitting in the car, half naked and soaked and –"

"Uh huh. Half naked, huh?" Brenna asked, smirking.

Annie ducked her face, embarrassment coloring her skin as she struggled to maintain a serious expression. "Anyway, by then the storm was really raging, so Malik offered to go find the keys while I waited in the car. He found them pretty quick and he'd turned back to hold them up so I could see. And Brenna, I hope I never see anything like that ever again."

"Don't even tell me –"

"He was struck by lightning," Annie broke in.

"You've got to be kidding me!" Brenna said, her eyes widening in horror.

"Nope, it fried his one arm, the one he'd been holding the keys up with. Burned him really bad; he hit the ground hard. It was horrible, the most horrible thing I'd ever seen. I think I'd rather have to catch Chase cheating again than have to see that."

"I don't blame you," Brenna said quietly. "What happened next?"

"After that, everything's kind of a blur really. But I remember running to him and I was just soaked, water in my eyes, my hair flying everywhere. And it was that kind of storm that's scary, where the rain's so cold and the ocean's crazy, waves crashing everywhere."

"And you, unable to swim," Brenna said. "I bet that was scary."

"Yeah, especially because I couldn't just leave his body there. And we hadn't brought any phone with us, and everything was so loud. There were tons of these giant heavy waves, just rolling in and out constantly. It was so loud, Brenna, and the top of the water was almost totally white with foam."

Brenna smiled. "I love storms like that."

"Not me!" Annie said, shaking her head, her eyes wide with the memory of that horrible experience. "But I don't remember much after that other than being angry. I was so angry, and I was like, trying to drag his body back to the water. I think I was a little crazy for a while. I got caught up in the undertow, I think. After that I don't really remember anything other than being scared. Grieving."

"You really thought he was dead?"

"I thought he was," Annie answered. "I couldn't find any pulse, couldn't feel any breath. We hadn't brought any cell phones or anything with us, and I just remember feeling like my chest was being ripped open with the shock of it. I thought he was dead," she finished, her eyes filling with tears as she remembered that horrible night.

"But he wasn't. He came here."

"No, he was just stunned by the lightning, he said. He says selkies are immortal," Annie said, lowering her eyes. She wasn't quite ready to share her own immortality yet.

"Mmhmm," Brenna answered, lowering her own eyes, tilting her head thoughtfully. "I've always wondered how long it would take me to become filthy rich. You know, if I were immortal. I think it'd be cool to have infinite savings, or like, really old investments. You know, like vampires do?"

Annie laughed. "It's not quite like that with the selkies, I think."

"You've met some? More than Malik, I mean?" Brenna perked up, sitting straighter in her seat as her fingers wandered through Lugus's fur.

Annie nodded. "Some of his family members actually found us, from what I'd been told. Malik said they brought us back to where they live. And that's where I woke up, in a little bed in a little cave room."

"A cave?"

"Yeah, the room I was in is where his aunt and uncle live. They have this maze of underwater caves right off the harbor that the clan lives in together."

"The clan?" Brenna asked, her voice wary. "There's a clan?"

"Yeah. I think of it as sort of like old Celtic legend meets our perception of the old Native Americans," Annie laughed. "They even have sort of a shaman."

"Hmm. Uh huh. Okay," Brenna said, taking in everything Annie said. Her eyes were wide, her face pale with surprise.

"It's a lot to take in, huh?" Annie asked. "Want me to stop there? Because after that it only gets crazier."

"Please, Annie, I'm Irish," Brenna laughed, waving a hand through the air to disguise her obvious discomfort. "Myths and legends come alive? That's my world. Tell me the rest," she finished, bringing her knees up to her chest and wrapping her arms around her legs. Lugus grumbled, settling deeper into the groove between Brenna's body and the side of the chair.

"Okay, but this is the part where it gets weird," Annie said, her eyebrows lowering as she watched Brenna. "Are you sure you're okay?"

Brenna wriggled her shoulders, settling her arms more comfortably. "Yeah, I'm as ready as I'm likely to get," she said.

Annie nodded, unconvinced. "Okay, so they live together in the caves, like I said. The clan is their family unit, but I don't know how many generations there are. There are some young ones, kids, you know, but most of the ones I saw looked like they're our age, maybe older. None of them look very old, though I did meet some that are very old."

"Like how old?" Brenna asked, perking up slightly.

"Well, I met some of the young guys, and I thought they were really young. But then Malik said they're like seventy-five."

"Hmm, that's impressive. They don't look it?"

Annie twisted in her seat, curling her legs underneath her body and stuffing a throw pillow behind her back as she brought Bryce and Finnigan's faces to her mind. "No, I thought they were in their twenties."

"That's cool though, right? To be that old and not look it? That must be awesome for the women," Brenna laughed, running her fingers through her cloud of red hair. "I hope I still look young when I'm not anymore. Tell me more about the clan."

"From what I can tell, I think clans are mostly like the way we think of the Native Americans. They're the same in a lot of ways, like the different tribes of Native Americans. They have their allies and their rivals, groups that work together and groups that don't. I think each clan has their own council, like their government. Kind of the same way that separate Native American tribes had their own tribal governments."

"Okay," Brenna said, her brow furrowed as she listened. "So there's a lot of them, then?"

"Oh yeah, from what I hear. And the shaman guy, his name's Tiernan. And he's like some kind of prophet or something. He has this giant book of his visions, and they check them all the time to see if they come true or not."

"And do they come true?" Brenna asked.

"Always," Annie said, widening her eyes dramatically. "That's the part that's gonna creep you out."

"Oh wow," Brenna said wryly. "After all this, with the pregnancy and the dead Malik and the selkie clans and the shaman, now you're going to creep me out?"

"Well when you put it that way …"

"I was kidding, I was kidding! Go on," Brenna answered, laughing.

"I'm in the book. Tiernan's book," Annie said, flinching slightly as she felt the baby twitch again. "Well, the baby is in the book. This baby is foretold, I guess. The whole human mother situation has been in Tiernan's book for decades or something."

"It is?"

Annie nodded, turning her arm over and showing the fine scar that crossed her wrist. The slice from the blood exchange had healed within a few days, but the scar was there, slightly raised as it circled the underside of her wrist. "And there's more," she said.

"More than an immortal selkie child that was prophesied however many years ago to be born to the very first human mother ever?"

"Did you ever read anything about humans turning into selkies, Brenna?"

"I've heard before that sometimes selkies would take human prisoners into the water, but never specifically that the humans were changed. I guess I just always thought they kept the humans prisoner or maybe killed them or something. What are you saying, Annie?" Brenna asked, a hint of suspicion in her voice.

Annie waited silently, giving Brenna time to think and process what she was being told. Brenna's blue eyes met Annie's sparkling green, awareness dawning in her face. "Are you one of them?" she whispered. "Can that even happen?"

A jet of fear pierced Annie as Brenna's eyes lowered again, making her wonder if she'd made a mistake. She'd trusted Brenna, believed in their friendship; but she'd been betrayed before. Would Brenna now turn on her, too afraid to accept Annie's new existence?

"I am," Annie whispered, feeling her shoulders tense protectively. Her womb tightened, cradling the child within.

"Holy shit." Brenna whispered, her eyes darting around the living room. "Holy shit."

"Brenna?" Annie asked, leaning forward slightly.

"I have a selkie woman in my house. An immortal. A pregnant immortal. A prophesied, pregnant human-selkie woman?" Brenna spoke slowly, as if the act of forcing the words to flow from her lips and into the room would make them sound more possible.

"Yes. To all of that, apparently." Annie waited, watching Brenna's eyes cloud as she faded into her thoughts. She whispered something to herself and then she was there again, her eyes clear and her face calm.

"Tell me more about the prophesies, Annie," Brenna said. "What do they say, exactly?"

"There will be a war among the selkie clans," Annie said quietly, knowing that this was the part where she had to trust someone again, the part where she had to count on a friend.

"Over what?" Brenna asked.

"My baby," Annie said. "Apparently, the baby will grow up and somehow bring the clans together. There are other clans who wouldn't want that happening, who like things just fine as they are. Tiernan says they'll want to kill me, or kill the baby to stop the prophecies from coming about. And so now –"

"It's all about protection now," Brenna broke in, straightening her shoulders. Her face hardened; she sat up taller in her chair, her blue eyes turning to ice. "Are there other clans after you already?"

"I don't know," Annie said, fear taking hold in the pit of her stomach as she watched Brenna lose her softness, becoming harder, colder, more fierce than she'd been before. "But Malik says I need to be watchful."

"Well, you certainly aren't the most boring friend I've ever had," Brenna said. "But I'm an easygoing kind of girl. Is there anything I can do to help protect you or the baby?"

"Just like that?" Annie asked, her tension draining away as confusion took over her emotions. "You just believe me? Just like that?"

Brenna laughed, her fierceness falling away again to reveal the softer Brenna, though she remained somewhat more stiff than she had been before. "Well you're my friend Annie, and that's your child we're talking about. I can't ever be 'Auntie Brenna' if someone comes along and kills the baby, can I? Besides, I told you I was steeped in Celtic tradition. I grew up believing in faeries and everything. This isn't that much of a stretch for me, I guess."

"You guess?"

Brenna sighed, her eyes wandering over to the photos of her late husband on the wall. "You know," she said, "When I lost Tommy, that was probably the hardest time in my life. Maybe even harder than when my mom died, because by the time Tommy was gone, I was a little older, a little wiser. I knew what death was and by then, I knew how long forever could really be."

"Well you're taking all of this a lot easier than I did," Annie said dryly. "When I was sure about what Malik was ... that day that I finally decided to confront him? I thought for sure he'd have me locked up and it'd be all over the news, you know? 'Crazy author locked up, insane, trapped in a fantastic delusion.' And waking up in the caves with his family there, and they were arguing for him to turn me, and –"

"They argued?" Brenna asked.

"Yeah. Malik says it has never been known to work before, but his aunt was saying that it was the only way to be sure I wouldn't die or lose the baby," Annie explained.

"How does it work?"

Annie held her wrist out again, turning it over to run the finger of her other hand over the scar. "I'm not really sure," she said softly. "He said we're handfast now. And there was a blood vow kind of thing. He cut me, licked the blood." Annie's mouth went dry at the memory, her nose wrinkling slightly as her tongue remembered the rusty warm taste of Malik's blood. "He cut himself too, and he held his wrist to my mouth; I had to swallow it. Then he strapped our wrists together. I got tingly there, where the cuts were pressed together, and then it got more and more tingly, up my arm, all over me. Sort of like being numb but at the same time I was in pain all over. The way pins and needles are if your foot goes to sleep, but worse. And it was everywhere. Later, I itched all over -- like my skin was crawling or something."

"And you're selkie now?"

Annie nodded. "Pelt and all."

Brenna laughed, the sound of her giggles ringing through the room as Annie watched, confused. Finally, Brenna wiped the moisture from her eyes and straightened in her seat. "Well," she said, her lips still twitching with suppressed laughter. "I guess you've finally learned to swim then, huh?"

***

"How were things with Brenna?" Malik asked nervously that night, as they sat together for dinner. They were sitting on a bench by the Bar Harbor pier, sharing a sandwich-and-chips picnic.

"It was good, better than I expected," Annie answered. "Honestly, I'm a little surprised by how well she took things. I think I surprised her a few times though."

"And she didn't maybe, um, add … anything? To the conversation?" He kept his eyes focused on the water as he asked this new question. Annie watched him, her eyebrows rising in suspicion.

"What would she have added?" she asked.

"Annie, let me ask you something. Where are Brenna's parents?"

Annie settled back on the bench, letting her sandwich rest on her thigh. "Her father is still in Ireland, I think. But I know her mother is dead."

"How did she die?" Malik asked, not noticing Annie's growing anxiety.

"I don't know, Malik," she said. "It's not a happy topic, so I never really asked her a lot about her mom."

"I can tell you what happened to her, because my family knew her. Tiernan knew her," Malik said, his hand darting forward to catch Annie's sandwich as her sudden jolt sent it sliding from her lap. Her eyes flew to his, her mouth forming an 'o' of surprise.

"Brenna's mother? How would Tiernan know Brenna's mother?" Annie asked, tilting her head as she narrowed her eyes at Malik.

"When clan Killian was still living off the coasts of Ireland years ago, Aislynn left the clan. She'd met a human and wanted to stay with him instead of leaving Ireland with the clan. She left the caves, and we never saw her again. I never knew her myself, but my mother had known her for a while."

"Aislynn?"

"Brenna's mother," Malik said, nodding. "They say Tiernan took it hard when she left; he aged a good deal in the months after she was gone, and they never heard from her again."

"What does this have to do with Tiernan?" Annie asked.

"Aislynn was his betrothed."

"She left him?" Annie asked.

"She left him," Malik answered. "Tiernan is our prophet, our healer. She was a seer, and as his wife, her responsibilities would have been very heavy on her shoulders. They would have been the most powerful visionary team among our people, but many think she couldn't take the pressure. So she left."

"And he's still alone?" Annie asked.

"He has a strong soul. But like I said, it did age him for a while."

"Is she a selkie, too? Brenna?"

"Most likely. Sometimes a selkie child is born to a selkie woman, sometimes a human child, if the father is human."

"Would she know?" Annie asked.

"How do you think she knew about me?" Malik laughed, leaning over to nudge her with his elbow. "Her heart recognized her blood. If she is a selkie, we are of the same clan. We are family. I don't know how she knows though, or whether her mother told her much about us. But yeah, she knows."

"She would be on our side then, a member of our clan." She spoke definitively, but Malik heard the question in her words.

"She would. She loves you as a human friend, and she would love you as a selkie clan member. She will help protect our child, Annie. It is part of why the clan leaders allowed us to come back up here at such an unsure time. We need all the allies we can get, and if she has her mother's powers ..."

"That would be very helpful." Annie said, watching as Malik nodded silently. Turning her face to the water, she took her sandwich and bit off a piece, chewing quietly and swallowing before she spoke again. "What about your dad? How did the visit go with him?"

Malik nodded, allowing her to change the subject to something more comfortable. "He's fine. He's angry with me for not telling him our plans, but he forgives easily. Then again," he continued, laughing quietly as he twisted the cap from a bottle of water, "He has to forgive me; he's my father."

"Did you tell him about the baby?"

At this, Malik threw back his head, laughing. "Well, of course I told him I'm about to be a father, my love. He says he can't wait to watch us parent our child together, and that if we go away again without telling him first, he'll kill us for taking his grandchild."

"Oh I see," Annie said, laughing at the idea of the little old man being stirred to violent anger. "And what else?"

"And I told him you took the change safely, that you're selkie now, like me. I told him that we're handfast."

"And what did he say to that?" Annie asked.

"He said it's a good thing I did it before he could," Malik laughed, throwing his arm over the back of the bench and pulling Annie close to him. He pressed a kiss to her forehead, tucking her into the curve of his shoulder with one hand as his other slipped around to cup the slight curve of Annie's lower stomach. "It seems like everywhere I turn, someone wants to steal my woman from me!"

"Well, we've had that talk, remember? I think you're safe from woman-thieves. At least for now," she said, laughing. "What else did your dad say?"

"He also says he's here if we need him. Either of us. For anything. This child will not go unprotected, and neither will you." He grew serious as he spoke, his voice lowering as Annie's face rose to meet his. "My life is attached to yours now, Annie; we are bound together until the end of time, and I will let no harm come to you. I would give my life for yours, protect your body with my own. All that I am is yours; all I have is yours. Always."

"Well I love you too, Malik," Annie whispered, her breath hitching as she sighed. "But really, are you sure we're going to be okay? Are the prophecies really so terrible?"

"They are," he answered. "But you don't have to be afraid. I know that any member of the clan would give their lives for you, for this child, for what the baby represents to our people. I will give my all to protect my family, but should I not be enough, there are many more behind me."

"Wow, I have legions," Annie said dryly. "But I don't want all that. I just want to know it'll be okay."

"I can't promise that. There will be war, Annie. I won't lie and candy-coat it; it will be a fearsome time and there will be many clans that will die out entirely, wiped out by the rage and fear of change and the iron swords of unrest. But clan Killian will live on. The prophesies promise that the clan will survive, to seek peace under the leadership of our child. And no matter what happens, I promise that you will be safe. Our child will be safe."

Annie rested her head under the shelf of Malik's chin, safe in his arms, her child still safe in her womb. And she tried to ignore the fact that he hadn't promised not to die in the war, or to be there for her afterward.

***

The next morning rose with rapid banging on the front door of Annie's house, ripping her from a sound sleep. Her eyes opened to find Malik already awake, donning his shorts in the middle of the room. "Get under the bed," he commanded, his voice still raspy with sleep. "Wait there until I call for you, and don't come out until then." And with that, he was gone.

Annie's breath caught; she wanted to call him back to her, to cling to him. She had no weapons, no knowledge of how to protect herself from selkie warriors. *How could they have found her so quickly?* But that didn't matter now, all that mattered was protecting her child. She scooted to the edge of the bed, dropping off the side of the mattress with a slight thump, lowering into a crouch and rolling herself into the space under the bed, careful to arrange herself in the middle to avoid notice.

She waited, desperately trying to keep her breathing calm as she thought of Malik, alone in the house without a weapon. *"Was he an able fighter? What would he do?"* She didn't know; she'd never seen him fight before. She'd only ever seen him angry once, and even then, she'd never seen any threat of violence in him. Voices sounded in the living room, the different tones of several men speaking. They were all calm, though. Perhaps all was well, then.

"Annie!" Malik called. "Come on out, we have company!"

Heaving a sigh, Annie lay still under the bed, gathering her courage. Her eyes filled with tears of relief, but she blinked them away – there was no time to fall apart. "I'm coming!" she called back. Slithering out from under the bed, she reached for a robe hanging by the door and shoved her arms into the sleeves, pulling the fabric close around her body and cinching the fabric belt. She ran her fingertips through her hair and sighed again, a deep cleansing breath that loosened her chest relaxed her tense shoulders. "Okay, here we go, then," she muttered as she started down the hall, surprised when she reached the kitchen to find Angus standing there. Tiernan stood by his side, nodding quietly to Annie as she entered the room.

They were out of place in her warm New England kitchen; Angus's tall frame seemed to fill the space completely, his broad shoulders and long dark hair bringing an element of fury into her peaceful home. Beside him stood the wiry shaman, his muscular body compact while still obviously powerful. His dreadlocks had been tamed, pulled back and tied with a strip of leather, the kinked hairs of his goatee emphasizing the delicately beautiful structure of his smooth, dark face. Tiernan looked odd without the shimmering mystique that surrounded him in the caves, dressed in regular clothes and without the sheen of oil. Fear widened his black eyes, and the tension of his body brought a heavy feeling to Annie's heart.

"Someone knows, don't they?" she asked, her hands going immediately to cradle her stomach, as if to protect the life held within. "Someone knows about my baby."

Tiernan nodded, looking to Angus before speaking. "The word has reached us. You are no longer a secret, and the enemy clans will be coming. It is best you stay here for some time. Avoid the caves. We will send men for you when it is time to come home to the clan, when you are no longer safer here. In my visions, I have seen war. Those old visions rise up fresh and now it surrounds us; the war surrounds us, it fills us. The time is coming."

"Will we prevail?" Malik asked, one eyebrow quirking higher than the other as he tilted his head toward Tiernan. "Will my child survive?"

"Whatever the visions, we will prevail," Angus said, determination lowering his voice to a hard growl as he answered before Tiernan could speak. "We protect what is ours. And in preserving the child, we protect the future of the clans, the peace of our people. If many lives are lost, the child will not be one of them."

From behind Angus, Tiernan gasped. Every face turned in his direction; every eye watched as his hand rose, shaking slightly. His elegant fingers closed around a picture frame propped under the kitchen window.

"Aislynn," he said softly, smiling gently down at the photo in his hands. His eyes darted to Annie and then back to the photo again. He held it out to her, questioning.

"That is her daughter," Malik said, stepping closer to touch Brenna's face in the photo, close beside Annie's, their eyes bright, their faces laughing. "Her name is Brenna."

"She is like us, isn't she?" Angus asked, his expression horrified as he watched Tiernan.

"She is one of us," Tiernan said, nodding. "You must protect her as family, Malik. She is family. She is clan Killian blood." As he spoke, his fingers slipped softly over the surface of the glass as if to stroke the softness of Brenna's cheek. He closed his eyes, shaking his head slightly as he replaced the frame on the windowsill. "Brenna."

"Would – would you like to – maybe meet her?" Annie asked.

"After. I should like to meet her after," Tiernan said, turning to pat Annie's face lightly with the flat of his palm, the lightness of his palm contrasting with the coffee color of his skin. In the caves, he'd always shined with oil, shimmering like polished bronze in the light of the fires. In the morning sun, shining in through the kitchen window, his skin was darker and less luminescent without the oil, like strong coffee laced with the slightest drop of cream. Exchanging a silent glance with Angus, Tiernan cleared his throat and turned his face to the window. Angus nodded, closing his eyes silently for a few seconds before turning to Malik.

"We have to get going, Nephew," he said, clapping his hand down on Malik's shoulder. "We are needed in the caves, to prepare. But --"

"You needn't worry, Angus." Malik replied. "I will watch over them. Both of them. They are my family, my life. And no clan, no battle, no war will take them from me."

"And Brenna?" Angus asked.

"She will be guarded as well," Malik promised. "I'll find a way to get her here."

Angus nodded again, his conflicted thoughts warring on his face. Finally, he turned to go, Tiernan walking silently behind. Annie and Malik saw the leaders of their clan out the door, and then Malik went to the kitchen to start breakfast while Annie went to get dressed. "What the heck do we do now?" Annie muttered, standing alone in front of the full-length mirror in the bathroom.

Brenna …

"Yeah, I know, right?" Annie answered without thinking, turning from the mirror to step into a pair of jeans. "I still can't believe she's a selkie. I mean, she's been a selkie all this time? I can't even get my head wrapped around that. This whole thing is just insane, and even though Malik told me, having Tiernan react like --"

Brenna …

"I really need to just go over and talk to her. I can't believe she didn't come clean with me yesterday, you know? Maybe she doesn't trust me?" Annie asked quietly, unsure whether she was talking to her child or herself as she slipped her feet into a pair of yellow sandals.

Trouble …

"You're right, baby. She is gonna be in huge trouble. How could she not tell me about this? Especially after I told her everything?"

Trouble. Now.

"Big trouble," Annie answered, her temper heating as she tugged her fingers through her hair. "I really think I'm going over there. I just can't believe she didn't tell me."

"Annie?" Malik asked, tapping from the other side of the bathroom door. "I think you should come out here. I need to talk to you."

"Everything okay?" she asked, yanking her yellow-and-white-striped tank top over her head.

"Not really," he answered, his voice muffled through the door. "Doyle just called, and he says Brenna's in trouble. He's been down the street from her house since last night, keeping an eye on her. He says two members of clan Conway are sitting outside her house, too, in a car across the street. They just pulled in an hour ago, and he says they're watching her house. He thought they weren't there for her, but them he recognized one of them."

"Is she okay?" Annie asked, whipping the bathroom door open and stepping out into the hall, her eyes narrowed. She followed Malik to the living room, where her shoes were already waiting.

"Doyle says she's okay right now, and he's still watching. But we should go get her and see if she'll stay here with us. If we're all in one place, it'll be easier for Doyle and me to keep everyone safe. Do you think she'll come?"

"I guess that depends on whether or not she's ready to tell me the truth," Annie said quietly, her anger dissipating, leaving only hurt behind. She'd trusted again; she'd given Brenna the whole story. Why hadn't Brenna told her? And what would she say when she knew that Annie knew the truth? Turning to Malik, Annie scooped her keys up from the entry table and said, "But I'm going by myself. Brenna and I have to clear some things up between us."

"Annie, you really shouldn't be over there alone with members of an enemy clan nearby. They're already watching Brenna, and you going over there alone is asking for trouble."

Stepping forward, her eyes flaring with anger, Annie poked her finger at Malik's chest. "I'm going. And you're not. I'm already hurt that Brenna didn't come clean with me, and I'm angry that you had to tell me things she should have said. So I'm going, and heaven help anyone who gets in my way. I'm a grown woman, Malik. I've survived drowning, I've survived a change no one else has lived through, I'm pissed off and I'm immortal. What more protection do I need right now?"

Stepping back, Malik crossed his arms over his chest. "Damn stubborn woman," he muttered.

***

"Annie?" Brenna asked, opening the door to the lighthouse with one hand while struggling with the other to hold her damp curls back from her face. "I, uh, just got home from walking the path out back. Not that you aren't welcome here, but … what're you doing here? Should you be running around alone out there? I thought you said Malik's clan had enemies that might come for you and the baby?"

"Brenna," Annie said warningly, her head held high, her green eyes flaming. "You know about how my marriage ended with Chase. And you know that he betrayed me with someone who was supposed to be my best friend. She didn't have the guts to tell me what was going on, even when I'd been telling her that I suspected him. She didn't tell me the truth even when I'd been crying over it on her shoulder. And I don't need another friend like that right now. So tell me, is there something you'd like to talk to me about?" As she spoke, Lugus cowered behind Brenna quietly, whining slightly.

Sighing, Brenna looked around the yard, her eyes narrowing slightly as she took in the blue car parked on the side of the street. "Maybe there is. You'd better come on in," she said, backing away from the door to make room for Annie.

Annie followed Brenna through the lighthouse and down the hallway to the bathroom, Lugus's claws clicking softly along the floor as they walked. In the bathroom, Brenna moved to pull a little bench away from the wall. The room was the same as before, with the little shelves floating above the bench, heavily laden with bottles of nail polish. But with the bench moved away from the wall, Annie was able to notice the silver grate attached to the wall behind the bench.

Closing her eyes, Brenna licked her lips and lifted the grate easily away from the wall, edging Lugus out of the way and reaching into the opened hole to pull out ...

"My pelt," she said, turning and flicking her wrists, snapping the pelt open so that it flowed from her hands and down to the floor. Lugus yipped softly, sitting near the door of the bathroom, his body tense and shivering.

Watching the dog's strange behavior, Annie whispered, "Brenna, why didn't you tell me? I told you everything yesterday. Everything."

"Annie, this isn't something we just tell everyone," Brenna said quietly. "Even Malik, he only told you because you knew."

"Yeah," Annie retorted, crossing her arms over her chest, her heart aching from Brenna's secrecy even as her mind understood the reasoning. "Because *you* told me."

"Annie, don't do this. Especially not now. I could give you a hundred reasons for not telling you, but none of them will make it any better. But you couldn't know what a huge thing this is to share with anyone. So I'll leave it with this: I'm sorry, Annie. I know it's a big thing, and I'm sorry. I didn't keep it from you to hurt you or because I don't trust you. I just keep that to myself because I've never told anyone. I never told Tommy either," she finished with a shrug. "I just sort of made it a point to go on water retreats as often as possible."

"So that you wouldn't age as quickly, or because the water calls you?" Annie asked, curiosity covering her anger.

"Both."

"What would you have done if he'd lasted long enough to die of old age?" Annie asked, reaching out to stroke the top of Lugus's head as he ventured into the bathroom again, passing Annie to sit beside Brenna's feet.

"I have no idea. I'd probably have died along with him. I'm still fairly young now, but losing him nearly killed me."

"Hmm," Annie said. "And how old are you?"

Brenna sighed, pursing her lips in thought before she answered. "I'm fifty-seven."

Annie's mouth fell open. "Wow, you're hot for fifty-seven!" she laughed, the sound bringing Lugus to his feet again. He yipped softly, sniffing the edge of the pelt still flowing through Brenna's hands as Annie said, "But I'm still mad that you didn't tell me. No more secrets."

"I know, and you have a right to be. I really am sorry. Forgive me?" Brenna asked, dropping the pelt so that it hung limply from one hand, stepping forward to place her empty hand loosely on Annie's forearm.

"For now, at least," Annie answered, finally remembering the original purpose of her visit. "Right now we have other things to deal with."

Brenna stiffened, her face hardening, the change in demeanor causing Lugus to back away again. "I know," she said. "I saw them out there; they've been there all morning. But I saw them in a dream last night; I think they're from clan Conway." She dropped her pelt to the floor and reached for the top of the toilet tank. Lifting the cover, she withdrew a dagger from within, replacing the lid on the toilet and turning to Annie as she said, "And they're here because they know about our friendship. They've come to see if I'm willing to sell you out, to trade you for them and help them kill you to stop the prophecies."

Annie swallowed nervously, dragging her eyes away from the gleaming dagger to meet Brenna's fierce blue gaze. She'd just explained everything to Brenna the day before, and suddenly the enemies were upon her. *"Is there a connection? There can't be ..."* Taking a breath and steeling herself to run, hoping Lugus wouldn't trip her, she said, "Well, if you haven't done anything yet, I have to assume that they've wasted their time in coming here, that our friendship has come to mean something to you, and that you, as a member of clan Killian, wouldn't want an end to a prophesy that promises peace for our people. Brenna —"

Brenna laughed. "Let it rest, Annie. I'm not trading that baby for anything. My mother didn't tell me anything about the selkies until just before she died, but she did tell me some things once we knew she was dying. She told me enough to instill clan loyalty, at least. And as my mother's daughter, as the direct descendant of a clan Killian warrior, there's no force on this earth or under the sea that will take or harm that child while I'm around."

Annie gulped, her heart swelling in relief, the baby twitching in her womb.

Brenna ...

"And there's another reason I didn't tell you about this," Brenna said, waving her hand toward Annie's stomach as if to indicate the baby – as if she'd heard the baby. "I saw how much you loved Malik, and I knew from the beginning what he was. But I needed to see how you'd react to him, and how he'd react to your knowledge. If you knowing about him destroyed the relationship, you'd have needed my support. Especially with the baby coming. The prophecy stands, whether you'd stayed together or not."

"Well, I suppose you're right about that ..." Annie muttered. "I did fall for him pretty fast, huh? But you said --"

Brenna nodded, tucking her dagger into a sheath from the bathroom drawer and smoothing the leg of her jeans before strapping the blade to her thigh, the hilt just within reach of her hand. "I knew about the baby too, even before you did. I could hear her, and I knew about her from the first time I heard her. My mother said once that a child is my destiny. She used to tell me someday I'd be given a purpose, a fight to win," Brenna said. "I never understood her, but I do now; I know what she meant. And I have for a while." Finished with the knife harness on her thigh, she stood, taking in Annie's expression of shock.

"Her??" Annie asked, her green eyes widening, flaring in surprise. "It's a her? The baby's a girl?"

Brenna smiled, catching her bottom lip between her teeth. Nodding her head slightly, she said, "It's funny what we want to know, isn't it? But yeah, the baby's a girl."

"How do you know that? And how can you be sure my baby is your fight? And you said you knew about the guys outside?" Annie asked, her hands covering her stomach, her eyes dropping in wonder even as terror filled her mind. A daughter. She would have a daughter. And there were enemies already coming for her.

"If you know about me, you probably already know that my mother was a seer with the clan," Brenna answered, shrugging her shoulders dismissively. "She was one of the only ones in the entire selkie population, from what I was told. And she passed her gift to me. Truth be told, Annie, I knew before Tommy left on that last trip that he wouldn't come back alive. I begged him not to go to Cambodia, but he said he couldn't abandon his calling. And I couldn't tell him what I knew. And I knew about Malik from the beginning … I saw him rescue you before he'd done it. I knew him through my visions; that's why I never freaked out about some strange guy staying with you."

"Oh, Brenna," Annie whispered, stepping forward just as Brenna stiffened, her eyes on the window that faced out behind the lighthouse. "You've —" her voice was cut off by a sudden burst of barking from Lugus.

"They're coming," Brenna said, her words fast and frantic. "Come on, let's go. Lugus!" she commanded, quickly dropping to the floor to shove the grate back into the wall, pressing the bench back into place. Annie gathered Brenna's pelt, clutching it tightly to her chest as if to protect her baby with it, as if the mystical power of the selkie pelt could save them.

"What do we do?" she asked.

"The closet. Open the closet," Brenna said, stepping back to check that the bathroom was neat and tidy. Lugus came bounding back into the room as Annie opened the closet and Brenna stepped inside, pressing the false back away from the wall to reveal a steep, dark staircase. "Get in, and go as fast as you can," she commanded, snapping her fingers toward the dog and then pointing toward the stairs.

Lugus rushed forward, obviously having done this many times. Annie took a deep breath and followed him into the dark, shoving the pelt across her middle to rest in a bundle under one arm. She used the other to feel her way along the wall, cautiously working her way down the stairs. A click sounded softly behind her, and then Brenna was there.

"They'll find it eventually," she whispered, "But they're both in the house looking for us, and I think that'll give us a break. At the end of this, there's a door; we can get out into the yard and take your car, but you have to be quick. Ready to run?"

Annie nodded, remembering that Brenna likely couldn't see her in the dark of the tunnel. "Yeah, I'm ready. I think I am, anyway," she whispered.

"Okay. We won't have a lot of time if they notice us, so keep following with me," Brenna said, stepping around Annie, each of them struggling to maintain their balance as Lugus worked his way back and forth between them. Annie followed Brenna through the tunnel, curving slightly as they worked their way under the lighthouse. Finally, Brenna held a hand out, pressing slightly against Annie's stomach to stop her. "The door is here. How fast a runner are you?" she asked.

"I was a track runner when I was young, but Malik was outdoing me that night on the beach. The night we burned his pelt," Annie answered, her skin tingling with fear. This was a side of Brenna she'd never seen, and she couldn't deny the niggling fear that maybe she'd trusted the wrong person – again. Still, she had no choice now, and her heart told her that Brenna was on her side.

"Okay, that should do," Brenna said, "And I think you'll likely be faster now with selkie blood. When I say 'run,' you run. As fast as you can, no stopping for anything. Not me, not Lugus. Not anything. Just run. I don't know if they'll still be in the house or not, so just go straight to your car, get in and start it. And get home to Malik, whether I make it to the car or not. You got me?"

Again, Annie nodded, forgetting again that she couldn't be seen in the dark. "Yeah, I got it. But you're coming, right?"

Brenna chuckled softly. "Yeah. If I get there first, I'm driving. And I'll bet my mortgage that Lugus and I beat you and the baby to the car, ten to one. But just in case, Annie, move fast. You ready?"

"Yeah," Annie said, digging her keys out of her pocket and feeling for the car key in the dark. She pressed it into Brenna's hand. "You have to come with me; you've got the keys."

"Alright, get ready, Annie," Brenna whispered, her hand on the door handle, Lugus shivering at her feet.

"I'm ready."

"Okay," The door flew open, burning Annie's eyes with the sudden blast of bright sun. "Run!"

Brenna and Lugus shot through the door and into the daylight, bursting toward Annie's car with amazing speed. Annie was right behind them, and they reached the car together. Brenna opened the driver's door, standing back for the half-second it took for Lugus to launch himself into the backseat. By the time Brenna dropped into the car and closed the door, Annie was already seated beside her, her eyes wide with fear, her breath coming in short gasps.

"You're gonna want a seat belt," Brenna suggested, turning the ignition of the car as two burly men ran through the open front door of the lighthouse. Tires squealed, the rear end of the car spinning around as Brenna backed out of the driveway, kicking the car into drive.

"Brenna!" Annie shouted, bracing herself against the door of the car as they sped down the road, sliding around a corner.

"They can't follow if they can't catch up in time," Brenna muttered, her eyes focused on the street in the front of them, the heel of her hand pressing the horn as they sped around another corner.

"Oh, God, I'm gonna die. Again," Annie mumbled, closing her eyes against the sights flying past her window.

***

"Back already?" Malik asked, looking up from the table as Annie and Brenna rushed through the door. Lugus was calm for once, padding quietly into the kitchen and settling in a heap next to the coolness of the oven door.

"Yeah, there were some guys at my house," Brenna answered. "Not really the friendly types, either. Apparently not fond of knocking."

"I know, that's what Annie was there for. To get you and bring you here," he answered.

Brenna turned to meet Annie's eyes; Annie shrugged, lowering her eyes to avoid Malik's steady gaze. "We didn't get that far before they were breaking into the house. We kind of had to escape."

"Were you followed?" Malik asked, stiffening in his seat. His eyes flickered to the door before moving back to Brenna's face.

"No, I don't think so. I dreamed they were coming, so they weren't as much of a surprise as they wanted to be."

"Men from clan Conway, most likely. But if you're here," he said, gesturing to Brenna with a raised eyebrow, "I take it you two had time to talk some, though. Are we all fully informed of where we stand, then?" he asked, pushing away the magazine he'd been reading, his eyes flickering over to the door again.

"Yes, we talked," Annie laughed, sweeping her fingers through his hair as she walked behind him. Moving to the sink, she opened the cupboard and removed two glasses, turning to raise a questioning eyebrow at Brenna.

"Just water please," Brenna said, moving to the back door, her eyes scanning the back yard. Annie nodded, heading to the refrigerator to fill the glasses with water before carrying them back to place them on the table.

"Okay, so we're all clear about everything?" Malik asked, tracing the upper rim of his glass with his fingertip. He looked to the door again, and Brenna raised an eyebrow at him.

"Yeah, she knows about me now," Brenna said, nodding as she sank into a chair across from Malik. "You waiting for someone else to appear?"

"My cousin Doyle was watching your house; I kind of thought if anything happened, he'd be coming here, too."

"I didn't see anyone else," Brenna said, shaking her head slightly. "Maybe he'll come soon." She tipped her head slightly, smiling as she said, "In the meantime, I was able to tell Annie a little something new about the baby."

His dark eyes rose, shooting up to meet Brenna's steady blue gaze. "What new thing?"

"The baby's a girl, Malik," Annie murmured, adding a plate of fruit and cheese to the glasses on the table. She plucked a strawberry from the plate and dropped into the chair beside Malik, turning to watch his face light with wonder.

"We're having a girl," he said dumbly, smiling as he took Annie's hand. Turning, he looked to Brenna for confirmation. "A girl?"

"A girl," Brenna laughed. "I heard her once, before Annie even knew she was pregnant, and I just knew. Like I could feel her inside my mind. That night I dreamed of her."

"Well you did a great job acting surprised then, when I told you I was pregnant before," Annie snorted.

Brenna laughed, raising her glass in Annie's direction. "I couldn't very well answer back with a stout, 'I know,' now could I?"

It was Malik's turn to laugh then. "I'd have liked to see Annie's face though, if you'd said that. Then again, a lot has happened and she's been steady, so maybe she wouldn't have reacted at all."

"Oh believe me, I'd have reacted to that," Annie laughed.

Malik leaned forward, bracing his elbows on the table as he reached for a piece of cheese. "But how are you able to know so much about the baby? And before Annie, even?" he asked, nudging the plate in Brenna's direction.

"I'm able to know a lot of things. My mother was a seer, Malik."

"Like Tiernan, I know," he said. "I didn't know she'd passed it to you."

"Who's Tiernan?" Brenna asked, her eyebrows lowering in confusion.

"You don't know about him? Aislynn didn't tell you?"

Brenna shook her head; Annie looked silently back and forth between Brenna and Malik.

"She didn't tell me what?" Brenna asked warily.

Malik sighed. "Your mother was betrothed to Tiernan when she left the clan. He's a seer too, a prophet. If she was a seer, then they would have been the most powerful couple in the entire selkie population, Brenna. Did she see the distant future, or the near future?"

"Near," Brenna said. "Did her leaving kill him?"

"No, he still lives," Malik answered. "He was weakened for a while and he did age some, but he is well now. He still leads the clan Killian; he's my uncle's most trusted advisor."

"Does my mother have anything to do with the prophecy about the baby?"

"No," Malik shook his head. "That's all Tiernan's vision, but the prophecy is an old one. Aislynn may have been there when he had the vision, or she may have known about it."

"Is that why she left him? Fear of the battle? The war?"

"No one knows," Malik answered. "And I don't know how much she may have told you, but the prophecy terrifies our people. They are all afraid of a war between the clans, but there are many willing to murder Annie in order to prevent the prophecy. To prevent the clans coming together. To prevent change, I guess. Fear of change affects us all Brenna, and there are many clans who don't want the prophesied reunion of the clans. There will be war, but there wasn't a time limit on Tiernan's prophesy. They didn't know it would be now, and maybe they were afraid then that the war would come soon. Maybe she was afraid. No one knows."

"And now, what? Am I called back to the clan or something? Is that why I'm having visions sometimes too? Does Annie need me?"

"Everyone needs you," Malik said. "If you are having visions and you are willing to share your gift with Tiernan, it could save us all. Your power combined with his would give us better warning times."

"Well, then, I guess it's time for an introduction, isn't it?"

As if on cue, heavy pounding sounded on the front door of the house, startling them all. As one, they left the kitchen and entered the living room, Brenna pressing Annie back into a corner, standing guard over her as Malik opened the front door, poised for battle. Peering around the corner of the door, Malik relaxed, releasing his breath in a heavy gush.

"They are our men," he said, turning to wave at Brenna, who took Annie's hand and led her to the couch. Malik opened the door to admit the waiting members of clan Killian: Angus, Tiernan and Doyle.

"The clans are fighting already," Angus said, his gaze landing immediately with recognition on Brenna. "And we need your help."

"Me?" she squeaked. "Already?"

"How willing are you to protect your mother's people?" Angus asked, his voice hard. He watched Brenna, raising a brow as he flicked shoulder-length waves of dark hair impatiently away from his face.

"Plenty willing," Brenna answered breathlessly. Her eyes had settled on Tiernan as he stepped forward, tall and proud before her.

"Good," he said, his dark hand outstretched, the light skin of his palm exposed as he offered his hand to Brenna. She looked to Annie; Annie nodded and Brenna took his hand, the white cream of her hand disappearing in his dark grasp.

"Good," he said again, tugging her hand and bringing her up from the couch, drawing her close to him. He studied her, running his palms up her arms, over the curve of her shoulders, his fingers losing themselves in the wild red of her hair. Brenna stood as motionless as if she were hypnotized, his hands finding the curves of her face, molding over the roundness of her cheeks. "You are Aislynn's daughter," he said.

"I am," Brenna breathed.

"I am Tiernan." His fingers stroked her cheek gently, tilting her face to look into her eyes. "And you are a seer also?"

"I am."

He smiled, straight white teeth shining out of his dark face. "Come with me," he said, drawing her into the center of the room. He crossed one foot in front of the other, lowering himself to the floor without letting go of Brenna's hands. Brenna met Annie's eyes, both women confused by the silence that had settled heavily in the room. Swallowing, Brenna closed her eyes, took a deep breath and crossed her feet as Tiernan had done, lowering herself to sit across from him.

He smiled again, edging himself closer until his knees touched hers. Taking her hands, he lay them palm up on his knees, smiling as he lay his own hands palm up on Brenna's knees. "Close your eyes," he whispered, and Brenna's eyelashes fluttered down to sweep her cheeks. Annie looked around; Angus and Doyle closed their eyes also, followed by Malik, who winked at Annie before they closed their eyes together.

Tiernan began to hum loudly; Annie opened her eyes as Brenna's eyes flew open. Brenna gasped, her hands jerking slightly away from his knees. He stopped, watching her as she resettled her hips on the floor and closed her eyes again. Tiernan's humming resumed and then grew louder, steadier. His energy filled the room, buzzing through Annie's body, tingling over her skin. Angus joined the hum, the sound low and heavy, rumbling out of his chest like the growl of a ferocious beast. Soon, Doyle and Malik were humming too, and it wasn't long before Annie was compelled to join in also, lending her own energy to the process, though she did not understand what was happening.

The humming rumbled through the room, circulating, building until finally, Brenna – who had not joined the humming -- broke away and lay back softly on the floor, her eyes wide, her breath coming in wild pants. Annie's eyes flew around the room, taking in the lack of concern among the men. She froze as the sound of the humming died slowly away. Tiernan remained motionless, his eyes closed.

"I see …" Brenna said, her voice disembodied and gravelly. "I see them; they're coming, six of them. They have five men and a woman. She is a warrior, a fighter in their clan. She is the one who will take the child, who will slice it from the womb of the mother and remove it to be murdered."

"No," Annie gasped, falling to her knees, her arms circling her abdomen, her eyes filling and spilling over with tears. "No, they can't take my baby."

Brenna rolled, pressing herself up from the floor and coming to her feet, crouching slightly in the middle of the room. "They can't if we stop them," she said, standing and moving purposefully toward Annie. Taking her upper arms, Brenna pushed her toward the coat closet in the living room and opened the door. Whipping the bottom of her shirt almost completely up to her chest, she revealed a belt encircling her waist, fully equipped with several small, sheathed daggers.

"Where did those come from?" Annie asked, her eyes widening as she took in Brenna's arsenal of blades.

"The linen closet at my house," Brenna shrugged. "Like I said, I'd had a dream that something was coming. I had to be prepared for anything. But listen, they're coming now," she said urgently, pressing a dagger hilt into Annie's hand and closing her fingers around it. "Take this, get in there and be quiet. The next time that door opens, you may be safe or you may be on your own, and I don't know which. So don't put this down, don't open that door no matter what and don't let down your guard." Turning to the others, she nodded toward the short swords

Angus had shared with Tiernan and Doyle. She stepped closer to Malik, offering him two of her daggers, keeping the last two for herself.

"A warrior," Angus whispered, standing motionless as he stared at her. "You are both a seer and a warrior. Like your mother."

"Apparently. And I'm not going down today. So let's not make this easy for them, shall we?" she asked, kicking the closet door shut and closing Annie in alone.

A scratching at the window caught the attention of the group, and as the window burst into the living room, Annie opened the closet door slightly, silently. Peering through the crack between the door and the jamb, she watched her friends form a tight circle of bodies, each facing out, protecting each other's backs as they readied themselves for the battle.

"And what the heck do I do now?" she whispered, her breathing coming in short frightened gasps. Annie pressed her back against the wall, spreading the coats hanging on the rail as far as they would go to give herself more space. The crash and the tinkling of the glass terrified her, the sounds of fighting filling her ears. Grunts and shouts coupled with metallic clanging, and Annie stood helpless, waiting to see if the closet door would be opened by friend or foe.

"They've broken in," she whispered to herself, one arm still clenched protectively around her stomach as she palmed the hilt of the dagger in her other hand. "And I don't even know how to fight. Oh, what I wouldn't give for a secret tunnel."

Safe, mama ...

"That's right, baby, I'm gonna keep us safe," Annie whispered, not believing the words even as she uttered them. Something slammed against the closet door, and moans and various shouts filtered in through the door. Annie squeezed her eyes shut, desperately hoping that her loved ones would survive the battle. There was another slam against the closet door, a grunt, and a horrifyingly final cry. Annie braced herself, crouching as she had seen Brenna crouch earlier, the dagger held out defensively in front of her body.

Annie listened as Brenna shouted to Lugus, "No! Lugus, go!" There was a bark, a snarling growl. Shrinking back into the corner of the closet, Annie heard the dying cry of the dog, followed by Brenna's furious roar. A number of shouts rang out after that, and then there was nothing but silence.

Finally, Brenna's voice sounded through the door. "Come out, Annie, come on. We need to get you out of here." The door wrenched open and then Brenna was there, taking the dagger from Annie's hand. She guided Annie quickly through the living room as the men formed a wall of muscle along the way, their backs turned to her as they stood shoulder to shoulder, blocking her from seeing the carnage.

Only Lugus lay exposed, his body ripped open along one side. Brenna looked over to him once, her chin trembling, but then she closed herself away again, her face hardening, her eyes turning to ice as she steered Annie away from the fallen.

"Are the warriors all dead?" she asked, touching the warm heaving backs of her still-living loved ones as she passed them. Tiernan's dark skin had taken on a paler tint as he stood, leaning slightly against Doyle, who was in turn leaning against Angus. Angus stood proud and tall, his back broad and strong, his muscled arm tight around Malik's waist. "Oh God, oh God," Annie murmured thankfully, gasping for air as her panic fell away, leaving her trembling in Brenna's arms.

"Yes, they are dead," Brenna answered quietly, wiping blood away from her weapons and stowing the daggers into her belt again, raising her forearm to wipe away a smear of blood on her forehead. "But our men are fine, you are fine, and there will be more coming for us. Many more are coming, so we need to go."

The group moved as one, leaving the house and moving into the driveway. Brenna passed Annie to Malik as they climbed together into Annie's car. Tiernan took the wheel, climbing into the front seat of the car with Brenna. Doyle and Angus followed in the truck owned by clan Killian, the bright red paint flashing in the sunlight.

"Why was Brenna the one to have the vision?" Annie asked, curled in the back seat with Malik. As she spoke, she was anxiously inspecting him, running her hands up and down his arms and pushing him forward so that she could see his back before allowing him to rest against the back of the seat. Finding a tear in the side of his shirt, she sucked in a breath, letting it out again in relief when she found only a minor cut concealed beneath the fabric.

"I have no idea," Brenna said. "I've only ever had visions in dreams before."

"What made it change like that? Maybe it was because you were with Tiernan?" Annie wondered.

Unable to answer the question, Brenna flicked her eyes toward Tiernan, who took a deep breath as he gathered his thoughts. "I am a prophet, a seer who has visions far into the future. I see the way things will be, if they remain as they are. My visions change; they follow the course of current events to predict the coming decades or centuries. That's why we write them down, because they are so far off as to possibly be forgotten, leaving the clans unprepared. But any change today can alter or outright cancel a vision in the distant future because it alters the course of time."

"Is that why you can't see how the war will end?" Annie asked.

Tiernan nodded, saying, "But Brenna is not like me. Instead, she is like a copy of her mother, both a warrior and a seer. She will have ease in battle, a clear head and a powerful fighting strategy. More importantly, she sees the immediate future, most likely with no visions more distant than a day or two." At this, he turned to glance at Brenna, who nodded to confirm the truth in his words. "Because of this, she can be counted on to tell us what is coming in the battles. When our power is combined, the visions become clearer, stronger. With enough concentration, they can be called."

"Did you see her, Tiernan? Brenna, I mean?"

"I have seen her face many times, listened to her voice, her laughter. I have —" he broke off, his eyes darting over at Brenna before turning again to focus on the street. "I have seen her, yes, but I did not know who she was. I believed … I believed Aislynn would —"

"Come back," Brenna said. "Is that what kept her leaving from killing you? Hoping for her?"

"It is, maybe. You look so like her; my visions of you gave me hope that she would come back, because I believed it to be Aislynn in my visions. But you? You are a sight to see, a balm to my wounds. She left me, yes, but she did well. She loved and she created beauty before her soul left her body. She created a new destiny for me."

Her face flushed, Brenna tightened her lips and kept her eyes lowered, her fingers working nervously together in her lap. In the back seat, Annie and Malik exchanged a silent look, each of them with one hand guarding the fragile womb that housed their child.

***

The walk through the tunnel and back to the selkie caves was terrifyingly dark, the eerie echoes of shuffling feet bouncing ceaselessly along. Clan sounds from the caves filtered through the tunnel too, assailing Annie, Malik and the others as fear and anger spread like plague through the clan.

As they approached the caves that housed most of the clan, Annie was kept sheltered in the middle of the small group, carrying Brenna's pelt bundled in her arms. Angus led the group, followed by Brenna, both with Brenna's daggers in hand. Annie walked behind Brenna, her mind flying with thoughts of the battle, anxiety for the future, and fear for the safety of her unborn child. Malik walked silently behind Annie, his shoulders rounded in the dark with the weight of his own burdens, the muscles of his arms bunched as he, too, wielded a pair of Brenna's daggers. Doyle followed, also armed, and Tiernan brought up the end of the line, listening closely for sounds from behind, his arms corded and heavy with the weight of Angus's swords.

As they left the darkness of the tunnel, Doyle heaved a sigh of relief. "At least in here, we're among our own. And we can see each other," he said, tucking a blade into the sheath at his ankle before standing and gesturing to the cave walls, lit by the natural gas fires. The large open room of the cave was a mass of bodies, most carrying their pelts under their arms for safekeeping.

"Okay, everybody, listen up!" Malise called, wandering among the crowd. Her youngest son, Doyle's younger brother, Bryce, walked a step behind her, carrying his pelt in the crook of one arm, hers in the other. Catching sight of Angus, Malise nodded briefly to him, her face softening in relief as she looked over him and found him without injury. "Okay!" she shouted, clapping her hands to draw the attention of the crowd. "The boys are back, so let's hear what Angus has to say!" Everywhere, people stopped walking, their faces turning questioningly to their leader. Some women held the hands of their children, their bundled pelts barely contained as they juggled their burdens.

Annie looked around the cave, taking in the meager size of the clan. She hadn't spent much time there and hadn't had a chance to meet many of the people, but the time she had spent in the caves had been peaceful and quiet. The selkie clan was a generally peaceful group of people, mostly independent though they did live together for safety. But now, in the face of the coming war, Annie felt as if she were looking at an entirely different place; the cave was warm now, filled with the crowd of frightened people who stood in small groups together, fearfully leaning on each other for support.

They were afraid, but they were also a logical group; they accepted the risk of a war they could not prevent. Clan Killian was grieving in advance for losses they could not stop, for death they could not hold back, and for a child they were not sure they could save. Annie stood silent, swept into a strange new people, her belly swelling with a future they'd only dreamed of, her heart breaking for those who would not survive.

"Clan Conway has already come to attack," Angus said, stepping forward and projecting his voice so that it bounced loudly around the cave. He stood tall as he addressed his people, and they watched him silently as he spoke, waiting for his orders. "We have defeated the first wave, but more men will come; more clans will come in waves and waves of men, and it is our destiny to hold them back. They will come for us, and we must fight fiercely to protect the child of the prophesy. In the coming years, many warriors will come upon us, attempting to stop the prophesies from coming to pass, attempting to stop the birth or end the life of the child. They will come to fill us with fear," he said, turning to pull Annie closer to him. She looked up into his face, his dark hair pouring over his broad shoulders, his face solemn as he presented her to his people.

Pressing his hand to her abdomen, he scanned the crowd with his eyes, calling on the loyalty of his men. He continued, "Other warriors will come to murder this child of our clan. They will come for each of you, because you aid us in this battle. But we have watched for this day for decades; we have waited for this moment of truth, this moment of war. We have all awaited the coming time of peace, the joining of the clans and the unity of our kind. But first, we fight for the future of our people; we protect what is ours. We give our blood for the blood of the child; we give our lives to protect this life, to make a better way for the new generations. We give our bodies if we need to, for the sake of peace."

Pausing, Angus waited as his men nodded, some giving shouts of approval. "Alright then," he said, "Who will fight with us?"

Annie's heart leapt as several men stepped forward immediately, vowing to lend their courage to the safety of her child, willing to give their lives for the sake of hers. Other men seemed to hesitate briefly, but within moments all the men in the cave stood together, shoulder to shoulder -- an army of angry fear and protective rage. "Clan Killian has risen to battle!" they shouted, tightening their ranks, the echoes of their shouts rumbling fiercely through the depths of the caves.

"I will fight as well," Tiernan stated, stepping forward. Angus shook his head, his mouth tightening, but Tiernan continued. "My sight is too distant to help us here, Angus, because the coming war can change what I have seen. I cannot predict anything of use, but I can lend my body to the battle. I can give my life, my loyalty to the child. This is a worthy battle," he finished, nodding toward Annie. Finally, Angus tipped his head in agreement, clasping hands with him in acceptance of his pledge.

"I will fight too, for my child's future," Malik said. He pressed a lingering kiss to Annie's forehead, his hands covering her cheeks, holding their foreheads together. He swallowed, kissed her lips gently and then turned to join the ranks of the men, his eyes fierce, his posture determined.

"I am a skilled fighter; I will stay and fight as well," Brenna said, drawing a gasp of shock from the crowd in the cave as she stepped forward.

Angus took her arm, stopping her. "No," he said, raising his hand to silence her as she drew a breath to protest. "I can see that you are a warrior, and I do not doubt your abilities to help our people. But if you're willing to stay, I have another plan for you."

Brenna waited as Angus turned to draw Tiernan close to them. He took their hands in his; meeting Brenna's blue eyes and then Tiernan's dark ones as he joined their hands together. "Together, you are a formidable force, an unstoppable power," he said. "You shall be the protectors of the next generation of clan Killian. You will stand beside Annie and guide her into the birth of the child when it is time. You are her personal guard for as long as she needs you; you will form the advising team to the child. If the war is lost, you will be the battle line, the final stand. The life of the child is yours to protect."

"This is assuming that Brenna is willing to stay that long," Tiernan said quietly. "The child is conceived, but there are many years ahead of us before she is able to rise to her power. And Brenna has lived as a human; she has ties to the human world, not ours. She doesn't know our world."

"She is here now," Angus said, lifting his eyebrow.

"She has come to help protect her friend. This is not her promise to join us, or her vow to live among us."

"Have you not seen her?" Angus asked. "In your visions?"

"My visions do not always come to pass."

Looking to Brenna, Angus lowered his brows, studying her. She met his gaze steadily with her own, unwavering, unintimidated in the face of the clan leader. "I am here now," she said, standing tall as she lifted her chin defiantly. "And I will stay as long as I am needed. The child will not be unprotected, nor will her mother be left alone," she vowed.

Angus nodded, turning back to Tiernan as he said, "Hmph. She appears willing enough for now, and we'll just see what *she* decides as the time unfolds. We are not barbarians, after all." Finished, he turned away to give orders to the clan. His shadow bounced darkly along the wall with his steps as he wandered through the crowd speaking to his wife. Malise joined him as he walked, and together they gathered the children of their clan, choosing women from among the mothers and guiding them all toward Annie, Doyle, Brenna and Tiernan.

Watching Angus weave through the crowd, Brenna turned to Annie. "I take it this hasn't happened before?" she asked.

"Not that I know of," Annie answered. "I think there have always been clan rivalries, but nothing like this."

Gesturing for Malik to leave the men and come back with him, Angus led the mothers and their children back toward Annie. Bryce took Malik's place among the ranks, hugging his mother before she followed Angus. Reaching Annie, Angus clapped one hand heavily on Malik's shoulder, his other hand clenching Doyle's upper arm. Looking to Doyle, he said, "You will guide them, son. You are their leader, for now."

"Father –" Doyle started.

"No," Angus answered, his voice thick and gruff. "Take them. Lead them. You are second in command, Doyle, second in line. I need you to do this. It's your duty to lead the clan if we fail; it's your duty to rebuild our people. I need you to lead the young ones now, and watch over them. But I *will* see you soon, when the battle is done."

Doyle chose not to speak; instead simply grunting as he turned his face away. "Let's go, then," he said, gesturing to the women crowded around him.

"Take them to your old place, Malik," Angus said. "It's a small place; it's well-hidden. No one will expect to find them there."

"They'll be fine with us, Uncle," Malik nodded. "And I'll come back to check in when I can."

"You be careful and stay safe," Malise said, taking Annie's hands in her own.

"I'll do my very best," Annie said. She took a steadying breath and stepped between Brenna and Tiernan, enclosing herself in the circle of her guards. Joining hands with one of the mothers, she urged the small group of women and children to crowd behind Doyle and Malik, who guarded them from the front. Behind them, Tiernan and Brenna followed, their hands still clenched tightly together.

***

"What will happen now, Malik?" Annie asked, later that night. She lay enclosed in his arms, his fingertips sweeping steady circles around the rise of her lower stomach. Her pregnancy was only a few months along, but selkie babies were large and no one was sure if Annie would make it to the full term of the pregnancy. She was already larger than she would have been with a normal human pregnancy, and as Malik swept over her stomach, Annie felt the flutter of their daughter moving in her womb.

"I wish I did but I just don't know," he answered, his fingers still stroking the flesh that protected his daughter. "The others are settled in, so I guess now we wait. Doyle and I will alternate with Brenna and Tiernan, keeping guard over you and the others. We'll take turns hunting to bring back food, and in a few days I'll go check in with Angus and the others."

"You will be the one to go?" Annie asked, tensing slightly in his arms.

"I have to. I'm the most disposable among us," Malik answered. "Brenna and Tiernan have the combined power of their visions, and neither of them apart will be as strong as the two together. You obviously are not disposable, even if you did know where to go. And Doyle is the new clan leader if Uncle Angus doesn't survive the war."

"But you aren't disposable to me, either," Annie said quietly.

"I know. But it's battle logic, and there isn't any other way to do it," Malik sighed, his fingers tightening on her skin as he pulled her closer to him.

"I think a change of subject is in order for now, but I'll plan to protest your logic later on. In the meantime, how are the children? Where are they, while we're here enjoying ourselves?" she asked, tilting her face up to meet his eyes.

He chuckled slightly. "They're the same as the mothers. They are all afraid, but being together seems to be helping. Some of the children are struggling with being separated from mothers called to fight, but the mothers that are with them are handling things well. They didn't want separate rooms though, so they're all camping together a little down the tunnel. Brenna and Tiernan are with them."

"They're trapped, away from their mothers, away from their homes, afraid because of me. Because of us," she whispered quietly, a shimmering tear leaping from the edges of her eyelashes to fall on the bare expanse of his chest.

"You know that isn't true, Annie. This is just the way things are. There's no blame here; neither of us knew what would happen, neither of us knew this is where we'd end up."

"And how many of them will die because we didn't know, Malik? How many of those children won't grow up, for the sake of our child? How many will be fatherless within days, or motherless? And if the war lasts longer than that? If we win this battle only to put off the facing of another? We should just leave," she whispered. "Just the two of us. Wouldn't that protect them better, if they weren't all protecting us?"

"No. Annie, the clans would sweep through them all, seeking just one who might know where we are. Better to be here, where I can fight with my people. Our people. This is our destiny; this is our daughter's destiny. She will be a leader, Annie, a ruler."

"If she survives to be. And what if we can't protect her?"

"She will be protected. She will be safe," he whispered, his lips moving over her hair as he drew her close. "She will be loved. That is her destiny too. Tiernan has seen her as the selkie queen."

"But his visions —" Annie started, interrupted by a shriek in the tunnel. Malik jerked, covering Annie's mouth with his hands before she could cry out. Her eyes widened, jerking around the room before settling fearfully back on Malik's face.

"There's nowhere to hide in here but under the cot," he whispered quickly, his voice harsh. "Slip under and roll all the way back to the wall. Stay there, and stay silent until I come for you. Not one sound, Annie, no matter what you hear. No matter what, just be still and be quiet."

Nodding desperately, Annie clung to him, but he kissed her face and pulled away, leaving a dagger on the edge of the cot before slipping silently toward the door of the cave room and sliding it open. Annie followed his instructions; clutching the dagger in one hand, she held her other arm in a tight band around her stomach. In the sudden cold of Malik's absence, she curled around her baby, the blade of the dagger kept close to her body to prevent it reflecting the firelight into the room. Still and silent, she lay watching the doorway, listening for signs of Malik's return.

In the tunnel outside the room, Malik crept quietly up beside Doyle, touching his arm softly to draw his attention. They watched together as two seals slid out of the water, shedding their seal pelts quickly and leaving them piled on the ledge. Naked, they crouched and moved forward as one, unarmed but no less mighty. They were empty-handed but each one was as large as two men, each of them swift and entirely silent as they approached the mouth of the tunnel. They gestured to each other as they moved; one pointed toward the tunnels where Malik and Annie had been lying together. Watching the other man smile wickedly, Malik raised his arm to a ledge above his head, his fingers closing over the short sword he kept hidden there.

Doyle saw him; he smiled as he brought his own arm forward, revealing an identical short sword in his own hand. "Are they alone?" he asked.

"I think so," Malik said. "But I can't be positive. I heard something and came running, but I didn't see anything out of place until I saw them. They hang with Sloane. Remember him?"

"I remember. The jerk that used to dive with us?" Doyle asked.

"Yeah. I think the youngest one is his brother, but I can't be sure. He could be here somewhere, or there could be more in the water," Malik whispered back.

"Well, one threat at a time, cousin. You ready?" he asked.

"Ready," Tiernan whispered from behind them. He grinned as they both jerked in surprise. Holding up both hands, he showed Brenna's daggers clutched fiercely in his grasp.

"Where's Brenna?" Malik whispered.

"Moving the children deeper into the tunnels," Tiernan said. "She'll be coming back for Annie."

"Alright, then. We can't be everywhere at once, so let's just do this and then we can check on the others," Doyle said. Together, the men advanced, moving closer to the mouth of the tunnel, closer to the invaders. Malik followed Doyle into battle, the two of them pressing their backs close together to protect each other while Tiernan circled around, trying to catch one of the intruders unaware. The pair descended on Malik and Doyle, ducking and shifting to avoid the wicked slice of Malik's short sword.

"Is that all you've got?" the smallest of the two men laughed, shifting again to avoid the sword and then barreling forward, his meaty fist grazing Malik's chin. Doyle stepped forward menacingly, rotating his sword to plunge it into the attacker's belly. Swinging a vicious right hook, Malik connected with the stabbed man, shaking out his hand as the now-unconscious intruder slipped to the floor.

Doyle's sword was ripped free of the injured flesh, and he grinned at Malik. Grinning back, Malik spun on his heels to take a stance beside Doyle, where he found himself face to face with red-hot fury, slowly taking over the face of the man in front of him. "That was my brother!" he growled. "You killed my brother!"

"Well, we thought he was someone else's brother," Malik answered, his voice low and calm as he gauged the other man. "Not to mention, he'd come for my wife and daughter, which I will not allow."

"Allow? You think you will have a choice? You have murdered my brother, and I will see you bound and gagged as I murder all of the daughters of clan Killian," the other man sneered, disgust melting into surprise as the pointed tip of a dagger suddenly appeared in his chest.

"I doubt it," Tiernan said, ripping the dagger free and watching the man fall at his feet.

Daddy …

"Annie!" Malik shouted, looking around. Frantic shuffling could be heard from in the tunnel. Panic filled him, stealing his good judgment; he ran recklessly into the mouth of the tunnel as he shouted Annie's name again.

The shuffling became louder down the tunnel, a broken grunt followed by a muffled cry feeding Malik's need to find his mate. As he rounded the bend, the door to his cave room opened, sliding slowly aside to reveal Annie, her green eyes wide in terror, her fingers clutching desperately at the arm of the man who held her. His arm was fitted snugly under her chin, cutting her air supply as he shoved her along from behind. His eyes were on Annie's terrified face as his free hand snaked along under her arm to grasp her breast.

"Don't worry, peach," he murmured, the tip of his tongue snaking out to stroke the side of Annie's face. "I'll take good care of you. My friends are making sure your little baby needs a new daddy soon, and I'm applying for the job."

"No," she cried softly as his hand left her breast, snaking down over the bump of her belly as she turned her face away from his, her body freezing as she caught sight of Malik.

Looking up to follow her gaze, the man saw Malik watching, standing with Tiernan and Doyle at his sides. "Want her to live, Malik?" he asked. "Want to know that she's alright and well cared for? That your daughter is well?"

"You will never take them," Malik growled, his body trembling with the force of his rage.

"I can, and I will," the man answered, tightening his hold on Annie. "You can't win this, so just turn around and walk away. You took something from me once, remember? That dive, all those years ago? You had to be the star; you had to beat me to the jewels. But I told you, you can never steal from me without repaying the debt. And now, you'll pay handsomely. The only clan that will benefit from the birth of this prophecy is mine. I will lead the child, raise her as I wish her to be raised, use her to ally my clan with the Conways. And – oh yes – I will be happy to introduce this wife of yours to the attention of a real selkie man. Finally, something more than a half-breed for her. Hmm, sweetheart?" He looked back to Annie, wrenching her face back to him, driving his tongue into her gasping mouth as he clutched her womb, dragging her tightly against his body.

An enraged sound escaped Malik, his body shaking with the need to lunge forward and murder the enemy. "Sloane, you bastard. Let her go."

"Steal my jewels, I steal yours, remember?" Sloane answered with a triumphant grin. "You will never see the child, living or dead. Nor will you ever possess anything again without me coming for it. Now you have two choices; I can walk out of here with my new wife and child, or you can stand in my way and watch me murder them both." As he spoke, he gripped Annie tightly with his arm around her throat, his other hand producing a rusty blade, which he held in front of Annie's face. She whimpered fearfully, her hands lowering from his arm to cover the swell of her child protectively. "Two choices, one choice. You have no choice, really," Sloane chuckled. "Surely you aren't heartless enough to let them die just to keep their rotting bodies."

"Take her then," Malik whispered, his eyes pained, his face pinched. Annie gasped, shaking her head frantically until the press of Sloane's blade against her throat froze her again.

Sloane laughed. "Take her? Oh yes, I plan to do just that," he said. His breathing grew ragged as he groped Annie's swollen breasts again, the blade at her throat holding her effectively enough for him to remove his arm, lowering his fingers to squeeze viciously at the pregnant roundness of her breast. She moaned, her face flushed with fear, her body trembling visibly. "And boy I'm going to have fun playing with her. My new toy."

Turning, Malik watched as Sloane passed him. Tiernan stood rooted to the floor of the cave as Malik and Doyle followed Sloane down the tunnel to the ledge where the cave met the water. Passing his dead comrades, Sloane froze and then turned back, "Oh, yes, Malik. She and I will have lots of fun. I'll make her beg for mercy and I will show none, as you showed no mercy to my friends. She will beg for the release of death, she will beg for murder, and I will deny her."

"How do you expect to get her out of here without her pelt?" Malik asked.

"I guess she'll have to hold her breath and swim along," Sloane replied, laughing. Turning dismissively, he shoved Annie to her knees, moving to pull his own pelt from a crevice in the cave wall.

Malik's motion was swift and smooth, rage and fear giving his grip surety and his timing perfection. The dagger he'd taken from Tiernan's hand flew through the air, spinning end over end in a clean arc, finally lodging in the side of Sloane's throat. He uttered a short cry, the force of the dagger's entry throwing him over the ledge and into the water. Tiernan shouted in triumph, his feet swift and sure as he followed Doyle and Malik. They raced to Annie, taking her arms and lifting her back to her feet. She pressed her hands to her face, sobbing uncontrollably as Malik gathered her into his arms.

"It's okay, we're safe now, they're gone, we're safe now," he whispered. "We're safe now, we're safe now."

Tiernan turned back to the tunnel, cupping his hands around his mouth, pursing his lips and whistling shrilly, the sound vibrating between his lips like the chirping of a bird. Before he'd ended the sound, Brenna stepped out of the shadows, a line of mothers with all the children trailing behind her.

"I know you told me to go further into the tunnels, but the truth is this place isn't safe either. Is it?" she asked.

"We won't be safe anywhere," Annie answered, struggling to control her emotions, her hands firmly covering her stomach. "They'll keep coming for me. They'll keep coming for my baby. And no place will be safe until she has come to her power. She may never be safe."

***

"There has to be some other way," Annie said, turning pleading eyes toward Doyle and Tiernan. "Isn't there any other way to handle this?" They'd been sitting grouped together for over an hour, cross-legged in the mouth of the tunnel, trying to decide where they should move the selkie children to keep them safe. "I know we need to contact the others, and I agree that we need to move, but why should only one of us go? What ever happened to the concept of 'safety in numbers?'"

"I explained this," Malik said, taking her hand in his, his thumb stroking circles along the back of her hand. "In open water, we're all in danger; but someone has to go, and I'm the most disposable candidate here. I know it isn't what you want to hear, and it definitely isn't something I like to admit, but it's true and we all know it. If we're stuck here, we're no safer than if we just turn ourselves over, and if one group can find us, another could too. But we can't go anywhere else without letting Angus know and checking on the rest of the clan."

"Do you really have to go alone?" Annie asked, her eyes filling with tears again.

"Malik, you know –" Doyle started, but Malik cut him off again.

"No, it's the way it has to be, Doyle; you know it is. You're the next in line to lead the clan. You need to be here because in the end of this, those women and their children might be all that's left of clan Killian. Tiernan is beside you, your prophet. You'll need him. Brenna doesn't know where to go, and you'll need her fighting skills if I don't make it back. Obviously, Annie needs to stay here where she can be protected. That leaves me."

"Much as I hate this for you Annie, Malik's right," Brenna said, draping her arm around Annie's shoulders as Annie lowered her head, crying. "But I don't think he should be alone. I could go with him; he shouldn't have to be out there alone."

"No!" Tiernan shouted, his sudden volume causing everyone to jerk in surprise. Clearing his throat, he calmed himself and said, "Brenna, you're needed here; you're a warrior. You are a seer, not a babysitter. Malik is a skilled fighter in his own right and will be fine, but you are needed here. This is where the clan needs your gifts."

"Exactly," Malik nodded, satisfied that everyone was finally in agreement with him, though his victory was bittersweet.

"Here we are then," Annie murmured. "Your kinsman, your prophet, your friend, and your wife, sending you off to what could be your death."

"It isn't," he answered, taking her face in his hands. "I will come back with guidance from Angus and word of the others. And I will be here, for her, all of her days," he finished, lowering one hand from her cheek to her stomach. "I will come back to you. I will."

Lowering her face into his palm, Annie closed her eyes, her lips trembling as tears ran freely down her cheeks. She nodded, turning to kiss his palm before scooting away from the group and climbing to her feet. "I'll bring your pelt for you," she said.

Watching her leave, Malik waited until she rounded the corner before turning his attention back to the others. "Take care of her, all of you," he commanded. "Don't let her worry herself to death. And if I'm not back in twenty-four hours …"

"We will flee from this place," Tiernan said. "We could take shelter on the land, maybe even crossing to find other waters. Annie and the child will be well cared for among your people, and the child might lend healing to her heartbreak."

"Okay, this is it then," Malik said, rising to his feet and pausing to wait for Doyle to stand with him. They clasped hands, the handshake a gesture of respect and brotherly love, each refusing to speak such a final word as 'goodbye.' They'd been the best of friends since Malik had first come to clan Killian; they were much more like brothers than cousins.

"Be safe," Doyle said. "And that's an order from your leader, Malik. Check on the clan, speak to my father, and get yourself back here quick."

"I will be back," Malik answered. "This will only take a few hours."

"Then go, speak your goodbyes to your wife."

Malik looked at Brenna and Tiernan, still sitting with Brenna's hand swallowed in Tiernan's larger one. He nodded to them, waiting long enough to remember their faces, and then turned to go. Walking down the tunnel, he approached the ledge where the dead bodies of the rival clan had been cleared away and thrown into the water. Annie was there, holding Malik's pelt in her hands. Tears streamed down her face, her lips trembling with the sobs she held back from him. "I can't believe you're leaving," she said, her voice shaking.

"I'll come back," he told her, stepping close to fold her into his chest. "This is not forever, but I have to check in with Angus."

"Don't you die again, Malik. I thought you were dead once already. We need you."

"I know you do, and I'll be back," he said. "I'm not leaving, I'm just checking on the others. I love you." He folded her more snugly into his arms, pulling her tightly against his body. "I will be back for you, I promise. Both of you." Annie pressed her face into his chest, his pelt bunching up between them, her sobs finally breaking loose. His lips moved over her forehead, crossing her temple and following the tears down her face to her mouth.

"I love you," he whispered against her lips, the tip of his tongue coaxing her to respond. "Believe me, Annie, I'll be back. I will." He stepped away slowly, reluctantly, taking his pelt from her hands and swinging it over his head, settling it around his shoulders. Turning, he lowered to the ground, the pelt closing up around him as he took on the form of the seal. Butting his nose against Annie's thigh, the deep, dark pools of his eyes met the shimmering green of Annie's own eyes one last time before he turned away and was gone.

***

"He should have been back by now," Doyle said, for the third time. He'd been pacing back and forth on the ledge by the water for several hours, periodically stopping to peer into the water in search of Malik. "He should have been back by now."

"What should we do?" Brenna asked, from her place on the ledge. She'd been sitting there for hours while Doyle paced behind her, daggers in both hands as she stared at the water as if willing Malik to appear.

"We wait." Annie spoke from the shadows at the mouth of the tunnel. "I'm not leaving here without him. He said he'd be back for me."

"Well, I'm sure it'll be soon. Maybe he's just been held up, talking to Angus or something. We'll give him another two hours and then we have to leave," Doyle said gently, turning to look at Annie. "It's what he'd have wanted, Annie. For me to move you, protect you from being found."

Suddenly, Brenna fell back, her head knocking sharply on the rock floor of the cave. She moaned, her hands shaking, her daggers falling to the floor beside her as she rolled, curling into herself. "No," she whispered. "No, no, not now, not this, no."

"Brenna? Brenna!" Annie shouted, running across the cave and dropping to her knees beside her friend.

"Brenna!" Tiernan echoed, falling beside Annie and reaching for Brenna's hands. He'd been sitting in the shadows, trying to call a vision to himself, but when he saw Brenna fall, he scrambled to his feet and rushed to her aid, lifting her head into his lap as she writhed on the stone floor.

"Malik," she whispered. "He's taken; Malik's been taken."

"Oh God," Annie whispered, falling back, nearly toppling over the ledge and into the water. "Oh God no. Not again, not now." Tiernan released Brenna's hands to catch Annie, drawing her away from the water. Doyle settled beside her, his heavy arm falling over her shoulders as she sobbed.

Tiernan brought his attention back to Brenna, pressing her back along the floor of the cave. He flattened his hands on her stomach, humming slightly as he closed his eyes in concentration. She whipped her head back and forth, her hair a wild spill of red on the stones beneath her. Her eyes flicked open and then closed again, her guttural moans morphing into a steady and terrifying keen that corresponded with Tiernan's humming. The humming continued for several minutes before Brenna calmed, her body stilling until she appeared to be sleeping.

Doyle moved to squat beside them, watching Tiernan carefully. "Were you able to share her vision?" he asked.

"Clan Conway," Tiernan said, his black eyes popping open suddenly, his words causing the cave to spin as Annie's vision faltered. "Malik has been taken by members of clan Conway."

No, my Daddy ...

At the mournful sound of her child's cry, Annie's vision swam; her heart dropped as the contents of her stomach rose. Turning away from the water, she reached for Tiernan, her eyes rolling back as she collapsed to the floor.

INTERMISSION TO SELKIE II

Malik Is Taken

I didn't think it would happen this quickly. I thought that I'd at least make it back to the clan before being attacked again, that I would be able to alert the others that Annie and the wives and children were in trouble. I thought maybe then that even if I was taken, my people would know that Annie was in danger.

I was wrong. They were there even before I could enter the main caves of the clan; the warriors of clan Conway were upon me. It was as if they'd been lying in wait, and after the previous attacks, I wasn't really surprised to find myself completely surrounded. They were as unarmed as I was, but there was only one of me, and I counted at least twenty of them. They were swimming above me, below me, in front of me, nipping behind me to keep me moving.

Annie's face flashed in my memory, and I tried not to think of how broken she would be without me. My heart was squeezing in my chest, the idea of never meeting my daughter crushing the air from my aquatic lungs. I had failed them. Annie would be alone, and it made me ache to think of how frightened she would be when I didn't return to her as I'd promised. Guilt settled on me, weighing me down; she was now an entirely new creature – a selkie – and she'd left her previous life behind her to join with mine. And now, I wouldn't even be there. Would we really lose what we'd shared, after we'd had to fight so hard to survive together? Was the last time I saw her really to be the last time that I saw her?

I consoled myself with the knowledge that Annie would not be totally alone. Brenna would be there for her, I knew, to support her and help protect her, to watch over her and guide her. Tiernan had taken a special interest in her also, almost like a father figure, and I knew that she would be loved and cared for with the selkies of clan Killian.

But would I ever love her again? Would I ever touch her again, would I ever listen to her breathless gasps as we lay together? Would I ever see her swollen with the weight of our child?

As the members of clan Conway surrounded me, nipping at me, nudging me away from the caves of my own clan, I felt the ache of her loss filling me. I thought of Tiernan and wondered how he had survived the loss of Aislynn, Brenna's mother, the woman who should have been his wife. But then I felt his hope surround me, the hope that I would see Annie again, that I would hold my child after all.

Hope that I would escape.

Hope that I would find my way home.

On the journey to the Conway caves in the upper mid-Atlantic, I held that hope tight inside my heart, inside my mind. When we reached the caves and I was allowed to take my human form, I held hope that I would see my family again. When I was taken to the leaders of clan Conway to be interrogated, I maintained silence; I held tight to my memory of Annie's face as I was beaten, shackled, starved. When the weight fell away from my body, when my hair was shaved away, when I was ridiculed and humiliated in front the members of clan Conway, I held tight to that same sense of hope, waiting for the moment when they would let down their guard, when I would escape this miserable place and find my way back to my love, my wife.

Soon.

Soon, my moment will come. Soon, I will find my way from the Conway clan and back to the safety of my people. Soon, I will stumble back into the arms of my wife, and I will cover her with kisses, I will shower her with words of love. I will reach for my daughter and run my fingers over the smooth roundness of her face. I will pet the silken fur of her pelt. I will teach her to hunt; I will teach her the ways of our people.

In the cold-water caves of clan Conway, hope is the only thing that keeps me alive.

ABOUT THE AUTHOR

Brandi Kennedy is an American writer who is finally living her childhood career dream. As a child, books were her world, and through adulthood, that love of words has never changed. Brandi is now a contemporary romance novelist and poet with a deep love of writing -- and a curiously adventurous desire to someday write in several other genres.

A woman of varied interests, Brandi loves photography, music of all kinds, knitting, crochet, and of course, mothering her two young daughters. Currently, she finds her home in the heart of Knoxville, Tennessee, among the mountains and the members of her extended family, where she spends her days at the computer, bringing fresh and incredibly real characters to life.

FOLLOW BRANDI KENNEDY ON THE WEB

On Amazon, http://www.amazon.com/author/brandikennedy
On Facebook, http://www.facebook.com/AuthorBrandiKennedy
On Blogger, http://authorbrandikennedy.blogspot.com/
On Twitter, http://www.twitter.com/BrandiKennedy84
And On Goodreads, http://www.goodreads.com/AuthorBrandiKennedy

OTHER TITLES BY THIS AUTHOR

The Selkie Trilogy
Selkie

The Kingsley Series
Fat Chance, Book One
Prescription For Love, Book Two

Coming Soon
Fighting For Freedom